PRAISE F

"Mary Ellen Taylor writes comfort reads packed with depth . . . If you're looking for a fantastic vacation read, this is the book for you!"
—Steph and Chris's Book Review, on *Spring House*

"A complex tale . . . grounded in fascinating history and emotional turmoil that is intense yet subtle. An intelligent, heartwarming exploration of the powers of forgiveness, compassion, and new beginnings."
—*Kirkus Reviews*, on *The View from Prince Street*

"Absorbing characters, a hint of mystery, and touching self-discovery elevate this novel above many others in the genre."
—RT Book Reviews, on *Sweet Expectations*

"Taylor serves up a great mix of vivid setting, history, drama, and everyday life."
—*Herald Sun*, on *The Union Street Bakery*

"A charming and very engaging story about the nature of family and the meaning of love."
—*Seattle Post-Intelligencer*, on *Sweet Expectations*

The Words We Whisper

"Taylor expertly employs the parallel timelines to highlight the impact of the past on the present, exploring the complexities of familial relationships while peeling back the layers of her flawed, realistic characters. Readers are sure to be swept away."
—*Publishers Weekly*

"A luscious interweaving of a spy thriller and a family saga."
—*Historical Novels Review*

Honeysuckle Season

"This memorable story is sure to tug at readers' heartstrings."
—*Publishers Weekly*

Winter Cottage

"Offering a look into bygone days of the gentrified from the early 1900s up until the present time, this multifaceted tale of mystery and romance is sure to please."

—*New York Journal of Books*

"There is mystery and intrigue as the author weaves a tale that pulls you in . . . this is a story of strong women who persevere . . . it's a love story, the truest, deepest kind . . . and it's the story of a woman who years later was able to right a wrong and give a home to the people who really needed it. It's layered brilliantly, and hints are revealed subtly, allowing the reader to form conclusions and fall in love."

—*Smexy Books*

AFTER PARIS

OTHER TITLES BY MARY ELLEN TAYLOR

The Promise of Tomorrow

When the Rain Ends

The Brighter the Light

The Words We Whisper

Honeysuckle Season

Spring House

Winter Cottage

The Alexandria Series

At the Corner of King Street

The View from Prince Street

The Union Street Bakery Series

The Union Street Bakery

Sweet Expectations

AFTER PARIS

MARY ELLEN TAYLOR

 Montlake

This is a work of fiction. Names, characters, organizations, places, events, and incidents are either products of the author's imagination or are used fictitiously. Otherwise, any resemblance to actual persons, living or dead, is purely coincidental.

Text copyright © 2025 by Mary Burton
All rights reserved.

No part of this book may be reproduced, or stored in a retrieval system, or transmitted in any form or by any means, electronic, mechanical, photocopying, recording, or otherwise, without express written permission of the publisher.

Published by Montlake, Seattle

www.apub.com

Amazon, the Amazon logo, and Montlake are trademarks of Amazon.com, Inc., or its affiliates.

EU product safety contact:
Amazon Media EU S. à r.l.
38, avenue John F. Kennedy, L-1855 Luxembourg
amazonpublishing-gpsr@amazon.com

ISBN-13: 9781662513442 (paperback)
ISBN-13: 9781662513435 (digital)

Cover design by Shasti O'Leary Soudant
Cover image: © Leonardo Baldini / ArcAngel

Printed in the United States of America

AFTER PARIS

CHAPTER ONE
DOMINIQUE

Outside Avignon, France
Tuesday, October 2, 1945

I should have stayed away.

For months, I'd lingered on the farm and avoided people. In a small village, there are few secrets. And though the townspeople knew of my return, I'd reasoned I would be safe if I stayed out of sight.

But existing in the shadows was never easy for me.

So, on this bright, warm day, years of hiding and grieving became too much to bear. I styled my hair and donned my best dress, determined to see Avignon on market day and the bookstore and cinema. I rode my bike into town, confident I deserved this small liberation from seclusion.

I tucked a strand of brown hair behind my ear, but I grew nervous when I arrived at the thick medieval walls of Avignon and saw several men in a truck watching me. I kept pedaling through the gates of the ancient walled city and soon found the market in the shadow of the Palais des Papes, a palace built for a papacy long returned to Rome. Today the market bustled with farmers and shoppers.

I dropped my gaze low as I moved along the farmers' stalls lined up in the courtyard. The war was over, and though they had more goods to sell this year, their offerings remained limited. Several farmers and their wives stared as I purchased olives, cheese, and salt. They remembered me, knew my family, but where I'd been during the war remained a mystery.

With my purchases in my bike basket, I hurried away from the market down toward the tree-lined Place de l'Horloge, toward the Cinéma le Vox. A vibrant red poster advertised the movie *Carmen*, a film based on the opera that was released last year.

I had not visited this movie house in years and was struck by how small it felt. Before the war, it had been my portal to the world.

In the days when I had no money for movies, I'd brandish a bright grin for the young boy taking tickets, and he'd let me slip inside. I'd sit in the back and watch films that would transport me into alluring worlds.

Now, the cinema doors opened, and people exited the theater. Couples were laughing and smiling, each dressed in their best prewar fashions. The women, deeply tanned after five years of working in the olive groves, had pinned sprigs of lavender on lace collars or attached brightly colored ribbons to their hats. The men, many still gaunt and too lean, had been released from German work camps or military service. They wore polished but scuffed shoes, and most tucked a neatly folded handkerchief into their breast pockets. Fashion and style were a way of reclaiming their lives and papering over the five years of a devastating war.

We'd all made choices and compromises to survive the German occupation. Many French people wanted to forget, but for me, memories remained so heavy I almost buckled under their weight.

A warm breeze brushed the edges of my skirt as a man paused to glower at me. His frown deepened. The leaves rustled in the trees, whispering a warning woven with dread: *Foolish woman. Leave while you can.*

But pride silenced the cautions. I stayed on the sidewalk as carts rumbled past on cobblestones, a truck engine roared, and laughter threaded through conversations. I'd so missed the sounds of a city, people, and life.

"Don't I know you?" a man shouted.

Tension hardened my spine, but I pretended not to hear his question. I walked away from the theater and pointed my bike down a side street toward the city's walls.

Gravel crunched under my bike's tires as I walked it through the gates and around the train station. The journey to the farm would take a half hour, but I still had enough daylight. If the war had imparted any lesson to me, it was to not linger.

"Mademoiselle," another man said, his voice echoing off stone walls.

I cut my eyes and realized the speaker was a French-uniformed policeman. Flinching, I continued as if I hadn't heard him. Many of his kind had worked with the German occupiers and assisted with arrests and roundups. Given my actions during the war, associating with the police was unwise.

The wooden soles of my shoes scuffed against the dirt as I climbed onto my bike. I calmed bowstring nerves and channeled a peaceful and easy demeanor. Perception was reality, no?

"Mademoiselle! Stop. Now!" His voice sharpened. Men, resenting the war's damage and clinging to shreds of authority, could be as cruel as the Nazis.

I stopped. As I turned toward the policeman, I kept my smile soft and demure as I slipped into the role of the humble farm girl.

The policeman's rawboned features bore the worn appearance of a war-battered soldier or work-camp survivor. Many men and women who'd returned from the war or work camps were angry and restless souls looking for a reason to lash out or justify sins.

"Excuse me?"

"What is your name?" he asked.

"You know me. I'm Madame LeClaire. I live on an olive farm near town."

He stopped within a foot of me, squaring his shoulders, when he must have realized he loomed over my petite frame. "What business do you have in Avignon?"

I dipped my gaze toward the goods in my basket. "It's market day."

"Why were you staring at the cinema?"

"I was curious. I don't get into town often." I wrapped the words in softness, just as I had when I wooed men in Paris. *Paris.* To think about Paris was dangerous. That part of my life needed to remain buried. "If you don't mind, I must return home. My husband is waiting."

He stared at me for a long moment. Taking that as an excuse, I turned and pedaled down the dusty road. I didn't bother to admire the vivid blue sky or glance back at the stone city's sun-bleached walls. Heart thrumming in my chest, I listened for footsteps or an order to stop. But I heard neither and kept pedaling until I reached the farm's twin vine-wrapped pillars.

The stone house had a sloping Roman tile roof. The house and the acres of olive orchards had been in the LeClaire family for seven generations. My husband, Daniel LeClaire, had run away at fifteen and served in the French navy during the Great War. He'd lost a leg in service to France and, upon his return, took work in the port of Marseille. He only revisited the farm during harvest season.

Last year I'd returned during the harvest, and when I saw Daniel, he'd said, *"Look at us. We ran but could not outrun ourselves. And now here we are."*

I crossed the front courtyard, parked the bike, and grabbed my packages. I reached for the door handle. As rusted hinges groaned open, a vehicle's sputtering engine roared in the distance. A glance back revealed a cloud of dust swirling around a truck barreling toward the farm. Several men stood in the open bed.

Fear fingered along my spine. I could reason with one man. But a group who'd been drinking could become a dark and dangerous pack more threatening than wolves.

I hurried inside and locked the door, sliding the wieldy bolt in place. I dropped my goods on a wooden table and backed across the main room toward the cold stone hearth. I grabbed a fire iron and pressed my back to the wall.

A heavy fist pounded on the door as I stood in stagnant, shadowed air. "Mademoiselle, I order you to open the door!"

Drawing in a breath, I didn't speak or move.

"Open the door! Now!"

I'd grown to despise orders and was well practiced at ignoring them.

"I know this house." I recognized the policeman's voice. "It's the LeClaires' farm, but he has no wife!"

Daniel had cautioned me many times about going into town. He'd warned me that the country, shackled between war and peace, remained unstable. *"Give it time. Be patient."*

The cottage's back door opened, and I whirled around to see two men. One leered at me as the other threw the bolt on the front door. Three more men stepped inside.

"I know more than you think, Mademoiselle Dupont," the man closest to me said. I recognized him. He was Charles Roche, the oldest son of a farmer whose estate was on the east side of Avignon. He'd always been big for his age.

"And what's that, Charles?" I gripped the iron tighter.

Hearing his name caught his attention as the group of men grew closer, each staring at me with narrowed gazes. Three wore suits, one a butcher's apron, and the policeman wore his oversize uniform. Dirt dusted their coats, sweat stained their shirts, and they smelled of wine. Daniel didn't want me venturing alone into town because of men like this.

"I need to see your identification papers," the policeman said.

"I dropped my papers while boating on the Rhône," I lied. "I've applied for new ones under my married name, but the paperwork is difficult to get."

The policeman looked pleased to have found this infraction. "I can arrest you for this."

"It was a foolish accident," I conceded. "I'm a little scattered." Most men calmed down if I assured them that I accepted their superior intelligence.

"She's a Dupont," Charles said. "One of the two sisters. They moved to Paris before the war."

"I'm Daniel LeClaire's wife," I said.

The policeman's frown deepened as if he'd discovered another incriminating morsel. "Paris?"

I remained silent. Explaining my life in Paris would mean nothing to him. As far as they knew, I'd left Provence for the north, and for the narrow minded, that was sin enough.

The policeman moved within inches of me. "Are you the older or younger sister?"

I was weary of playing the fool for simpletons. The war was over. The Germans were gone. And I'd abandoned my sins in Paris.

Charles grabbed my arm. He moved quickly for a man his size. He wrenched my hand hard until pain shot up my arm. My grip slackened and I dropped the iron. "What's your name?"

"Does it matter?" the butcher asked. "I hear both sisters slept with Germans. They ate well and lived better than kings while we suffered." His face was puffy, and his eyes were bloodshot.

The policeman's eyes brightened. His day had begun with the monotony of market day. And now he had found a woman who'd collaborated with the Boche—the common slur for German soldiers.

Hardships, tough choices, and humiliations festered in France under German rule. And to vent their anger, the population was cornering vulnerable Frenchwomen suspected of collaboration. Neighbors became judges, juries, and punishers. No one cared why women had made the choices they had during the war.

"Paris," the butcher snarled. "So many Boche in Paris."

The policeman's face was within inches of mine. "Tell us the truth. How many Germans did you fuck?"

I held his gaze as the irony of this moment settled. "I've done nothing wrong."

He pressed the knife blade to my cheek. One of the men yanked off my scarf, exposing my brown hair I'd arranged with care into a topknot this morning. I'd been so excited to see the city. Another man grabbed a handful of my hair and pulled. Pins fell and pinged against the floor. My hair tumbled to my shoulders. The policeman smiled as the knife's metal glinted in the afternoon sun.

During the war, I'd grown accustomed to fear, scarcity, and watching neighbors betray neighbors. I'd thought I'd find safety when I returned home. But I'd discovered men searching for dignity in my shame.

The same restless energy that had driven me out of this little town, praying for a bigger life in Paris, rallied. My distaste for the small minded balled my fingers into a fist, and I drew back. I aimed for the policeman's aquiline nose and slammed my knuckles into it. He howled in pain and immediately slapped me so hard I lost my balance and fell to the floor. The men circled like wolves around an injured doe.

A fat fist grabbed a massive chunk of my hair and jerked my head back, pulling so hard my scalp burned. As my throat lay bare, the policeman brandished the knife's sharp tip in front of my face. He watched closely and waited for my fear. He wanted me to beg. He wanted me to cry, wail.

I did neither.

The blade's pointed tip scraped against my throat, pricking the tender flesh. Liquid warmth trickled down my neck and stained the white collar I'd ironed last night. Still, I didn't flinch but instead held his stare until his annoyance had turned to pure rage.

The policeman raised the knife. "This is what we do to Nazi whores."

CHAPTER TWO
RUBY

Norfolk, Virginia
Monday, June 30, 2025
6:00 p.m.

My love of fashion reached beyond personal pride to obsession. I dressed well for any occasion and took too much time choosing the right dress, skirt, or slacks. Shoes, purses, and jewelry were never afterthoughts but well-thought-out parts of the ensemble. I never "threw on" sweatpants and a T-shirt, even if I was having drinks with my older brother, as I was tonight.

I scrutinized my off-the-shoulder black dress. I wondered if I should change into the red silk sheath. The black dress was more forgiving and draped softly over my thinning frame. The red dress didn't draw as much attention to my diminutive breasts, which was good. All the Nevins women had arrived on this earth with the almost certain guarantee that their bosoms would be ample. I was the exception. That left a few female cousins to wonder if I was adopted, which my parents assured me I was not. I stayed with the black dress.

A teardrop necklace, created from a purple healing stone, dripped toward my scooped neckline and the PICC line scar inches below my collarbone. I tugged the fabric up and then slipped on lavender earrings that drew attention to my short black hair à la Leslie Caron in *An American in Paris*. Maybe I'd keep it short and not bother to grow it out.

After grabbing my purse, I hurried out of my apartment and headed toward my MINI Cooper parked out front. The normalness of this moment felt awkward. I'd grown accustomed to living with my parents over the last two years and had forgotten what it felt like to be alone. They'd wanted me to stay with them, but I'd countered their worries with assurances that I was ready to strike out again.

Three years ago, on a hot July day, I was newly graduated from college and working as a tour guide in Paris. My specialty tours focused on films made in the City of Lights. That day, I'd been escorting twelve people in their late fifties and early sixties. Most were from the East Coast of the United States, but there'd been a couple of Canadians and a gal from Texas there. This was their second or third day in Paris, and they'd shaken off their jet lag and were eager to explore.

Our tour had started on the Champs-Élysées. I began with a brief film history in Paris. I spent extra time discussing movie production during World War II and the challenges of the German occupation. As we moved down the long tree-lined boulevard filled with shops and restaurants, I felt like I might have been getting a bug. I mentioned the films *Taken* (2008) with Liam Neeson, *Charade* (1963) with Audrey Hepburn and Cary Grant, *The Bourne Identity* (2002) with Matt Damon, and *The Da Vinci Code* (2006) with Tom Hanks. We moved down the iconic boulevard past the Place de la Concorde, and I pointed out the filming locations for *Emily in Paris*. I joked that my thick-soled athletic shoes weren't nearly as posh as Emily's high heels.

Usually, when I finished a three-hour tour, I was ready for a café, water, or maybe a croissant. And until the last couple of weeks, I could turn around and give another tour within the hour. But that day I was exhausted.

As I sat in the café with the group, I smiled but felt dizzy and was sweating too much. Many in the group lingered as they practiced their high school French, which was often difficult for French people to decode. When I finally said goodbye to my group, it took everything I had to get to my small fifth-floor walk-up apartment in the fourteenth arrondissement.

I'd assumed I'd have an energy rally. But when it still hadn't arrived a week later, I found myself in the doctor's office, waiting for a quick fix. When the doctors couldn't figure it out, they sent me for more tests. Two weeks later, I was on a plane headed back to the States with my boyfriend, Scott, and a cancer diagnosis in hand. Mom and Dad picked us up at the Norfolk airport. Our journey through Cancerland had begun.

Now, my phone buzzed with a text from Scott.

He'd been good enough to travel with me back to the States. And he'd stuck around for two months, attending doctor's appointments, comforting me after the grim forecasts, and bolstering my family with his positive visions of the future. But the demands of my failing health were hard on him, which he covered up with extreme positivity. And then one day, he said he couldn't do it anymore and returned to Paris.

Scott: Going to be in DC this week. I'd love to see you.

His casual message glossed over my broken heart, which for a long time had been held together with gum and fragile stitches.

Sudden breakups, like ours, were usually final and complete. But our situation was more complicated. After my first consultation with doctors, I'd learned my treatment would leave me sterile. If I wanted children, I'd need to harvest and fertilize my eggs. Scott was enthusiastic about it. Using his sperm made sense, he'd said. We were a team. So, I had twelve eggs harvested. Six remained unfertilized, and to boost my odds of motherhood, I had six fertilized with Scott's sperm.

Even if I never saw Scott again, our potential children would link us. I didn't answer his text and shoved the phone in my pocket.

Scott and Cancerland were in the rearview mirror. The past was the past. Eyes forward. And until I opted to use one of the embryos, I owed him nothing. I slid behind the wheel of my car, started it, and pulled out slowly into traffic.

I hadn't driven in three years, but I was relearning traffic patterns, left-hand turns, and parallel parking. The drive to Norfolk's Waterside restaurant and bar district located on the Elizabeth River took twenty minutes.

When I pulled into Buzzy's bar lot, I said a prayer of thanks when I found an end, pull-through parking spot, a rare beast this time of day in the city.

Out of the car, a warm breeze blew off the river, catching the edges of my A-line skirt as my heels clicked on the sidewalk. As I approached the bar entrance, a man dressed in khakis and a T-shirt paused to hold the door open. I smiled, thanked him, and noted interest flickering in his gaze.

Sandy-brown hair. Dimples. Clean shaven. He was cute. I could smile back. He could ask me to have a drink. I could say yes. We could chat and laugh and have a blast. And then there'd be the inevitable conversation about what each of us had done lately. I'd say "cancer," as if it were a brief side trip to the mountains. He'd try to be cool about it. But reality would sink in, and then he'd ghost me. I wouldn't be mad because life with me was too risky.

As the sun hovered in the sky, I breezed past him into the bar. I glanced into the crowd. It took me a moment to absorb the noise and chatter of people enjoying their lives. It was such a contrast to silent hospital rooms filled with beeping machines.

"Ruby!"

I turned and immediately spotted my brother, Eric. He was five years older than me, but he had a youthful, almost naive way that always made me feel as if I should take care of him. He was an electrical/mechanical engineer who was a rock star in his field. He was tall, with a runner's build. His thick black hair swept across his forehead, drawing attention to vivid blue eyes. When he smiled, his cheeks dimpled.

As he swooped in for a hug, I noticed he'd taken my fashion advice. He'd swapped a favorite ten-year-old MIT jersey for a tailored shirt, new jeans, and docksiders. He hadn't combed his hair carefully or straightened his collar, but he'd made great strides.

Crooked collar and flyaway hairs aside, Eric was the best catch. Still, he'd barely dated in the last few years. Part of his lack of feminine company was due to my illness. He'd dropped his personal life to care for me, just like our parents had. Now it was my turn to take care of him. Hence, tonight's meetup was to plan Operation: Find Eric a Girlfriend.

I wrapped my arms around him, taking in the spicy scent of the aftershave I'd given him for his birthday. "My, my, you do clean up well."

He grinned. "You spoke, and I listened."

I'd been raising fashion standards since I was ten. Even when I was at my sickest, I always combed my thinning hair and donned a bright Hermès scarf and red lipstick. "Are you willing to admit that Ruby knows best about film, fashion, and love?"

"Yes to the first two, but the latter might be a bigger hurdle to jump."

"Nonsense," I said in all seriousness. "Finding love for you won't be hard at all, especially since you ditched the MIT jersey."

He pretended to look wounded. "I love that shirt."

"You've loved it since college, and that's fine as long as you don't wear it around any woman who you'd like to have sex with."

He grinned. "Duly noted. I got us a table, and drinks are on the way." He led me to a round tabletop overlooking softening light dripping on the river.

"How early did you get here so you could grab this table?"

"I came by at lunch and tipped the headwaiter fifty bucks to hold it for me."

"Wow."

"Only the best for my baby sister."

I looked out at what was one of my favorite views in the city. The river was always busy with tankers, ships, sailboats, and people traveling to far-off places.

A waitress arrived with three drinks: red wine, beer, and scotch. I accepted the wine and knew the beer was for Eric. "And who are the scotch and third chair at this table for?"

"Jeff," he said.

"He's in town?" Jeff Gordon had been Eric's roommate at MIT. Since their graduation, he had set up a computer company in Washington, DC. Mom had said it was doing very well.

When I'd first met Jeff, I was in middle school and he was a freshman in college. Almost immediately, I'd developed a crush on him. But timing was never our strength. When I arrived in college, he was off building a new company. And then I was off to Paris. Then I met Scott, and then the cancer. Now we were both back in the same town. "I've missed Jeff."

Jeff visited me several times when I was in the hospital. He'd always come armed with chocolates and an obscure French film he knew I would adore. "He's thinking about setting up an office in Norfolk. Something to do with defense contracting. Hush-hush, from what he says."

"Even if you outlined all the details, I wouldn't understand. Not my wheelhouse." I sipped the wine, a smooth cabernet. "Delicious."

"Have you called Mom and Dad lately?" he asked.

"We spoke two days ago, and they're supposed to be on vacation." I swirled the wine.

"And they text me every hour on the hour when you don't touch base. You know Mom worries."

I pulled out my phone. "Take a picture of us. Your arms are longer than mine."

He held out the phone, both of us smiled, and as I held up a thumb, he snapped the picture. I texted the picture to Mom and Dad, and ten seconds later, a heart emoji popped up. That was Mom's way of playing it cool, but she and Dad were in Germany, making it well after midnight in her time zone. I pictured the phone charging on a nightstand near Mom's head.

"Does she sleep?" I asked.

"No. And those eyes in the back of her head still have twenty-twenty vision."

"Good. She needs it to keep Dad from getting lost." Ever since we were kids, Mom had been the navigator who kept Team Nevins on track. Dad was always the dreamer. A former navy sailor, he was the creative advertising executive who sketched squid and shells on our trash cans and painted a large-scale can of Campbell's soup for my dorm room.

"Is he ever going to retire?" I asked.

"He's talked about it enough," Eric said. "But he still needs a place to be, so likely not."

"His life is back to normal, and he wants to keep it that way."

Eric sipped his beer. "A toast to normal."

I raised my glass and clinked it against his beer bottle. "The purpose of tonight's meeting isn't about me but you. This is Operation: Get Eric a Girlfriend."

Cringing, he gulped another sip of beer as he looked around the room. "I have no idea how to start."

"That's why you have me," I said.

A midsize guy with light-brown hair brushing his shoulders approached us. He wore faded jeans, a black Star Wars T-shirt, and flip-flops. Five o'clock shadow darkened his chin.

It had been a few months since I'd seen Jeff, and I immediately smiled. I rose, ignored that he looked like he'd slept in his clothes, and hugged him close. The scent of soap lingered on his skin. He hugged me tight and lifted me off my feet.

"Ruby, you look amazing as always." His voice was deep, rich, and full of joy.

"Of course I do," I said.

He chuckled and kissed me on the cheek. "I gather we're here tonight as Eric's wing people. Operation: Get Eric Laid," he joked.

Eric cringed. "Bro, that's my baby sister."

Jeff waited until I'd sat and then took the chair beside me. "She's younger than us, but in the spectrum of life, she's wiser than both of us combined."

Jeff had a way of making anyone feel like they were the one. All the women he'd dated had said so. Anyone who did business with Jeff reported he could charm a $100 million contract out of the toughest CEO.

Jeff sipped his scotch, held it to the light, and admired the marbled browns and golds. "Nice."

Eric held up his beer. "To my two favorite drinking buddies."

I took a sip. "To the two best men in the world."

"So, what's the game plan?" Jeff asked. "How do we go about getting someone for Eric?"

My gaze roamed the room and settled on the long mahogany bar, where a group of three women stood. They were traveling in a pack. But I could tell by how they looked at the crowd that they were open to a lovely man approaching them.

The redhead in the group twirled her manicured finger around a thick curl. She shifted back and forth on her high-heeled wedge sandals. Her blouse was tight, her capri pants snug. The brunette wore an A-line dress that dipped past her calves toward sensible tan flats. Next to them was a blond in a pink sleeveless blouse that revealed muscled forearms and skimmed the top of white shorts. Flat sandals completed what appeared to be a relaxed look.

"There are three women at the bar," I said. "Redhead. Brunette. Blond."

"And your assessment?" Jeff asked.

"The blond. Pink top. One o'clock." As Eric turned to look, I added, "Don't look over your shoulder."

"Why not?" Eric asked. "Is she looking this way?"

"She's scanning the room. So be cool. Don't turn this into a big deal," I said. "The goal is to look confident. Self-assured."

"What's wrong with the other two?" Jeff asked.

"They're putting off nervous vibes," I said. "They're lovely, but for the purposes of this exercise, I pick the blond."

Jeff grinned. "You're objectifying them."

"We're in a bar that caters to singles," I replied. "We're all doing it to each other right now."

"Point taken." Eric sipped his beer.

"Walk up to the bar and order a beer while standing beside the blond."

"You make it sound easy," Eric said.

"It is. Order the beer. The woman will notice you, and then you say, 'I'm Eric, what's your name?'"

"And what if she doesn't tell me?" Eric asked.

"She'll bite."

"I'm not so sure."

"*When* she tells you her name, tell her you're here with your sister. Otherwise, you'd buy her a drink now. Could you get her number for coffee or a drink later?"

"'Sister.'" Jeff chuckled. "Good play. Sounds disarming, bro."

"Exactly," I said. "It'll make you sound like a good guy. And if you want to mention we're celebrating me beating cancer, then do it."

Eric's forehead furrowed. "Not funny, Ruby."

I smiled. "Too soon?"

"It will always be too soon," Eric said.

Joking about cancer had been my default from day one. I'd refused to cry or cringe. "Now that you're pissed and not nervous, go talk to her."

"Fine, I will."

"Good."

I sipped my wine as my brother moved toward the bar. Annoyance tightened his spine, and he reminded me of the guy who could design complex engineering systems.

"You think he'll get her number?" Jeff asked.

"I'm about seventy percent sure."

"I'm glad you didn't tell him that. He'd spend the next hour analyzing the remaining thirty percent."

"He tends to overthink."

Jeff chuckled. "I'm cursed with the same kind of brain. We operate in facts, methods, and systems."

"And you both have done well with those brains." Jeff had put himself through college and risen to the top of his class his freshman year. He'd earned his PhD by twenty-five. I was always so proud of his accomplishments. "Eric tells me you might open an office in Norfolk."

"I'm here enough for work. It makes sense."

I held up my glass. "Welcome to the beach."

"Thanks." He clinked his glass against mine. "Looks like you've gotten back to yoga. You look great."

I smiled, realizing the compliment felt good. "I rejoined the studio about a month ago. I'm getting fitter and back in the swing of things."

"You got the all clear from the doctors?"

I glanced toward Eric at the bar. "I'm not sure I'll ever get an 'all clear.' But so far so good."

"Well, you look great."

"Thanks."

"What're you working on these days?" Jeff asked.

Mention of work was now actually a welcome topic. Like Dad and his job, I needed to work. "The Virginia Tourism Bureau has hired me to write a series of articles for next year's spring French film festival. They want me to write a profile on their feature film, *Secrets in the Shadows*, which stars the French actress Cécile."

He met my gaze, his interest keen. "A woman with only one name is always a little dangerous."

I laughed. "Cécile was the 'it' girl from 1938 to 1942. She burst on the movie scene in 1938, made five films, and then, after shooting *Secrets in the Shadows*, she vanished in 1942."

He swirled his glass. "A dangerous woman who disappeared. The world loves a mystery."

I pulled up a picture of Cécile on my phone. Her blond hair swept in gentle curls over high cheekbones and an angled jawline. She'd painted her full lips red, and diamond teardrops dangled from her earlobes.

"Wow, she's a looker," Jeff said. "Why did the festival choose her?"

"I pitched the idea during my interview. If this gig works out, I could end up with a full-time job with benefits."

"Score."

"Cécile was beautiful, mysterious, talented, and she vanished during World War II. She's the complete package."

He handed back my phone. "How do you even start to write about someone who went missing in 1942?"

"Sylvia Rousseau, her dressmaker, moved to the United States after the war. Rousseau's passed away, but her daughter lives in the DC area. I contacted her, and she's agreed to see me. I'm driving up tomorrow."

He raised a brow. "Does Eric know?"

"Not yet."

"I'm not trying to get into your business, but you should tell him. He worries."

"I want to be the girl no one stresses about. I want people to say, 'Ruby is skydiving? No worries, she's got that. Snake wrangling? Knife throwing? She's a natural.'"

A slight smile tipped the edges of his lips. "You're cursed with people who care."

"Not complaining. But I want to be the girl I was before Paris."

"That'll require a time machine. And even if you could go back, the future would always loom on the horizon."

"Stop being analytical."

"Don't get me started on the complexities of time travel."

If I could look into the future, would I? Doubtful. Too much downside. I looked toward the bar. "Eric and the blond are chatting. Both are smiling."

Jeff didn't bother to glance over his shoulder. "Your matchmaking skills are legendary. How many couples can you claim as yours?"

"A few."

"Twelve by my count."

"You're keeping score?"

"I track everything. For example, it's been exactly sixty-nine days since I last saw you. I logged fifteen miles of jogging last week. The cost of bread has risen twenty-six percent in the last four years."

I was touched he remembered our last meeting. He was in town for work. Mom and Dad had hosted him, Jeff, and me for dinner. I wore a red crocheted bucket hat to cover my sprouting hair. He wore his Star Wars T-shirt, and I thought he looked amazing. "Do all those facts bump into each other as they rattle in your head?" I asked.

"It gets crowded up there sometimes." A waitress arrived with a tray of appetizers. When she set them down, Jeff thanked her. "I called ahead and ordered. I can't drink and not eat." He handed me a stack of cocktail napkins. "Eat. You look thin."

"I've gained five pounds," I said with pride.

"Still a tad underweight."

"I thought I was looking sleek."

He lifted a fried shrimp. "Your Cécile had curves."

I took a shrimp. "How can you tell that from a headshot?"

"Eric might have mentioned the project, so I might have done a quick online search." He took a bite of shrimp.

"I didn't think you'd be that interested."

"Why wouldn't I be? It's a fascinating topic."

When Eric returned to the table, his cheeks were flushed. "Susan is meeting me for drinks tomorrow."

"Susan?" I said, as if testing the name. "Nice."

Eric crunched a nacho chip. "Yeah."

"What can you tell us about Susan, other than her name?" I asked.

"She's an attorney. She's new in town. The rest to be determined."

"Excellent," Jeff said.

I took another shrimp, realizing I was hungry. I listened as Jeff and Eric discussed office spaces and places to live. "By the way, I'm heading to DC tomorrow. I'm freelancing an article."

Eric paused midsentence. "By yourself?"

"I'm twenty-five, Eric. And I've been to DC before."

My brother reached for his phone. "I can clear my calendar."

"No," I said. "I'll be fine." Before he could make a rebuttal, I added, "And if I feel bad, I'll call you."

Eric frowned. "No, you won't. You'll tough it out like you did in Paris."

"I called when I needed help."

"You ignored the problems for too long."

"Well, I've learned my lesson. For the most part."

Jeff tore off a piece of bread and buttered it. "She'll be fine, Eric. DC is a four-hour drive away with traffic."

"And there's always traffic," Eric muttered.

"Aren't you going to ask me what I'm writing?" I asked.

Eric shrugged. "The French actress, right?"

"You make it sound boring and sad," I said, laughing.

"Not at all," Eric said. "I know France and film are your things. This article should be a cakewalk for you. Am I wrong?"

"I'm not going to get rich writing this piece, but I'm reclaiming my life."

"Can't you do this via Zoom?" Eric asked.

"No." And the point was to get out of town on my own. "The woman I'm interviewing doesn't do technology. She has a landline and an answering machine. It took me several days to set up this appointment."

He took a long drink from his beer. "I won't tell Mom and Dad."

"I mean, you could, but it might be easier if you don't," I said. I felt a little like the kid who'd opened all her Christmas presents early, rewrapped them, and put them back under the tree. Everyone knew what I'd done, but everyone pretended I hadn't.

"You're going to have to call in each day," Eric said. "And how long will you be gone?"

I looked at Jeff. He looked amused. "Are you going to help a girl out?"

The grin tugged Jeff's lips higher. "She'll be fine, Eric. She said she'll call you if she needs you."

"I will. And I'll be back Sunday or Monday. And I will call if I need help." It would have to be a five-alarm fire for me to call for help, but if a raging inferno broke out, I would at least text. Brush fires I could handle.

"Fine. But be careful."

"Look at it this way: If you're stressing about me, you won't be uptight about your date."

"'Date'?" Eric asked. "I'd already forgotten about that."

"Put a reminder on your phone," I ordered. "This is going to be a good thing. I have a great feeling."

"Ruby is part white witch when it comes to making couples," Jeff said. "Trust her."

Jeff had always taken my side when Eric was overprotective. It was one of many reasons I adored the guy.

Eric rubbed his index finger over his left eyebrow, like he did when he faced a problem that he couldn't fix. "Okay. Go to DC, and I'll go on a date with Susan. But I'm going to worry."

"Worry is your thing," I said, smiling.

"Your next project will be Find Ruby a Guy," Eric said.

"Right." Scott's unanswered text on my phone was proof that I could choose for others but not for myself.

CHAPTER THREE
RUBY

Tuesday, July 1, 2025
7:00 a.m.

I was packed, ready to go, and anxious.

For all my talk of bravery and "please don't worry about me," I was nervous. It had been years since I'd driven more than twenty miles. And now, just before the July Fourth weekend, I planned to drive through the Hampton Roads Bridge–Tunnel, likely clogged with vacation and commuter traffic, and then up I-95. The sooner I left, the better chance I'd have of making it to Northern Virginia before noon.

I pushed down hard on my travel bag and leaned into it as I zipped it closed. I'd be gone for over a week, but choosing what to wear was more difficult than I'd imagined. Was I going to select business attire, Paris chic, southern casual, or something more formal? I was interviewing the daughter of a dressmaker who'd outfitted one of the most beautiful actresses in Paris during the height of World War II and the German occupation. As I'd packed, I couldn't choose the appropriate style, so I didn't. Better to be ready for any scenario that might arise.

I hefted the suitcase, grunting under the weight, and set it hard on the floor. Pulling up the handle, I allowed the wheels to do the work.

My front doorbell rang. I glanced at my slim gold wristwatch as I hurried to the door. I wasn't shocked to find Eric standing on my doorstep.

"I'm fine," I said.

"I know. I'm helping you load your suitcase, which weighs three tons."

That teased a smile. "Two tons. And thanks. I wasn't excited about dragging it down the stairs."

Eric hoisted the bag. "Bricks, bars of gold, rocks?"

"Chiffons, jeans, silks, and, of course, shoes."

"You always look nice," he said.

"Thanks."

Today, I'd chosen white capri pants and a lightweight beige safari top. I had on my favorite Dior scarf, wedge sandals, hoop earrings, and a collection of gold beaded bracelets. My cross-body purse was a vintage Saint Laurent I'd found in a Paris thrift shop. A wide-brimmed hat rested by my front door. Of course I wouldn't meet Madame Bernard in this outfit. But no reason to miss out on any chance to dress well.

Eric walked me to my MINI Cooper and loaded my suitcase in the trunk with an exaggerated grunt. "When you get to your hotel, have someone lift this for you."

"Will do."

He met me at the driver's side door and hugged me. "Call me if you need help."

"I will. I promise." I settled behind the wheel and started the engine. I rolled down the window. "Don't worry."

He shoved his hands in his pockets. "I'll do my best."

"Take Susan out."

"Will do."

I pulled out of the spot and wound through the parking lot toward the main road that would take me to I-64 West. I made good time for about ten minutes. Then traffic stopped closer to the Hampton Roads Bridge–Tunnel. I took the chance to set up one of Cécile's movies, which I'd downloaded to my phone.

I'd seen all her movies at least three times, but *Secrets in the Shadows* was by far my favorite. It was a murder mystery set in wartime Paris and centered around a woman accused of murdering her older husband. Cécile played Françoise, the sultry accused. Actor Louis Lambert played Guy LeRoy, the private detective who was a cynical World War I veteran.

There was nothing remarkable about the story. But each of the actors brought an intensity to their parts that was gripping even after eighty years. But when Henri Archambeau wanted to cast the sultry Cécile in this role, film producers, directors, and movie reviewers questioned his choice. No one believed the star of four romantic comedies would have the acting chops to pull it off.

But Cécile had proved them all wrong. Reviewers after the war would later link her intense performance to how Paris had reacted to the Germans tightening the noose around the city. If she had not disappeared, she would have been a worldwide star.

In the movie, Guy believes Françoise is guilty, but he needs her money to pay off his gambling debts, so he takes her case. As Guy digs into her story, he grows closer to Françoise. Her demeanor is impossible to ignore, and he falls for her. But, when Guy discovers proof that Françoise is the killer, he must choose between hiding the truth or turning her over to the police. In the end, Guy takes justice into his own hands.

Funded by the German occupiers, the film upheld the values of duty and honor despite personal cost. Symbolism was in every frame of the movie. Françoise represented wanton France bent on ruining German values. Guy epitomized the hardworking German soldier mesmerized by the Parisiennes who dyed their hair, painted their nails, and wore makeup.

I'd watched this film so many times I could picture the scenes as the audio played while I drove. Françoise's smoky voice evoked images of her walking into Guy's office, tears spilling down her cheeks as she slid off her coat. Nearly naked in a sheath, she insisted she loved him. The viewer almost believed the two would have their happily ever after.

After Paris

The sensuality, pain, and loss embedded in the scene always held my full attention.

Rumor had it that Cécile and Louis were having an affair at the time of the filming, so their relationship had bled onto the screen. Others said their *affaire* was propaganda designed to boost ticket sales. If they weren't an item, their talents were underrated.

I'd analyzed the movie too much. But Françoise had spoken to me as I'd lain in hospital beds hooked up to IVs. She, like me, found herself trapped in a world not of her choosing.

After four hours and two replays of the movie, I approached Northern Virginia and entered the Beltway encircling the DC metro area. I sat straighter and gripped the wheel a little tighter. My phone's Maps app interrupted the *Secrets in the Shadows* finale and directed me toward Old Town Alexandria and the narrowing streets of the historic city.

I'd booked a hotel room in Old Town Alexandria on Union Street in the heart of the historic district. I parked in the hotel's underground lot and hefted my suitcase out of the trunk.

Good Lord, what had I packed?

Dragging the suitcase, I made my way to the lobby. When I reached the front desk, I was more tired than expected.

I squared my shoulders and smiled at the young woman dressed in a burgundy jacket bearing a gold name tag that read **JOANIE**.

"Ruby Nevins. I have a reservation."

When I first arrived in Paris, I was overwhelmed by the city. But in a few weeks, the ancient buildings and winding streets and I had become good friends. By the end of that first month, Paris had felt like home. But I was healthy and believed I was indestructible like all early twentysomethings.

Now I understood how fragile life was. A few cancer cells could topple any life. Cancer had derailed mine, and though I was in remission, the chances were that it would get me one day.

However, that day wasn't today.

I smiled at Joanie as I handed over my credit card, filled in the information about my car, and took my key. I rode the elevator to the fifth floor and walked to room 512. When I swiped the key and the lock didn't open, I rested my head against the door.

"We're not doing this," I muttered at the key. "You're going to let me into my room." I swiped the card again, and this time, the green light appeared, and the lock popped open. I dragged my suitcase into the room and let the door slam behind me.

I moved toward the window, overlooking the meandering waters of the Potomac River.

Several sailboats glided on the water, and pedestrians walked along the winding path. Blue skies, white puffy clouds, and a gentle breeze teased the treetops on the Virginia side of the river.

I kicked off my shoes near a small round table flanked by two chairs.

Tugging off my earrings, I slid off my capris and let them fall to the floor. I hung them up, unbuttoned my blouse, and laid it on the double bed closest to the door. I opened my suitcase, hung up my clothes, and changed into an oversize T-shirt and gym shorts.

A sigh slipped over my lips as I pulled back the coverlet of the bed closest to the window and slid under the sheets. I'd just opened my phone, ready to watch the finale of *Secrets in the Shadows*, when it pinged with another text message from Scott.

Scott: Not sure if my last message went through. I'm in DC this week for work. Before I fly back to Paris, I'd like to drive down to Norfolk to see you.

I let my head fall against the headboard and then texted: **Why the interest now?**

Scott: Do I need a reason?

I could've written a long paragraph summarizing how little I thought of him and his newfound desire to see me. If he'd been honest from the beginning and said my illness was too much, I might have been more forgiving. But he'd sworn up and down that we were in the fight together. We'd made embryos. And then he'd left and hadn't responded to any of my messages.

But I didn't have the energy to fight with him now, and I didn't want to waste time.

My near-death experience had sharpened my capacity to cut through bullshit and protect myself. I'm out of town. Another time.

I then texted a smiling selfie to Eric and Jeff, assuring them I'd arrived in one piece, and I put my phone on "do not disturb."

All that mattered now was this article.

CHAPTER FOUR
RUBY

Wednesday, July 2, 2025
9:00 a.m.

I didn't sleep well.

When I woke up in the hotel room last night, it was past 1:00 a.m. For several minutes, the sterile surroundings had thrown me off. I blinked, searched for my bearings, and then remembered.

It was a nice hotel. But its decor and furnishings were industrial enough to evoke memories of strange hospital rooms. The beds were always too hard, the side rails too restrictive. My mother tried to make my room friendlier with a favorite quilt, a stuffed bear, and even a few Taylor Swift posters.

Sometimes, when I'd wake in the middle of the night, I'd panic. Then I'd see my mother sleeping in a recliner or on a cot, and I'd calm.

But as hard as Mom tried to soften the experience, she couldn't go with me to all the tests, blood draws, and scans. I started to send her home, insisting she sleep in a real bed. There was no reason for my cancer to kill her. On those nights, I'd wake to the beep of machines, the rumble of carts, or the quiet conversations of nurses and doctors. And on those nights, my darkest worries would creep out of the shadows and circle my bed.

That's when I'd text fellow patient Jason, who was often on the same ward as me. Jason was forty-one and fighting non-Hodgkin's lymphoma. So far, the "foma," as he called his disease, was winning.

Me: Tell me something funny.

Jason: Why was the calendar afraid?

Me: Why?

Jason: Its days are numbered.

His brand of dark humor made me laugh and slew the late-night dragons. When he graduated from the ward, I followed him into the hallway, waving a handmade sign that read **BON VOYAGE**. The nurses and doctors cheered him on as his parents wheeled him out of the hospital.

After Jason left the ward, we rarely communicated again. There's this weird barrier between the living and the dying, and as much as we pretend that we're all on the same team, we aren't. He'd hopped to the living side of the line, while I remained with the sick and dying.

I rose early and took a long hot shower. After drying my hair, I applied makeup, choosing understated beiges and browns for my eye shadow and minimal blush. The point was for the red lipstick to pop. I scrutinized the foundation with a critical eye, pleased it covered the circles under my eyes.

My outfit debate had finally ended. I chose a white linen blouse, a blue Hermès scarf, fitted black pants, tan ballet flats, and an oversize brown purse. Gold hoops dangled from my ears, and a small gold cross settled in the hollow of my throat. Effortless chic took work.

I double-checked my bag for my notepad, covered with questions and ideas, and headed out.

I considered getting an Uber but opted to walk the five blocks north along Union Street to Michele Bernard's town house.

The air was softened by a cool river breeze. I enjoyed the historic brick buildings with wrought iron railings, the small cafés with outdoor seating, and the elegant trees dating back centuries. It was reminiscent of Paris, though if I'd made the comparison to someone from France, any one of them would have raised an eyebrow. *Three centuries versus fifteen. Ridiculous.*

I was breathless when I arrived at the three-story brick town house at the corner of Union and Cameron Streets. I knew Madame Bernard was a widow, and her late husband had been in commercial real estate. Beyond that, I knew very little about the woman. Her mother was Sylvia Rousseau Talbot, who had dressed Cécile circa 1940 to 1942, not only for her most iconic roles but also for galas, parties, and photo shoots. Based on Cécile's fashion photos, Sylvia Rousseau Talbot had been an enormous talent.

I climbed the ten brick stairs, breathless, wishing I'd taken the Uber. I still struggled with stamina, which could be elusive. I pressed the doorbell. If Jason were here, he'd have another corny joke: "My husband said I should do lunges to stay in shape. That would be a big step forward."

Smiling, I straightened my shoulders, and I heard music drifting toward me. I recognized the French singer Édith Piaf. She was crooning her most famous song, recorded in the late 1950s, in the final years of her career. In the refrain, she continued to emphasize that she'd regretted nothing.

Was Madame Bernard getting into the mood of my interview, or was the idea of my questions stirring up something?

Determined, heeled footsteps moved toward the door. It opened to a petite woman attired in a stylish black dress. Silver hair twisted in a chignon, diamond studs winking from her ears. I was a little shocked at her clear, direct gaze. Madame Bernard was at least eighty, but she had the vitality of a woman twenty years her junior.

"Madame Bernard, I'm Ruby Nevins," I said. "I'm here to talk to you about your mother and her work with Cécile."

"'Madame'? I like it." The woman looked me over. "Are you French?"

"No, but I lived in Paris for several years."

A brow arched. "And why did you leave?"

"Family matters. It made sense to come home."

Madame Bernard inclined her head forward. "Of course. Family is everything. Please come inside."

The entryway was long and thin, and a Turkish runner stretched over oak floors toward a white kitchen. On my left was a parlor decorated in French country style, complete with white pillows, soft pastel paintings, an ornate chandelier, and a white marble fireplace. It was lovely.

I followed Madame Bernard into the parlor. After she beckoned me to sit, she sat on the white cushions on the couch across from mine. Between us was a Louis XIV table with a silver tray holding coffee and cookies.

My mother loved white furnishings. But she said that with two active children and two golden retrievers, they had only been a dream. She had vowed to redecorate once her children left for college, but the thick, durable navy blue fabric remained. Trips to Johns Hopkins in Maryland, hotel stays, food, and deductibles had drained their wallets. So, chic whites remained a dream.

"Could I record our conversations?"

"Perhaps later. Today I thought we could take some time to get to know each other," Madame Bernard said.

As I set my purse by my feet, I was fearful I might forget key details. "Of course."

"Coffee?"

"That would be nice."

"Cream, sugar?"

"Yes."

Nodding approval, she poured two cups of coffee, flavored with both cream and sugar, and set a napkin alongside my cup and saucer. "Help yourself to the cookies."

"Thank you." I set a cookie on my napkin and imagined my mother warning me about crumbs and stains. "I love that song you're playing."

"It's one of my mother's favorites," she said. "You live in Norfolk, you say?"

"Yes. I grew up there. My dad was navy, and now he's an advertising executive. Mom was a teacher, then stayed home with my brother Eric and me." I considered sipping the coffee but opted to wait until my nerves settled.

"What does your brother do?"

"Eric's an engineer," I said. "Lives in Norfolk too. Very smart."

"And you?"

"I graduated college early, moved to Paris, and was a tour guide there for several months. My specialty was French film tours, and I wrote dozens of online articles on the subject." I hesitated a fraction. "And now I'm back in the States, revisiting a subject I love."

Madame Bernard sipped her coffee, her lined hand as steady as a surgeon's. "For the tourism department's French film festival?"

"Yes. The Virginia Tourism Bureau is my boss and the sponsor of the festival. There will be five festivals across the state next spring." Did she see freelance writing falling somewhere between work and a hobby? "If all goes well, the bureau might hire me full time to coordinate more festivals."

Madame set her cup in the saucer so gently there was no sound. "I was surprised your event chose to feature Cécile. She's all but forgotten by most today."

"I pitched the idea. I'm kind of a Cécile superfan."

"Ah, so I'm not the only one who admires her work."

"Cécile had so much talent, unfulfilled potential, and beauty, and then she disappeared. I've read all I can about her. Several articles credited your mother's designs. I found a photograph of Cécile. It was never published but was part of a French *Vogue* fashion shoot in 1941 on the Passerelle Debilly footbridge."

In that image, Cécile was wearing a black off-the-shoulder dress with a fitted waist and a flared skirt. Sylvia was fussing over the lines of Cécile's skirt. She had glanced at the photographer, who had snapped the picture.

Madame didn't stifle a weary sigh. "My mother wouldn't like the idea of me talking to you. She never talked about Paris."

"Why? Her work was excellent."

"The war. The occupation in Paris forced many to make choices and keep secrets. It was difficult for so many, and my mother was no exception."

"How did she come to fashion?"

"Ah, her father was a tailor in Warsaw. He was one of the finest. She said his address book contained contact information for the city's most elite men. My mother learned from him. And, of course, from her mother, who was French and a talented seamstress in her own right."

"When was your mother born?"

"1918. My grandmother died when my mother was fifteen. In the midthirties, the situation in Poland was deteriorating, so my grandfather sent his only daughter to Paris. She was seventeen. She didn't want to leave him. But he insisted and set up an apprenticeship for her with his old friend Aleksy Jarek, who owned a lingerie factory in Paris."

"When did your mother arrive in Paris?"

"1935. My mother sewed and cut patterns and later sketched designs at the factory for five years. She also began to help Mr. Jarek with the incoming Polish refugees he often employed."

"'Sylvia Rousseau' doesn't sound like a Polish name."

"By the mid-1930s, many from the east were fleeing to France. The French government, fearing overcrowding, began deporting foreign nationals. My mother decided to get forged papers that stated her name was Sylvia Rousseau. Zofia Rozanski, the daughter of a French Catholic and a Polish Jew, ceased to exist."

"What did her father say about her name change?"

"He supported it. The Germans were stirring more trouble in Germany by 1936, and he feared they'd come for the rest of Europe one day."

"When the Germans took over Paris, she must have been terrified."

"If she was, she never said. She refused to leave her job and the Polish nationals who needed her help."

"How did she help them?"

"Mama worked with a French forger, Marc LePen. He made false travel papers all through the war. He also ran a small boulangerie and employed a young woman named Emile Dupont."

"Cécile's sister?"

"Yes. Emile always disliked the film industry. But she followed her sister to Paris and became committed to Monsieur LePen and the French Resistance."

I'd tried to dig up information on Emile Dupont but so far had yet to find anything. "Did your mother ever speak of the sisters to you?"

"No. She would talk about the lovely fabrics and the dresses she made then. However, she never discussed her clients, politics, or the difficulties during the occupation. She began keeping secrets at a young age, and years of staying silent left a mark on my mother. Up until the day she passed, she was cautious and never discussed anything related to the government."

Tension crept into Madame Bernard's features, and I shifted topics. "What was the first film that your mother worked on?"

Her taut smile softened. "Cécile hired my mother to dress her on *Too Many Choices*. That was the fall of 1940."

"The Germans were in Paris in 1940."

"Yes. They'd been in the city since June."

"The Germans closed the film industry for months," I said. "It didn't reopen until the following year."

"The film's director had connections in Germany. They allowed him to finish *Too Many Choices*."

That explained why, when movie production officially began again in 1941, Cécile was one of the first actresses to be rehired.

"Why did your mother leave the lingerie factory?"

"The factory closed when the owner, Monsieur Jarek, died in June 1940. For a few months, she sewed piecework, often for German officers or their wives; then her friend Emile arranged a meeting with her sister."

"That must have been difficult for her."

"She never said if it was or wasn't. She was on her own and didn't have the luxury of awkward conversations. By 1940, her father had died, and whatever assets he'd had in Poland had been seized."

"Did your mother date? Was there anyone she fancied?"

Madame Bernard smiled. "She was always a very passionate woman. She and my father were always kissing. So, I suspect she had her share of lovers during the war."

"When did she meet your father?"

"In 1943. She sailed out of Marseille to Portugal and then later to England. That's where they met. After the war, they returned to America. She often joked that England was swimming with American GIs. And all she had to do was pluck out her favorite."

Her tone had lightened. I suspected this was a favorite family story. It was much like when my mother and father talked about their first meeting. They'd met in a downtown Norfolk bar. Mom had asked Dad to dance, and he'd said yes so fast she'd laughed.

"Did your mother ever return to France?" I asked.

"No. When my French club planned a trip to Paris in the early sixties, I had to beg my mother to let me go. My father finally convinced her, but she insisted I call her each evening while I was there."

"Tell me about your father."

"He was an airman who survived twenty-five missions and then asked my mother to marry him. I was born in England."

"How did you learn about your mother's work with Cécile?"

"I knew my mother could make anything from fabric, but again, she said little about Paris. When she passed in 1982, my father couldn't bear to handle her belongings, so the task was mine. I found a leather-bound diary, and inside was the original picture you mentioned. It showed Cécile and my mother on the Passerelle Debilly bridge, with the Eiffel Tower in the background. The photographer had scrawled on the back: 'Fashion shoot, 1941. Cécile with her dressmaker.'"

"Your mother kept a diary?"

"Yes. From the day she moved to France until the day she left Europe for good. Over ten years."

Madame Bernard rose and walked to a desk tucked in the corner. She lifted a small leather-bound book and gave it to me. "Handle it with care. The pages are quite delicate."

"Yes, of course." I skimmed my fingers over the soft, stained leather. The book's spine had broken, and many of the pages were no longer bound.

"We all think we know our parents. I thought I had a mother who worried too much and made me wear homemade, albeit elegant, clothes." The silence grew thick with her regrets. "What I wouldn't give for one of the dresses she'd made me. They were far beyond anything a girl could find at the mall, but I was a teenager, and we aren't our brightest at fourteen."

"When I was fourteen, I rocked the Taylor Swift look like no one else. I begged my mother to let me dye my hair blond, but she wouldn't hear of it."

Madame Bernard smiled. "Your mother was wise. Your dark hair suits you, and I like the short cut. It's very chic."

"Thank you."

After Paris

I looked down at the neatly penned entries. The closely spaced lines of text saved paper too precious to waste. The first entry was June 2, 1935.

Paris, like Warsaw, shares similar traits of a busy capital city. People hurry about. And there's a delightful blend of rumbling horse-drawn carriages and roaring car engines. France has an air of old-world elegance, as one would expect. Poland's Second Republic, like me, was born in 1918, and has a youthful brash energy. If Paris and Warsaw were family, Paris would be the older sophisticated sister. Warsaw would be her vibrant, less polished younger sibling.

In Paris, the women move with a confidence I envy. They paint their nails and wear silk stockings and makeup. I want to look like them. I'm in love with Paris.

I glanced up at Madame Bernard. "She wrote her diary in English."

"Her father insisted she not write her letters to him in Polish, French, or German. Of course, writing down any thoughts could get anyone arrested. Using English was no guarantee of safety, but so few people read it in those days. If one were to get a hold of the journal, it would take time to decipher. The French were already censoring her people when Mama arrived in Paris in 1935."

"Before the war? I had no idea."

"It was a different time."

"What were your mother's impressions of Cécile?"

"Mama said in her diary that Cécile didn't have as extensive an education as she did, but Cécile had a brilliant memory. Her recall was photographic. What she lacked in education, she made up for in raw brainpower, cunning, and bravado. Though Cécile couldn't read German, she learned how to speak it fluently when the Germans arrived."

I smoothed my hand over the worn pages. So many questions bombarded me. I wanted to read this journal and dissect every line. "Did your mother save anything else from that time?"

"A few letters," she said as she sat on the sofa again. "I've collected anything associated with the movies my mother worked on. I have ten dresses she made for Cécile."

"How did you find them?"

"There's quite the vintage auction market in Paris. And I put out the word that I wanted anything Cécile had worn. There were many fakes, of course, but I insisted on photographs of Cécile in the dress. The first few garments that came to me were from the 1940 film *Too Many Choices*. The costumes were nothing spectacular. My mother inherited the creations from the film's former dressmaker, but she managed to add her own flair. But word has a way of getting out, and about ten years ago, I received a call from a dealer. I flew to Paris to meet him. That's when he showed me these dresses from *Secrets in the Shadows*." From a folder she pulled out a collection of black-and-white photos featuring Cécile. "My mother always sewed her initials into my clothes. When I inspected these dresses, I discovered a very discreet 'SR' on the underside of the hem."

"It must have been thrilling."

"I was excited and sad. My mother kept so much of her life from me. I would've loved to have talked to her about her time in Paris. But she never discussed the occupation days."

I understood shutting the door on a troubled past. Pain and sadness were a part of life, but that didn't mean one had to keep reliving it.

"If you come back, I'll have the dresses ready to show you. I wanted to meet you before I got too far ahead of myself."

I smiled. "I understand. Could I take pictures of a few of these diary pages? I'd love to read them."

"Of course. But I would ask you not to share them."

"I won't discuss anything you don't want me to." I turned the pages, holding my breath when they creaked. I snapped a couple of dozen images. "Does your mother know what happened to Cécile?"

"Read those entries, and then we'll talk again. How about tomorrow?"

"Excellent. I have a meeting on Friday with Hank Johnson, a film expert at the Smithsonian national history museum."

"Lovely man. You'll enjoy him. Call me when you wish to meet again."

"I will. Thank you."

"I'm happy you called me about this article, Ruby. I rarely get the chance to talk about my mother."

"I'll bend your ear until you tell me to stop."

She sipped her coffee. "I'm sure I'll be able to handle it."

CHAPTER FIVE
SYLVIA

Paris, France
Saturday, October 5, 1940

When I wore my tailored scarlet jacket, I was Kobieta w Czerwieni, or the Woman in Red. The garment's vibrant color always stood out in crowds, and so made it easy for the Warsaw refugees to find me.

The coat's padded shoulders dipped into a fitted slim waist that enhanced my curved hips. Though it epitomized the current Parisian style, it was also very useful. Inside the jacket were a half-dozen pockets crafted to blend with the design. Hidden zippers secured identity papers, enough money to sustain me for weeks, a small knife, and lipstick.

The station was busy today, but it was not humming with panic and confusion as it had been in June. Then terrified French citizens had scrambled to escape the invading German army, dragging massive trunks, toting large bags, or carrying paintings as they crammed onto train cars. Ultimately, the lucky few who managed to obtain a seat on a train were forced to abandon their possessions in the station or on the platform.

Today, I was searching for a young couple with two small children. They were from Warsaw, fleeing the Germans, who were now walling off a section of the city.

I caught the gaze of a man in a dark overcoat wearing a wide-brimmed hat. He held a small sleeping boy with bright-blond hair and rosy cheeks. Next to him was a sturdy woman wearing a scarf and darned wool stockings and carrying a baby. I moved toward them, careful not to shout. As I approached, the man's scanning gaze settled on my jacket. Slowly, his eyes met mine.

"Albin?" I asked.

He stood straighter.

"Come with me," I whispered in Polish.

Hearing his native language eased some of the tension in his face as he nudged his wife. I knew little about the couple other than their first names and former jobs: Albin and Miriam. The couple had owned a shoe shop on the eastern side of Warsaw, near the Vistula River. Now in the shadow of the rising wall built to contain the Ghetto.

I led Albin, Miriam, and their children out of the Gare de l'Est. We crossed the cobblestone street and headed south toward the Marais district. The buses weren't predictable, and uniformed German soldiers often guarded the Métro. Many bicycles rambled past, but no motor traffic. The Germans had banned most car traffic in June. Our only option was to walk.

"It's a couple of kilometers," I said in Polish.

Albin and Miriam braced as if this was one of many hurdles they'd faced. They followed close behind me as we wove down a side street and cut to another. A half hour later, we arrived in the Marais district, the most ancient neighborhood in Paris. I guided the young family to a vivid green building that had no signs or markings. As we approached the front door, a man stumbled out, a scantily clad woman waving goodbye.

Albin took hold of my elbow. "What is this place?"

"It's a brothel," I said. "The owner was originally from Poland and is sympathetic to guests like you. She'll give you a place to stay while I sort out your papers. There's food, milk for the children, and a bed to sleep in."

Albin looked as if he'd argue, but Miriam shot him a look of warning. "A bed and meal would be very welcome."

We entered the house. The first sitting room to the right was decorated with antiques, gilded mirrors, and paintings of large-breasted women. "We'll climb the stairs to the third floor. It's quiet, and there's no business conducted there."

On the third-floor landing, I opened the door to a room with two double beds, a small table with four chairs, and a window that overlooked the back alley of another building. On the table was a man's dress fedora and a woman's black wide-brimmed hat.

As Miriam looked around the room, the baby began to stir. "I need to feed him."

"First, I must take your pictures for your new papers." I beckoned Albin to sit, and I bade him to swap his hat for the Parisian style. I removed a small camera from my purse and took several pictures. Next, I draped a white sheet over his chest, settled his oldest son in his lap, and took a picture. I did the same with Miriam and the baby.

"We are to wait?" Albin asked.

"Yes. Stay out of sight. The Germans have been polite since arrival, but they're always watching. You don't need to catch their attention."

"Polite Germans?" Albin's distaste was palpable.

"For now, yes," I said. "But we both know that will change."

Albin grunted. "When will you return?"

"As soon as your papers are ready, in a day or two. Then I'll take you to another contact, and you'll travel south toward Spain."

Miriam sat on the bed, and as the baby fussed, she unfastened her blouse and attached the infant to her breast. "I'm grateful to you."

Last year's bombings had crushed Poland. Warsaw had fallen under siege. Weeks later, the city surrendered, and its occupation began.

My father was a stubborn old man who'd refused to leave Warsaw, no matter how many times I'd begged him. It seemed father and daughter were no different.

"Do you have news from Warsaw?" I asked.

"It's bad," Albin said. "People are dying. There are roundups and shootings. Rioters burned your father's shop to the ground."

"You know my father?"

"The tailors' and shoemakers' families are well acquainted," Albin said. "It's how we heard about the Woman in Red."

"Is he alive?"

"No. But he died peacefully," Miriam said.

Unshed tears clogged my throat. So many regrets clawed inside me. But a part of me was glad he wasn't witnessing his city's destruction. "You were with him?"

"My mother was. Your father was glad you'd left Warsaw. He was proud of the daughter who wore the red jacket."

I couldn't speak for a moment.

"Do the people in Paris realize the wolf has cornered them?" Albin asked. "The beast is full and fat now, but when it gets hungry, it will strike."

"No one seems worried," I said.

France and England had declared war on Germany, but no one in Paris had exhibited any sense of urgency. They went about their lives as if Poland was a distant land and the Germans would treat France differently.

"They're fools," Albin said.

There was a knock at the door, and I crossed the room and opened it. A young serving girl with dark hair and pale skin handed me a food tray. "Thank you. Our guests will only be here a few days." My French now mimicked the best Parisian accent.

"Madame isn't worried," the girl said.

"You're very kind," I said.

When I closed the door, Miriam said, "You look like you were born and raised in Paris."

"Blending in to the city is important."

My former employer was Monsieur Jarek. He had spoken French with a heavy Polish accent, and he knew the police were watching him. "*Your French is perfect, and you look like a good Christian Frenchwoman. No one will question you. You could be of great help to others like us,*" Monsieur Jarek had said nearly five years ago.

"When we leave, wear these hats. There are French clothes hanging in the closet," I said.

Miriam glanced at her discarded headscarf. "What's wrong with this?"

"It's lovely," I said. "But as I said, it's important not to draw attention to yourself."

"We wait just a few days?" Albin asked.

"Yes. Have your money ready when I return." I rewound the film, removed the case, and tucked it into a pocket. The camera went deep into my purse. If anyone searched me, the camera would be cause enough now for an arrest. The German soldiers all had cameras and snapped pictures as if they were on holiday, but the devices were forbidden for the French.

"I can give it to you now," Albin said.

"No, keep it until I have your documents."

I'd met the forger Marc LePen five years earlier, when I'd determined that I needed French identity papers. When I first arrived at LePen's boulangerie, I was running late after my shift at the factory. A cigarette dangled from his lips as he unlocked the bakery's large wooden back door. Tall and lean and with dark hair, Monsieur LePen wore a shirt that was dusted with flour, and his fingertips were stained with ink. I tried to hand him francs, but he told me to wait until the papers were ready. When I returned three days later, I exchanged money for my new identity papers as well as sets for three of Monsieur Jarek's immigrant employees.

That day we'd barely spoken two words to each other, and now more than ever, we monitored our conversations whenever we made our exchanges.

"We'll do whatever you say," Albin said.

I uncovered the platter of cheese, bread, and sausages. We all lived under rations now, but food was still attainable. This brothel was a favorite of the Germans, and the madame was granted extra ration cards. "I'll return soon."

After exiting the house's side door, I moved along the city streets until I reached LePen's boulangerie in the Marais. I knocked on the back door. Moments later it opened to a grayer, thinner LePen.

"Sylvia."

Standing in the kitchen wiping down a butcher block countertop was Marc's lover, Emile. The young shop girl was tall and slim, with dark curly hair that skimmed her jaw. Last year, I was surprised to learn the two were sleeping together. Monsieur LePen liked his solitude and, given his work, had to be careful. But the young Emile from Provence had taken a job in his shop and soon found a way into his bed.

I entered the kitchen, savoring the soft scents of yeast and flour. The boulangerie had been swept and cleaned since the morning baking, and in these few hours, it was gleaming and waiting for the next round of baking.

Emile looked up from her worktable. "Sylvia. I was wondering if we'd see you again. We were sorry to hear about Monsieur Jarek's passing."

It had been a blow to us all. The older man had the constitution of a bear, and we'd all imagined him living forever. He'd died in mid-June.

Emile came around the worktable, and we kissed each other on the cheek. "How are you? I heard the factory closed," she said.

"Monsieur Jarek's wife and sons don't want to keep the factory. They're selling and leaving Paris for the south."

"You no longer have a job?" Emile asked.

"I don't. But there is plenty of piecework with the German soldiers."

"How can you work for them?" she asked.

Her hatred for the Germans had narrowed her vision of the bigger picture. "What's most pressing are the papers for my latest guests. I need to move them to Spain in the next few days."

"It may take longer," Emile said. "There's greater risk crossing the borders now."

"When do you think they can leave?" I asked.

"It will be several weeks," Emile said. "Do you have film?"

"I do."

I handed her the film case and followed her into a storage closet. Inside, she pushed back coats and opened a hidden doorway to a small windowless room with a tabletop press, ink bottles, and official government stamps. This was where Emile and Marc developed pictures and created forgeries.

"This is a list of their new names," Emile said. "They should all use these names now. It's important the children hear only their new names."

For security, I never shared a family's identity or where they were currently staying. "Thank you." I tucked the list in an inside jacket pocket.

"Of course."

Marc waved inky fingers. "Go, I have work."

As Emile and I left, he shifted his attention to his press. She closed the door behind her.

When we stood in the kitchen, Emile rested her hands on her hips. "You'll need work. The cost of food rises every day."

"It'll sort itself out."

"You sound so relaxed."

I was worried, but talking about it was fruitless. "Others suffer much more than me."

"You could work for my sister."

"The actress?"

"I still call her Dominique, but to everyone else she's Cécile. More mysterious and glamorous, I suppose. Cécile isn't happy with the man who dresses her."

Through the shop's back window, I noticed a French policeman lingering in the alley. I turned away, feeling the list of new names pressing against my body.

Emile was silent for a moment and then glanced over my shoulder. "He's gone."

"Good. We don't need the attention."

"They're everywhere now," Emile said with disgust. "All of them ready to turn us over to the Germans in exchange for a kind word or a favor. I've come to despise anyone in a uniform."

"Be careful," I said.

"You sound like my sister. She's always warning me to be more cautious."

I hadn't met the actress but had enjoyed her last film. "Why is your sister not happy with her dresser?"

"He's having trouble fitting her figure. He's enamored with her large bosom and seems to enjoy touching her. Yesterday, she walked off the set when her dresser kept fiddling with her cleavage. The director told her if she did that again, he would fire her. Now that you're free, you could be of help to her."

"I'm certain I'm better than anyone your director has hired. And I do need the work."

Emile regarded me. "It's not only the costumes. Cécile will need gowns for premieres and parties."

"That's what I do, but does she have the power to hire me?"

"That's up to Henri Archambeau, the director, but no man has told my sister what to do since she was young. If you're free, we'll visit her on set now."

I didn't know the world of movies, but I knew its production was now controlled by the Germans. I could point out that this job wasn't so different from mending clothes for German soldiers, but I didn't. "Introduce me to your sister and the director. They'll both see I'm the person to dress Cécile."

CHAPTER SIX
RUBY

Wednesday, July 2, 2025
1:00 p.m.

The July heat warmed my bones as I sat in the recliner by the pool, dressed in a red polka-dot bikini, a large white wide-brimmed hat, and dark sunglasses. I had returned from Madame Bernard's and discovered I needed to take a small afternoon break. My doctor had told me it would take time—months, even years—to regain my full strength. He'd insisted that whenever I felt tired, I should slow my pace.

Easier said than done.

In high school I'd loaded up on advanced placement classes and graduated with two years' worth of college credits. In college, I'd decided one major wasn't enough, so I majored in French and business and minored in public relations. I took the maximum number of credits allowed per semester and was doing fifty hours a week in the library. I had color-coded charts on my dorm wall and my phone to remind me of deadlines. I never got tired and felt a little lost when I didn't have a moment scheduled. Chaos and confusion were my jam.

If my parents saw me lounging by the pool now, they'd be glad, and then they'd wonder if the body snatchers had arrived and taken the real Ruby. I closed my eyes and tilted my face toward the sun.

I breathed in and then out slowly. *I'm healthy. I'm in remission. Think positive thoughts.*

As I repeated my mantra, I glimpsed Destination: Positive in the distance, but the winds shifted and knocked me off my path. Suddenly, I pictured a smiling Scott.

"Babe, I love you. I would do anything for you."

I'd had wicked nausea, and my patience was paper thin. "All I hear is the big 'but.'"

His eyes softened, and he cupped my face in his hands. Very gently, he kissed my lips, and I wished that I was feeling good so I could jump his bones. The sex between us had always been great, and I so missed having sex.

"I love you." His lips were flat, his gaze direct. "No 'buts.'"

We'd been together for a year, and I'd grown to notice the subtle changes in his expressions. When his brows rose, he was upset. When his lips flattened, he was angry. He never had to utter a word for me to know that the politics in his office had turned toxic, or a guy had grabbed his weights at the gym, or the buses were late.

His brow furrowed slightly.

Pending disaster had a coarseness that couldn't be smoothed. Silent, I waited.

"I'm sorry, but I need a break from this," he said.

"'This'?" I asked.

"The hospitals, the doctors, the endless bad news."

"I'd like a break too," I quipped. "We could go somewhere. A sandy beach would hit the spot."

The furrow deepened. "You have to stay here. You'll die if you don't."

I glanced at the IV connected to blue-green veins in my pale, thin arm. I wondered where I started and the machines ended. "I'm very aware."

He walked to the window and stared out over the parking lot. "I need time away."

"Time."

He hesitated, turned, and crossed to the bed. He took my hand in the now-damp grip of his fingers. "I love you."

"But this is too hard," I said. Later I would cry, but at that moment, I was so pissed. I didn't pull away from him. I wanted him to take me in his arms and hold me close.

However, guys don't give soul-searing hugs when ditching a partner. I desperately needed him to stay. He was a lifeline, but I would not beg.

"I'll be back. It's a break. I won't be gone forever."

"You're going back to Paris?"

"Yes. I've been away from work for two months. I'll lose my job if I don't go back."

We'd been living together when I received my diagnosis. I packed a bag but left behind clothes, mementos, and random items. I'd worried about losing my job, but my fear of cancer had swallowed that up. "Send me my stuff."

"What? No, babe. It's not forever."

A couple of months could be my forever. "Just go, Scott."

He stared at me for a long moment, and then he rose and kissed me on the forehead. "I love you."

A car horn honked on Union Street, pulling me away from the image still imprinted on my brain. I hadn't seen Scott in two years. Love or not, he wasn't coming back.

I reached for my phone and opened the pictures I'd taken of Sylvia's diary. As I leaned into the scripted words, the tension banding my gut eased. I stopped thinking about Scott, cancer, and where the hell I'd be in a year and slipped into her world. In these few pages, she had yet to meet Cécile. She'd stepped onto the path that would lead her toward the movie industry and, ultimately, here.

My phone rang, and I smiled when I saw Eric's number. "Big brother. I'm alive and well. You received my text."

"You're doing okay?"

"Yes. You saw me yesterday morning." His concern touched me, but I was also a little annoyed. "You don't need to check up on me."

"I wasn't checking up," he said. "Maybe I needed dating advice."

"Are we talking about the blond?"

"Susan," he corrected. "And yes, we're talking about Susan. We met. Had a lovely time. And we're having dinner."

"When?"

"Tonight."

"Nice. Where?"

"The same place where we met. Seemed like common ground."

"Good. And what're you going to talk about?"

"I have no idea," he said. "I used up all my ideas when we had drinks. If Susan wants to talk about the mechanics of bridge building, I can talk for hours, but . . ."

"Human interaction is a challenge. I got you. Susan looked fit. Does she work out? What's her favorite exercise routine? What's the best thing that's happened to her this year?"

"Not her job or zodiac sign?"

"No, not her zodiac sign. And jobs skim the surface. You want open-ended questions."

"For reference, what's my zodiac sign?"

"You were born March second, which means you're a Pisces, the fish, one of the water signs."

"Right. I want to make sure everything runs smoothly. I can already picture Susan stopping the date after fifteen minutes and leaving."

"What is it with the Nevins siblings? Why are we so convinced that the worst is going to happen?"

"Because it does."

"And sometimes it doesn't," I said. "And if it does, we keep going and look for the life on the other side."

"Are we talking about me or you?"

I chuckled. "Have drinks with Susan and enjoy yourself. Eric, you're a catch. If she doesn't see that, another woman will. I'm committed to getting you into a relationship."

"Now I know it's going to happen."

"Bet on it."

"Speaking of relationships, can you help Jeff out?"

"Help Jeff?"

"The dude had a bad breakup last year, and he's super gun shy. He needs to meet someone else."

"I'd forgotten he had a girlfriend last year." But, in my defense, I barely remembered last year.

"It was intense. Jeff was talking about marriage."

A twinge of jealousy tweaked my good humor. Of course he'd need and want a solid relationship. "I remember that now. I should have cared about Jeff's love life, but I didn't have the reserves. How bad am I? He's my friend, and I forgot he had a breakup. Maybe I'm not that different than Scott."

"You're nothing like Scott. If that ass dropped dead in front of me, I'd step over his body and never look back."

That prompted a small smile. "Cancer is a hard thing to put on any guy."

"Life is hard. He needed to sack up." Eric's tone had turned brittle.

And for whatever reason, I rose to Scott's defense. "There's extensive research about caregivers needing time away."

"A break or a vacation is one thing. But Scott never came back."

I drew in a breath, wondering why I was defending Scott. I was looking out for the biological father of my frozen embryos. "Yeah, well, life goes on. Now, back to Jeff. Does he need dating help?"

Eric cleared his throat. "Desperately."

"Remember when I took you to Butler's Suits and introduced you to Tommy?"

"I do. I felt like a piece of livestock with you two preening over me."

"And you looked like a million bucks the other night. I'd bet money Susan adored what she saw. So, you're welcome. Tell Jeff to see Tommy and tell Tommy to do what he did for you. It won't be cheap, but Jeff will walk out of that shop a new man."

"Jeff is loaded and doesn't care about money."

"That makes life easier." He could be attached by fall if he put out feelers in the dating market.

"And then he should see Stella at her salon?" Eric asked.

"Yes. He should get a haircut like yours. She'll know."

I hadn't had enough hair for a cut until a few months ago and watching Stella snip off the hard-won ends had been a little traumatic. But she'd been super cool, joked with me, and ultimately transformed my bird's nest into a chic style. "Jeff needs to tell Stella I sent him."

"Perfect. Thank you. Jeff will appreciate this."

"I'd do anything for him."

"He's a good guy."

Emotion clogged my throat. "He's one of the best," I said. "And he deserves to be happy like you."

"Fingers crossed Susan and I hit it off."

"Even if it's not her, Eric, there's someone out there for you and Jeff. You fellas are now my number one priority."

"We rank higher than your article?" he teased.

"Barely. But yes."

"Any luck on the interview?"

"I had a lovely meeting this morning with Madame Bernard. She let me photograph part of her mother's diary. I've been reading it all afternoon. I'm so intrigued already, and this article will be great."

"It will be."

"Thanks. It's nice to be working again."

My grandfather had set up a trust for me before he passed. And currently, it was supplementing my meager freelancing salary. That was fine for now, but I wanted to stand on my own two feet.

"Glad to have you back in the saddle."

I traced a cluster of IV scars at the crook of my elbow. "Good to be back."

※

Two hours later, I was settled in my hotel room bed, curtains drawn, pizza at my side as I hit play on *Secrets in the Shadows*. I knew the plot by heart and could recite lines before any character uttered them.

This time, I made notes on Cécile's costumes. She wore ten outfits, each reflecting the mood created in the scene. In the opening moments, Cécile, a.k.a. Françoise, entered the investigator's office. She wore a white dress with a fitted bodice and a pleated skirt that skimmed above her knees. Her accessories were pearl drop earrings, a simple gold bracelet, black shoes with chunky three-inch heels, and a slim black clutch that matched the belt hugging her narrow waist.

Anyone watching *Secrets in the Shadows* would never have guessed that Paris had suffered two years under German occupation. The director had created a world filled with stunningly beautiful actors, breathtaking fashions, gluttonous food displays, and the best bottles of wine. There were no hints of the long breadlines, coal or firewood shortages, Resistance bombings, or brutal retaliations. On film, Paris remained a glittering gem.

Secrets in the Shadows was almost not released because Cécile's disappearance and the director's sudden death had cast a shadow over the production. But the German-controlled movie company Continental Films, which oversaw French movie production, was making tremendous amounts of money. So, the scandals were swept under the rug and the film was released six months later. There'd been little publicity, and the distributors had dropped Cécile's name from above the movie's title to below. Still, the movie had done well. Rumors about the star's fate were all over Paris, and many were curious about her latest film.

Cécile was at her most stunning in *Secrets in the Shadows*. She was no longer the silly airhead searching for love in her romantic comedies. She was only twenty-two during filming, but she had matured into the dangerous blond who knew what she wanted.

I took screenshots of each outfit and hoped that Madame Bernard might have a tale or two about the clothes or the woman wearing them. Cécile was magical on the screen, but much of Françoise's allure was enhanced by Sylvia's costumes.

CHAPTER SEVEN
RUBY

Thursday, July 3, 2025
9:00 a.m.

Old Town Alexandria was crowded with Independence Day weekend out-of-towners, all wearing shorts, T-shirts, and vaguely confused expressions. They reminded me of myself when I'd first moved to Paris. Confusion coupled with missed Métro stops and constant stress had plagued those days.

Today, I'd chosen a red A-line skirt, a white collared shirt cinched at my waist, and the same ballet flats and purse. I knotted a red, black, and white scarf to the purse handle and wore a headband with a subtle flower off to the side.

When I rang madame's bell, quick steps followed, and the door opened to her.

Today, she wore navy pants that skimmed her trim figure, a loose Breton striped sweater, tucked only at the front of her waistband, and a chunky gold-link necklace. The scent of Dior drifted around her.

Madame Bernard's lips curved with a pleased smile. "Welcome, Ruby."

"Madame," I said, kissing her on the cheek. "I'm so glad you've allowed me to return. I was up late watching *Secrets in the Shadows*, but I marveled at your mother's work this time."

Madame closed the door behind me. "She took great pride in her creations."

I followed her into the same parlor. But this time, five outfits were hanging from silk-padded hangers. Tea and cookies rested on the table between the couches.

Immediately, the yellow tulle gown with the black lace embellishments around the waist caught my attention. "Cécile wore this during the cocktail party scene in *Secrets in the Shadows*."

Madame smiled again. "She did."

"How did you ever find these?" I asked.

"My mother died when I was forty, and I was raising a distant, moody teenager. I thought discovering my mother's past would give my daughter and me a common cause."

"Was your daughter close to your mother?"

"Yes. Sophia adored her grandmother. They were close from the day she was born. So, I became determined to find anything related to my mother and her life in Europe. So much of her past was a secret. As a child, I didn't give it much thought. But once she was gone, all those missing early years mattered so much."

"Sophia must have been excited for this adventure."

"Sophia, like most teenage girls, was dissatisfied with her life. At first, she had no interest in traveling to Europe, but I insisted. And off I went, dragging a sullen teenager."

"I gave my parents a run for their money in my teen years."

"I don't mean to give you the wrong impression of my daughter. Sophia was a typical child. I was also moody when I was young. It's the way, no?" She stood beside me, staring at the gown but not touching it. "This was the first gown we found of Cécile's."

"Where did you find it?"

"In a secondhand shop in the second arrondissement, near the Louvre. Once I found my mother's diary, I hunted down Cécile's films on VHS. I made Sophia watch *Secrets in the Shadows* before we left for France. And when we saw the gown, we both suspected it was one of my mother's creations. And then I found my mother's initials embroidered on the underside of the hem. I was so excited, and a miracle happened. My sixteen-year-old Sophia smiled."

Under madame's tone was a sense of finality. I didn't know the woman well enough to ask about her personal life. "Sophia is such a pretty name."

"My mother suggested the name. A very romantic name from an efficient woman."

"Does Sophia live nearby?"

She cleared her throat. "My daughter died of cancer two years ago. She was forty-seven. She never married or had children."

"I'm so sorry." My whisper-soft voice slipped over my lips, and a chill puckered my skin. I immediately pictured my parents sharing similar news about me one day.

A slight shrug lifted her shoulder. "We all die."

I sat straighter. "I was diagnosed with cancer three years ago."

Madame's brows drew up in a frown. "How are you doing?"

I crossed my fingers. "In remission now. Hoping it holds."

She didn't offer any platitudes because, like me, she understood that all the best wishes in the world couldn't stop a disease if it came to claim a life. "Feel free to touch the gown."

I cleared my throat. Speaking about my illness to a near stranger felt good, much like dragging a demon from the shadows into the sunlight. "I don't want to damage it."

"It's survived a war and over eighty years. Despite it all, it still exists, like you and me. I think it can withstand your touch."

I captured the tulle and lightly rubbed the textured fabric between my fingers. "Cécile was so beautiful in this gown. The lighting, the camera angles, and the dress made her glow."

"My mother wrote about the fitting in her diary. It took her days of adjustments to fit Cécile's waist. Cécile kept losing weight, according to my mother, and each time she tried on the dress, it was a little looser."

"This would have been early 1942," I said. The faint scent of lavender drifted from the gown. "I know there were food shortages by then, but she lived well, didn't she?"

"She lived in a rarefied circle."

"The articles I've read about Cécile claimed she was a collaborator."

"Who wasn't in those days?" madame said. "Survival, for most, requires giving the appearance of getting along. Yes, there were traitors, but most were simply trying to survive. These people fell into gray areas." She twisted a simple gold ring on her index finger. "Germany and France shared close ties before the war. For those in the upper classes, there was a real connection, even a kinship, with the Germans. Some women slept with the soldiers willingly. For others, their affairs with a German were strategic. An occupier provided access to food, protection, comfort, and sometimes military secrets."

"Was Cécile a spy?" What a twist that would be for my article.

"Cécile was a practical woman. She understood how to get what she wanted."

"What did she want?"

"Who's to say? She vanished, and we cannot ask her."

I turned my attention to a smooth brown velvet dress. It had a high collar, fitted sleeves, and a skirt that floated over her knees. "Where did Cécile wear this dress?"

"Cécile wore that frock to a midday party at the German embassy. I have a photograph of her wearing it next to Otto Abetz, Hitler's ambassador to Paris."

"She moved in elite circles."

"Yes, she did."

The other three dresses were just as elegant. One was a rich ruby gown with a cross bias and long skirt, and the other two were suits.

Sylvia had created all this beauty during the German occupation, when silk went to parachutes and wool to military uniforms. Many seamstresses recut and repurposed older clothes.

If Cécile moved easily among the Nazis, Sylvia must have been concerned for her own safety. "You mentioned your grandfather was Jewish."

"Ah yes, he was. And as you can imagine, my mother guarded that secret during the war and ultimately to her grave."

"She never told you she was Jewish?"

"No. I learned of this while reading her diary. I wish she'd been honest with me, and for a long time, I was angry that she hadn't told me. I would like to have known more about my grandfather. But some secrets hide under so many lies there's no retrieving them."

If I ever had children, I'd have to explain Scott, the biology of their connection, and the choices I'd made long ago. Regardless of how I felt about Scott, his genetics would be a part of my children.

Madame reached for a folder filled with photographs. "I have many dresses dating back to this era, but these are the only ones with provenance."

I flipped through the photos, marveling at how they captured the glamour in such a dark time.

Several images showed a German officer with short blond hair, a straight nose, and a strong jaw. He wore SS insignia and an Iron Cross and appeared to be over twenty years Cécile's senior.

In one photo, he had his hand on the base of her back, and she was smiling. Photos didn't tell the entire story, and she'd been an actress, but she looked relaxed and happy. "Do you know who she's pictured with here?"

"Oberst Johann Schmidt."

"Oberst. A colonel."

"A decorated Luftwaffe World War I ace who commanded a squadron during the Blitz over London and crash-landed in Brittany in late 1940. As a reward for his service, he was sent to Paris in 1941 to recover. In 1942, he returned to Berlin."

In another image, Cécile sat beside Oberst Schmidt in a nightclub. She leaned close to him, gazing into his eyes, a cigarette dangling between two manicured fingers. "She looks totally in love with him."

"Before you judge her too harshly, read my mother's diary. I made copies of it all, and I also have a few letters that Cécile wrote but never mailed."

"Why didn't she mail them?"

"The censors opened and reviewed all letters as a matter of course. And some of the information in the letters could have gotten her arrested. Many women were transported north of Berlin to Ravensbrück prison camp for less." She handed me a folder with neatly bound pages. "That might explain who she was and why she did what she did."

"Thank you."

"Please sit, and let's have a coffee. I ordered the cookies special from my favorite bakery in Old Town. I've always counted my calories carefully, but today, I wonder why I worry about fitting into my clothes."

I laughed. "I never say no to a cookie."

We sat, and I set the file aside. I no longer brushed aside quiet moments like this as I had before. "Tell me about yourself. Wife, mother, daughter."

"That about sums me up." She poured a coffee for me and handed me the cup and saucer. "I went to college but dropped out when I met my husband. We had one child, Sophia, after several miscarriages and twelve years of marriage."

"How awful. Did your mother have a difficult pregnancy?"

"She never said." She drew in a breath. "My husband, daughter, and I lived a wonderful, charmed life. My parents lived close to us, and I saw them often. And then I lost them all one by one. Now it's just me and my collections."

"What else do you collect?"

"Only my mother's creations." She poured herself a coffee and selected a cookie. She took a bite, and for a moment, her face softened with pure pleasure.

"Did your mother say anything about living in Europe?"

"On infrequent occasions, she spoke about her early years in Poland. She adored her father and her mother. It broke her heart when her mother died."

"Did your mother give you any lasting advice?"

The question gave her pause. "Once, when I was a child and told a friend that my mother lived in Paris, Mom later cautioned me not to share details about my family. One never knew who in their circle could turn against them. I've stuck to that advice until now."

"Her war experience had a profound effect on her."

"Read her words and Cécile's. They can tell you more about that life than I ever could."

We spent the next hour chatting about fashion, movies, and a trip madame was planning to the South of France in the fall. For all her losses, she kept her life full and busy. I admired her fearlessness in the face of so much loss.

I wanted to embrace life and plan my future, but I was like the little child too afraid to jump into the pool. As I hemmed and hawed at the water's edge, time passed, summer ended, and the water grew cold. The opportunity to enjoy my life would pass.

CHAPTER EIGHT
SYLVIA

Saturday, October 5, 1940
3:00 p.m.

The crowded Métro ride to the Boulogne-Billancourt studios in the western suburbs took over half an hour. The guards waved Emile and me through the gates, and we wound our way to the dressing rooms.

We found Cécile standing on a small box. She looked annoyed and tired as a thin man regarded her too-tight blouse. Well into his fifties, he wore a tape measure around his neck, sharply creased pants, a white shirt rolled up to his elbows, and a fitted vest. His thinning black hair was parted neatly on the side.

He reached for the button between her breasts, released the straining fabric, and exposed her cleavage, contained in a satin brassiere. Standing in a corner was a young man, holding extra fabric and keeping his gaze averted. He was lean and gangly and couldn't have been more than fifteen.

"They throw off the entire look of the dress," he said. "They're more suited for the Moulin Rouge than a virginal movie character."

Cécile rested her hands on her hips, mindful that the move exposed her breasts more. "Monsieur Richards, that's why it's called 'pretend.'

I'm pretending to be Babette, a virgin who can't choose between three men who all can't live without her."

"You as a virgin," Monsieur Richards scoffed. "What do you think of that, Rupert?"

The boy kept his gaze down. "I-I'll . . ."

"Don't put the boy on the spot," Cécile ordered. "Assertions of my intact virginity are as preposterous as you claiming to be a dresser."

Rupert's face flushed as he dropped his head to hide his smile.

The lines on Monsieur Richards's face deepened as he frowned. "I've been dressing women for three decades."

Cécile rolled her eyes. "That long? Who would have known?"

His frown deepened. "We'll bind them. Once they are flatter, they'll fit into the blouse."

She waved him away with long, manicured fingers. "Why should I have to change because you can't measure?"

Emile and I stood by the door. Emile grinned at her sister's boldness, while I was annoyed with the small man who didn't know his craft.

"Let the fabric out," I said.

Cécile looked past Monsieur Richards toward Emile and me. When she saw her sister's familiar face, she smiled. "Finally, help has arrived."

As if Cécile had not spoken, the dresser said, "Binding them will be more efficient. Besides, all the dresses made for you won't fit those." He waved his hands toward her chest as if it were an unwelcome anomaly.

"*They* are called breasts," I said, aware the young boy was blushing. "You shouldn't hide an asset. Men like large breasts, especially when a woman seems pure." I approached Cécile and her dresser. "Did you measure her?"

"Of course I did," Monsieur Richards said. "I stand by my work."

"I didn't sprout these overnight," Cécile said.

"I don't have time to remake the dresses," Monsieur Richards ground out. "I'm already behind schedule."

Cécile stepped off her block and walked toward Emile. When the actress hugged her sister, the shirt fabric strained across her back. "You haven't been here in ages. I missed you."

Emile tightened her hold around her sister's neck. "The boulangerie is always busy."

The two sisters were quite different. Emile was as tall as her sister, but her hair was dark brown and twisted back in a tight chignon. Emile's features were more angular, her demeanor sterner. She had the air of a much older woman, whereas Cécile, who'd dyed her hair a light blond, had an electric, youthful energy. I could no sooner picture Cécile escorting refugees over the border than I could Emile flaunting her breasts.

"Can you give us a moment?" Cécile asked Monsieur Richards and Rupert.

"We are on a tight schedule," Monsieur Richards countered.

"Only because you can't measure," Cécile said. "Be off with you. And Rupert, would you be so kind as to get me a coffee?"

The boy bowed as if grateful for the task. "Yes, mademoiselle."

"Don't get her coffee," Monsieur Richards shouted.

Cécile smiled at Rupert in a way few men could resist. "Off with you. I'll handle Monsieur Richards."

"The boy works for me!" Monsieur Richards said.

"No, he works for me now." She waved the boy off with a flick of her fingers.

"You overvalue yourself," he countered. "Actresses like you come and go. You're disposable."

Cécile looked amused. "Someone is disposable, but it's not me. Go get the director, Monsieur Archambeau, and we'll have this discussion with him."

"We don't need to get him involved."

"We do," she insisted.

Monsieur Richards muttered under his breath and stomped off the set.

Cécile glanced in the mirror. "The hairdresser, the makeup artist, and the acting coach are all trying to fix something that's wrong with me. But I draw the line at my breasts."

Emile kissed her sister on the cheek. "I want to introduce you to Sylvia Rousseau. She's a seamstress."

Cécile regarded me as she extended her hand. "I gathered as much. It's a pleasure, Mademoiselle Rousseau. So, do you think this blouse is too tight?"

"It's a miracle you can breathe," I said.

"You should hire her," Emile said. "She's very talented."

"What kind of experience do you have, Mademoiselle Rousseau?"

I detailed my work in the lingerie factory, my boss's passing, and my desire to find new work. "I'm very familiar with fitting a woman's body."

"What have you made that I could see?"

I had not made my suit, but I'd stitched all my undergarments. I stepped back, removed my jacket, and slipped off my shirt. "I made this."

With a critical eye, Cécile studied the chemise that glided over my body. She leaned closer, inspecting the stitching. "Very nice. But I'll need more than undergarments."

"I can make anything out of fabric." I buttoned my blouse and tucked it into the waistband of my blue skirt.

"I'm sure you're wonderful, but sadly, I don't make production decisions. The director does."

"He listens to you," Emile said.

"From time to time."

"Does Monsieur Richards know how to use a tape measure?" I asked.

My question coaxed a smile. "Monsieur Richards assures me that he can."

"That tight bodice contradicts his claim." I motioned her to spin. "Would you turn around for me?"

Cécile turned, and I asked her to stop. I ran a finger along the seam running down the center of her back. I suspected the crooked seam was unfinished inside. "Assuming Monsieur Richards created moderately generous seams, I can let out your shirt and have a fitted version within an hour."

"He says he doesn't have time to fix anything," Cécile said.

"Monsieur Richards is lazy," I said. "I'll fix this in an hour. The rest won't take me more than a few days."

"You make your statements with such confidence."

"I'm that good." I was unsure about much in this world, but I knew needles, thread, and fabrics.

"What do I do with Monsieur Richards?" Cécile didn't sound concerned.

Emile scoffed. "Talk to Henri. You can convince him of anything."

Cécile's shoulder lifted in a slight shrug. "Where are you from, Sylvia?"

"Paris."

She regarded me. "Your pronunciation is flawless, but I detect a slight accent."

"No," I said. "I'm French. I have all the paperwork that's required."

"It's not for me to cast stones, Mademoiselle Rousseau," Cécile said. "Reinvention is my specialty."

I waited for her to press me on my background, but she didn't. Instead, she unbuttoned her blouse and handed it to me. Dressed only in a brassiere and skirt, she looked perfectly comfortable, as if being half-naked didn't bother her.

"Where is the sewing room?" I asked.

She grabbed a silk robe, slid it on, and beckoned Emile and me to follow. We wound our way down a dimly lit hallway toward a door that led to the costumer's office. When we entered the sewing room, Monsieur Richards sat beside a sewing machine. He wasn't ripping seams but drinking a cup of coffee. When he saw us, he didn't bother to stand.

"Have you spoken to Monsieur Archambeau?" Cécile asked.

"Yes." Monsieur Richards reached for a cigarette case and lighter. "He's on his way."

"Give us the room," I said.

He lit the tip of his cigarette and puffed. Even the smoke swirled unhurriedly around his head. "This is my room. My domain."

"We're simply borrowing it," Cécile said.

"To what purpose?" he demanded.

"You don't need to worry, Monsieur Richards," Cécile said. "Now, move."

His face reddened with outrage. "I inherited this job from my uncle, and you cannot challenge my position."

"You may be right," Cécile said as she coaxed him out of his chair. "We'll see."

"The director won't stand for this," Monsieur Richards said.

"Go on, tattle to Monsieur Archambeau before he arrives."

Monsieur Richards stormed toward the door and then paused. "Do not touch anything."

As soon as he was gone, she closed the door. "Do your magic, Mademoiselle Rousseau. I suspect we'll have him charging back through that door with Henri in tow any moment."

I moved toward the silver sewing machine I'd seen Monsieur Richards hunched over. I sat and brushed off cigarette ashes. Then I reached for a seam ripper and skimmed the sharp edge through the threads on each side of the blouse. I'd done this thousands of times before, and my fingers needed little direction. Once I'd freed the fabric, I stood and beckoned Cécile forward.

She slipped off the robe and slid the partly constructed blouse on. I repinned the seams in a matter of minutes and then ordered her to give me back the blouse. I returned to the machine.

"It's refreshing not to hear comments about my body or to feel hands lingering on my waist or the underside of my breasts," Cécile said.

As the machine whirled, Emile smiled. "He's a pig. I've told you that."

"The movie industry is full of them," Cécile said.

"You accept too much," Emile said.

Cécile smiled. "And you've been fighting since you could walk. How did you meet Sylvia? Please tell me it wasn't at one of your meetings."

Emile attended many late-night gatherings focused on ways to resist the Germans. "She's a customer of the boulangerie."

It was a small lie, but better than the truth. Cécile didn't need to know about my work with the refugees and Marc. Even Emile and Marc didn't know all my secrets, and that was how it would remain.

"Sylvia. May I call you Sylvia?"

"Of course."

"Are you a gossip, Sylvia?"

The machine stopped, and I stood. "No."

Cécile studied me a beat. "I suspect you're good with secrets."

I didn't probe deeper but quickly finished the seams. "Try this on now."

Cécile slid on the shirt again and buttoned the front. The fabric joined easily and held without any gaps. She turned toward the full-length mirror. I stood behind her, smoothing my hands over her shoulders and waistline as I critically studied the fabric and then analyzed the overall shape of the blouse.

The door opened abruptly. Monsieur Richards and a short balding man dressed in a well-made suit loomed at the threshold.

"Cécile, why are you being difficult?" the bald man asked.

"I'm not being difficult, Henri." Smiling, she moved toward him slowly and then kissed him on the lips.

"Then why is this man pestering me?" he asked.

"He measured all my costumes incorrectly. He wants me to bind my breasts so I can fit into my clothes." She cupped her bosom, drawing his attention to them. "I thought you said they were my best assets."

He cleared his throat. "They are."

"Then why should I hide them?"

He studied the fabric contoured to her chest. "This blouse fits perfectly."

She continued to grip her breasts. "Mademoiselle Rousseau fixed the blouse in less than ten minutes. Monsieur Richards says redoing my wardrobe would take too much time. But mademoiselle thinks she can do it in less than a week. We'll remake the outfits in order of the scenes you wish to shoot. You'll lose no production time."

Monsieur Archambeau grumbled an oath. "Monsieur Richards has been with my company for years, as has his uncle."

"He has grown lazy," she said. "And I like Mademoiselle Rousseau. She hails from one of the haute couture dress shops in Paris. Her clientele is exclusive, but she's hungry for a challenge."

He looked past her to me, his frown deepening. He'd been casting and categorizing faces for two decades and had a keen eye for small differences. "She does not look French."

"She's from Alsace," Cécile lied easily. "Which I suppose for you is like another country, but I can assure you it's very French."

"What do I do with him?" He jabbed his thumb toward Monsieur Richards.

"Can't you send him somewhere?" she asked. "I'm sure there is a movie that requires ill-fitting clothes." She ran her fingers down his chest to his belt buckle. "Please?"

"Stop," he warned.

She pouted. "Are you sure?"

"Not here."

I'd seen men like him before. They brought their mistresses to the lingerie shop and lavished them with lovely intimate apparel. And by the following season, the same men would return with a different young woman. Like them, Monsieur Archambeau would most likely grow tired of Cécile, but she still held his attention for now.

"Later?" she coaxed.

"Yes."

"So, I get Mademoiselle Rousseau as my dresser?"

"If she lives up to your promises, she can stay," he said. "She has one week to make good on her claims."

"And I don't want Rupert fired or reassigned. I like the boy. He lives close to the studio with his mother and sister, and he works hard."

"You ask so much," Monsieur Archambeau complained.

"*Merci, mon cœur*," Cécile said.

Monsieur Archambeau turned toward Monsieur Richards and pointed toward the door. "Out."

The man's face reddened with outrage. "This is my office."

"No longer. Go! Now!"

As Rupert entered with a tray holding a cup and saucer, Monsieur Richards glared at the actress. I knew then she'd made an enemy.

Unmindful of Monsieur Richards, Cécile accepted the cup from Rupert. "Thank you, my darling. You'll be working for Mademoiselle Rousseau now."

Surprise flashed across the boy's face, but he was quick to hide it. "Of course."

"Excellent. Now, leave me with the mademoiselle to finish my fitting. She'll find you when she needs you."

When the men cleared the room, Cécile faced me. "He's a good boy and will work hard for you."

"I've never had an assistant before."

"You do now. So do not disappoint me."

She'd done me a huge favor but would release me if I didn't deliver. "I will not."

She studied my round face and very blond hair twisted into a bun. "Henri is right. You look foreign, and these days, that can draw unnecessary attention. Sylvia, we'll visit my hair salon. I think you need a more sophisticated cut."

I touched a blond strand that had escaped its pins. I had my mother's thick wavy hair, and I hadn't cut it because it reminded me of her. "Why?"

"We want you looking like the Parisienne I know you are."

I'd said the same to Albin and Miriam. Something about me suggested I wasn't French. "If you think it'll help."

"It'll make you a new woman." She glanced toward Emile and then leaned in close to me. "The better job we do of hiding you, the better for us both."

Unspoken secrets clawed at my insides. Cécile was right, of course. A storm swirled around Paris, and I feared it would wipe everyone out.

CHAPTER NINE
RUBY

Thursday, July 3, 2025
3:00 p.m.

The influx of information from Sylvia was intoxicating and overwhelming. Her English was perfect and her handwriting precise. I'd read the diary pages several times. Then, finally, unable to retain all the little details, I pulled out a pad and began taking notes. When I'd first had the idea for this article, I wasn't sure what type of person I thought Cécile was. And I'd sure not expected to meet Sylvia. But I liked these women more than I'd imagined.

In the late 1930s, Cécile had been an outlier. Few women in that era escaped the rural southern farming communities. When she'd moved to the capital city, she'd shattered tradition in many respects.

I could imagine Cécile growing up with a restless spirit in a small community, always testing the bounds of society. Women in Paris enjoyed a more accessible lifestyle. They visited cafés, wore makeup, and even took lovers, but in the country, all this was taboo.

And for Sylvia, to travel alone from Warsaw to Paris was also unique. Her father had sent her away from family, friends, and Poland so she could have a better life. Sylvia's father had seen the dark future coming and hadn't been afraid to act on behalf of his daughter.

My phone dinged with a text from Jeff. I almost didn't answer, assuming Jeff was checking on me so he could report back to Big Brother. Still, Jeff had never joined forces with Eric against me. He'd remained beautifully neutral or on my side.

I glanced at the text.

Jeff: I'm in DC today negotiating contracts. Please save me from a night alone and have dinner with me.

Cracker crumbs peppered my green oversize T-shirt from eighth-grade soccer camp. I brushed them away before I hovered nervous fingers over the keys.

Me: Knee deep in research. Fantastic finds.

Jeff: That's Terrific. But you must eat. Crackers don't cut it.

A smile teased my lips as I picked a few remaining crumbs from my shirt and dropped them onto a piece of paper.

Me: Very funny.

Jeff: But true.

He knew me too well. Eric and even Scott noticed some of my quirks and successes, but Jeff had an inventory of them all.

Jeff: There's a French restaurant two blocks from your hotel.

I knew the place. It took months to get a reservation.

Me: If you can get a reservation, I'm in.

Jeff: See you at your hotel at 6:30 p.m. Reservations at 6:45 p.m.

Me: No way.

Jeff: Way. CU

I laughed. Leave it to Jeff to pull off a miracle.

Me: Done.

When I was in the throes of chemo, Jeff once texted me and told me to look out my hospital window. I was so sick and weak, but Mom pushed my wheelchair to the window overlooking the parking lot. And then I heard a horn and then a drum. And then, a marching band paraded across the parking lot and stopped below my window. The band played the Beatles song "Twist and Shout." I'd laughed and clapped, and even though I still felt like shit, I was a little better.

Eric had asked me to find Jeff a woman, which seemed the least I could do for my best friend.

🦋

Dressing for a French restaurant on the eve of the July Fourth weekend required a cocktail dress. I selected a navy blue halter dress with small white polka dots. The full skirt skimmed my calves and flowed as I moved.

I wrapped a red belt around my slim waist, slipped my feet into tan pumps, and grabbed a sweater to hide all the IV scars on my arms. The doctors said to give the blemishes time and they'd fade, but they remained a tangible reminder that I'd nearly died. I slid on the sweater.

When I walked into the lobby at 6:28 p.m., Jeff was waiting for me. He was wearing khaki pants, a crisp white shirt with a red tie, and a blue blazer. Polished loafers and a short haircut completed the look. I almost didn't recognize him.

"I'm sorry, I'm looking for Jeff," I said.

He smiled, proud of his appearance. "Clean up pretty good, don't I?"

As I straightened his already-square tie, the faint scent of aftershave wafted around him. "You've been talking to Eric, I see."

"He gave me my marching orders yesterday."

"That was a quick turnaround. You must be serious about finding a lady friend."

"I am."

"Well, you've come to the right place. I'll be your teacher."

He winked. "I'm counting on it. Ready for dinner?"

"We really do have reservations?"

"Of course. I wouldn't kid about something like that."

"How did you get a table on a holiday week? With such short notice."

"Got lucky, I guess."

"That's some luck."

We strolled down the brick sidewalk past sunburned couples dressed in shorts, T-shirts, and ball caps. I caught a few admiring glances directed at us. I smiled and slipped my arm into the crook of his.

"What's so amusing?" he asked.

"The difference a year makes. I never could've pictured myself here last summer."

"It's been a long road."

In the July-evening heat, the light cotton sweater felt heavy on my skin. I was already counting on the restaurant's air-conditioning.

"It's all in the past," he said.

"That's the hope."

He frowned. "It's more than hope. It's science. Eric told me your last scans were clean."

Hope and science were so tantalizing. I wanted to believe it was over, but I'd met several people on the ward who'd been, as they joked, "repeat offenders." They'd all had at least one relapse and had rearmed to fight their newest brand of cancer.

One gal I'd met, Brenda, was twenty. She had leukemia, and she'd been fighting it since she was fourteen. She'd been cleared and declared healthy right up until six months before she reentered the hospital. We became friends as two young hairless women fighting cancer. Brenda beat the disease a second time, weeks before I received my all clear. We'd been out of the hospital for seven months by now, and as close as we'd been, we hadn't talked since she'd left the hospital. I needed to call Brenda. She was turning twenty-one in a few days. How could I be such a bad friend?

"Where did you go?" Jeff asked.

I grinned. He'd caught me overthinking. "My mind has always drifted. It's worse these days."

Jeff opened the restaurant door for me. We walked up to the maître d', a tall man with jet-black hair brushed off an angled face. He greeted us with a wry smile as if braced to tell us there were no tables.

"Good evening," he said.

"Good evening," Jeff said. "Reservations for two, under the name Gordon."

The man dropped his gaze to his computer screen. "Yes, it's right here."

The maître d' collected two menus and beckoned us to follow. I glanced at Jeff, shaking my head and mouthing, "Oh my God!"

He winked.

The restaurant was full of people, the din of their conversations, and the clink of glasses. A circular chandelier dangled from the center of the room and cast a warm glow over white tablecloths, sparkling glasses, and shiny silverware. We were escorted to a corner table covered with a crisp white cloth.

The maître d' pulled out the table so I could slide onto the cushioned seat backing up to a mirrored wall.

Jeff sat across from me and smiled. He had pulled off a miracle and was proud of himself. He accepted the wine menu and ordered red for me and a bourbon for himself.

After the maître d' left us, I leaned forward, feeling like a kid who'd sneaked into a room reserved for adults only. "Well done, Mr. Gordon."

"Luck has always been on my side." He looked a few years older with his short haircut, and his new tie added a flattering pop of color.

"We need to find you a woman. You're quite the catch. Though I miss the Star Wars T-shirt."

He chuckled. "I'll never get rid of that shirt. It's damn near sacred."

"Like my soccer camp T-shirt."

"You still have that?"

"It's holding on by a few threads."

The waiter brought us our drinks. In the French tradition, the waiter allowed us time to enjoy our drinks for at least fifteen minutes before the menus arrived. The French took their time with meals.

I sipped the burgundy and paused as the rich flavors rolled over my tongue. "Amazing."

"Good?"

"Yes."

He sipped his bourbon and set the glass down. "How goes the research?"

"This has turned out to be very fascinating." I recapped my visit with Madame Bernard, the clothes, and what I'd read in the source material.

"Sounds like you've hit a gold mine."

"There's so much to dig through, but I'm getting an idea of what Cécile was about. I suspect she was complicated."

"Well, she was French."

I chuckled. "True."

"Let me offer my data mining skills. I can dig through many historical statistics and digital records if you need me to."

"That's very kind."

"Distilling information is my superpower."

"Is that why you're in DC on a holiday weekend?"

"Top secret business. Need to know, Nevins," he joked.

I winked. "Ah, I got ya."

The waiter arrived and gave us our menus. We chatted over the food selections, and I translated a few for him. He selected salads and the beef entrée. I chose the salmon. Once we were alone again, we chatted about Eric and his wine date with Susan. When he asked me about my parents, I shook my head.

"The purpose of this meeting, Mr. Gordon, is to find you a lady friend. Do you have a dating profile?"

He rolled his eyes. "I do."

"But?"

"As a computer programmer, I understand the connections apps create. But I've always felt a little funny putting my data online."

"It's a few pictures and a bio," I said.

"Understood. But discussing me feels awkward."

"Can I see your profile?"

He removed his phone from his coat pocket, unlocked it, and handed it to me. I opened his profile. The picture of him looked like it had been taken in college, and his bio was nonexistent.

Shaking my head, I opened the bio and began to type: **Owner of a software systems company, MIT graduate, triathlete, sucker for the original Star Trek.** When I read it out to him, he laughed.

"Okay. That's factually correct."

I scrolled through the pictures he'd selected. Nothing was acceptable. "Hold up your drink."

He did, and I snapped a picture of him. The result was a super-hot blend of Data and James Bond. I swapped my image for the existing photo.

I swiped through his pictures. I selected images of him at a 5K charity race and riding on his mountain bike, and a PR photo of him working at his desk. "Too bad you don't have a picture with a puppy."

"I'm allergic."

"I know. And cats give you hives. That's okay." I kept swiping until I came across a picture of the two of us. An Hermès scarf covered my bald head. I'd been in the throes of chemo treatment. He was wearing a red band leader's hat and grinning like a fool.

I laughed. Tears welled in my eyes.

"What?" He took the phone. "Ah, I remember that day."

"I'd been so sick to my stomach, and I'd been angry at the world. Not one of my finer moments."

"I thought you were the bravest person I knew."

"I didn't feel brave."

His gaze lingered on the photo. "You didn't let it show."

Even now, my stomach soured as I remembered the day. "I was trying so hard not to throw up on you."

"You managed to keep it together really well."

"You're welcome."

We both lost interest in his profile, and we spent the next twenty minutes discussing his hunt for new office space. I learned he now employed twenty people. The appetizers arrived. He had a pissaladière, a puffed pastry with cheese and olives, and I ordered the snails. We both marveled at the plating and presentation. When I was in Paris, food had been an obsession, and I was glad my appetite had returned.

Whenever I had an American tour group in hand, I had to remind them to slow down and enjoy the process. I fished out a snail, dipped it in garlic butter, and placed it on a small piece of bread. It melted in my mouth.

Jeff chatted about work, and his plan to buy houses in the Washington and Norfolk areas. The entire time, all I could think was that he would be a great catch.

Before I got sick, he'd told me a few times that he wanted several children. He'd worked hard to get through college and build his business, and he'd had no time for anything beyond work for so long.

That obsession with work, he conceded, had been the cause of last year's breakup.

Now, he was ready for it all.

If it were a different time, I might have made a move on Jeff. He was the real deal. But I likely couldn't give him children, or even guarantee I'd be alive in a decade. He needed someone who was healthy and could give him what he wanted. I couldn't be that person, but I could find a woman who could.

After what had turned into a three-hour meal, Jeff walked me back to my hotel room. The night air was exhilarating and the sky clear. Stars winked by a half moon. It had been a lovely evening.

"I feel normal," I said.

Jeff's brow rose. "You are normal."

Memories pulled me back to the lost days. "I haven't felt that way for a long time."

There had been nights when my only companions were beeping machines and IVs. I'd been hairless, my blue-lined skin thin as tissue, and I'd felt closer to ninety than thirty. But tonight, a night I hadn't dared dream was possible again, I was my old self.

Jeff tapped his finger against the side of his glasses, a nervous habit he'd always had. "It's been a long road, but you've reached the end."

"You've been talking to Eric too much."

"What does that mean?"

"My parents and brother want to believe I'm perfect and all better. But there's no guarantee."

"No one is looking for assurances, Ruby. No one has one."

"We all want them. We all want to believe in the proverbial happily ever after." The best I expected was "happy for now."

Jeff frowned. "No operating system is perfect, Ruby." He tended to use my name when he had a point to make.

"But some systems are so flawed we must return them to the factory. They're held together with duct tape and gum."

The tension edging his smile carried hints of determination. "You had a close call. It's normal to be apprehensive."

Some fears couldn't be discarded. "I'll worry about every ache and pain for the rest of my life. My muscles were sore from a yoga class last week, and I freaked out and wanted to call my doctor."

"Did you?"

"No, but I was close. I hate worrying because I never worried in the Before Times."

"'Before Times'? Sounds mystical."

"The years on the other side of the Great Divide, before the Scorched Earth days, were magical and innocent."

"You read those fantasy novels I sent you, didn't you?" he asked.

He'd sent me twenty audiobooks. They all featured heroines who'd slain an actual or metaphorical dragon. Because the earbuds hurt my ears, I'd just let the books play on my phone. Often, a nurse or doctor would linger until the narrator had reached the end of a chapter. When I eventually checked out, the nurses had wished me, the Dragon Slayer, bon voyage.

"If a dragon showed up now, I could ride it," I joked. "I know the moves."

He laughed. "That, I would pay to see."

A smile teased my lips. "Stop making me happy. I'm trying to wallow in self-pity and fear."

His brow furrowed as he studied me. "You're not doing an excellent job of it."

I drew in a breath. "Give me a minute or two. I'll get the self-pity back."

A breeze caught the scent of his aftershave. Maybe it was the wine or my very long sexual dry spell, but he struck me as so sexy. When I first met Jeff, I was thirteen, and he was eighteen. He'd treated me like a kid sister and teased me like Eric had.

When I was eighteen and he was twenty-three, we were going our separate ways. I went to college, and he set off to create his company. And then Paris. And then The Cancer.

For a long time, I'd listed him in the brother-ish column. But now, fraternal love was the last feeling that came to mind. And now here we were. I was twenty-five and he was thirty. And we were both dressed and ready to impress the opposite sex.

"Did I tell you how nice you look?" I asked.

"You did."

"It's worth noting twice." I leaned closer. Suddenly, kissing him made total sense. The combo of alcohol and a desire to feel alive had created a potent mixture. I would analyze it later during one of my many sleepless nights.

But for right now, I wanted to know what he tasted like. When we reached the entrance to my hotel, I asked, "Can I kiss you?"

He stood very still, barely breathing. He didn't say yes, didn't say no, but he wasn't backing away.

I stepped toward him and, rising on my toes, pressed my lips to his. I savored hints of bourbon and traces of chocolate cake.

His hand came to the small of my back as he stared at me. Was he steadying me or himself?

"You can kiss me back," I said, my lips close to his.

He tilted his head and kissed me. It was slow and steady, executed with the technical precision of a computer expert, and it felt good.

"Is this part of helping me find a date on the app?" he asked.

"A girl likes a guy who can kiss." I pressed my body against his and wrapped my arms around his neck. I'd missed intimate human contact.

"Practice makes perfect?" His voice was rough.

"Exactly," I murmured as I kissed him harder.

"Get a room!" a guy shouted from across the street.

I didn't immediately break contact before whispering, "Kids today."

"Can't do anything with them." His hand remained on my back, his nose inches from mine.

"I had a perfect time," I said.

"You said that."

Had I? "Want to come upstairs?"

His gaze sharpened, and I'd never seen him look so sexy. "You've had three glasses of wine tonight."

"It was so delicious. And what's wrong with me being a little tipsy?"

"Nothing. You're very charming. But I'm going to table your request. I want to revisit this proposal when you're sober."

Only he could make a rejection sound okay. "Why?"

"We both have early-morning meetings, and you'll have a better time in bed if you're sober."

"Not my first rodeo."

He traced his finger along my jawline. "I want it to be special and unforgettable."

I found his confidence hot. "You're that sure of yourself?"

"I am."

"Now I really want you to come upstairs."

"Anticipation is half the fun." He kissed me again on the lips. "Call me after your meeting tomorrow. I'm fascinated about this history mystery you're chasing."

"It's odd how people who lived so long ago can now feel so real and suddenly mean so much to me. I'm not sure Cécile was the heroine I first thought she was."

"No one is perfect."

"There's not so perfect, and then there's ties running deep with the Nazis."

His head cocked. "Do you think Cécile collaborated?"

Cécile suspected Emile's meetings wouldn't have met with German approval. She'd already noted that Sylvia wasn't born in France and carried a dangerous secret. All this pointed to a softness toward the Resistance. Yet she worked for Continental Films, a German-owned and -controlled company designed to spread propaganda. "Like I said, complicated."

"Complicated sells tickets, right?"

"Very true, though it could destroy the whole 'Cécile the headliner of the festival' narrative."

"Story's not over yet."

"How long are you in town?" I asked.

"A few days. The big presentation is on Monday."

"Got time for another date? Doesn't have to be as fancy as this one."

His gaze grew questioning. "You didn't like it?"

"I loved it. But you don't have to go all out like that all the time."

"Why not?"

"Dating lesson number one. A date doesn't always have to be a huge extravaganza—although extravagant can be amazing. A date can be quiet and simple." I glanced toward the hotel.

He chuckled. "That falls under the 'extravagant' category."

I laughed, but suddenly I was unsure. Had I overplayed my hand? Perhaps Jeff felt weird about the kiss and was trying to be nice. "Simple can also mean a walk in the park. Pizza. A drink."

"Ah. Understood."

I'd agreed to find Jeff a girlfriend, not make a run at him myself. He was letting me down easy. Swallowing some disappointment, I smiled. "Jeff Gordon, any woman who doesn't swipe right is a fool."

His laugh was full and deep. "I'll call you tomorrow after your meeting."

"Sounds like a plan." I kissed him on the cheek and moved through the hotel's revolving doors.

I was halfway across the lobby, but despite my best efforts to play it cool à la Cécile, I stopped and glanced back. Jeff smiled, waved, and turned and walked into the shadows.

I immediately stepped out of my heels and rubbed my toes when I walked into my room. I hung up my dress before stripping off my shapewear and bra. I then slipped on my oversize soccer camp T-shirt. After I washed my face, I brushed my teeth and took my nightly meds.

I clicked on the TV in bed, muted it, and opened my phone. I'd missed three calls. They were all from Jason. We'd been chemo buddies last year. For hours, we'd sit side by side, our arms hooked up to IVs, chewing on ice chips or ginger chews and trying not to be ill.

"You're such a vixen," Jason said. Before cancer, he'd been a muscular six-foot-two man with a washboard stomach. (He had the pictures to prove it.) He and his boyfriend had broken up the previous year. And our relationship miseries had bonded us in a way the cancer could not.

A red, white, and brown Hermès scarf covered my bald head. Gold hoop earrings dangled from my ears. I'd always insisted on dressing for events and had determined that chemo treatments would be no different. "Thank you. That's the nicest thing anyone's said to me today."

"You have standards, kiddo." He, too, was bald, and though some men could pull off a bald dome, it made him look sicker.

"You can rock a suit. I've seen the pictures."

"Hard to get motivated when I feel like a truck hit me, backed up, and ran over me again."

He was right. The endless cycle of sickness, semi-wellness, and more illness was exhausting. "When's your last treatment?"

"Two weeks," he said with a smile.

"And what's the first thing you're going to do?"

"Fly to the Caribbean, order a large mojito, and find a hot guy."

I barely had the energy to tie a scarf and put on earrings, let alone fly to an exotic beach. "What about Robert? He's called you a few times."

"No. He doesn't deserve this."

I didn't know what to say. Scott couldn't do this, and maybe Robert couldn't either. "What movie are we going to watch today?"

He chuckled. "I'm into a classic phase. The Way We Were."

Barbra Streisand and Robert Redford played the unfortunate lovers. "Ah, Babs. She's always a classic. But the title is too obvious."

"How so?" He almost sounded offended.

"Who cares about who we were?" I asked. "It matters who we are now."

"Speaking of now," he said, "Robert texted me."

"Robert, the ex?"

"He wants to see me."

"You broke up with him. You just said—"

"I know. But I want to see him. But God, I look like a horror show."

"You look fine."

Jason laughed.

"Hey, if he dares enter the inner sanctum of the cancer ward, let him see you. Not everyone is so brave."

"I don't know."

"Introduce him to me. I can spot when a couple belongs together. I'm a bit of a matchmaker in my circles."

He laughed. "It would be nice to have backup."

"I got you. Now find a new movie. One that's a love story with a happy ending."

"Why are you so convinced we'll have a happily ever after?"

Negativity and nausea went hand in hand. I got it. I'd had my share of my own fears, but I'd refused to acknowledge them out loud. "At the end of every day, we will feel something, Jason. We can choose to feel bad or good and optimistic."

He was silent for a moment.

"Get a spray tan, a mani-pedi, and drink sparkling water with a slice of lime. Then tell Robert you want to see him."

He cleared his throat. "And the movie selection?"

"*About Time,* with Rachel McAdams and Domhnall Gleeson. The men in the hero's family are time travelers. But there's a hitch."

A wry smile tugged his lips, adding a slight spark to his pale-blue eyes. "There's always a catch."

"It's what makes life interesting."

"If you say so."

I hadn't seen Jason in over a year. That was our last shared treatment together. Before Robert could visit, he'd been released. And though we'd promised to write and keep up, we hadn't. Everyone on the ward desperately wanted to get well, and when health was finally before us, it was hard to look back to those who were still so ill.

And now he'd called but hadn't left a voicemail. I could almost imagine Jason and Robert sitting on a Caribbean beach, sipping umbrella drinks. I could also picture him lying in another hospital bed, drained of color and dying. The second image terrified me. It brought home the fear I doubted I'd ever shake.

Right now, with my world feeling so normal, I couldn't bring myself to call him yet.

CHAPTER TEN
SYLVIA

Tuesday, November 5, 1940
7:00 p.m.

I'd met my initial sewing deadline and was hired as Cécile's dresser. I'd now been redesigning and sewing new outfits for Cécile for four weeks. My days began early and ended late. But I was grateful for the work and the place I was earning on the production crew. Even Monsieur Archambeau had accepted my talent.

The streets were quiet when I left Cécile's dressing room and the movie studio. Young Rupert, who had been so silent around me at first, now tended to chat about his ailing mother and his sister, who was attending university. I'd grown fond of the boy.

"Mademoiselle," he said.

"Yes," I said, smiling.

"I found something that might be of interest to you."

He carried a large bolt of fabric covered in muslin under his arm.

"Did you find my red silk?"

He unwrapped the fabric. It was a white silk that was soft, smooth, and perfect.

"Oh, this is amazing! Where did you find this?" I asked.

He grinned, proud of himself. "There's a butcher shop that sells just about anything on the side."

"Can you find more fabric?" Supplies were growing scarcer by the day.

"It'll cost money," he said.

Monsieur Archambeau had allotted me a generous budget for fabric, but shortages made finding it difficult. "I have money in my dressing room. Follow me."

We hurried back into the darkened studio. Only a few crew members remained as they repositioned cameras for tomorrow's shoot. I unlocked a drawer under my sewing machine and removed a roll of francs. "How much for a bolt of silk fabric?"

"One hundred francs."

"It was twenty last year."

Rupert shrugged with a youthful arrogance I found very charming. "The black market never has deals."

"No matter. I'll transform this fabric into a magnificent dress. Can you get more?"

"Whatever you need."

I handed him another twenty francs. "For your mother and sister."

He puffed up his chest. "I'll find anything for you, mademoiselle."

"One day, Rupert, I predict you'll be running an empire."

A blush warmed his face. "Thank you."

I left Rupert on the sidewalk by the studio and hurried to the Métro. By the time I arrived, it was almost curfew.

I had a stale baguette from the morning shoot tucked in my pocket. I kept my head low as I moved through the shadows with quick, self-assured steps. Couples were walking hand in hand as they left cafés. Soldiers patrolled in pairs. And policemen stood guard on several corners.

Thanks to Cécile's hairdresser, my shorter style allowed my blond hair to curl above my shoulders. Cécile had been right. The new look was more sophisticated and drew attention to my green eyes. I'd always been confident in my skills, even in how I dressed and carried myself, but my hair had been a throwback to my past. Now, when I looked in the mirror, I didn't see the girl from Warsaw but a Parisienne. Oddly, in the realm of moviemaking, which sought the world's attention, I was beautifully invisible in Cécile's shadow.

The Marais was the city's oldest section. I'd chosen it years ago because of its narrow cobblestone streets, centuries-old mansions, and hidden courtyards. They reminded me of Warsaw.

I hurried past a café now filled with German soldiers and headed toward Marc's boulangerie. The shop was dark now. But when the clock struck midnight, Marc would set aside his inks and stamps, leave his secret room, and rekindle his ovens. He'd spend the next few hours kneading, shaping, and baking dough. The man rarely slept.

I hastened down the back alley, then knocked on the shop's double back doors four times. It wasn't a complicated code, but it alerted Marc that it could be me.

Seconds later, a light flickered on, and I saw Marc's slim figure moving out of the shadows. When he opened the door, he wore a leather printer's apron smudged with ink over a black collarless shirt rolled up past his elbows, showing muscular arms.

He still regarded me with some skepticism, ever since I'd cut my hair four weeks earlier. "I'll never get used to it."

"It's effective." I followed him into the kitchen, infused with the scents of yeast and flour. "Is Emile ready to guide my family to the border?"

"Yes. We just received word that German security checks at the border and train stations will be lighter this week."

The wait had been stressful on the family and me. Each day, we feared discovery. "My charges and I will meet Emile at the Gare de l'Est." Emile didn't speak Polish, and we'd found that if I at least accompanied my charges to the station, there was less chance of confusion and discovery.

"Good."

He walked to a bin marked "Sugar" and opened it. He burrowed his ink-stained hand deep into this familiar hiding spot, now filled with graying sugar. He removed a small cloth bag. "There are four sets of papers. Mother, father, children."

I accepted the bag, opened it, and thumbed through the four sets. The work was immaculate. Only a very trained eye would spot the forgery. I handed Marc a roll of francs I'd collected from Albin at the brothel yesterday.

He pocketed the money. "How do you like working for *them*?"

"I don't work for them. I dress Cécile."

He sniffed. "Is there a difference?"

"Emile has confidence in her."

"Emile loves her sister. She can be blindly loyal."

"You don't trust Cécile?" I asked.

His shoulder rose with a shrug. "I trust no one."

"A good policy."

"How will refugees find you now? I don't see you donning a red jacket and wandering the train stations anymore."

"Slipping away is becoming harder. They watch us."

"We must be more careful than ever now."

"If I visit the boulangerie, I'll see only Emile, my old friend." When he grunted an approval, I asked, "Where is she?"

"At one of her meetings."

"Again? The police stopped her last week."

He rolled his head from side to side as worry weighed down his shoulders. "I've warned her. She never listens to me. Forbidding her is a waste of words."

"Will she be here in the morning? We must leave once curfew ends." The Germans changed the curfew times often, leaving us guessing and worrying that we'd be out past the deadline.

"She'll be here."

If she wasn't arrested or shot. The Germans were cracking down on Resistance members. A soldier had fired into a crowd last week.

The circles under Marc's eyes were darker than I'd ever seen. "How are you doing?"

"It's getting harder to find flour and salt. The costs are rising fast. I'll have to increase my prices soon." His patrons couldn't afford him now, so most made do with fewer baguettes.

"I have a contact in the black market, if you need . . ."

"No," he said. "Keep your distance from those markets. The Germans have spies there."

My thoughts went to Rupert. I would warn him.

A year ago, this city had been filled with laughter. Now, the shadows whispered betrayals. "Thank you for the papers."

"Of course."

I was quiet as I hurried down the alley toward the street. Past the café, I heard the laughter of men and inside saw the Germans sitting as if they were at home. The Nazi banner hung above a fireplace.

I hurried down the street toward the brothel. As I reached for the front door, it opened, and a German soldier was bidding good evening to one of the ladies. The woman saw me and kissed her soldier, giving me time to hide in the shadows until he'd left.

As soon as he was gone, I dashed inside, thanked the young woman, and rushed up to the third floor. I knocked on Albin's door, and he opened it immediately.

He breathed a sigh of relief when he saw me. "You got them?"

"Yes," I said. "We leave at six in the morning, as soon as the curfew ends." I reached into my purse and pulled out the small cloth bag. "They are all there. I checked, and they look good."

Albin opened each booklet, studied the pictures, and traced his fingers over the paper. "It feels real."

"The paper is genuine. And the stamp official. No one will question it."

He hugged the packet to his chest. "Thank you."

"Of course."

"We'll be ready at first light." He embraced me. "You have saved us."

"Don't thank me until you cross into Spain."

As he unwrapped his arms from around my neck, I removed the bread from my bag. "For you. When you travel."

Tears glistened in Albin's eyes. "The children will appreciate this."

I left him and hurried back to my apartment, located around the corner. When I stepped inside my building, a clock tower chimed ten times, announcing curfew.

I hurried up the center staircase to my fourth-floor apartment. Inside, I drew my thick curtains closed and then turned on a small light. I shrugged off my coat, hung it up, and moved to the kitchen, where I put a kettle on the gas stove. With gas so expensive, I heated up only a cupful of water at a time. As the water warmed, I set out a blue-and-white teacup and filled a small strainer with tea leaves. I switched on my radio and finagled the dial until I found the BBC evening broadcast. Once the water was boiling, I poured it into the cup and shut off the gas.

Sitting by the radio, I sipped the hot tea. Weak orange and allspice flavors warmed my chilled bones. The tea was a moment's break from the world around me.

Over a year ago, Britain had joined forces with France and declared war on Germany. When the British king had spoken to his people, he'd called for bravery and resolve, even as daily German bombings turned England to rubble.

Last year, Poland suffered similar air raids and bombings. These attacks scattered or killed many citizens before the German army had even entered Poland. Even before the Warsaw Ghetto wall, the Poles had suffered mass executions and arrests. A year ago tomorrow, 183 professors from the Jagiellonian University in Kraków had been arrested. They had been sent to concentration camps or shot.

Tears welled in my eyes as I sipped my tea, which had already grown cold. I couldn't help the incoming refugees now, but I could do something to help France.

After finishing the last few sips, I rose and set the cup in the kitchen sink. I unfastened the buttons of my jacket and slipped it and my skirt off. I hung both carefully on the back of the chair. I shut off the radio and lights. How much longer before the German noose strangled France to death?

Footsteps sounded in the hallway, followed by four knocks on my door. Wrapping a blanket around my shoulders, I opened the door. Shadows silhouetted Emile's slim body. "I didn't mean to wake you," she said. "Marc told me that you were worried about me."

"Curfew must have started."

"I have a few minutes."

"Still, it's not safe out at night," I said.

"I couldn't sleep until I spoke to you."

"Come in." I closed and locked the door behind us.

Emile pulled up a small chair and sat. "How does it go on the set?"

"Well enough. There's pressure to finish the film by the end of next month. The producers want the movie in theaters by spring."

"Have you finished altering the costumes?"

"Almost. I'm also making a dress for Cécile to wear to a party next week."

"A party?" Bitterness shadowed the words.

"It's part of the business. It's important to attend the right events."

"Where is it?"

"At the German embassy."

"What kind of dress?" she asked.

"White silk, bias cut and off the shoulder, I think. Her figure is amazing." Thinking of the rich white silk fabric bolstered my mood.

"She's had a woman's body since she was twelve. Men have always noticed her."

I chose my words carefully, because Emile and Cécile were sisters. "She wants to succeed."

"Yes, she does. And she will. But I worry she's sided with hazardous people."

I allowed the silence between us to linger before saying "You aren't afraid of danger."

Emile sighed. "I'm afraid. But what choice do I have? A growing number of students are joining the Resistance."

Resistance. It sounded so passive. So easy.

I thought about the Kraków professors. Most were likely dead by now. "Be very careful."

"I'll be fine," she said. "My sister isn't the only clever Dupont."

"I need to sleep, and so do you. We meet at the train station at six in the morning."

"I know. I must hurry home. I only have a few minutes." She stared at me. "You do know that I'll never pass on whatever you share with me. I understand the value of silence."

I had no doubt she meant her words. But the police were as clever as they were brutal. And few people remained silent under such punishment. It was best we shared as little as possible. "The devil is here, Emile. He's greedy. And he'll crush us if we aren't very careful."

CHAPTER ELEVEN
RUBY

Friday, July 4, 2025
9:00 a.m.

Last night with Jeff was fun. I hadn't laughed like that in a long time. But he was right about the third glass of wine. It was a bridge too far and made me bolder than I should have been.

Even after a couple of aspirin and coffee, my head still pounded. My body was reminding me that the balance I enjoyed between illness and health was fragile.

Outside, it felt good to smell fresh air. I walked up King Street to the Blue Line of the DC Metro. It would take me across the Potomac River to the Federal Triangle stop in the city. I'd been in contact with a film historian, Mr. Hank Johnson. He said he had information on the production of *Secrets in the Shadows*. His office was in a building across the street from the Smithsonian. Though his directions had made sense at the time, I realized they were a tad vague.

Out of the Metro stop, I walked toward Constitution Avenue, the National Mall, and the Smithsonian National Museum of American History. The Mall was filling up with tourists snapping pictures and wandering toward the Capitol or the Washington Monument.

As he'd explained, I entered the front building and crossed to the reception ticket desk. To an older man dressed in a security guard uniform, I said, "I'm trying to find a Mr. Hank Johnson. He has an office in the building."

"He's in the basement level. Ride the elevator to level two, take a right, and you'll see his office."

"Thanks." I rode the elevator to a bland gray hallway decorated with posters of moments in American history. My red heel clicks echoed down the hallway as I passed posters depicting Washington crossing the Delaware, Harriet Tubman leading the Underground Railroad, and World War II–era women working in a factory. I'd chosen a navy blue dress that skimmed my waist and flared slightly at my knees. A red scarf tied to my purse was the extra pop of color that tied my outfit together.

I found Mr. Johnson's door and knocked. There was no answer, so I knocked a second time. Inside I heard pages rustling, so I took the chance and opened the door. "Mr. Johnson?"

A big guy with wide shoulders and a thick shock of white hair sat behind a desk piled high with papers, magazines, newspapers, and metal 8 mm movie canisters. With earbuds implanted, he faced away from the door and toward a computer screen. He wore a bright-blue T-shirt.

I knocked again on the door and waved. He turned, pulled out the earbuds, and stood so quickly he knocked over a pile of old *Look* magazines. I saw that his shirt had what appeared to be Rita Hayworth on the front.

"Hello," I said. "I'm Ruby Nevins. I contacted you about an article I'm working on about French film."

He glanced over half glasses, and I sensed he was trying to place my name as he stared. "Right. Right. Glad to meet you."

I extended my hand. We shook. "Thank you for seeing me on such short notice."

He grinned. "Not a problem. As you can see, there's not a lot of folks beating down the door to talk about old movies."

"Lucky for me."

"Please have a seat."

I glanced at the single chair, filled with files. "Mind if I move these?"

"Oh, let me get those." Hurrying around the desk, he scooped up the files before dropping them on a bookshelf to his right.

When I sat, I had a chance to look around the room and take in the framed movie posters on the walls. "*Casablanca*, *Notorious*, and *Citizen Kane*. American classics."

"But you're here for the French films made during the Second World War."

"Specifically, the actress Cécile."

"Ah, star of *Secrets in the Shadows*. Mysteriously vanished in mid-1942."

"Yes. I'm trying to piece together her life while she was acting. A local French film festival will feature her work this fall."

"Cécile isn't the obvious choice for festivals because her career was so short. But she was stunning, and she vanished. People do love a mystery."

"Do you have any idea what happened to her?"

He sat and adjusted his glasses on his nose. "It was the height of the Nazi occupation in Paris. It didn't take much to disappear."

"But she was so famous. Her disappearance would've been noticed, wouldn't it?"

"She'd finished filming *Secrets in the Shadows*, and she was in contract negotiations for her next film. Perfect timing for an arrest."

Sylvia's diary suggested that Cécile wasn't afraid of taking risks. Had she taken one too many? "Why arrest her? She made romantic comedies and a mystery movie. Was she involved in anything else?"

He thumbed through the large pile of files and pulled out a thick folder. The entire stack wobbled and teetered but managed to stay upright. "You know she was working for the German-controlled Continental Films."

"Yes."

"As you must also know, American films were banned in France in 1940. But because the Germans' films weren't hugely popular with the French, they let French movie production resume, but on their own terms."

When the Germans invaded France, the country was split in two. Germans controlled the north and the French Vichy government the south. Vichy called themselves free, and during the earliest days of the invasion, the south was the only place to make movies. Then by the fall of 1940, film production in Paris resumed.

"Cécile's star rose quickly after the Germans invaded," I replied. "She went from a supporting actress to starring roles in 1941."

"That's exactly right." He thumbed through the pages of the thick folder. "When you called, I dug out this file."

I scooted toward the edge of my seat.

"Cécile was close to director Henri Archambeau, who, until his death, collaborated with the Germans during the occupation. And because Cécile was his favorite actress at the time, her star rose with his."

"They were lovers."

"Yes. She was beautiful, smart, and, like Monsieur Archambeau, willing to sacrifice to obtain her dream."

"A very common dynamic in Hollywood."

"It's a tale as old as time."

"How did he die?" I asked.

"Murdered. No real details in the police reports."

"No suspects?"

"I'm sure there were some. No arrests, but that didn't mean someone wasn't hunted down and killed."

Could Cécile's disappearance have been linked to Monsieur Archambeau's death? "What was it like working with Continental Films?"

"In some ways it was business as usual. Continental Films had access to raw film and camera equipment. Supply shortages weren't that bad in late 1940, but over the next few years, they grew much worse.

Production managers had to deal on the black market more often. Cécile was assigned a German driver, but his real job was to spy on her."

"Someone was watching her?"

"The Germans wanted to make sure their up-and-coming star didn't cause the Reich any issues." He flipped through a few pages. "Cécile's monitor was Hauptmann Otto Wolfgang. Otto was born in 1905 and came from a farming family in eastern Germany. He was young enough to miss World War I, but only barely. He worked in a series of jobs in the 1920s while trying to attend college. He even made it to Paris in his youth. But like most in Germany after the Great War, he was scraping by—depression, hyperinflation, that kind of thing. He married, but his wife and child died during the birthing. Shortly after, he joined the Nazi Party because he needed the paycheck. I don't think he was ever an idealogue like the hardcore members. But he managed to win the favor of someone, because he was deployed to Paris in 1940. A Paris posting was a plum assignment."

"I can only imagine."

"The Reich assigned the good captain to follow Cécile and ordered him to take note of her actions while also keeping her safe. The French and Germans didn't want any nasty surprises." He peered over his glasses. "Otto Wolfgang was the man for this job. He was very diligent when it came to tracking her movements and those of her dressmaker."

"What did he say?"

"Lucky for you, I translated his reports into English years ago, when I was writing a book on French film."

"You wrote a book?"

"Sadly, I never finished it. Life, work, a divorce. The pages stopped flowing."

"I'm sorry to hear that."

"It happens. These translated accounts will give you a glimpse into Cécile's life through Otto's eyes."

"Can you give me a hint?"

He laughed. "That would be spoiling the read. But I'll warn you: Otto will drown you in the details. Quite the historian. He also took pictures. The German soldiers acted more like tourists when they first arrived in Paris. And Otto, like many of his countrymen, was enthralled."

"Madame Bernard gave me a copy of her mother's journal. Sylvia hasn't mentioned Otto yet."

He sat back in his chair. "Madame let you see the journal. I'm jealous. She only offered me snippets, but that was years ago, and her daughter was still alive. Now that it's just her, I suppose whatever secrets she's protecting don't matter as much anymore."

"'Secrets'?"

"Keep reading the diary, and cross-reference it with Otto's notes. Both should give you a good perspective on the women. I took photos of Otto's scrapbook, but I'm going to have to dig for those. I buried them somewhere in my computer."

"That would be great. I'd love to see them. Do you have anything Cécile wrote?"

"No. Nothing in her handwriting." A look of resigned envy crossed his gaze. "If madame is letting you read her mother's journal, she must see something special in you."

"I like her." I accepted the reports. "What else do you know about Cécile?"

"She was from the South of France. It was a rural area, and everyone knew everyone."

"Do you know anything about Cécile's sister, Emile?"

"Otto does mention her. He suspected she was part of the Resistance."

"Emile told Sylvia she was."

Mr. Johnson wagged a finger at me. "Keep reading Sylvia's diary. I don't want to spoil it for you."

"Do you know what happened to her?"

"I do."

"But not telling. You and madame are very much alike."

He chuckled. "I'll take that as a compliment."

"What drew you to all this?" I asked.

"You mean why would a good old boy from Texas care about a French film star?"

"Basically, yes."

"Cécile was a looker and could have written her own ticket to stardom. But she vanished at the height of her fame and after the war was blackballed. *Secrets in the Shadows* almost didn't get released."

"Do you think she collaborated with the Germans?"

"So many living in Paris bent the rules during the occupation. Buying on the black market, giving accurate directions to a German soldier, sleeping with a German to feed a child, or having a boarder, albeit forcefully, in your home were all considered cooperating by some after the war. Did this mean they gave away secrets or betrayed neighbors? Not necessarily. But many in France didn't make distinctions between traitors and those trying to survive. Two different apples, if you ask me."

"Women, especially, suspected of collaborating didn't fare well after the war."

"No. The French, men and women alike, turned on them. Shaved their heads, burned swastikas into their bare skulls with tar. Suddenly everyone was a moral authority."

I'd made all kinds of deals and bargains with the Almighty when I was sick. What would I have traded to stay alive? I cleared my throat. "What was it like during the occupation?"

"In 1940, the German soldiers were polite, well mannered. The charm offensive. But as the occupation continued, the Germans began stealing the city's art, fine wines, and food. They took anything they could send back to Germany. Food shortages became common for the French, while the Germans ate well. Resentment grew. When the Resistance became increasingly violent, the arrests began. And then thirteen thousand Jews were rounded up in July of 1942."

"Sylvia's father was Jewish. Her mother was a French Catholic."

"I didn't know that." He sighed. "Whatever fears the average Parisian had during the occupation, someone like Sylvia would have been doubly terrified."

Sylvia had never told any of this to her daughter. She could have destroyed her diary and buried her secrets forever. But she'd kept her journal carefully tucked away in a closet, knowing that after her death, her daughter would learn the truth she couldn't speak.

"You need to read those papers," he said. "Dig into Otto's mind, and if you have any questions, ask away. I'm here all the time for July, and then I retire."

"Retire? Then you'll have time to write that book."

He grinned. "I'll leave that to you. I'm going to be fishing and watching old movies."

I held up the letters and translated reports. "Thank you for this information."

"Keep me posted."

I wanted to think this story would end well, like Cécile's romantic movies. But happy endings were generally the exception to the rule during the war.

"Thanks, Hank. I'll be in touch."

He regarded me. "You've been to Paris, haven't you? I can tell by the way you dress. Very Leslie Caron."

I chuckled. "Thank you. I lived in Paris for a year. French film tours were my bread and butter, and I'd still be there if I could."

He folded arms over his chest. "What brought you back to the States?"

I could have lied or made up a polite story, but it was important I remembered what had altered the course of my life. "I was diagnosed with cancer."

He frowned. "How's it going?"

I held up crossed fingers. "So far, I'm in the clear."

He was savvy enough not to pretend I was cured forever. "Your illness might help you understand these women."

"How so?"

"Cancer's a little like an occupying force. Until it leaves, you can't breathe, and even when it does depart, you're never quite the same after."

"That's very true." His insight suggested a deeper understanding.

"I look forward to hearing back from you," he said.

"Maybe I'll find Cécile's happy ending."

"Happy endings are rare, but they do happen for the lucky few."

CHAPTER TWELVE
HAUPTMANN OTTO WOLFGANG

Wednesday, November 6, 1940
6:00 a.m.

My assignment to Paris was unexpected and very appreciated. Not only was I fluent in the language, but I'd traveled here ten years ago, several years after the Great War ended. Though I had no money in those days, I was young and ready to discover the City of Lights. After my return to Germany, I studied all I could about Paris. I immersed myself in the language, art, and culture. I'd always wanted to return to Paris but needed the means.

Now, Germany had laid this lovely city at my feet—so many sights and wonders. I couldn't stop snapping pictures.

The French exit from Paris was chaotic as the Germans marched in neat rows down the Champs-Élysées on that hot June day. Millions fled in cars, in carts, and on foot. The evacuees littered the roads with discarded suitcases, musical instruments, hatboxes, and stacks of books. The fools couldn't even prioritize their survival needs.

Primarily women, children, and old men remained in Paris when we arrived. Our commanders ordered us to be polite. For a few months, we shared an uneasy peace.

After Paris

My first few nights in the city were a visual and gastronomic delight. I dined in several charming cafés, paying with reichsmarks worth twice as much as the French franc. The high command had assigned me a four-bedroom apartment in Neuilly-sur-Seine. The large rooms were adorned with splendid furnishings and art finer than I'd ever seen.

In the early days, the Frenchwomen tended to look away from me. But as fall cooled the air and the Frenchmen didn't return from labor camps or military service, the lonely and overworked women took more interest in the German men.

Now, whenever I walked down the street out of uniform, appreciative glances followed me. It was an intoxicating rush that I'd never enjoyed before.

Street and restaurant signs were changing into German, the Nazi flag hung in many shop and hotel windows, and officials moved the clocks forward an hour so that Paris and Berlin would be in sync. German foods were now easy to find, and the cinema featured German-language films.

On a more disturbing note, I'd heard tales of resistance. They included the sabotage of the Eiffel Tower's elevator, stolen street signs, painted **V Is for Victory** on walls, and manhole covers being removed. Yesterday, a car hit an open maintenance hole cover. The impact flipped the vehicle and injured the soldiers inside. We were now on the hunt for the pranksters. And the Wehrmacht government installed a curfew between 10:00 p.m. and 5:00 a.m. to cut down on nighttime mischief.

I'd been ordered to work with Continental Films, which was technically a French-owned company, but the Reich controlled it. My orders stated that I was to monitor the actors and ensure they made movies that would distract the population and bolster the values of the Fatherland.

The first day on set, the filmmaking immediately fascinated me. However, I soon discovered that the process was far more tedious than I'd first thought. But these French did create stories that dazzled audiences.

The movie in production was a romantic comedy called *The Orphan's Folly*, which featured a young woman, Babette, who was working in a hotel as a chambermaid. The charming staff were more like a family to Babette, who was determined to build a better life for herself. The role of Babette was played by a new actress, Cécile, who, even dressed as a maid, looked utterly stunning.

According to the script, three men loved the same young woman. Each man wooed her. And she juggled their affections until she finally chose the sober, hardworking hotel chef. She learned that material items were dazzling but were fleeting in the face of good, steady work. It was an acceptable story.

Cécile was always on time, dressed in costume, and not only knew her own lines but often those of her fellow actors. Though I strove to remain impartial, I could admit she was a marvel. If she were to visit the Fatherland, her blond hair and lovely face would win the hearts and minds of the Germans.

Over the last two weeks, I'd watched as Cécile delivered her lines easily and quickly while her costar stumbled over his. I suspected the lead actor was hungover. The director, Henri Archambeau, was frustrated with him but was doing his best to cover. Archambeau wanted this movie done as soon as possible because *The Orphan's Folly* was one of Continental Films' first releases. He understood that his livelihood—his life—depended on this opportunity.

Today as Cécile left for her dressing room, I stepped directly into her path. When she stopped and looked up at me, she blinked and then smiled, but I couldn't tell if it was genuine or the reaction of a talented actress. I accepted the warmth in her eyes as genuine.

"Good afternoon," she said.

"I'm Hauptmann Otto Wolfgang. I'm the Reich's representative on the film set," I said in what I'd been told was flawless French.

"I'm Cécile," she said pleasantly.

"Yes, I know. You were perfect today."

"Thank you."

"My job is to ensure nothing stops you from working."

She was silent for a moment. "That's very kind."

"If you ever need anything, please let me know."

"Of course."

I didn't take offense to her reserve because a discerning, wise woman was careful. "Are you finished filming for today?"

"No. Costume change," Cécile said. "My dressmaker awaits."

I looked over my shoulder and saw a woman hovering near Cécile's dressing room. A white smock fitted her slight body, a measuring tape was draped around her neck, and a pincushion banded her thin wrist. Blond hair framed her face. In the right light, she could have been confused for Cécile, but I immediately noticed her nose was a little flatter, her face rounder, and her breasts slightly larger. I conceded immediately that the dressmaker was more to my tastes.

"Well then, I'll let you get back to your work," I said.

"*Merci.*"

As she passed, I inhaled the faint scent of a costly perfume. I admired how well the dressmaker had fitted the costume to the actress's narrow waist and full hips.

The dressmaker, who had joined the production crew recently, glanced in my direction. When my gaze locked onto hers, she looked away quickly and ducked into her sewing room.

I found her modesty charming and stopped a young boy carrying a box of cables. "What is your name?"

The boy's face blushed. "Rupert."

"Rupert, who dresses Cécile?"

"That would be Mademoiselle Rousseau."

"What do you know about her?" I asked.

Rupert looked a little desperate to say something worthwhile. "She stays in her workshop all the time and rarely speaks to anyone unless it's related to the film."

"Why not?"

"She's very busy."

I made a note to keep my attention focused on Mademoiselle Rousseau. People who favored the shadows were often hiding something. She could be just a hardworking seamstress, or she could be trouble for Cécile.

CHAPTER THIRTEEN
RUBY

Friday, July 4, 2025
2:00 p.m.

I spent my afternoon sitting under the bedcovers, eating popcorn, and reading the captain's reports. He was fascinating, in a creepy stalker kind of way.

I glanced at my phone several times, half expecting to see Jason's name. But he didn't call me again. I needed to call him. I would call him later today as soon as I'd discarded this raging sense of avoidance. I didn't want to hear any bad news. I wanted to write this article and grab my chance at a new life.

I flipped through the diary and thought about the pages I'd already read. Otto had lived in a different time and place, under different circumstances. That might have explained his attitude, but he annoyed me. He said he'd been a clerk and university student and then had joined the Nazi Party for more significant opportunities. And now he was in Paris, France, wielding power over an actress and her seamstress.

When my phone rang, my annoyance snapped. And then I saw Jason's name. I should have called him back first. Damn it.

Drawing a breath, I held very still, bracing for the worst. "Jason? It's good to hear from you."

"Ruby." His rough, graveled voice hadn't changed. "You didn't call me back."

"I'm sorry." What could I say? I was working. How often had someone annoyed me when I'd been sick? "Will you forgive me?"

Because I hadn't tossed him an excuse, his voice softened. "Yes, you're forgiven. God knows I owe you a thousand apologies."

"Because you ghosted me?"

"Oh. That cuts like a knife."

"In Jason's words, 'Life is too short for little, polite lies.'"

He chuckled. "You're right. It's short."

The papers on my lap slid onto the bed as I sat up straighter. "Why the call now?"

"I wanted to know how you were doing. I had a dream about you last week."

"Tell me it was a good one."

"None of my dreams are good anymore. They tend to be a bit dystopian."

"I told you to stop reading those novels," I said. "They always put you in a difficult mood."

"I gave them up, but the themes linger."

"What's going on with you? You haven't called in a year. How's your health?"

"Bit of a setback." He sounded weary. "The beast caught me off guard, and I needed a friendly voice from the good old days."

Our old days had been grueling and challenging. A chill iced over my skin. "What kind of setback?"

"The demon is alive and well. It had been waiting for a new moment to strike."

"Where are you? I can come see you."

"Nothing to see right now. I'm headed into the hospital for more tests tomorrow. My parents and husband are here. They've been amazing and do their best to cheer me up."

"But they don't quite get it, do they?" I loved and appreciated my family. And I wouldn't have survived without them. But, in the end, the battle was between me and the cancer. Jason understood. So did Clara, Brenda, and Bob, our cancer partners in crime. The five of us were as different as anyone could be, but we shared the same struggle, and when it was us, we could drop the pretense and share our fears.

"No. And I hope they never do understand," Jason said.

"I'm in Alexandria right now. I can drive out to your house in Fairfax." The distance was less than twenty miles. "What about tomorrow?"

"What are you doing in Alexandria?"

I explained my article and the French film festival I hoped to manage one day. "It's a small restart, but I'll take it."

"It sounds amazing and right up your alley." His tone lightened. "Don't tell me, *Secrets in the Shadows*."

I chuckled. "Yes."

"Congratulations."

"Thanks. I'm keeping my fingers crossed that I'll pull it off." Asking questions and gathering data was one thing. Turning it into a piece that people would enjoy was another.

"You will. I always said you were the smartest of our merry band."

I chuckled. "What have you been up to the last year? You were going to return to the law firm." Jason was one of the best copyright lawyers in his field.

"I did. But I was never committed to working the insane hours like I used to. It was too much, and I have enough money." A bitter chuckle rumbled over the phone. "I'm forty-two, but there are days when I feel eighty."

"We know rest is a big part of recovery."

"I hate it. All the mandatory downtime feels like a ball and chain."

"I know." I glanced at the blanket over my feet. In college, I'd never have been caught dead—no pun intended—in bed at 2:00 p.m. on a Friday.

"What are you doing today?" he asked.

"I'm reading historical journals by Cécile's dressmaker. I'm also reading reports written by a German officer circa 1940. I need good questions to follow up with my contact, Madame Bernard."

"A lady with a plan."

"Remember, 'We don't make plans. We focus on today.'" Repeating the counselor's mantra on our ward made me smile.

He chuckled and then coughed. "Planning a follow-up interview is safe enough."

"And because we're bold, we'll make plans for tomorrow?"

"I'd like to see you."

He gave me his home address. We'd never met outside the hospital. It felt oddly personal to stare at the scrawled address on my pad.

"I'll find you."

"Bring me good stories. I need entertainment."

"I will. I love you, Jason."

He hesitated. "I love you too."

When the call ended, a restless energy consumed me. I couldn't sit on this bed and hide away from the world wrapped in a blanket. It was a beautiful day outside, and a clock ticked somewhere in my head.

I pushed aside my notes, showered, washed, dried my hair, and applied my makeup just right. I glanced at my clothes in the closet, running my fingers over the selection. What did I feel like? I chose a white dress with a ruffled hemline that put off a positive, flirty vibe. I accented the dress not with wedge sandals but with whimsical white thick-soled sneakers. Red earrings added a final pop of color.

I had no idea where I was going, but I needed to start moving for myself and Jason.

CHAPTER FOURTEEN
SYLVIA

Monday, December 30, 1940
7:00 p.m.

The occupation had settled into an uneasy, troubled existence. Most days, it felt like we were all staring into the eyes of a hungry tiger, ready to pounce.

The lines for food were getting longer. The ever-changing curfews were frustrating. And the Nazi banners adorning most stores, hotels, and landmarks were chilling. The few times I saw Emile at the boulangerie, I could see that her hatred for the Germans was growing. Last week, she'd bragged about giving two German soldiers who had Paris guidebooks the wrong directions. She'd stolen a briefcase from another and punctured the tires of several Reich automobiles. She also flaunted the curfew hours often and routinely assembled in small apartments with others who felt as she did.

I couldn't fault Emile's resentment. In some ways, I admired her boldness. But she wore her anger on her sleeve. I'd cautioned her to take care, to bide her time, but she was so righteous. She believed good would triumph over evil. Her certainty reminded me of my father's warning: "The virtuous tend to die first."

Tonight, Cécile was attending another party at the German embassy. She wore a vivid green gown with a full skirt that grazed the tops of silver heels. The dress's bodice had a teardrop opening that revealed only the skin trailing between her breasts. I'd dressed women long enough to know that everyone noticed hints of the forbidden.

"Have you heard what they're saying about me?" Cécile asked. We were in her new apartment in the eleventh arrondissement. The couple who'd lived in the seven-room flat for decades had moved to the free zone in southern France last May. Monsieur Archambeau had given the apartment to his newest rising star two months ago.

Cécile stood in front of a tall mirror. I hovered behind her, fussing with the small shoulder pads and the alignment of the teardrop cutout dipping to her belly button.

"I don't pay attention to people's gossip," I said.

"Very diplomatic."

"What is troubling you?" My gaze met hers in the mirror's reflection.

"Emile and I had lunch, and she left in a terrible huff. She's furious that Monsieur Archambeau encourages my association with the Germans."

I pretended to drop a pin and knelt to pick it up. I wasn't fond of Monsieur Archambeau, and I could see he was using Cécile to solidify his grip on power. Her last film, *Too Many Choices*, released two months ago, was a tremendous success. Overnight, she'd become a sensation.

"She's passionate about her causes."

"She's made it clear I'm dancing with the devil."

"We all are," I said.

I disapproved of how Cécile smiled and flirted with the Germans when they visited the set. But this job was sustaining me. It provided me with money and food to pass on to the refugees. Emile saw the world in black and white. Good and evil. She didn't care about getting caught. But I knew the best work was often done in the shadows.

"Does she listen to you?" Cécile asked.

"I have warned her to tread carefully," I said.

"And?"

"Her jaw sets, and I can see her digging in her heels."

"My sister has always been like that. What does Emile do in her spare time?"

The lie tipped over my lips. "Emile stays very busy at the boulangerie."

"I don't believe that. Emile has never been one to sit on the sidelines and bake bread."

"You know her better than I do."

"I'm not so sure." She skimmed her manicured finger along the teardrop opening. "Would you consider moving into these apartments with me?"

The offer caught me off guard.

"Henri lives across town with his wife and lately never visits me here. He's grown tired of me and found a new actress. But such is the way with his kind." An edge sharpened her light tone. "If you lived here, it would save you riding the Metro each evening."

"I hadn't thought about moving," I said.

"You mustn't think about it but do it. I'm rattling around alone with only a maid who spies on me." She shrugged. "I'll need more clothes," she added. "Henri is trotting me out in front of his new German friends at their embassy tonight, a salon next week, and a Strauss concert." The German composer was brilliant. Many French people still enjoyed his music, but they were now cautious with their enthusiasm.

Dressing her well would mean sourcing more materials and repurposing what she already owned. The creative challenge was thrilling and consuming, but it would mean more trips to the black market for Rupert.

Living in the Marais put me in the center of the masses, making it easier to distribute food. But it also positioned me close to whatever troubles Emile might find.

"It's a natural choice," Cécile said. "I need clothes. The best designers have either left Paris or closed their doors. And I'm not overly fond of Lucien Lelong's designs. You know my body better than anyone, including Henri. And you won't have to race home to avoid the curfew."

It was a practical choice. "What will Emile say if I move in here?"

"Tell her to come along if she wishes. You both will be safer here."

"She'll never move."

"Or leave her boulangerie lover."

At first, Marc and Emile had been careful and secretive about their affair. But lately, neither seemed worried about who saw them kissing. "Time," Emile had said, "is precious, and I refuse to waste it on silly rules."

"When would you like me to move in?" I asked.

"Tomorrow. There's no time to waste."

She was so like her sister. Impetuous, determined, and driven.

Living here would distance me from Emile's activities, but I'd be a fool to think Cécile could shield me completely. "I'll bring my things tomorrow."

"Excellent." Her smile turned radiant. "This is going to be a very productive arrangement. By the way, I have a food package for Emile. I doubt she'd accept it from me, but you can convince her to take it."

"I'll deliver it on my way home tonight." I stepped back for a full view of the gown. "Amazing."

Cécile inspected her reflection. Yes, appreciation flared, but she understood she possessed an unusual, striking beauty. Her high cheekbones and full lips, combined with her vivid blue eyes, was a stunning look. For Cécile, her beauty was an asset and a weapon she wielded freely in her quest for fame. "Henri should be pleased."

"Yes, indeed."

As she reached for long white gloves, I glanced at the shadowed impressions on the walls and tabletops. Over the summer, the Germans had taken paintings and objets d'art from apartments like this, and if not for Monsieur Archambeau, this place would have been stripped bare. He wielded influence, but how long it would last was uncertain.

I laid a black velvet cape on her shoulders and tied the bow so that the strands angled between her breasts. No man in that room would miss her when she entered, and I took some pride in knowing I'd created this look.

"Wish me luck. If the producers like what they see, we'll have our funding for the next movie."

"Once you remove that cape, no man will be able to string two thoughts together."

"I need them infatuated and a tad stupid. Men say the most amazing things when a woman shows off her breasts."

It was nine thirty when I arrived at the boulangerie. I'd walked briskly the last few blocks from the Métro. I was grateful the curfew had been extended to ten. And the last thing I wanted was for the police to question me.

Cécile had instructed her maid to give me a container with roast chicken, a thick slice of bread, and butter. Food like this was becoming a scarce luxury.

At the boulangerie, I hurried up the side stairs and entered the door. I knocked on Emile's door, but when she didn't answer, I tried the handle. I found Emile sitting on her bed. She'd removed her shoes and jacket, but her blouse and black skirt were dusted with dirt. Red scrapes covered her knees, and blood trickled down her legs and stained her white socks.

I set down my parcel and hurried toward her, kneeling to get a better look at the terrible wound. "What happened? Are you hurt anywhere else?"

She raised her chin. "No."

I took a damp cloth from her and began to clean up the streaks of blood along her shinbone. I was careful to avoid the raw flesh. "How did this happen?"

"I fell."

"This is a nasty wound."

"I was running and fell."

My breath caught. I hesitated to ask. The less I knew, the better. But I'd long ago learned that ignoring trouble didn't make it go away. "From?"

"The police," she whispered.

"What were you doing?" I'd avoided asking for so long, but now I couldn't ignore this anymore.

"I was handing out flyers."

"If the police catch you with any information critical of the Germans, they'll put you in jail or shoot you on the spot."

"Why would they shoot me for handing out paper? I'm telling the truth."

"The truth doesn't matter. You're challenging them, and they don't like opponents." The cloth brushed close to a deep gash. She hissed.

"You're hurting me."

"If the police arrest you, they won't be as gentle as me. The Gestapo never ask nicely."

"I know. That's why I ran. Others weren't so lucky."

"Was anyone arrested?"

"No. We all escaped this time."

"And Marc?" He took significant risks with his forgeries. But he was always careful about attending meetings.

"He wasn't there."

For Emile, I feared there would be a next time, and tonight's escape would make her bolder.

Outside, a police whistle blew, and men shouted. My breath held until the street had grown silent again. "Emile, your sister has invited us to come live with her. It's time we leave this district."

Her eyes went a little wild as she stared at me. "I can't. I must stay here. I have work to do."

"If you continue as you are, the police will arrest you. And when they turn you over to the Germans, you'll be tortured or killed. I've heard too many terrible tales of those who go against the Germans."

"I don't care. I can't give in to these monsters like my sister has. I'd rather be dead."

She was so full of bravado. She was so sure that she would prevail. Maybe she would, but the chances were against it.

"I'm going to move in with her," I said. "I won't say anything about what you're doing. Your secrets will always be safe with me."

She cupped my face in her hands. "It's safer for us both if you leave. This occupation is all going to get worse before it gets better." She rose, limped toward a little round rug, and lifted the carpet. "I can't kneel, so would you lift the floorboards for me?"

I put the bloodied cloth into a porcelain basin filled with water. Then I knelt and opened the loose board. Underneath was a small compartment with a bound roll of francs and several sets of identification papers inside. All this was enough to warrant an arrest.

"If you or my sister need to get word to me, put the message here. And if I should sense trouble coming, I'll try to leave something here."

My face flushed red, and I closed the small compartment as if I expected a hand to reach out and pull me in. I replaced the rug, careful to smooth it out. I wanted to assure her that she was overreacting, but she wasn't. People had been vanishing from Paris lately.

"Don't tell Cécile about this compartment unless it's dire."

"Is it dire?" Forces of destruction could build without anyone noticing. And then, in a snap, they exploded.

She paused. "So far, I'm fine. Good people that I trust surround me."

"Everyone has a breaking point, Emile. The police can make the most loyal talk," I said softly.

She stared at me for a long moment. "I've never asked you about your past, but Marc says you are excellent at keeping secrets."

I had to guard my secrets. As much as I wanted to tell her about my father, our Jewish heritage, and the friends in Warsaw who'd vanished, I didn't dare.

"Never let your guard down." My voice was rough, strained.

"I've heard you speak Polish when you worked with refugees."

As much as the Germans terrified me, the French, tortured or not, were also turning on neighbors. France deported foreign nationals to the work camps daily. "I've always had a talent for language."

Emile dug a finger into her thumb's cuticle. "I would never betray you."

The swell of emotions clogged my throat. Of course, in this moment, she meant that. "The less we share, the better. No one can extract what we don't know."

"But I must trust someone," she said. "I can't talk to my sister anymore, but I would hate it if I vanished and she never learned of my fate. Promise me you'll check this compartment if you can't find me."

"I promise," I said.

Emile's smile hinted at her relief. "I'm being dramatic. Life is never as dire as I imagine."

I wanted to believe she was right, but the world had grown too ominous to think otherwise. "I pray you're right."

CHAPTER FIFTEEN
HAUPTMANN OTTO WOLFGANG

Monday, December 30, 1940
9:00 p.m.

I stood at attention in my dress uniform at the German embassy in the Hôtel Beauharnais. It was in the seventh arrondissement, near the Right Bank of the Seine. My waistband had grown snug, a sign I'd enjoyed too much French food in the last few months. The city was a delight, and I refused to be shy about devouring its fruits.

My commander had ordered me to wait here for Cécile, who was arriving with Henri Archambeau. The couple was late, but Frenchwomen had a reputation for their dramas and imprecise schedules. And if there was a woman who epitomized Frenchwomen, it was Cécile.

The mansion's interior would be impossible to describe to anyone who hadn't been to Paris. A white marble entryway gave way to parlors trimmed in gold. Each wall showcased intricate murals of bare-breasted nymphs, angels, and goddesses. The furniture, trimmed in gold and upholstered with the finest silks, was flush against the walls to give the guests plenty of room to mix and mingle.

I wondered how a modest man, the son of a farmer, could find himself attending such a lavish event. I'd joined the Nazi Party for a job, never realizing it would carry me to such heights. Before the war, I would never have been welcome in these elite circles or an event like this. The war had changed everything for the better.

The men wore their pressed uniforms, Iron Crosses, medals, braids, sidearms. Jodhpur-style pants tucked into knee-high black leather boots so polished they reflected the chandelier light. Many wore the red-and-black swastika armbands with pride.

The women wore the finest silks and furs. They styled their hair in loose curls, painted their nails and lips red, and encircled slender necks with diamonds. Some women were the officers' wives, but many escorts were younger and French. Though German women were far superior, a Parisienne was a delight to see and enjoy.

There was a flurry of whispered conversations by the main double doors. Cécile's escort, Monsieur Archambeau, helped her remove a black fur-lined cape, and when he did, a hush fell over the room. Green silk skimmed her curves and tiny waist. But what drew my attention was the cutout. It trailed from her neckline down between her breasts. Her dressmaker was indeed clever, and her indecent mind had me shifting in my too-tight jacket.

Immediately, several colonels and a general approached Cécile, their cheeks pink like lads in short pants. When she smiled, all of them melted. If given the chance, almost every man in this room would have taken her upstairs now.

A tall, lean man with crisp blond hair and blue eyes extended his elbow to her, and she accepted it with a grateful smile. He was Oberst Johann Schmidt. He was a Luftwaffe colonel who'd distinguished himself by downing twenty enemy planes. A battle-hardened man didn't have patience for parties like this, but Cécile had transformed boring into exciting.

Henri Archambeau remained behind, pleased to chat with several men wearing uniforms and others in ties and tails. The French peacock was looking for money for his next film and using his lead actress to win over hearts and minds.

I moved into a room where a string quartet played. Oberst Schmidt swept the actress into his arms before she could grab a glass of champagne. The two were waltzing on the dance floor, moving in perfect time as if they'd been a couple for years. The oberst pressed his hand into Cécile's back, trapping her close. He held her slim hands in a loose grip that nevertheless suggested he could snap bone in the blink of an eye.

When the song ended, Schmidt escorted her toward a waiter bearing a silver platter with champagne flutes. The oberst plucked two glasses from the tray and handed her one. He stood close to her, and if she took a half step backward, he closed the gap. Several times, she stole searching glances, but Monsieur Archambeau was nowhere to be seen.

I moved toward the couple. "Excuse me, Oberst, but Henri Archambeau has a request of Mademoiselle Cécile. There's a director he'd like her to meet."

The oberst's smile vanished, and those cold steel blue eyes cut across me. In a different place or time, he'd have struck me to the ground.

Cécile placed her hand on the oberst's chest as if taming the beast roaring inside. "Henri is on the verge of closing a deal. He wants to make an introduction. I won't be long."

The oberst captured her hand, kissed it, but held it tight. "I'm counting the minutes."

"Good. I'd also like another dance."

Her words softened Oberst Schmidt's hardened features. He noted the time with a glance toward a gold mantel clock.

As we moved away, she took a long drink from her flute. "Where is Henri?"

"I'm not sure."

"What do you mean? You said he wanted to see me."

"I thought you might wish a break from the oberst."

She guarded her expression. And I couldn't tell if she was angry or relieved. "I've seen you on the set every day, Hauptmann Wolfgang."

I was pleased that she'd remembered. "I'm the monitor for Continental Films."

She leaned a fraction closer. "Does that make you a spy?"

"A spy works in secret. I've never hid my job or intentions."

She sipped more champagne, and the tension arching her back eased. "Ah, I'm glad you explained the difference."

We stepped out of the parlor into the main hallway and the long marble stairs. "I see Monsieur Archambeau. I'll speak to him. Thank you for the rescue, Hauptmann Wolfgang."

"My intervention wasn't intended as a rescue." But, of course, that was what it was. And by intervening, I'd come to the oberst's attention.

"You don't need to worry about me," she said, smiling. "But thank you."

"My compliments to your dressmaker." It was a bold statement that crossed too many lines.

"I'll tell her."

My mouth had gone dry. "Good evening to you."

She stared with an intensity that jumbled my thoughts. "I trust you'll be close."

The hints of a rich perfume swirled. "Of course."

Her lips spread into a bright grin. I'd seen that smile on the movie screens when I watched her last film, and it was intoxicating. Mademoiselle Rousseau was too severe to smile with such charm. But I imagined if she did, it would be brilliant.

With long, manicured fingers, Cécile brushed back an already-perfect lock of hair. "It's nice to know I'll always have a shadow protector, Hauptmann Otto Wolfgang."

CHAPTER SIXTEEN
RUBY

Friday, July 4, 2025
4:00 p.m.

My walk about the city had lasted only an hour. Summer heat and humidity had made it more exhausting than I'd imagined. So, I returned to my hotel room, changed, and pulled out my historical diaries.

When my phone rang, I almost didn't bother giving it a glance. The captain's report of the embassy party consumed me. But for some reason, I looked over, and when I saw Scott's name, my laser attention vanished. The man had a talent for ruining a good thing.

Drawing in a breath, I accepted the call. "Scott."

"Ruby. I wasn't sure you'd answer."

"You got me. What do you want?"

"Did I catch you in the middle of something?"

"Working. What can I do for you?"

"Working on what? Did you get a job?"

I brushed back a strand of hair, annoyed that I cared that he seemed to care. "Communications for the Virginia Tourism Bureau."

"That's great, babe. You always wanted to be a writer."

I had been writing and selling articles when we were together, but I didn't bother to point that out. "And here I am. Scott, what do you want?"

"Your brother said you were in Northern Virginia."

"You called Eric?"

"You weren't answering, and I was worried. And for the record, he wasn't outing you. He let it slip."

Eric had been sad when Scott broke up with me. They'd shared interests in computers, Star Trek, and chess. "Don't worry about it."

"I'm in DC, fresh from Paris. It's a quick trip, but I wanted to see if you had time for a coffee."

Coffee was cheap and easy. Not even lunch. "I only have a few more days and several more interviews to do."

"Come on, Ruby. You have an hour for me, don't you?"

"Since when was it so important for you to see me?"

"I know it didn't end well, and I've always felt bad about that. This next meeting will end on a better note."

Eric and Jeff had said a few times that I needed closure with Scott. I couldn't spend the rest of my life thinking of him as "The Asshole." Well, I could, but maybe they had a point. Perhaps untangling my knotted anger would make life easier. Positive thinking was good for overall health.

"I can meet you in about an hour. I'm in Old Town Alexandria."

"Excellent. Where do you want to meet?"

"There's a bakery on Union Street. They serve coffee."

"Excellent. I'm looking forward to seeing you."

"See you soon." I ended the call and tossed the phone on the bed, allowing a groan to rumble unrestrained in my throat. I didn't want to deal with Scott. I wanted him never to have happened. But he had. Time to act like a big girl and face him again.

Forty-five minutes later, I walked down Union Street's brick sidewalk. The sky was a brilliant blue, and the Potomac meandered on my left. I'd changed into black capris, a white off-the-shoulder shirt, gold hoop earrings, and red flats.

Outside, the heat felt good. When the hospital released me, I'd sworn I'd spend every waking minute in the sun. But lately it seemed I'd spent too many days inside, on a computer screen. Mental notes: More time in the sun. More fun. More laughing.

When I spotted the bakery shop sign, my stomach clenched. Not even sunshine could take away this tension. Scott. I loved him so much. When he'd said forever, I'd believed him. And then he went on a permanent break.

I opened the bakery's front door and found him sitting at a small round table. He'd ordered two decaf coffees and chocolate croissants. Damn. He would remember my favorites.

When the bells above the door jingled, he looked toward the door. For a moment, he stared. My hair wasn't as long as it had been in Paris, but it also wasn't thinning, and I wasn't deathly pale and doubled over with nausea. This Ruby hovered between the versions in his memories.

Widened eyes reflected relief as he came toward me. He wrapped his arms around me, and I leaned into him out of habit. He still wore the Chanel aftershave I'd bought him three years ago. And the top of my head still fit right under his chin. His hug was firm, and it annoyed me how good it felt.

Finally he released me, and when I stepped back, my cheeks felt slightly flushed. "Scott. You look as amazing as ever."

He stood a couple of inches over six feet, with wide muscled shoulders. His hair was still thick and blond, his skin tanned.

"I ordered for you. I hope you don't mind."

"Not at all." I took a seat. Coffee with cream steamed in a porcelain cup. Beside it, a rose-shaped pat of butter topped the croissant.

"This is a surprise," I said.

He took a seat, his brow quirking with amusement. "Not exactly. I've been calling."

I set my small square bag on the table and sipped my coffee.

Scott was putting on a show like he had in the old days. "I like the short hair."

I resisted the urge to touch it. "All systems are a go. I received a clean bill of health at the last doctor's appointment."

"It's hard to reconcile you with the gal who was so sick." Admiration sharpened his stare. "I don't know how you survived all that."

I thought about the selfie that Eric and I had taken for our parents. There were still times when it felt as if I were staring into a stranger's face. "I turned a corner after the bone marrow transplant."

"Bone marrow."

"Eric was a match. Big brother to the rescue again."

He frowned as he traced the side handle of his cup. "I'm glad he was there for you."

"Me too."

"How are your parents?"

"Taking their first vacation in years. Last I heard, they were in Rome."

"Nice."

I sipped the coffee, loving the taste and needing something to do to fill the silence. "So, what are you doing in DC?"

"Grant presentation."

Scott worked for the American University of Paris. His job was to obtain educational grants for students who couldn't afford a semester abroad. "Right. You made this trip before about three years ago."

He seemed surprised that I remembered. "We'd only been dating a few months."

"That's right."

He tapped his right hand on his thigh, the tell he was nervous. He wasn't here to catch up on old times. And he sure didn't want to reconcile. But he wanted something.

"Spit it out," I said. "I can tell you have something important to say."

A half smile curved his lips, and his tapping fingers stilled. "You know me so well."

I did. And if I was honest with myself, our breakup would have happened eventually, even if I hadn't gotten sick. Scott liked to go out with the lads to drink, and they could be gone for days. He also wasn't good about remembering special moments, like our meet-a-versary or my birthday. But when he was with me, he was so engaged that I forgot about the times I went to bed angry. My illness sped up the clock. "I met someone," he said.

It wasn't unexpected, a natural progression, but it made me angry. A part of me wanted him to stay frozen in time, forever tortured and longing for me.

"Congratulations. Who?"

"Her name is Bridgett."

"You work with a Bridgett, from what I remember."

"One and the same."

Tall, blond, slim, big boobs, Bridgett was from Nice, France, and had moved to Paris in her early twenties. "Are you happy?"

"I am." He did his best to look a bit ashamed.

"You could've texted me all this. We didn't have to meet."

"You know we have unfinished business as well as I do."

"Do we?"

His gaze hardened. "The embryos we made."

He'd agreed to donate his sperm so I could have fertilized eggs. I also had unfertilized eggs, but the embryos would have a better chance of making it to the finish line than they would. Eric had cautioned me against using Scott as a donor. He'd wanted me to use a sperm bank. But I'd thought my brother was worrying over nothing. "What about them?"

"We aren't together. And you could have my child."

"You signed over full custody to me." Once Eric had accepted that he couldn't change my mind about using Scott's sperm, he'd lined up the lawyers. Again, I'd thought he was overreacting, but as always, my brother was thinking five chess moves ahead.

"They're my children," I said.

"They're my children too."

"They have your DNA, but they're *my* children." A protective ferocity burned in my chest. "You're not going to take my chance of motherhood away."

"What if you meet someone? What if your stored eggs fail to fertilize? Is this guy going to want to raise another man's child?"

"I'll cross that bridge when I come to it, Scott."

"Are you dating anyone?"

He thought he could still ask me anything, but that window had closed when he'd left. "That's none of your business."

"It is."

Scott was always good at getting what he wanted. He could always coax me into caving on a thousand different little choices. But looking back, I was the one who always chose not to stand my ground about restaurants, movies, or vacation choices. I wasn't upset or bitter that I'd given in because, deep down, I knew I could have said no at any time. He'd asked. I'd given. And it was okay.

But this wasn't okay. Somewhere deep in my brain, an impenetrable line had become etched between us. "Our legal agreement is ironclad."

He softened his voice and leaned closer, just like he used to. "I was hoping you'd tear it up."

I sipped my coffee and regretted such a lovely croissant would be wasted. "No."

"This question is bigger than a quick yes or no, Ruby."

I reached for my purse. "You can make the question as big or small as you'd like, but it'll always be a no. My embryos. My babies." I rose again, feeling a primal sense of protection for children who were years from birth.

Never a fan of public displays, Scott stood. "You're being selfish, Ruby. You're betting on a long future that might not happen."

"And if I live to be one hundred?"

"If you're wrong, the child will suffer."

His quietly spoken words hit their mark.

"Bridgett and I are getting married. She's pregnant."

The one-two punch struck hard. He added, "You sure you'll live long enough to raise a baby?"

"We all die, Scott."

I moved toward the door, and Scott hurried after me. "I did this all wrong. I hit you with too much, too fast. I'm sorry. Let's sit down and talk more."

"We've covered the main points and low blows." Bells jingled over my head when I opened the door. "Have a good life, Scott."

"I have a legal right."

"No, you don't. You willingly signed your rights away. No one twisted your arm."

"I was trying to be nice."

I stared at him. "Your sperm was a parting gift?"

"You're not being fair."

"'Fair'?" I couldn't hide my disgust. "Do you think life has been fair to me?"

"I don't want to fight."

"If you press this, you'll get a big one."

He reached toward me, but I angled away. "Scott, you offered to donate, even if you saw it as a consolation prize," I said. "I know my illness was hard on you. No harm, no foul. But you won't steal my chance to be a mother."

"I don't think you're being reasonable."

Again, we were talking about *fairness*. "We're done."

When I stepped into the late-afternoon heat, my chilled skin soaked up the warmth. I hurried down the brick sidewalk, unmindful of the tourists enjoying the holiday weekend. Cars rumbled by, and several people on bicycles dashed past on the cobblestone road.

I didn't look back at Scott and hoped he didn't follow. I wasn't in the mood for a public fight. He wouldn't give up this easily, but any more talking would be through lawyers.

When my phone rang, I almost cried with relief when I saw Madame Bernard's name. "Bonjour, madame."

"Ruby. Where are you? How was your meeting with Mr. Johnson?"

"It went well."

"Where are you?"

"I'm a few blocks from your town house, enjoying the afternoon."

"Do you have plans?"

"Reading the reports from Otto Wolfgang."

"Mr. Johnson gave you the captain's reports?"

"He did. They are an amazing find."

"Join me for a drink and tell me what you've learned. This hunt of yours is very exhilarating. I was so motivated I spent the afternoon in the attic."

"In this heat?"

"I sent a young man up there to bring down items. The poor fellow ended up soaked in sweat, but I paid him well. You'll love what he found."

CHAPTER SEVENTEEN
RUBY

Friday, July 4, 2025
5:00 p.m.

My heart raced as I stood on Madame Bernard's front stoop. I was doing my best not to replay Scott's request in my head. Each passing second, I grew angrier.

"Be positive. Be positive." I drew in a breath. With an exhale, I shoved out the words, hoping the negativity would drift off into the universe. "My life is good. I'm moving on. Scott doesn't matter."

The door opened to Madame Bernard. She wore black cotton pants, a silk blouse, and flats. She'd styled her hair and makeup perfectly. She had to be close to eighty-five, yet she had a youthful energy I loved. I hoped I made it to eighty-five, though at this stage of my recovery I'd take whatever time I could eke out.

Here I was busting on Scott and ready to protect my future baby, when I didn't even know if I had a future. I wasn't willing to commit to a cat, but a potential child was on the table.

"I can see you have a great deal on your mind," Madame Bernard said. "Not the article, I hope."

"No, no. Working on this article has been a great experience. I can't wait to get to the end of your mother's and Otto's diaries."

She stepped aside and beckoned me to pass. "Otto."

"A captain in the German army. His orders were to keep an eye on Cécile while she was contracted to Continental Films."

"Ah, yes. My mother mentioned him several times. Hauptmann Wolfgang, or 'the captain.'"

I noticed she'd opened a bottle of red wine and had set out two gleaming glasses. "I didn't think to ask, but do you drink?"

"I do."

"Excellent. I enjoy a glass every day. My treat to myself." She motioned for me to sit across from her. "I opened the bottle an hour ago, so it's had plenty of time to breathe."

The label told me she was very serious about her wines. "I had friends in Paris who wouldn't consider drinking a bottle if it hadn't been opened and had a chance to breathe."

"Wise friends," she said.

She handed me a glass. I held it up and admired the way the soft evening light made the ruby hues sparkle. When I sipped, I wasn't disappointed. This wine was as good as, if not better than, the wine Jeff had ordered last night.

"Did you know the Germans loved French wine?" Madame Bernard asked. "As soon as they invaded the country, they raided the vineyards and the cellars. So many bottles taken."

"Some families hid their best bottles behind false brick walls or buried them deep in the ground."

"So much destruction." She sipped. "Where are you in the diary entries?"

"Late 1940. I'm reading Otto's and your mother's entries at the same time and creating a timeline of their lives during the war."

"Experiencing the war through their eyes is excellent. What do you think about the captain?"

"An average guy who saw his station rise because of the war."

"While so many fell, many did rise."

I sensed something under the words but opted not to press. "Your mother made a dress for Cécile for a party at the German embassy."

Her features softened. "That was the green silk dress."

"Yes. Captain Wolfgang noted it and said every man in the room did as well. He also praised her dressmaker."

Madame smiled with pride. "My mother was an artist."

"Did your mother move in with Cécile?"

A slight smile teased her lips. "You'll have to keep reading. It's a dramatic story. I knew nothing of her past until I found her diary. I had so many questions, but she wasn't alive to answer them."

"She said nothing about Paris or the war?"

"You think like a modern woman accustomed to sharing thoughts and feelings. That generation wanted to forget the war." Madame lifted her shoulder in a slight shrug as she sipped her wine. "Times were very tough. Working in film helped shield my mother somewhat. But no one in Paris during the early 1940s escaped difficulties."

"She took great chances delivering identity papers."

"Others were arrested or sent to concentration camps for less. But whatever pushed her never left. In high school, I had a friend who'd lost her mother. My mother insisted Kate come live with us. Kate stayed with us for three years." She sipped her wine. "Kate was one of my best friends. She passed away two years ago."

It appeared Madame Bernard had lost everyone, but I suspected she would not have appreciated my pity. "I've read several old articles about all the parties Cécile attended. She was as famous as the actress Arletty and the designer Coco Chanel. She was often photographed at the Ritz, the theaters, and the finest restaurants. She always wore Van Cleef & Arpels diamonds and pearls. When others were starving, she was living like a queen. Did she collaborate with the Germans?"

"Accusations like that are easy to make, but as always, the story is far more complicated than a quick headline. You must keep reading."

"No clue or hint?"

Madame Bernard chuckled. "I cannot do justice to the events. You must experience them in my mother's and Otto's words."

"Did Cécile ever consider other designers for her costumes and gowns?"

"No. Cécile trusted my mother, and trust was more important than a designer name. Despite Cécile's youth, she was very focused and headstrong."

"Your mother met Emile through Marc."

"Marc had his fingers in many circles in Paris during the war. He continued running his boulangerie and forging papers until he passed in 1969."

"And Emile?"

She sipped wine and then set the crystal glass on the table. "You must keep reading."

I always peeked at the last page of a book before I committed. "How did your mother meet your father?"

"She'll tell you."

I laughed. Madame Bernard was enjoying herself, and my spirits and hers lifted.

"It's important to walk in their shoes as they traveled their path and not jump ahead. You can't appreciate the tension if you know the ending."

"I know your mother escaped, but Cécile . . ."

Again, the shrug and a caution to keep reading. "I found my mother's oldest photo album." From the secretary, she picked up a small leather-bound book and set it on the table between us. The spine creaked as she opened the faded red cover. Black-and-white photos were tacked onto dark-gray pages. The first image featured a tall, thin woman with sweeping blond hair that skimmed her jaw. Her expression showed hints of amusement as she gazed over her shoulder toward the Eiffel Tower in the background.

"I've seen this picture before. That's Sylvia helping Cécile?"

"Yes. Quite handsome, don't you think?"

"Yes."

"Up close, no one would ever have confused them, but as you said, in the shadows, she could be her double." She sipped her wine.

The neat handwriting at the bottom read "1942."

"Don't be fooled by their beauty. Together, they took great risks. The SS were all over Paris in 1942 and would have shot them on sight if they knew the truth." She kissed her fingertips and pressed them to her mother's face. "My father says he fell in love when he first saw her."

I turned the page to an image of Sylvia with a young US serviceman. He had dark hair, a square jawline, and a small mustache. Judging by the uniform, he was an airman. "Where did they meet?"

"Keep reading."

So frustrating. I wanted to skip to the end of the story and read the ending, but madame wasn't giving anything away. "How long were they married?"

"Forty years. They were happy, and I couldn't have asked for a better life." Her tone turned melancholy. "Once you've finished the diary, ask me any questions you want."

"I'll keep reading, and I'll call again. A friend of mine from the cancer ward is ill, and I need to see him tomorrow. I'll be heading home Tuesday."

She frowned. "When my daughter was ill, she had several lapses. And she beat all until the last."

"My friend isn't dramatic, and for him to call after a year means it's serious."

"You haven't spoken in a year?"

"He was healthy and living his life. I understand he didn't want to look back."

She closed the scrapbook. "We ignore painful pasts for many reasons."

Sylvia couldn't revisit Paris. Jason couldn't look back at cancer. And I was afraid of the future.

"Do not borrow trouble," Madame Bernard said. When I looked up, she smiled. "My mother used to say that often. She said life gave us plenty of trouble, and we didn't need to search out more. Still, when I was a teenager, I never met an argument I didn't like."

"I can't believe that."

She chuckled. "Believe it. I was a little difficult. My mother was patient with me but didn't indulge my dramatics."

"I was the teenager most likely to find a party or join friends for a road trip to New York. I felt as if I were running out of time. I guess I was right."

"We're all running out of time, Ruby. You're squeezing the most out of what you have, and that's all you can expect."

CHAPTER EIGHTEEN
SYLVIA

Wednesday, March 12, 1941
2:00 p.m.

Bitter cold winds had swept from the east over Paris, gripping the city. No cars or taxis ran, and most people traveled on foot, on the Métro, or by bicycle. Long food lines were now standard. The majority waiting were women. All their husbands, fathers, and brothers remained in prison or conscripted to German work farms. We all knew someone who'd been arrested, deported, or beaten up by police. And resentment toward our well-fed occupiers grew.

The black markets, now considered a necessary evil, flourished despite their high prices. Rupert had discovered some of his best fabric finds through questionable contacts.

Five days ago, the captain had insisted on driving Rupert and me to Les Halles. I hadn't been in a car since I'd ridden in a taxi to the Warsaw train station. That old car had been clean and well cared for, but the seats were threadbare, and a spring had poked me in the back the entire ride. In those days, I believed I would return home soon.

Hauptmann Wolfgang's Mercedes was pristine. The black exterior glistened in the morning light, the seat leather was smooth and soft, and the mahogany console was well polished.

Neither Rupert nor I spoke as he drove. When the captain parked across from the shops, Rupert promised to return immediately. Minutes after he'd vanished into the crowded market, German soldiers marched in behind him.

"Rupert," I said, reaching for the door handle.

The captain extended his hand over the seat and took my arm. "Stay."

I jerked away. "I can't. I must warn him!"

As I spoke, soldiers marched six Parisians onto the street. Rupert was one of them. The boy glanced toward the car, and I could see resolution hardening his face as he and the others were lined up against a brick wall.

"They can't shoot him," I shouted. "He's done nothing wrong!"

"You can't stop them." He grabbed my arm. "You'll be shot if you try."

"I need to help him."

His grip tightened, his biting fingers holding me in place. Seconds later, the soldiers fired, and the six French people fell to the ground, dead.

Disbelief numbed my body. Rupert had done nothing wrong. He was a boy. He had a family to care for. "Did you know this was going to happen?"

"This, no. But I know the streets are dangerous now. There will be more of this if the Resistance continues."

I stared at the bodies crumpled on the street. Two old men, three women, and young Rupert. I willed the stilled bodies to move, but I saw no signs of life.

The captain released my arm, but I was too stunned to move. He drove us back to the studio, neither of us saying a word.

I should have been immune to death by now, but Rupert's loss stung. When I told Cécile about him, she left the set, went home, and got drunk. She'd refused to leave her apartment for two days.

I'd attended Rupert's funeral three days after his death. When I called on his mother later, she'd given me a pouch filled with faux pearl buttons. He'd been carrying them when he was shot. They were for a gown I was creating.

When I'd visited the boulangerie yesterday, Marc was behind the counter. Though he was quick to discuss the scarcity of flour and sugar, he said nothing about Emile's errands. I'd once welcomed Marc's willingness to skirt the law, but ever since the executions, I feared his influence on Emile would get her arrested or killed.

I visited Emile's room and opened the panel under her floorboards. I found a jotted note from her wishing me a good day and thanking me for the food. It was her way of letting me know she was alive.

After her short retreat from the world, Cécile jumped back into her life as if nothing had happened. She flirted with Germans on the set and resumed her party schedule, and, when Oberst Schmidt arrived in Paris, she went to him willingly. A few in the production crew grumbled about her growing attachment to the Germans, but no one was brave enough to speak up. In her shadow, they were unnoticed.

Since the executions at Les Halles, Hauptmann Wolfgang's gleaming black Mercedes had arrived each morning to pick us up. Always formal and polite, the captain was the perfect gentleman. Could the monsters who'd shot Rupert in cold blood have been capable of politeness too?

Small red Nazi flags mounted on either side of his hood flapped as the car drove along quiet morning streets toward the western suburbs and the Paris film studios in Boulogne-Billancourt. With the captain behind the wheel, neither Cécile nor I felt comfortable discussing anything beyond costumes and makeup.

The movie studio was housed in a long gray industrial building. But inside, set designers created countless worlds where the French had been making films since the 1920s.

Most days, we were on the set for at least ten hours. Scenes had to be shot from several angles, which meant that when one vantage point was complete, we'd have to wait until the cameras could be repositioned, and then the same lines would be repeated.

Cécile's recall was so remarkable that several times, she fed lines to her new costar, Louis Lambert. Lambert had light-brown hair, a square jaw, and a slim mustache. Chiseled good looks combined with his tall muscular frame to create a purely masculine male. The two were a dashing couple.

Now as Cécile filmed on set, I sat in the dressing room repairing the hem of a navy blue skirt torn during filming yesterday.

As I concentrated on angling my sewing needle into the heavy wool fabric, I became aware of someone standing in the doorway. When I looked up, Hauptmann Wolfgang's sturdy body filled the frame. Sharp eyes added menace to his frown.

Before the war, I guessed he was a humble man with little power, and the occupation had provided him with new adventures and purpose. Since Les Halles, he had taken a particular interest in me, and I often caught him staring.

"Mademoiselle Rousseau," he said.

I set the garment aside and stood, knowing that ignoring him could be seen as a provocation. "Hauptmann Wolfgang. How are you today?"

"I'm well. I'm checking to see if you have all that you need. Some others on set have complained they can't get the required supplies."

I doubted he could fix our shortages. And I suspected he was more interested in gathering complaints for future reference.

"I have all I need, Hauptmann Wolfgang. Thank you for the inquiry."

Instead of leaving, he lingered. "I'm sorry about the boy's death. He was a good, hardworking young man."

His reference to Rupert rekindled grief, sadness, and anger. "Yes, he was."

A heavy silence fell between us before he broke it with "Did you see Emile Dupont yesterday? I know you visit her on Tuesdays."

I stilled. "Is there a concern?"

He adjusted his cuff, pausing before saying, "Emile has been known to associate with the Communist Party."

All questions from a German had to be handled carefully. "Whenever I see Emile, we only discuss her sister."

"So, Emile hasn't seen her sister?"

"No. There's been no time. Cécile works here all day. And if she has a spare evening, she's with Oberst Schmidt."

"She rarely rests."

"I must work doubly fast to keep up with her."

Curiosity hardened his eyes. "You'll let me know if Cécile and her sister meet."

Many French people were whispering secrets to the Germans to gain favors or extra ration cards, but I'd refused. "Yes, of course."

"Excellent. We must keep our star safe and out of trouble."

"Of course."

Cécile appeared at the doorway, her breathless smile flickering when she saw the captain. "Ah, Hauptmann. How are you today?"

Ever since Rupert's execution, she'd been extra friendly with him. He stepped aside, giving her a wide berth. "I'm well. And the filming is on schedule?"

"Of course. It's all perfect."

"Your costar forgets his lines," the captain said.

Cécile waved her hand. "Words can be coached. What can't be taught is the chemistry with the camera and a well-timed delivery."

Like everyone else on set, the captain had seen the magic on screen between Cécile and Louis. They were both physically beautiful and shared a restrained, captivating passion for film.

"Sylvia, you must change my dress. The director wants to reshoot the scene from yesterday," Cécile said. "Hauptmann Wolfgang, please excuse us." Even as she spoke, she was kicking off her shoes and reaching for the buttons of her blouse. For all his bravado, the captain was at his core a good country Lutheran. His well-fed cheeks flushed as he turned, closing the door behind him.

Cécile peeled off her blouse and handed it to me. Her expression sharpened. "What's this about Emile?"

I carefully snapped the wrinkles from the blouse and hung it up on a padded hanger. Fabrics were growing ever more precious by the day, so each piece had to be treated with care. Most of Cécile's wardrobe items were either mended or repurposed from another costume, and many carried the faint scent of stain remover.

"He thinks she associates with dangerous people."

She huffed as she shimmied out of the skirt. "My sister is going to get herself killed." She sat in a silk tufted chair and carefully unrolled her stockings. "Will you see her next Tuesday?"

I accepted the stockings. "Yes."

"She doesn't think well of me these days. She hates that I work here. Hates who I associate with. And there are days I can't blame her."

I hung up her skirt and reached for the polka-dot dress for the reshoot. "She leaves the notes, so you know she's well."

"Perhaps the notes are more for you than me."

"No. She cares and worries about you."

"When you visit Emile again, I'll have a note for her," Cécile said.

This was the first time she'd sent a note to her sister. "Of course."

She lowered her voice to a whisper. "Don't show anyone my note, and guard it closely. It'll contain personal information I wouldn't want anyone else to see."

Cécile had always been savvy about maintaining her position in the world. For her to take any risk was a shift. "Of course."

She stared intently into my eyes. "Why do I trust you, Sylvia?"

Dozens of refugees had put their trust in me, but they'd had no choice. Cécile didn't appear desperate, and she had many options before her. "I don't know."

"I shouldn't. No one can be trusted now." Her tone sounded sad, but she was right.

"But?" I asked.

"You hold secrets close. There's been no whiff of gossip about you on the set. You stay in the shadows."

Was she being honest or seeking information for her German friends? Until now, we'd done nothing but discuss fashion, deadlines, and the weather. I didn't ask about her evenings out. And she never inquired about how I filled my precious free time.

"You should visit your sister," I said.

Resolve settled on her shoulders. "It's too dangerous now. The captain's questions prove it. A visit from me would draw attention to us all. We must be careful."

Cécile was right. She couldn't go anywhere in Paris now without being noticed by Hauptmann Wolfgang or the public. Communication with her sister would have to be via me.

As if sensing my apprehension, she said, "I would like to wear the black silk dress tonight for my dinner with Henri. The one with the plunging back. I find that dress makes men delightfully chatty and silly."

"I added a row of pearl buttons along the back and cuffs. It's a very striking effect." They'd been Rupert's pearls.

"Henri will love the detail. He loves the dramatic."

"Of course." Lately, Monsieur Archambeau had shown little interest in Cécile. Rumor had it he was drawn to an even younger woman with dark hair and long, lean limbs. Cécile didn't seem to mind that his attentions had shifted elsewhere or that their conversations were focused on business. Her interests rested on Oberst Schmidt.

"Henri wants tonight to be perfect so that when his associates return to Berlin, they'll have nothing but glowing words about Henri Archambeau and his films."

"And his lead actress."

"I'm the shining star now, but I can be erased like everyone else."

"You erased? You have an entire career ahead of you."

"I don't think so. Some flames burn bright and hot, and then they're gone."

I held up the polka-dot dress, and she stepped carefully into it. I fastened each of the twenty-five black buttons. "And what does Monsieur Archambeau say about a dramatic movie?"

"Henri doesn't want to upset anyone. Especially considering how the war is going in the east."

"What does he say of the east?" I asked, carefully.

"Cities leveled. Ghettos built. He believes the violence is headed toward Paris, and only the movies will save us."

Once-vibrant cities were now crumbling. So much waste and loss. Too many good lives destroyed. "You speak so calmly."

"Tears fix nothing," she said. "Only the calm and calculated win. And I'll win."

"What are you saying?"

"Men talk, too much sometimes. And I remember it all."

Cécile, through Oberst Schmidt, had access to high-ranking Germans. She'd likely heard secrets that only a privileged few were privy to. Was she ready to communicate some of these secrets to her sister? She'd said she couldn't contact Emile, but I could. Now, I had a chance to strike back for Rupert.

I adjusted the seams of her shoulders. "I'll deliver whatever you have for Emile."

She smiled. "Good."

CHAPTER NINETEEN
SYLVIA

Tuesday, March 18, 1941
6:30 p.m.

As promised, Cécile had a letter ready for me late Monday. She had asked me not to open the letter, but she'd also not sealed the envelope. I wasn't sure if this was a test or a statement of her trust. Either way, I didn't look at the letter. In case I was arrested, the authorities wouldn't be able to extract what I didn't know.

When I arrived at Emile's, the sun was low on the horizon, and the streets were quiet. I hurried. The last Métro car left at 8:00 p.m. and would deliver me home before the curfew.

I dressed simply, selecting my oldest suit, and brown shoes that had been resoled twice. I hadn't sewn extra pockets into this jacket, but I would make that a priority. My blond hair was tucked under a simple hat. I wore no jewelry.

The boulangerie was dark. I guessed Marc was catching a few hours of precious sleep before baking began at midnight.

The exterior stairs creaked as I climbed to the second-floor apartment. Inside the hallway, I knocked on Emile's door, and when I didn't hear a response, I opened it.

Emile sat at her small table. A lantern glowed and cast light on her pale features. There was a dishcloth wrapped around her hand.

"Emile?" When she didn't look up, I closed the door and crossed to her, setting my basket on the table. "Emile."

She looked up with hollow, bloodshot eyes. "Sylvia."

I removed my gloves and jacket and set them aside before I reached for her hand. She flinched.

"Let me see. You must let me help you."

Nodding, she braced.

Very carefully, I unwrapped her hand. My stomach roiled at the sight of her twisted index and middle fingers. They looked as if they'd been smashed.

"Who did this to you?" I asked.

She wiped a tear with the back of her other hand. "The police."

"The French police?"

"Yes."

"What happened?"

"I was at a meeting."

"Emile . . ." I carefully lowered her hand and crossed to the sink. I filled a white porcelain bowl with warm water and returned. I lowered her injured hand into the water. She hissed and tensed but didn't draw back.

"How did they do this?" I asked.

"With a hammer." Tears welled in her eyes as her jaw set. "We were doing nothing wrong," she said. "We were simply discussing ideas."

"Ideas are dangerous. Being seen with the wrong people is perilous. Rupert was shot because he was in the wrong place at the wrong time." I ripped a washcloth into several uneven strips. "What happened?"

"The police raided the meeting. Marc escaped. So did several others. But I tripped, and the police caught me and threw me on the ground. One policeman held me down while the other struck my fingers."

I swirled the water around her hand until the water had turned red with blood. "Did they ask you any questions?"

"No. They said this was a warning." She narrowed watery eyes on me. "They said they've been watching me."

I sat in the chair across from hers and, lowering my voice, asked, "What did they see?"

Emile stared, blankly searching for a logical answer. "They caught me handing out flyers and newsletters."

I'd had friends like her in Poland. In their letters, they'd told me they weren't afraid to challenge authority, believing justice would prevail. I'd heard from none of them in years. "Newsletters against the Germans, no?"

"Of course."

"And you don't think that won't get you killed? I've told you this before."

Regret mingled with the classic Dupont stubbornness. "I didn't believe you."

I gently dried her fingers. They were badly bruised and bent, and she would lose the nails. Emile sucked in a breath, her fingers stiffening. Fresh tears spilled down her dirt-streaked face.

"Consider yourself lucky," I said.

"'Lucky'?"

"They've done far worse to good people."

"How do you know this?"

Hangings, mass graves, torture, the camps. Poland was a preamble to what had arrived in France. "France isn't the first country they've taken over. They know what they're doing."

Panic brightened her gaze. "Is Marc back?"

"I saw no sign of anyone downstairs."

She ran her left hand over stray strands that had escaped a bun. "He must be in hiding."

"Or dead or in prison. They won't hold back on him if they did this to you. And if they discover he's a forger, they'll come for us all."

She set her jaw. "He's a good man."

"History is littered with the deaths of good men."

Neither of us spoke as I dried off her injured hand and gently wrapped it in the clean linen. She could hide the bandage if she kept her fingers curled up under a coat, but when she worked at the boulangerie, if it ever opened again, everyone would see she'd been marked as trouble.

"Your sister sent you a letter, and she also sent along food."

A childish scowl crossed her face. "Food paid for by Henri or the German film industry."

Her cheeks were hollowing, and her collarbones were more pronounced. "It's food, and you need to eat. If you starve to death, then they win." I unwrapped the bread and cheese and set it before her. "Eat. If you're too weak to function, you're of no help to anyone."

"The food is tainted."

"Food is food. It'll keep you alive, and that's the goal. Live for another day."

She accepted a piece of bread I tore off for her. "What does the letter say?"

"It's intended for you."

"She trusts you, or she wouldn't have asked you to deliver it. Read it to me."

I opened the letter.

> E—
> I hope this note finds you well. Stay in touch with me. Though we can't see each other now, I miss you. I have so much to tell you about the fantastic people I've met.
> —DD

DD. Dominique Dupont. Did she hope that using her real name would reconnect her with Emile?

"What is she trying to tell me?" Emile asked.

"She has access to many high-level people. And her memory is excellent."

"She never forgets," Emile scoffed. "Parties with German officers."

"And industrialists and French government officials." I handed her another piece of bread as if she were a child.

A slight bitter smile curled her lips. "If she's paying attention, she'll remember every word. Men rarely look past her beauty. They don't realize how brilliant she is."

"And now she wants to correspond with you," I said carefully. "She trusts you. And as we both know, trust is rare. Could you pass on information to the right people?"

She cradled her injured hand. "Marc has connections outside this country in Spain, Britain, and Switzerland. Has she told you what she's heard?"

"We didn't speak in specifics. Unless you agree to hear her out, we won't know what she has to say."

Provided Marc was still alive and willing to operate as a courier, the connection between the sisters could be productive.

Emile's gaze sharpened with more questions. "Why's she doing this?"

"She's always smiling and seems carefree, but she's been more guarded since Rupert's death. She's different. She's not so different from you."

"We've never been that much alike."

"In this, you might be."

Emile carefully flexed her fingers. "How do you know she's not working for them?"

I'd seen families turn on each other. "I don't, I suppose. We won't know unless we test the waters."

"If you're wrong, it could be very costly."

"To do nothing is wrong."

She glanced at her fingers. "What should I do?"

"Stop attending these meetings. They draw attention to you. Work in the boulangerie. Become invisible. And wait."

"It's hard to remain silent."

"Loud and angry gets attention for a short time, but those voices are often silenced first. The quiet ones can get a great deal accomplished."

"You're saying I'm loud?" Bitterness wrapped around the words. "My sister is on every screen in France."

"Playing the roles of silly women. Cécile is clever. She understands how to play the game, but your moral outrage makes you scream."

She flexed her fingers, winced, and rested her hand on her lap.

"Write your sister a note and tell her you want to rekindle your relationship. Tell her you've missed her."

"I've been saying that in my letters."

"It'll be different this time. She'll understand you're responding to her offer."

"If it's an offer."

"Either way, we'll wait for her to write another letter to you, which I'll deliver."

Emile rose and crossed the room to a small dresser. She removed paper and pen, sat, and, with her injured hand, carefully wrote out a simple message.

> D.
>
> Your kind words mean a great deal to me. I always welcome hearing from you. Get in touch with me as often as you'd like.
>
> Your loving sister,
> E.

Heavy footsteps sounded on the stairs. Emile folded the letter and tucked it in the envelope that had carried her sister's letter to her. I pushed it deep under the lining of my basket. If it were found, what would be the crime? Two sisters talking was normal. If these sisters were going to pass secrets, I would have to find shrewder hiding places for the messages.

A fist pounded on the door. Emile drew in a breath and smoothed her hand over her disheveled hair. She looked toward me. I nodded.

When she opened the door, Marc rushed over the threshold into her arms. She gripped him tightly, burying her face in his coat. His dark hair was disheveled, and his pant leg was torn. He looked at me, his eyes dark with questions. Then he noticed the bowl and the rag bandages.

"What happened?" he asked.

Emile raised her hand. "The police gave me a warning."

He lifted her wounded hand. "They're trying to get to me."

"Why?" I asked. "Do they know what you do?"

"They know there's a forger providing papers to refugees and Jews. They're trying to shut this counterfeiter down."

"Why would they suspect you?" I demanded.

"The police have conducted many sweeps. Someone could have said something."

"But they don't know it's you?" Emile demanded.

"Not yet." His voice was brusque and harsh.

"You must be more careful," I said.

"I won't stop doing what I do," he said. "You, of all people, should understand that."

"Emile's smashed fingers was a gentle warning," I said.

"So leave," he said. "We'll be fine."

"There's a greater prize to be had," I said. "I'll let Emile explain. I must go before I'm caught by the curfew."

CHAPTER TWENTY
RUBY

Saturday, July 5, 2025
7:00 a.m.

When I woke up the following day, I was exhausted. I'd spent most of the night staring at the ceiling. I'd been so damn angry. Every time I closed my eyes, I saw Scott.

Scott had known me well at one time, and he still knew which buttons upset me. I hadn't given in to his demands, but when he called me selfish for wanting a baby, I'd started to have doubts. My future was so uncertain, and I could be setting my child up for loss.

Three years ago, I'd have brushed off his comments, confident I could tackle anything. But I couldn't conquer everything. I'd won this round with cancer, but like Jason used to say, that disease loved rematches.

It was frustrating not to be able to live like I had. I sat on the edge of the bed, glaring at my harried expression in the mirror above the dresser. I wanted the old me back.

My phone chimed with a text, and when I saw Jeff's number, I nearly cried. Such a good man. He deserved more than I could give.

Jeff: Any breakthroughs yesterday?

Me: Making progress.

Jeff: Breakfast?

Me: Pass. Sorry. Exhausted.

Jeff: Dinner?

Me: Headed to Fairfax to see an old friend, Jason.

After a moment's hesitation:

Jeff: The Jason with non-Hodgkin's Lymphoma?

What a memory.

Me: One and the same.

Jeff: I'll drive.

Me: You don't have to.

Jeff: What time?

As much as I wanted to be the brave soul, a little backup now would be excellent.

Me: 11 am

Jeff: CU

When he arrived precisely at eleven, I was waiting out front of the hotel wearing white linen pants, a black off-the-shoulder top, and flats. I'd tied a yellow scarf to the handle of my purse, which matched daisy-shaped earrings.

He rose out of a black Mercedes and approached the passenger-side door. "You look amazing," he said.

"Thank you." I slid on dark oversize sunglasses. "When did you start driving a fancy car?"

"The 2000 Toyota finally gave out."

"Got your money's worth."

"Always." He regarded me a moment and then opened the car door. Once I was settled, he came around and slid behind the wheel. He asked for Jason's address and plugged it into his GPS. Seat belt on, he pulled out and said, "Want to tell me what's eating you?"

I clicked my seat belt. "Hearing from Jason again has thrown me for a loop."

His head cocked. "That's all it is?"

"Isn't that enough?"

When he reached a red light, he glared at me. "It's more, Ruby. Remember, I'm a Jedi when it comes to your moods."

I shifted, feeling a little like a bug under the microscope. "You're a mind reader now?"

The stoplight turned green, and he drove through the congested city traffic. "How sick is he?"

"He won't tell me. That's why I need to see him."

"That's kind of you. I don't remember seeing much of him at all the last year you were in treatment."

"You were traveling for work."

"Eric and I talked."

"Don't be mad at Jason. He was free of cancer and running toward life. I'll never fault him for that."

"You aren't running away."

I sighed. "Don't paint me as brave. I'm very average and doing the best I can."

His jaw pulsed, and then he changed the topic. "Tell me about Cécile."

The conversation shift was so welcome. "It looks like the story's star is Sylvia, her dressmaker. I'm unsure what her full story is, but she appears to be a woman with many secrets."

"Secrets make for a good story."

"Yes, they do."

"She made many costumes for Cécile's movies, right?"

"She did."

"Could you arrange to show some of the costumes at the opening nights? A traveling tour?"

"That's a good idea. But I'm not sure Madame Bernard will agree."

"Doesn't hurt to ask."

The busy streets of Old Town fed into the Beltway, and Eric eased into traffic.

"You get up here often, don't you?" I asked.

"The company took on a few accounts in the area last year, so yes, I've been up here a lot. Let's say the car knows the way."

I glanced out the window, watching the highway rush past tall buildings that all looked identical.

"Scott called me yesterday," I said.

Jeff's fingers tightened on the steering wheel. "And?"

"He's in town for work. Lucky me. I agreed to see him to close the door on us for good."

"But?"

"He's more of an ass than I remember. I'm not sure why I thought I loved him once."

"But?"

I stared ahead as we moved past brick buildings. "He wants to destroy the embryos we created. He says it's selfish of me to consider having a baby because I could die. And he's now engaged. And he doesn't like the idea of his and my biological child walking the face of the earth."

Jeff muttered an oath. "He didn't say that, did he?"

"Not exactly, but close. He wants all his children with the new pregnant fiancée."

Jeff stared ahead, calculating the angles. "I saw the contract Eric drew up. It's ironclad."

"And I'm grateful my brother was thinking ahead when I couldn't."

"But?"

"But maybe Scott is right. Maybe I am being selfish."

"How so? Those are your embryos."

"But what if I end up like Jason? What if I get sick again? It's feeling a little selfish to expect a long future."

"We can all say the same. No one has a lock on tomorrow."

"My future is on shakier ground than most people's."

"Scott's gotten in your head." His jaw pulsed. "What an asshole."

"Yes. But even an asshole can be right."

"Kick him out of your head, Ruby. He doesn't deserve the space."

He pulled off the Beltway and headed down a series of highways. We pulled into a tree-lined neighborhood. He parked in front of a brick colonial with a neatly trimmed yard, an aggregate driveway, and boxwoods cut into identical rounds.

"He talked about his yard a lot. He loves working in the garden."

"Are you much for gardening?"

"No. Dirt under my fingernails, clunky shoes, bugs . . . not my jam."

He chuckled as he shut off the engine. "I'm a big fan of air-conditioning."

"And fireplaces that can be flipped on with a switch. Gourmet kitchens rock. And I do love balconies overlooking a lovely garden."

I remained in my seat, staring at the house. My heart thumped faster. "What am I going to find?"

"The only way is to go inside," he said.

A sigh rushed over my lips. "Right. Let's do this."

He got out of the car and waited for me to join him. Together, we walked to the front door. I pressed the doorbell button, and within seconds, steady footsteps echoed inside.

When the door opened, Jason's husband, Robert, stood at the threshold. He was tall and lean, dressed in crisp khakis, a white button-down shirt, and brown loafers. His hair was grayer and thinner than I remember from the pictures I'd seen of him, and dark circles smudged under his eyes. Robert and Jason had reunited right after Jason's treatment, and they'd married a month later. Jason had faced a tenuous future and had every reason not to marry. But he had.

He smiled. "Ruby. I'd know that face anywhere."

I hugged him. "I couldn't stay away."

"I'm glad you came."

I slid out of his embrace and held a trembling hand out to Jeff. "This is my friend Jeff."

Robert stepped outside and closed the door behind him.

"I'm glad you brought someone. Jason is in rough shape."

"When did he get sick again?"

"March. He had stomach pains, and I took him to the emergency room. The cancer had spread everywhere."

"What about his follow-ups with his doctors?"

"He wasn't going like I thought he was. He said over and over he wanted to be normal."

"I understand that."

"I'd be mad if he wasn't so sick." He fixed his jaw, found a smile, and looked at me. "You look amazing. How're you doing?"

I crossed my fingers. "So far, so good."

He reached for the door handle. "Please come inside. He's on the sunporch."

We followed Robert down a long center hallway through an all-white kitchen and onto a sunporch filled with plants. Jason sat in a recliner by a collection of ferns. Crosby, Stills, Nash & Young's "Our House" played. I knew the song because Jason loved hits from the 1970s.

Jason was painfully thin, and his skin was paper white. A thick patchwork quilt covered his skinny body. His eyes were closed.

With each step closer to the chair, my anger grew. We'd always promised never to talk about fairness and unfairness, but honest to God, this was unfair. Jason didn't deserve this.

I pulled up a chair, sat beside him, and took his cold hand. His eyes fluttered open. He smiled when they focused on me. "Ruby."

"Jason."

"You look the picture of health," he said. "And don't say that I do. I look like shit."

My frozen smile felt like a million others I'd seen when I was sick. "I imagined you on a sandy beach."

"Robert and I went to the South of France for a vacation. It was amazing. You were right about the beautiful coastline, the bread, and God, the olive oil."

"I still miss it all."

"Have you been back to Paris?"

"No. Just restarting life."

"You want to return?"

"Maybe for a visit. But I like being closer to home now."

"I understand." He rolled his head toward Jeff. "You her wingman today, Jeff?"

"You always had a great memory." Jeff shook Jason's hand.

"Both of you, sit. Tell me about this article you're writing."

I settled in an overstuffed chair by him. "I've gotten access to Cécile's dressmaker's diary. It's fascinating."

"It won't take you much to bond with a dressmaker. How many times did you talk about the clothes in *Secrets in the Shadows*?"

I laughed. "Fashion is its own form of resistance."

A sigh leaked over his thin lips. "What has the dressmaker told you about Cécile?"

"I'm not certain. She was either a collaborator or maybe a spy."

A thin brow arched. "A spy? Like a movie heroine. Very mysterious."

"I don't know Cécile's entire story yet. But espionage adds more mystery to her 1942 disappearance."

"The plot thickens."

"I can't wait to figure it all out."

"You will."

"Let's hope."

Jason shifted and coughed, wincing. He cleared his throat. "Jeff," Jason said. "Do me a favor and take Ruby back to Old Town Alexandria. She needs to work on her article. As much as I love seeing you both, sitting here with me won't do us any good."

"I like sitting here with you," I said.

Jason's eyes drifted closed briefly before reopening. "I can barely tolerate myself now. And as you can see, I can hardly keep my eyes open."

"I don't mind if you sleep," I said. "I'll hang out here."

"That's creepy," Jason said with a smile. "You and Jeff, get out of here."

"If you're sure."

"I am."

I kissed him on the cheek, knowing this was for the last time. "I love you."

"Back at you." He squeezed my hand. "Glad to see you and Jeff are finally together. He won my heart with the marching band."

"We're not together. We're friends."

Jason's gaze turned serious. "Don't waste any time, Ruby. Love him for as long as you can."

I swallowed a lump in my throat. *But what if I don't have that much time?* Of course I couldn't ask him, because I wasn't wasting any more time complaining about fears of death and dying. "I will."

Jason's grip grew surprisingly strong, and his tone became more urgent. "Promise me, Ruby."

"Promise you what?"

"That you won't withdraw and wait for it."

It. Death. "I'm not waiting around. I'm here. I'm living my life."

"Good. Squeeze every second dry."

CHAPTER TWENTY-ONE
RUBY

Saturday, July 5, 2025
11:30 a.m.

"How are you doing?" Jeff asked as he started the car.

"Okay. It was intense." I didn't want today's image of Jason to be the last one burned in my brain.

When a stoplight turned green, he took the right lane and merged into the Beltway. "That's an understatement. It hits at the core."

I drew in a breath and allowed it to bleed off. "He was on top of the world this time last year. And now he's got days, maybe weeks left."

"Here I was pissed at him for not touching base with you last winter."

"He must have known he was sick again. I wish he'd told me. Maybe I could have helped." My own platitudes sounded flat.

Jeff merged into traffic and headed south on I-495. "What would you have done if it were you?"

"I don't know. That's why I can't be mad. No one knows how they'll react until they're in the hot seat." Midsize high-rises blended with strip malls, storage buildings, and office parks. "Gives me a little appreciation for Sylvia, Emile, and Cécile."

"How so?"

"Death surrounded them. I'm halfway through Sylvia's journal, but I'm guessing it'll get harder for them. The Germans were 'playing nice' their first eighteen months in Paris, but that's starting to shift. Sylvia mentioned a young boy who worked on the set. He was shot and killed by the Germans. She writes about the police crushing two of Emile's fingers as a warning." I hated the idea that Cécile might have been murdered in a prison or concentration camp.

Jeff rolled his shoulders. "Why did they do that?"

"She was handing out anti-German propaganda. The French Resistance wasn't intense at first—women wearing large hats, singing 'La Marseillaise' publicly when told not to, or pretending to misunderstand German instructions. All this alone wasn't a big deal, but it annoyed the Germans. However, this mild form of resistance morphed into bombings and shootings. By mid-1942, the Germans were crushing Paris with retaliations, arrests, and roundups."

"Do you know what happened to Cécile or Emile yet?"

"No. Sylvia hasn't told me."

"You haven't peeked ahead, have you?"

I chuckled. "No. I promised Madame Bernard that I wouldn't. And honestly, if it's a bad ending, I'm not sure I could keep reading."

Two trucks rumbled past us, and the traffic slowed for a minute. Then, the pace picked up again. He said, "I'm doing a little cyber-digging. If any of these women were in a government registry, I might be able to find them."

"How do you do that?"

"I write a program."

I snapped my fingers. "Just like that? You make it sound easy."

He waggled his brows as he tossed me a grin. "It is for me."

I kept forgetting how purely brilliant he was. "Yeah, sure. That would be great. Sometimes, people aren't super honest in their diaries.

Especially then. A discovered journal could get you shot. But the Germans were excellent recordkeepers, so I'd love to see whatever you can find."

"If I get a bite on the cyber-feelers, I'll let you know."

"Thank you."

"What are you doing this afternoon?"

"Reading journal entries."

"Why don't you take a few hours off? Play hooky. I can do the same. Seize the day, right?"

Squeeze every second dry. "I'll agree on one condition."

"What's that?"

"If today showed me anything, I can't commit to anyone right now."

"I'm talking about lunch."

"I've known you for twelve years. You don't do anything without a specific goal in mind."

He glanced at me, amused. "And I want you?"

Color warmed my face. "I think you do."

"You wanted me the other night."

I closed my eyes, scrunching my face. "The wine made me do it."

"It was the wine, not you?" He sounded so pleased with himself. "What if I don't like you in that way?"

A smile curled my lips. "Your kiss in the hotel lobby said otherwise."

His shoulders straightened. "It was good, wasn't it?"

"It was amazing. Really. But I can't make any long-term promises. I can help you find someone who'll be there with you for the long haul."

"What if I don't want anyone else?"

"You will, once I find the right person."

His gaze sharpened. "You could be the right person."

"Sorry, no. I'm not. But when you meet The One, you'll know it."

Tension strained his expression. "This is the craziest conversation I've had in a long time."

"Did you get any pings on your dating profile?"

"I haven't checked."

"Why not?"

"Because I was focused on you."

"Let's direct our attention to a healthy woman who can give you children."

He wound around the Beltway toward the Old Town Alexandria exit. He slipped into an irritated silence as he took the off-ramp and merged into traffic. I sensed a barrier between us when he pulled in front of my hotel. I didn't like it, but it was for the best. He could design a software system that made billions of calculations. But casual conversation with a stranger wasn't in his wheelhouse.

"I'd still like to have lunch with you," he said.

"I need to work on the journal and article. But we can have dinner. We can pick the love of your life over pizza."

He shifted his gaze to mine, studying my face like he was trying to crack an algorithm. "If I let you help me, and that's a big if, you must meet each woman."

"That's a little weird."

"Not weird. You can show up or sit at an adjoining table if I have a date. You can't judge anyone based on a computer profile."

"You're not serious."

"I'm very serious," he said. "If you want to help me, you must actively participate. No half-assing the 'significant other' selection."

"You live in DC."

"And I just closed on a condo in Norfolk. We can work both areas if that helps, or we can stick to Norfolk, so you're close to home."

The condo was news to me. "Where did you buy a condo?"

"In Waterside. It overlooks the Elizabeth River."

"You must have paid a fortune."

Money was never a priority for him. "I know how to negotiate."

"Sounds like that's what we're doing now."

"I made an offer. You rejected it and then countered. Now we're working out the details."

"If I didn't love you, I'd say you were the weirdest guy ever."

A smug smile warmed his features. "You can't say you love me, remember? You're my official dating consultant. And I don't date people I work with."

"Right."

"As payment, I'll write a search algorithm for you and your project. Even Steven?"

He didn't mean that. He liked me way too much to accept my offer this easily. But I did love him and wanted him to have someone who could care for him for decades. With me, he could well be saddled with illness and sadness, like Jason's husband.

"Deal." All relationships are transactional on some level. And in this arrangement, today, we both received great value.

"Send me whatever names, dates, places of birth, et cetera, and I'll get on it."

"I'll do the same."

"I'm booked for the next few days with work, but you could get a date for us next week."

"Us, like as in the three of us?"

"You're my millennial matchmaker. I need you to vet these women for me."

"Technically, I'm Gen Z."

"Details."

My hand rested on the door handle, but I wasn't ready to leave. I wanted us on good terms. "You aren't mad, are you?"

"No. You've been very logical. And you know how much I appreciate logic."

"Can I hug you?"

"Is that professional?"

"Matchmakers can hug their clients. It's in the code of ethics," I deadpanned.

"As long as we aren't breaking a rule." He wrapped his arms around me. The scents of expensive aftershave and whatever scent made him *him* mingled. He was such a good man and deserved so much more.

I squeezed a little tighter and then pulled back. "I won't let you down."

"I know you won't." As I opened the door, he said, "What about pizza now? I'm starving."

"I have to work."

"So do I, but I think better when I'm not dizzy with hunger." When I hesitated, he grinned. "Come on, Ruby. Pizza, and you're back working at the grindstone in an hour."

"Can we look at your dating profile messages?"

"Sure. We can look."

"I don't hear much excitement."

"Takes me time to warm up to a new idea."

I closed the car door, and we drove ten minutes to a pizza shop off Duke Street. He found parking, and we only had to wait about ten minutes before we were seated at a table covered with laminated images of Italy.

"How do you know about this place?" I asked as I scanned a QR code and pulled up the menu.

"My office is in Alexandria. My apartment is down the street."

"Why didn't I know this?"

He scanned the QR code. "When I moved in a year ago, you had your hands busy."

Chemo. A good reminder of why I needed to find him someone solid to love. Pushing aside the thought, I glanced at the menu. "You like the mushroom and onion, right?"

"Yes. And I always ask them to go light on the cheese."

"Perfect."

"Sprite?"

"You know me so well." I'd lived on the stuff for almost two years but still couldn't get enough.

He placed our drink orders (mine had extra ice), and minutes later, we were sipping our drinks.

I stabbed my straw into the crushed ice. His phone was nowhere in sight. "Should we get down to business?"

"After the pizza. I can't talk on an empty stomach."

"You make it sound painful. It's going to be fun."

"If you say so." He slurped his soda to be annoying. "Cécile and Emile were born in Provence? Cécile also had a boyfriend, Daniel, who worked in the port of Marseille."

"That's right."

No sense in complimenting his excellent memory. We both knew he could recall the serial number of a car part from 2010.

"And Sylvia?" he asked.

"She was from Poland. She was a little older than Cécile. Born circa 1918, if she was in her midtwenties. I can get the exact date of her birth from Madame Bernard. She moved to France before World War II, in the mid-1930s. After Germany invaded Poland in 1939, she was stuck in France. Even if she'd wanted to go home, she couldn't."

"What did she do between 1939 and when she showed up in the Dupont sisters' lives?"

"She worked as a seamstress in a lingerie factory, but the shop closed when the owner died. She also helped Polish refugees who moved to Paris."

"Last name Rousseau, correct?"

"That's right."

"Doesn't sound very Polish."

"She was living under a false identity. Madame Bernard said her mother's birth name was Zofia Rozanski."

"Did Mrs. Bernard have more to say about her mother's past?" he asked.

"Sylvia talked a little about growing up in Warsaw. But she didn't discuss the war years. Madame Bernard only found the diary after her mother died."

"So, Mom didn't want to talk about her past. It wasn't uncommon in that generation, especially after the war," he said.

"I'll keep pressing Madame Bernard for more names and dates. She's kind of spoon-feeding me details."

"She's trying to figure out if she can trust you," he said. "She's protecting her mother's legacy."

"She's worried about what her mother was hiding."

"What do you think she was hiding?"

"I don't know." I added, "It's a fascinating project. It has it all. Mystery, fashion, film, and spies." I sipped my soda.

"A Polish emigrant moves to France," he said. "For five years, she helps refugees get false papers. Then she finds herself working with two sisters, one of whom was a famous movie star with access to high-level Germans. I'm not a fan of coincidence."

"What does that mean?"

"I'll check the records for the British and Polish intelligence officers assigned to France during the war. By now, everything is declassified."

"Do you think Sylvia was an Allied or Polish spy?" I asked.

"Polish nationals made it to France and Britain after the 1939 German invasion. They fought fiercely for their country with the help of whomever would support them."

I slurped my drink, feeling like a kid who'd found a hidden treasure. "That puts a different spin on things."

He shrugged. "Would explain why Sylvia didn't talk about her past."

"She was Jewish."

"Ah, another reason for secrecy."

Our pizzas arrived, and the scents of basil, tomato, and cheese made my stomach grumble. I'd barely eaten in the last two years, and my appetite was finally turning back on.

After I ate two slices, I wiped my fingers clean and searched for Jeff's phone. "Your phone?"

He reached in his pocket, handed it to me, and rattled off his passcode.

"You have five messages on the app," I said. "Nice."

"Please share." He took a large bite of pizza, seemingly more interested in the food than this conversation.

"Ellen, twenty-nine. Tall, dark-brown hair, publicist, lives in Virginia Beach. Loves long walks on the beach, dancing, and rock climbing."

Jeff took another bite, waving for me to give him the next.

"Sarah, thirty-one. Blond, five foot six, lawyer, swimmer, loves cycling, reading."

Jeff sniffed. "Let me see her picture."

I turned the phone around. "See, pretty?"

"Nice."

"But?"

"Who else?" He took another bite of pizza.

I read out the stats for the next two women. Jeff didn't yawn, but he looked about that bored. "This won't work if you don't try."

"I'm trying. I am. Let me think about the choices. It's a big decision."

"It's not. It's a date. A lunch or a dinner."

"I thought you were looking for my wife and the mother of my children."

I scowled. "I want you to have someone. I want you to be happy."

"I am happy. I'm eating great pizza and listening to you talking about secret spies and possible spouses."

I glanced at the next one who'd messaged him but rejected her. I handed him his phone back. "I'm not going to be defeated."

He leaned forward a fraction and grinned. "That's what I like about you. You don't give up."

"I don't."

An alarm chimed on his watch. "As much fun as this is, I have a meeting this afternoon. We can continue this discussion over dinner."

"Will you agree to take one of these women out on a date? One woman. One date?"

"Sure, fine. Pick one close to Norfolk, and we'll meet her in two weeks."

"You keep saying 'we.' I can't be there."

"That's the deal. You must check her out. Maybe you can grab Eric, and you both can bump into us. He'll run cover. Won't look weird at all."

"But it is weird."

"Friends check out their friends' dates all the time. Not any woman can be the mother of my children."

"Fine, it's Ellen in Virginia Beach. You can set up a date at Waterside."

"Can't you do that?"

"No. That's on you."

"Okay. Consider it done. Keep your calendar open the week after next. We have a date."

A waitress set the bill on the table. I tried to grab it, but Jeff refused. She boxed up the last slice of pizza for us, and he dropped me off at my hotel room.

As I opened the car door, he handed me the to-go box. "I'll get more intel on Sylvia. I'll report at dinner."

We weren't forever, but being around him was fun, relaxed, and easy. "Okay. Dinner."

"Pick you up at seven?"

"Perfect."

In my hotel room, I removed my shoes, carefully undressed, and hung up my clothes. No matter how tired I was, I always hung up my clothes. After donning my oversize T-shirt, I made decaf coffee and reached for Sylvia's diary.

"Who are you, Sylvia?"

CHAPTER TWENTY-TWO
SYLVIA

Monday, June 23, 1941
4:00 p.m.

Days of unseasonably cool temperatures and an overcast sky had added to the weight of growing restrictions. Despair was everywhere I walked.

Few Frenchmen were left in Paris, but the ones remaining were either too old or too young. The women left behind struggled under the extra weight of caring for small children or aging parents while chasing ways to make money.

Ration cards provided barely enough food for the average person, and the French queued in lines for hours, only to discover that the butchers, bakeries, wine shops, or cheese vendors had been stripped bare by our occupiers, whose appetites were never satisfied.

Despite all the hardships, the Frenchwomen kept up their appearances. Dresses and skirts might have been several seasons old, but hot irons pressed worn fabrics until they were immaculate. Charcoal masked scuffs on shoes, and any self-respecting woman who couldn't afford silk stockings painted her legs with iodine to mimic the appearance. Looking one's best was our form of rebellion.

Life on the movie set grew further and further apart from that of everyday Paris. The sets were staged with fruits and breads that could make any housewife weep with jealousy. Naturally, the crew took what they could, each having a hungry family at home. When it became impossible to shoot a scene before the food vanished, the set designer announced that he'd poisoned key pieces. The warning slowed the theft but didn't stop it.

So far, Cécile had written three notes for me to deliver to Emile. I never read a word unless Emile shared the letters with me. So far, nothing written on the page was beyond the chatter shared between sisters. If the Gestapo had read any of the notes, none would have sparked suspicion. Cécile was testing our new system and me before she risked more incriminating information.

When Cécile entered the dressing room, she looked annoyed as she sat and removed her shoes. She stood, and I unfastened the pearl buttons on the back of her blouse. She shrugged off the silk, unfastened her skirt, and shimmied out of the dark wool. She slid on a red robe.

We'd worked together for over eight months, and as I hung up the skirt and blouse, I felt comfortable enough to make simple inquiries. "Is everything all right?"

"Henri wants me to star in another film."

"That's good, no?"

"It's a comedy. I want a more dramatic role."

"The comedies sell well at the box office."

"That's what he keeps saying. But I might as well be in a factory making hats or shoes." From a silver case she removed a cigarette. "I've made them all a great deal of money. I live well, but what am I now? Their trained puppet? I don't need a lead role, but I want a part with more passion and depth."

Everyone in Paris guarded their words so carefully, and we stepped as if pins and needles lined the sidewalks. Still Cécile dared press against these restrictions. She was so like her sister.

"I'm going to a party tonight. Oberst Schmidt has returned to Paris. He's fresh from Berlin and sporting his new medals. And he insists on seeing me again."

"Berlin." We all feared vanishing into Germany on a crowded railcar. "What would you like to wear?"

"Something dark and smoky. Our German friend wants me to seduce him the instant I walk in the room."

Monsieur Archambeau had paraded Cécile in front of the Germans like a man dangled bait for fish. So far, she'd been clever enough to avoid their advances, but we all knew German patience thinned.

"I know the dress. It's the ruby silk that you wore in *The Orphan's Folly*."

Cécile lit the tip of her cigarette and inhaled. "Ah, yes. It was the dream sequence. The colonel will be impressed by an outfit that appeared on the screen."

"When will you get ready?" I not only dressed Cécile but also often styled her hair.

"We'll arrive at the restaurant by nine. We'll be late, which we know they hate, but this is Paris, and I'm French."

Cécile was often late now to the set, a lunch appointment, or a dinner. Making people wait had become a type of resistance for her. "Have you seen Emile?"

"Almost a week ago. Your sister looked well." The truth was she was thin and pale. I'd again cautioned her to restrain her nighttime activities. But she enjoyed knocking out streetlights, puncturing German tires with ice picks, or snatching shopping bags from female German soldiers. All these pranks could lead to her arrest, and none of them would win this war.

"She's staying out of trouble?" Cécile asked.

"For the most part."

Cécile drew on her cigarette and let the smoke trickle out. "The colonel will be in a good, chatty mood tonight. I should have a letter for you tomorrow to deliver."

"I'll be waiting."

☙

By 8:00 p.m., Cécile was wearing the red silk dress that floated over her curves. I'd grown accustomed to her shape and knew when to nip in a seam or let one out. Ever since Rupert's death, she'd been losing weight. She barely slept, spending her days on set and her nights flirting with the most influential.

She and I had moved into a more lavish apartment in the twelfth arrondissement. The rooms had high ceilings and gold chandeliers and overlooked the Place de la Concorde.

When we'd first entered the suite, Monsieur Archambeau had shown us around, proud of this new find for his movie star. All I noticed were photographs featuring a father, a mother, and their three children as well as letters tucked in a cherry secretary desk, lingerie in the dresser drawers, and dresses and suits in the closets. The house was frozen, as if waiting for its actual owners to return.

The front doorbell rang. Cécile glanced in the floor-length mirror and touched the diamond clip securing the left side of her hair. Pearls dangled from her ears.

"Stay in here. I'll answer the door," Cécile said.

"Are you sure?" She'd dismissed all the other servants, something she often did now.

"I am. I want the colonel to think we're alone."

"I'll wait for you here."

She closed the bedroom door behind her. Heels clicked against the parquet floors as she moved toward the front door. After a pause, old hinges groaned.

"Good evening," she said.

"Good evening." The male voice was deep, thick with appreciation. His French was almost flawless, barely tainted with a faint German accent.

"Oberst Schmidt. Please come inside. We'll share a drink before dinner."

"We'll be late." His voice sounded clipped.

"Let them wait."

"You're good at making men wait."

She laughed. "Anticipation heightens desire, no?"

The front door closed. "There are limits to any man's patience."

Her chuckle was soft and seductive. "You'll be glad you waited a little longer."

When German men first arrived in Paris, they were shocked by the Frenchwomen. Their makeup, fashion, smoking in public, and stylish tardiness didn't fit the German ideal. But Frenchwomen continued to believe the world should bend to them. Still, only a few women like Cécile could press as much.

Leaning close to the door, I listened as the champagne bottle popped, glasses filled and clinked. Laughter mingled with a record playing on a phonograph.

It was impossible to understand their quiet conversation, but I sensed an intensity in their low tones. Cécile's throaty laugh was enough to encourage the man and delay whatever was to come. Expectation was too exciting to be rushed.

When they left the apartment forty-five minutes later, I hurried to the window and peered through the slim opening between the rich yellow curtains. Cécile walked toward a waiting car, where Hauptmann Wolfgang opened the back seat door. The colonel wore a neat dark-gray uniform and pressed his hand to her back.

Once Oberst Schmidt had lowered himself into the car, the captain closed the door. For a brief instant, he glanced up toward the apartment, and I could swear he saw me. We'd barely spoken since the executions at Les Halles, but he was always watching me, always aware. My heart leaped in my chest, and I let the curtain slip from my fingers. As I drew back, I pressed palms to my flushed cheeks.

Cécile's flirting had constantly tested the bounds with men. I'd had a lover when I first moved to Paris but working at the factory and with the refugees left me little time for love. Over time, my lover lost interest in the affair and had moved on.

I realized now that I missed a man's touch. How could I be thrilled by a German captain's glance? And what did that say about me?

I spent the night sitting in the drawing room, fully dressed, and waiting for Cécile. I drifted off sometime after 2:00 a.m., but my sleep was light and troubled. I dreamed of Warsaw in the days when I was a child. In those golden years, my mother laughed a lot, I took drawing and piano lessons, and my father dressed the most sophisticated clients in Poland. I'd had all a child could desire. But in the next moment, my mother was gone, and the Germans were firing into the crowd of six innocents at the market.

I sat up, shaking off the dream as the front door opened just after sunrise.

Cécile wore her fur coat wrapped tight. Her hair was messy and her eye makeup smudged, but she'd repainted her lips a bright red. She slid off the coat, tossing it over a chair as she crossed to the secretary and sat. "Sylvia, strong coffee, please."

I hurried to the kitchen, set the kettle on the stove, and filled the press with fresh coffee grinds now worth a month's pay in Paris. When I brought her a cup of coffee in a delicate porcelain cup, she had already pulled out paper and pen and had filled one full white page with neatly scripted words.

"What are you writing?"

"There were so many conversations last night. Germans were discussing manufacturing plants and factories. I must put everything I heard on the page."

I sat at the table as the pen moved with great speed. "You can remember conversations like this?"

She sipped her coffee. "It's harder when there are so many distractions, and Schmidt never let me out of his sight. But I can recall most of it."

She didn't need to explain. "Where was Henri?"

"He never showed."

I took her now-empty cup and refilled it along with one for me. She was scribbling on a second sheet when I sat back at the table. She gulped coffee.

"Oberst Schmidt is a pilot?" I asked.

Cécile hesitated as if understanding that this conversation bound us in a new, risky way. "He's an ace in the Wehrmacht Luftwaffe. Apparently, he's quite skilled at fighting in the air. He and other officers were discussing bombing missions, and they also mentioned a Renault factory near our studios that supplies vehicles to the Germans. You must get this information to Emile, and she'll pass it on to Marc and his friends in England." Her eyes glowed as if this new danger had ignited a fire in her.

"Where is Oberst Schmidt now?"

"He had important meetings this morning, but he wants to see me again. For now, he's sent me back to the toy box to wait."

I noticed the small rip in her side seam when she leaned back to stretch. There were faint bruises on her forearms, as if Schmidt had held her on her back. "Are you all right?"

She stared momentarily at a bruise. "My mother said I was born to be a whore. And she was right. I've used my body ever since I allowed the baker's son to touch my breasts in exchange for bread. Parisian men and the Germans are no different. All men want the same thing, but my price has changed. Once it was stardom, and now it's revenge."

"For Rupert?"

"For all the boys and girls like him."

"If this information is as sensitive as you say, it'll be traced back to you."

"Maybe, but it'll take time. Everyone at the party didn't see beyond my dress or the size of my breasts. It would never occur to any of them that I could remember conversations so easily."

"Henri knows you have a good memory."

"He has no idea of how sharp it is." There was no bravado, simply a statement of fact.

"Finish writing down your thoughts, and I'll draw you a bath. Later today, I'll deliver your letter to Emile."

Her gaze lifted from the pages to me. "This is no longer a letter between sisters. What's contained in these will get you arrested, shot, or deported."

I'd accepted this consequence each time I'd delivered forgeries or escorted refugees. "Rupert died for less. I don't want Paris to become like Warsaw."

Her gaze lifted to mine. "You're Polish?"

Emile suspected the truth, but I'd never admitted it to anyone in Paris. "It was a long time ago."

"Do you receive news from home?" she asked.

"Not for some time." The Ghetto walls encircling a portion of Warsaw had cut off almost all communication. Refugees still escaped the Ghetto via the sewers, but I'd heard precious little lately.

"You understand why we must do this," she said.

"I understand very well."

She brushed back a strand of hair. "Let me finish my note."

"I'll draw that bath."

"Thank you. I want to wash off the scents of last night."

As I turned, I paused. "Was the colonel cruel?"

She showed no emotion. "I've had worse."

When I left the apartment at noon, Cécile was still sleeping, and the servants were going about their duties. A basket dangled from my arm. Inside was Cécile's letter tucked between two fresh baguettes and covered with apples, a wedge of cheese, and a precious sleeve of salami. As I stepped out the front door, Hauptmann Wolfgang approached me.

"Good afternoon, mademoiselle," he said.

I was surprised to see him. Had he been lingering outside the apartment all morning? "Hauptmann Wolfgang, how are you today?"

"I'm well." He fell in step beside me. "It's been some time since we spoke."

"Yes."

"And where are you off to today?"

"Have you been here since you dropped Cécile off?"

"It's important that someone keep an eye on our film star. Where are you going?"

The captain had been watching the apartment. Had Schmidt ordered this? Was he already suspicious? "To drop off a basket of food for Emile."

He matched my pace. "Your mistress is very generous with her sister."

"It's natural, isn't it?" Had he taken note of my visits to Emile?

"It is."

"I must hurry."

"Emile lives in the Marais. It's a long walk, and the Métro is not running today. And we know how dangerous it can be. My car is parked a few steps from here. I'll drive you."

"That's very kind, but it's such a lovely day. I need to stretch my legs."

"Nonsense," he said with authority. "There were more disturbances on the streets yesterday. Several arrests have been made already. I wouldn't forgive myself if you were injured on your way to Mademoiselle Dupont's residence."

To argue might have raised his suspicions and given him a reason to seize my basket and search it. "Thank you, that's very kind."

He opened the front passenger-side door, and I settled in, tucking my skirt close. I hadn't ridden in a car since the shootings at the market.

The faint scent of Cécile's perfume still lingered in the air, a reminder of why she'd gone out with Oberst Schmidt last night.

"You had a late night?" he asked as he started the engine.

"I would guess yours was later than mine."

"I've always slept whenever I can." His keen interest and unasked questions darkened his gaze.

"There can't be much to do while waiting on your clients."

"There are other drivers to talk to. I catch a minute or two of sleep, and there's always food to be had from the kitchen staff."

"We're indeed fortunate."

"I'm blessed." He drove past a line of women queued up outside a butcher shop. The women looked tired, their shoulders stooped, the baskets they held empty. Many appeared restless, glancing impatiently toward the front of the line. By this time of day, the shop would most likely be out of supplies.

As if anticipating trouble, six uniformed German soldiers moved toward the women. I tensed. But this time the soldiers didn't draw their weapons but announced that the food was gone, and it was time to move along. Some old women left in disgust, but others were bold enough to complain. However, no one was foolish enough to raise a fist. Every Parisian knew that the consequences of disobedience were severe. I held my breath until the crowd had cleared.

Hauptmann Wolfgang drove toward the Seine, glancing in his rearview mirror. "They must learn patience."

"Hunger breeds impatience."

"Discipline is important."

He spoke with such authority, but that was easy when his belly was full and his place in the world secure. As I stared out my window, the weight of the hidden note reminded me to tread carefully. We crossed the Pont Neuf toward the large markets at Les Halles. Only a few vehicles were on the streets, and most citizens traveled on bicycles or by foot.

"You don't agree?" he asked, breaking my silence.

As we passed the Les Halles market, my mind grew blurry with the sounds of gunshots and screams. This market looked very different to me now. I no longer approached it with anticipation or excitement. "I didn't say that."

He cast a sharp glance at me. "Your mouth flattens into a thin line when you're unhappy."

I moistened my lips. "It does not."

"It does. I pay attention to the details," the captain said. "Amazing what I see on the movie sets."

I intentionally softened my expression but suspected it didn't look natural. My father had warned me that I wore my emotions like a thick wool coat in summer.

"Do you want to know what I've noticed?" he asked.

I knit my fingers in my lap. "Do I dare ask?"

"You're not French," he said with conviction.

I squeezed my palms together. "Why do you say that?"

"Your paperwork is French, your name is French, but"—he raised his finger—"your very faint accent and your face remind me of my boyhood. I grew up on the eastern border of Germany, a stone's throw from Poland."

To admit to my origins was cause enough for arrest or deportation. So, as my false papers stated, I said, "I grew up in eastern France, in Alsace, on the German border. That must be what you're hearing."

He took a right at the next corner and followed the route leading out of the city along the river.

"I believe you need to go the other way," I said.

"There's a roadblock in that direction. If we don't take a detour, we'll get stuck."

Tension knotted my belly, sending bile up my throat. As we drove toward the suburbs, I wondered if we were nearing a police station or a Gestapo outpost.

"When were you last in your hometown?" he asked.

"It's been some time. What about you?"

"My parents passed, and I never had a desire to live on their farm. I moved to Berlin when I was young and then studied in Paris for a time."

"Do you miss home?"

"I do. But life moves on, does it not?"

"Yes, it does."

Up ahead, there was a roadblock and three German guards waiting with guns. Hauptmann Wolfgang seemed unconcerned as he slowed and waited for the signal to advance. When we pulled up to the guard, he rolled down the window and handed him his identity papers.

The guard glanced toward me. "And the woman?"

I removed my papers from my purse and handed them to the captain, who turned them over to the guard. I'd paid Marc a month's salary for the documents. He'd assured me they were near perfect. But in this world, the Germans didn't need a reason to detain anyone.

The guard looked at the papers and studied me. Seconds passed as his frown deepened. Finally, he handed the credentials to the captain, who tucked both sets in his breast pocket.

We continued, driving farther and farther from Emile's. Fear pressed against my breastbone. "May I ask where we're going?"

"It's a lovely day. We aren't on duty, so we have time for a short adventure. When was the last time you left the city?"

"It's not allowed." He knew this. "But I don't need to leave. I'm fortunate enough to have everything I need."

"Lucky indeed."

Under other circumstances, a trip to the country would be welcome, but this unexpected detour only stirred images of guards aiming rifles at the very old and young. "I cannot linger long. I must return and press Cécile's evening dress."

"She's very popular. Is she meeting anyone tonight?"

I deliberately unfurled my fingers around my basket's handle. Was the captain testing me? Or simply making conversation? "I don't know."

"Ah, well, we'll both know soon enough, eh?" He continued driving farther east. Taller stone buildings gave way to smaller-profile structures surrounded by more land that rolled and dipped into ravines. In Poland the gullies had been filled with bodies.

"Sir, I must make my delivery and return to work."

He continued to drive. The route he'd chosen would have been lovely with someone else. But with him all I could see were places ready to swallow a woman's body whole. The farther we went, the more tense I became. Finally, after another twenty minutes of driving, he pulled off the road beside an open field. "We must take moments like this whenever we can, Sylvia. I can call you Sylvia?"

"Yes."

He rolled down his window and inhaled the fresh country air. My own breath caught in my throat.

He shifted in his seat toward me. "Why are you nervous?"

The expanse of his chest blocked my view of the road. "I'm not."

He laughed. "Remember, I can read you so well."

I shifted. "The unexpected makes me nervous."

"You aren't afraid of me, are you, Sylvia?"

"No, of course not."

He stared ahead. "You have nothing to fear from me."

The captain had saved me at the market. If he'd let me rush inside, I would have protested the execution and likely been shot myself. "I know."

"Do you?" The question was tinted with doubt.

"Yes."

Hawk eyes studied me, and I struggled to read his expression as he had mine. But just as quickly, he shifted that searing attention to the road and angled the car back toward the city. A half hour later, when we were parked in front of Marc's boulangerie, the worry cramping my belly still lingered.

"I'll come in with you," he said.

"That's not necessary. I'll be quick."

He shut off the engine. "Nonsense. It would be rude of me not to escort you."

I glanced over at the empty shop. The morning bread was long gone, and Marc was in his basement making forgeries.

Several old women, who'd heard the rare rumble of a car engine, peeked out from between curtains. Were those who remembered me from my days in the Marais whispering words like "collaborator" or "traitor"?

Hauptmann Wolfgang approached my side of the car and opened the door. Nodding my thanks, I rose, holding the basket close.

"Let me take your basket," he said.

Worry razored up to a forced smile. "Thank you."

He accepted the basket in a gloved hand, and when we crossed to the side door, he opened it. "I've never been inside the building. I sat outside once or twice when Cécile still visited Emile, but that was last year. Why are the sisters not visiting each other anymore?"

"I don't know. Sisters fight, I suppose."

"You have a sister?"

"No."

"Brother, father, mother?"

"All gone."

"Like me." He motioned me to enter first.

I climbed the stairs, looking up toward Emile's second-floor door. She might have been expecting me, but indeed, not the captain. I had no idea if she was alone or had invited one of her Resistance friends or Marc to her room. As I flexed my fingers, the soft leather tightened against my skin.

Moving toward Emile's door, I wanted to put distance between the captain and me. But quick, determined steps kept him close.

I knocked on the door. "Emile, it's Sylvia. Hauptmann Wolfgang and I have brought you a few gifts from your sister."

The apartment's interior was quiet, and there appeared to be no signs of life.

"Perhaps she worked the early shift," I said. "And is sleeping now. Or she could be out for deliveries this afternoon."

"It wouldn't be wise to leave your basket in the open."

"No, it won't last an hour." I didn't begrudge a hungry soul who stole food, but once the letter was discovered, it wouldn't take long to trace it back to the source.

Finally, footsteps padded on the apartment floor toward the door. Chain locks scraped free of their holders, and the door handle turned. When the door opened, I saw that Emile wore a light-blue robe. Messy hair drew attention to the dark circles ringing under her eyes as she clutched the folds of her robe with her uninjured hand.

"Sylvia, this is a surprise." When she glanced toward the captain, her smile was apologetic and relaxed. Acting came naturally to both sisters. "Apologies, I was making bread all night and am now stealing a few hours of sleep. Marc should return with fresh bags of flour soon so we can begin work again."

Her story was as believable as it was likely false. I wouldn't have been surprised if Marc was hiding on the other side of the door with a gun in hand. But as tempting as it might be to kill the captain, his death would mean more reprisals and the death of more innocents like Rupert.

I held out my hand. "We won't trouble you, Emile. The captain and I must get back. There's much to prepare for this evening."

"Is this evening special?"

"There's a party." Always a party. "I believe Monsieur Archambeau plans to announce his next film."

"Good for him and Cécile. Thank you for the food. It's always appreciated."

The captain touched the bill of his cap, and Emile smiled and softly closed her door. Silence settled on the other side, and I could imagine Emile and perhaps Marc holding their breaths.

I turned toward the stairs, expecting the captain to follow. When he didn't, I paused. "Hauptmann Wolfgang?"

His frown deepened as he stared at Emile's closed door. He turned and silently followed me outside.

When we reached the bottom stairs, the joyous shouts of children echoed. To my right, three boys, all younger than ten, had dark hair, dirt-smudged faces, and clothes that seemed too small.

The boys kicked a patched ball back and forth. When the ball returned to the largest boy, he glanced at the captain and kicked it so hard it skidded past his companions and bounced off the captain's legs. The younger boys grew silent, and even the oldest froze as if he realized he hadn't expected the ball to hit with such force.

As the ball ricocheted forward, Hauptmann Wolfgang immediately trapped it under the sole of his black boot. He reached down and picked up the ball.

The two littlest boys stepped back, but the oldest stood his ground. Hauptmann Wolfgang moved toward him with slow, measured steps until he loomed over him. All traces of defiance vanished from the boy's face.

Hauptmann Wolfgang tossed the ball in the air and caught it several times. "What's your name, boy?"

The oldest boy swallowed. "I'm Anton."

"Do you live nearby?"

Anton puffed out his chest. "Several blocks from here."

"And who are the others with you?"

"They are my cousins. But I'm in charge of them today."

"You have quite the kick, Anton."

I stepped beside the captain. "Children can be reckless."

"So it seems." The captain shoved the ball into Anton's chest. "You have a good leg, young man."

The boy gripped the ball. "Thank you."

"Be more careful."

The boy and his companions turned and ran.

"They're careless children, no?" I noted with relief as they vanished around a corner.

"Children today, but young soldiers tomorrow," the captain said as he brushed the dust from his pant leg.

He was right. If this war raged for a few more years, the oldest boy would either take up arms or be shipped to a German labor camp. Childhood passed too fast in times of war.

The captain opened the car door for me, and I settled in the front seat. As he walked around to his side of the car, I glanced up toward Emile's apartment and saw movement flickering over the curtains. She was tracking our departure before she dared open her basket.

"That was very kind of you," I said.

He started the engine and glanced at me. "There's no reason not to be courteous."

It had been easy for the captain to be generous today. But he enjoyed this power that war had given him.

"You're nervous now," he said. "Your gloves stretch over your clenched fingers like a second skin."

I glanced at the straining seams and then worked the stiffness from the joints. "The boys and the soccer ball . . . not everyone would've let the slight slip."

"Was it a slight or a mistake?"

I didn't answer. Panic clawed.

"I made a few mistakes as a child," he said. "We all do."

"Do you have children?" Of course, I realized, he could have a wife or children back in Germany.

"Once. The child and my wife died."

"I'm very sorry."

He was stoic. "It's the past." After he drove for several minutes, he asked, "Do you speak German?"

"A little," I replied in German. "Why do you ask?"

"Nice to hear my mother tongue. It reminds me of home."

"But there are so many Germans in the city. German is a second language in Paris now."

"It'll soon be the first."

The offhand remark spoke to a terrifying scenario.

"Knowledge of the German language will make it easier for you in the summer," he said.

"The summer?"

"There's talk of organizing a tour for Cécile in Germany. She's quite popular in Berlin, and many important people want to meet her."

"Berlin?" I held my breath until I thought my lungs would burst. A trip to Germany would mean my papers would fall under greater scrutiny. "Does she know?"

"She was notified yesterday." He glanced at me. "She has not told you?"

Had she forgotten, or was she too distracted? "She was exhausted this morning and went to bed immediately."

"Perhaps today she'll give you the details."

I stared out the window, studying the ancient buildings awash in grays and afternoon shadows. She'd known about this trip to Germany, and yet she'd still written her letter. Many would have hesitated. Perhaps I would have. But not her. And now Cécile, Emile, and I were playing a very high-stakes game.

"I'm sure she will," I said.

CHAPTER TWENTY-THREE
RUBY

Saturday, July 5, 2025
7:00 p.m.

Dinner at the Indian restaurant with Jeff was terrific. Like in the old days, we recited *Star Trek* lines, we complained about our shared distaste for brussels sprouts, and we discussed which *Mission: Impossible* remake was the best. He offered a few updates on my brother's dating life. As it turned out, Eric had seen Susan twice since he'd first met her. My evening with Jeff was easy, fun, and flirty with hints of sexual innuendo.

When he walked me back to my hotel room, the air had cooled, and there was a soft breeze from the Potomac. We weren't holding hands, but I wouldn't have pulled away if he'd taken mine. As we walked through the hotel's automatic doors, I was ready to invite him up to my room.

"Ruby." Scott's voice cut across the lobby as he moved toward me with quick, frustrated steps.

My stomach dropped. "Scott."

Jeff's gaze leveled on Scott. His jaw pulsed with anger, but he remained silent. I'd often called this look Jeff's Death Stare. I'd only seen it a couple of times. Once, when a classmate claimed his dissertation didn't have proper sourcing, and another time, when a nurse was a little too aggressive while inserting an IV line into my arm. He'd never raised his voice, but in every instance, the other party had backed off.

"Scott," he said.

Scott glanced at him. "Who are you?"

"Jeff." He stopped short of saying "Ruby's date" because, well, we were friends who'd gone out for dinner.

"What do you want, Scott?" I asked.

"We have unfinished business," he said. "And it would be better if we had this discussion in private."

"Here is fine," I said. "I have no secrets from Jeff."

Scott's gaze scanned Jeff in a new assessing way. "Are you dating?"

"Not your business," I said. "We said all we had to say earlier."

"We haven't," Scott said. "We aren't close to a resolution."

"You don't like the resolution, but the matter is closed," I said.

Scott raised his chin a fraction. "I'm hiring an attorney."

"Feel free." I knew how much Scott made, and this wasn't an expense he could afford. He wasn't good at bluffing, so the comment made me wonder if the fiancée had underwritten this fight.

"This could get very ugly," Scott warned.

"It might be uncomfortable and expensive, but 'ugly' . . . that's a harsh word. I've lived through ugly, and this fight will be child's play for me."

Jeff remained silent, but he hadn't missed a word. He knew me well enough to know I could fight this battle.

"Is that a threat?" Scott asked.

"A promise. Why do you care?" I asked. "You're getting married and raising your baby. These eggs and embryos are my only shot at motherhood."

"You have your unfertilized eggs. I'm asking you to destroy the embryos," Scott said.

"You don't want to take all my chances, but you want to cut them in half."

"I don't want a kid of mine watching his mother die."

With care, I drew in a breath, absorbing the blow of his words. "You signed away all rights. As I remember, you didn't argue or ask for anything."

"I didn't understand," Scott said.

"Understand what?" I asked. "Is the fiancée worried about one of my children making a claim on your finances or showing up one day and messing up what you have? Or if I die, are you worried you'll have to raise this child?"

"I'll take responsibility for the child," Jeff said.

I looked up at Jeff, seeing the resolution etched in his features. He'd meant what he said. Emotion clogged my throat, and I couldn't speak.

"You can't do this!" Scott gritted his teeth and clenched his fists.

Scott had always lived a charmed life, using his good looks to boost his moderate intelligence.

"Leave," I said.

"I'm going to sue."

"That's your choice," I said. "I'll contact Eric first thing in the morning and alert him."

"Eric." He ground out my brother's name as if it were an oath. "He's not as smart as he thinks."

"He's a lot smarter," I said. "And you're about to experience the full weight of Eric's legal team."

"Time to go, Scott," Jeff said. "We can keep going around in circles, but it's redundant and boring."

"You don't get a say," Scott said.

"He does," I said.

"What gives him the right to weigh in?" Scott demanded.

"He cares about me more than you ever did, so that gives him the right."

"I stood by you when you were sick. I held your hair back when you threw up, hung with you while you took chemo, and gave up my life for months."

"And then you got on with your life. Which I don't fault you for," I said. "I'm getting on with mine."

"This is bigger than us," he said.

"You've made your point," Jeff said. "Time to leave."

Scott stood at least three inches taller than Jeff and outweighed him by at least thirty pounds of muscle. "Make me."

Jeff reached for his cell phone. "An arrest record isn't going to help your career. But if you want to press this, I'll file harassment charges."

"I'm not harassing you," Scott said.

"You're bothering me," I said. "I'll file the charges."

"This is bullshit," he shouted.

The clerk at the front desk had been watching us, doing her best not to stare. "Everything all right?"

Realizing an audience had gathered, Scott muttered an oath. "This isn't over."

"It is, but if you want to believe otherwise, go ahead," I said.

Scott stalked out of the hotel's front door, and his tall frame vanished into the day's dimming light.

"Sorry about that," I said. "You shouldn't have to deal with my drama."

"Not a big deal," he said. "I deal with Scott's kind of drama all the time."

"His kind?"

"Guys with an unjustified sense of entitlement." A wink wiped away all traces of the Death Stare. "Not my first rodeo."

"Not the best way to end the evening."

He took my hand in his, rubbing my palm with his thumb. It was subtle but sexy. "I want to kiss you."

He'd been listening to my dating advice to Eric. And he'd also internalized it and was using it on me. And it was working. I forgot about forever. I only cared about now. "Okay."

He leaned in and pressed his lips to mine. It was a soft, testing touch, but when I relaxed closer to him, he wrapped his arm around my waist and tugged me a little closer. We both deepened the kiss.

Desire rushed through me, warming my body. This feeling was so natural and right. "Come up to my room. I haven't had a drop of wine."

He traced a small circle at the base of my spine. "Are you sure?"

"Yes."

His gaze pinned mine. "Does this have to do with Scott?"

"No," I said. "It has to do with you and the heat."

"Heat?"

"Yeah. You know how to bring it."

"I do?"

"Yeah. You do." Tonight was just tonight. It wasn't forever. We were both healthy and young and willing. And that trifecta was hard to ignore.

"Okay."

I took him by the hand and led him to the elevator. We rode it to the fifth floor, and I swiped my key over the door lock. Inside the room, I dropped my purse on the unused double bed closest to the door and kicked off my shoes. He shrugged off his jacket and pulled me into an embrace. The kiss went on and on. He was in no hurry to stop, as if he had been waiting for this moment for a long time.

I unfastened the buckle of his pants. I didn't want to rush, but it had been a couple of years since I'd had sex. I missed the desire, the skin-to-skin contact, and the sense of connection.

During intense moments, Jeff often quoted *Star Trek*'s Captain Kirk. But he didn't say anything as he reached for the zipper skimming along my back. He pulled it down to my waist and peeled the dress off my shoulders until it puddled at my feet.

His gaze glided over the strapless black lace bra and matching panties to the PICC line scar under my left collarbone. "Stands to reason you'd choose something French and lacy."

"Of course."

He shrugged off his shirt and removed his pants. Soon, we were both naked and in the center of the bed. "I've dreamed about this for a long time," he said.

"You have?"

"I fell for you the day you came home from your sophomore year abroad. You were dressed like a French fashion model. All grown up in all the right ways."

In those days, Jeff had been Eric's buddy. He was another big brother whom I'd worshipped. I still adored him, but not in the old ways. Not ever again.

As he kissed each breast, I smoothed my hand down his muscled back. "You've been working out."

"I have." He continued to kiss me, slower again, taking his time just as he did when faced with one of those intricate math problems he loved so much. Each moment, each discovery was a thrill to him, and he didn't rush the process.

But right now, a faster pace would be okay. I guided him to my entrance. "Maybe a little faster?" I asked.

He hesitated, holding back, teasing. "What, you're horny, Ruby?"

"All the blood has rushed from my head."

"Sounds serious."

"So serious."

A sly smile added a devilish, sexy glint to his eyes. Very slowly, he pushed inside of me. My body, accustomed to celibacy, resisted, but he moved with calculated patience, content to wait for my body to open.

When he pressed in to the hilt, he kissed me. "All right?"

"Feels amazing." I'd feared I'd never feel something like this ever again. "So amazing."

A slight smile tipped the edges of his lips. "I'm just getting warmed up."

CHAPTER TWENTY-FOUR
SYLVIA

Monday, September 22, 1941
4:00 p.m.

As summer temperatures heated, the tension in the city rose. Food shortages were more acute, arrests increased, and breadline demonstrations were louder. I continued to visit Emile weekly, though of late, the letters I delivered weren't incriminating. Hauptmann Wolfgang drove me each time, and as much as I wanted to ask Emile if she'd passed along the letter discussing the Renault auto factory near the film studios, I didn't dare, knowing the captain was lurking outside her door.

Cécile finished her romantic comedy, and Monsieur Archambeau insisted she make another romp. With the success of Continental Films' *Premier rendez-vous*, starring Danielle Darrieux, those in Paris and Berlin realized French film could rival Hollywood. The newest movies in production not only distracted, influenced, and swayed audiences, but they also entertained and made money.

However, Cécile was adamant that another comedy wasn't best for her career. She and Monsieur Archambeau had many heated arguments in her dressing room. The crew heard glasses shatter and tables overturn. After he'd leave, I'd often question Cécile's audacity, but she wouldn't accept another silly role. Finally, the two struck a bargain. Monsieur Archambeau would scout for more scripts if Cécile promoted her latest movie. She'd agreed.

When *Vogue Paris* magazine offered a shoot to Cécile, she'd hesitated until Monsieur Archambeau said the magazine was also looking at Corinne Luchaire. The petite, fair-haired actress was one of Cécile's rivals on film and in her dealings with the German high command.

We spent weeks before the shoot reviewing designs, balancing timeless elegance with hints of wartime practicality. In the end, we settled on a dress with an off-the-shoulder neckline, cap sleeves, and a full skirt. With money from Monsieur Archambeau, I visited many of Rupert's contacts in the black market and finally found a rich blue satin in a shop in Les Halles.

Now, the final dress cupped her creamy shoulders, nipped at her waist, and flared into a lush full skirt that skimmed her knees. For the shoot, she wore a diamond necklace and earrings made by Van Cleef & Arpels, all gifts from Oberst Schmidt. The colonel had left Paris weeks ago, but he telephoned her several times a week. When she'd told him about the shoot, he'd asked her to wear her hair down.

I fastened the last satin-covered buttons cinching in Cécile's waist, growing narrower by the month. These days, she ate little but drank her champagne daily.

Outside, the photographer waited for us across a small bridge spanning the Seine. In the background, the Eiffel Tower dominated the skyline.

"I can share a secret with you," Cécile said as she met my gaze in a full-length gilded mirror tipped against a wall. "I've won. I'm to star in a mystery drama yet to be titled."

I caught her gaze in the mirror. "How did Monsieur Archambeau agree?"

"I mentioned my desire to make a drama to Oberst Schmidt. I declared that if I played one more orphan with two love interests, I might go crazy. The colonel laughed, but two days later, the new offer surfaced."

"What does he want from you?"

"He wants me in Berlin at the end of the summer."

This was the first time we'd talked about Berlin. "Are you going?"

"Most likely."

"You've created an image that few see as threatening. Do you want to change that?"

"They suspect us all," she said. "We both know the innocent are vanishing and dying. Rupert. Two writers. A cameraman. Parents and children are separated. I might as well have a little fun before they shoot me or send me to prison."

I adjusted the necklace's diamond pendant, so it pointed toward her cleavage. These gems were beyond a Luftwaffe colonel's salary, and I knew they'd been stolen and resold to him for pennies. "Be careful what you say."

She touched a sparkling diamond earring. "We're all going to die someday, Sylvia. Better our life counts for something. You understand this, no?"

I took risks in the shadows, and the idea of following her into the spotlight, or Berlin, terrified me. "Yes, I do."

She chucked me under the chin. "Don't look so glum. I don't think a movie role will change that much."

"What about Berlin?"

"We can weather one quick trip to the city. I hear it's lovely in the summer." A smile tipped her red lips. "As long as I remain the right kind of trouble for the colonel, he won't suspect."

"Berlin is an unfamiliar city, far from anyone who can help us."

She arched a brow. "And who would help me in Paris? Not Henri or my Nazi lover."

I reached for a white wide-brimmed hat, set it on the crown of her head, and pinned it in place. "All the more reason to be careful. Conditions in this city are getting worse."

The wealthy weren't feeling the constraints of the occupation, but I saw it daily whenever I bargained in the markets for buttons or bread. Refugees and Parisians alike now felt the hard, oppressive boot of the occupiers pressed against their necks.

"This is why we must make the best of what's available. And now I must be photographed." She appraised her dress in the mirror. "You're quite gifted, Sylvia."

I accepted the compliment. "I learned from the best."

"Where did you learn design? Not all in the lingerie factory." All this time together, and she'd never asked about my credentials.

This small opening into my fading past was too hard to resist. "My mother. And father. Both were very talented."

"They were designers?"

"My father was a tailor and my mother a dressmaker."

My past was an Achilles' heel hidden under layers of identities I'd created.

"They're gone now?"

I handed her white gloves and helped her pull them on. "Yes."

I opened the door, and a cool breeze stroked my cheeks. Outside, the photographer was checking his camera lens. He was a tall, lean man with stooping shoulders and a cigarette dangling from his mouth. When he looked up, a flicker of appreciation crossed his eyes. He tossed his cigarette aside.

"Beautiful. Please stand here." He pointed to the bridge's center, and Cécile moved to her spot. I followed, checking for flyaway hairs, readjusting a twisted earring, and fluffing her skirt. As I worked, I heard the click of the camera's shutters. And when I glanced over my shoulder, the photographer snapped another image.

"Stunning," he said.

I turned my face away from the camera and rose. "You're wasting your film on me."

"No, I don't think so. The world wants to see how a lovely woman makes another woman stunning. It's an interesting story."

"Cécile is our star." I stepped to the side. I didn't want my photo taken. If someone from my past recognized me, they could turn me in to the police.

The photographer raised the viewfinder back to his eye. *Click. Click.* "Mademoiselle Cécile, can you clasp your hands at your waist?"

Cécile was accustomed to direction and found her pose in seconds. When he asked her to raise her arms, she did. When he asked her to walk away from him and glance over her shoulder, she tossed back a carefree smile few in the city could muster. He took photographs for half an hour.

The photographer lowered his camera. "Perhaps another outfit."

"Of course," I said.

"A lighter dress will work better in the fading afternoon sun."

"Give us a few minutes." I had come prepared with several outfits selected from the set. We returned to the dressing room, and I helped her change into a smart white suit. She stepped into black heels, and I cinched a belt around her wait. A black fascinator sporting an ostrich feather finished the look. Outside in the dimming light, the sun caught the brim of her hat and cast a glow over her pale features and ruby-red lips.

A Mercedes pulled up behind the photographer. Hauptmann Wolfgang stepped out and opened the back door, and Oberst Schmidt exited the car. The colonel settled his cap on his head and tugged the visor lower. He was attractive, cold, controlled, and impressive in many ways. I might have admired him if I didn't despise his kind so much.

Oberst Schmidt strode up to me. "How's she doing?"

"Excellent." I was careful to keep my gaze averted.

"She's stunning. Your work with her wardrobe is top notch, Mademoiselle Rousseau."

Hearing my name from his lips unsettled me. "Thank you. You're very kind."

He continued to watch Cécile as she angled her face toward the camera. "How is her sister, Emile?"

My breath caught. "Work in the boulangerie keeps her busy."

"And you deliver food to her on Tuesdays?"

No surprise that he knew what was happening in Cécile's circle. Cécile was too precious a prize for her not to be guarded.

"Yes," I said.

"The sister can be troublesome. But I hope her gentle warning will discourage further problems."

The "gentle" warning had cost her two broken fingers. "I'm not aware, sir."

"When you deliver your next basket, make sure you impress upon Emile that I'm aware of her. The next warning will be more direct. I cannot afford any scandal."

I didn't respond. Had Oberst Schmidt ordered the attack on Emile? Or was he using the incident to his advantage?

"Nothing can tarnish Cécile. We have big plans for her this summer, so Emile needs to behave."

Blood rushed to my head, and my heartbeat raced. I'd been tamping down my rage for years. And now it was constricting my throat and robbing me of my voice.

"You understand, Mademoiselle Rousseau?" A slight smile suggested he'd interpreted my reaction accurately.

I wouldn't be so reckless as to confront him. But given the chance, I would kill him. "Yes, sir."

"Johann!" Cécile left her position just as the photographer clicked his camera. His flash of annoyance vanished when he saw Cécile kiss Oberst Schmidt. "This is a lovely surprise."

"I just returned to the city. I couldn't stay away."

She grinned. "Wonderful."

"Have dinner with me." He touched her necklace. *"Schön."*

"It's beautiful, isn't it?" she said, smiling. "I'll hurry home and change."

"You look flawless," he said.

"I'm a mess," she said. "And I want to be beautiful for you."

"You're perfect for my suite at the Ritz. I ordered room service dinner." Dark desire flickered in his eyes, and dinner clearly wasn't a priority.

"Of course, darling."

He offered his arm to her, and she took it as she followed him to his car.

As the car drove away, the photographer came up to me. His jaw tightened. Anyone witnessing this scene would claim she was a collaborator like Corinne Luchaire. The photographer spit on the cobblestone street, turned, and packed up his camera in a battered wooden case. When he stood, he shook his head. "Boche."

He fell silent after the muttered slur. Like me, he understood the Boche were no longer interested in playing nice.

"Thank you, sir," I said.

He grunted. "I'll send you the picture of you and the actress. You can show it to your grandchildren if we all live through this."

"That's very kind."

He grunted, lit another cigarette, and walked away. I returned to the makeshift dressing room and packed the rejected outfits, makeup, extra shoes, and jewelry. I wouldn't see Cécile this evening, but in the morning, I needed to be ready to deliver another basket to Emile.

Couriered espionage letters, false identity paper deliveries, and even clandestine BBC broadcasts were all flint strikes against dried kindling. Only one spark could catch my life on fire and reduce it to embers.

I held up a ruby Cartier bracelet. If I found a buyer, I would make enough money to leave France and remake myself. My father would tell me to run. He'd begged me to be safe and survive. And I'd done that. But where would I go now? The northern and southern ports were closed. My original travel papers issued in Poland were unusable, and my counterfeit papers might not hold up to scrutiny.

Even if I chanced an escape to Spain or Switzerland, what would happen to those I could still help? Who would deliver the letters to Emile? Poland and France had been my homes, and I would not disrespect either by ignoring her people.

"*We are all afraid, Zofia,*" my father had said when I'd hugged him so close at the Warsaw train station. *"Better to make peace with it."*

CHAPTER TWENTY-FIVE
SYLVIA

Tuesday, March 17, 1942
11:00 a.m.

The Allies bombed the Renault auto factory two weeks ago. The raids occurred over two nights and, according to witnesses, lit up the night sky. The facility, which made over twenty thousand cars each year for the Germans, was devastated. Because the studio was six kilometers from the factory, all movie production had ceased for several days. When crews returned, they found shattered glass windows, the lingering scent of smoke, and more German soldiers checking identification papers.

The information Cécile had gleaned from Oberst Schmidt last fall and that I'd passed on to Emile had led to the factory's destruction. Oberst Schmidt's commanding officers demanded an in-person report on the attack, and he'd left for Berlin last week.

Cécile had made a great show of crying when he'd said he was leaving. On the night before his departure, she had shown up at his room at the Ritz with a bottle of champagne. She'd worn only a thick mink fur and heels. He'd left Paris satiated and none the wiser.

Food grew ever scarcer. Although Cécile's cook could still get coffee, butter, and pâté, many in the city went hungry. My baskets to Emile fed her and the growing number of people Marc allowed to spend a night or two in the flats above the boulangerie. I never asked who these people were but had begun to stuff more cheese and dried meats into my basket. Cook was never happy with me, but she kept her complaints to herself because she had plenty of ration cards and banknotes for the vendors in the black market. She, of course, stole extra food for herself and her family, but we all turned a blind eye.

With Oberst Schmidt gone, the intelligence had dried up, so Cécile cast her net wider. She avoided music concerts, the opera house, and exhibitions at the Musée de l'Orangerie. These activities were favorites of the "gray mice," the locals' name for female German soldiers. Instead, she frequented locations favored by the male German soldiers. Her favorites were Coco Chanel's parties at the Ritz, Comédie-Française productions, and the risqué shows at the Folies Bergère.

"All men," she'd said days ago, "do their best thinking between their legs."

Cécile's role at Continental Films remained on the rise after the release of her last romantic comedy, which had been out for weeks and was already a hit. Her first drama, *Secrets in the Shadows*, would begin production in several weeks.

In *Secrets in the Shadows*, Monsieur Archambeau cast Cécile as Françoise, a young widow accused of killing her husband. Françoise hired a cynical private detective, Guy LeRoy, to prove her innocence.

Her favorite leading man, Louis Lambert, was cast in the role of the detective. The initial publicity shots of Cécile and Louis were already getting noticed by *Le Temps*, and many hinted they were lovers. Many suggested in private that the couple was reminiscent of American actors Clark Gable and Carole Lombard.

Once the production of *Secrets in the Shadows* wrapped in the summer, she was to travel to Berlin and tour Germany with eight actors and actresses. I'd agreed to accompany her, but I worried the Gestapo would realize my identity papers were false once I crossed into Germany.

My basket for Emile in hand, I left the apartment after eleven. Cécile was still asleep, having been out until dawn. This afternoon, we were to meet with the set designer and director to discuss costumes.

As I stepped onto the sidewalk, Hauptmann Wolfgang's gleaming Mercedes waited. He stood at the passenger-side door, a cigarette in hand. When he saw me, he tossed the butt aside.

I'd grown to expect the appreciation that flashed in his gaze when he saw me. In another time and place, I'd have been flattered, but under all his politeness and my obliged responses, he was German, and I was Polish.

After the recent bombings, the Germans chased all information leaks, no matter how small. If Oberst Schmidt had determined that he himself was the source, I doubted he'd be quick to inform his superiors. He'd use someone like the captain to make the problem go away.

"Hauptmann Wolfgang, good morning."

"Good morning," he said with a slight bow. "Are we headed to Emile's today?"

"Yes, that's right."

Each time he drove me to Emile's, he often found a detour and chatted as if we were touring the city for pleasure. He liked to share his discoveries, whether it was a museum or a new restaurant. He'd invited me once or twice to join him for dinner, but I'd begged off because of work. Thankfully, I had a meeting at the studio at five today, so we couldn't dally too long.

We never talked about the war. Most days, I listened to him reminisce about his hometown on the Polish border. He often described his family home as a quaint cottage surrounded by red poppies in the spring and summer. The pictures he painted reminded me of my own childhood. Our conversations were oddly normal.

At times when he spoke about home, I became terribly homesick, and painful longings tempted me to share the truth of my past. But each time I believed he might be an ally, I remembered the roundups, executions, or arrests.

The captain opened the car door. I no longer protested this kindness and now found it charming.

A woman passed us on the street. She was thin, and her coat was old and worn. When her gaze locked on mine, she telegraphed her disapproval. But with Hauptmann Wolfgang so close, she didn't dare speak, and I didn't show remorse.

More subdued, I settled into the front seat and tucked my skirt in as he closed the door. The car heater was running. The warmth felt good, and this small comfort shamed me.

The captain slid behind the wheel. "You have to be at the studio by five."

"Yes."

"I noticed that your schedule is clear a week from today. We'll go out to dinner. It's time we shared a proper meal in a nice restaurant."

I hadn't been to a restaurant in two, or was it three, years? Before the Germans, I had little money to spare, and after, well, I chose to stay away, knowing soldiers crowded all the cafés and restaurants. Eating good food served on a linen cloth was tempting but impossible.

"Ah, I can see you want to say yes," he said, pulling into the empty avenue.

"It's an extravagance," I said.

"That's the point. You work hard and deserve a nice evening out."

"I don't know about that."

"Nonsense. You've turned me down twice already, and my pride might be damaged if you refuse this offer."

To decline now with no tangible excuses would tempt fate and perhaps invite the suspicions of the Gestapo. "That would be lovely. Thank you."

He grinned. "It'll be an evening you won't soon forget."

"I have no doubt."

"Excellent."

I listened as he talked about home, a new café, and his plans for life after the war. He spoke as if the war had been settled, and it was just a matter of him moving on to his next assignment.

When he parked by the boulangerie and reached for his door handle, I said, "No, please, stay. I'll be in there for just a minute. Keep this lovely heater running."

He hesitated. "Don't be too long."

As always, I hurried up the back staircase, a little fearful of what I might find. Emile hadn't given up her Resistance meetings. And I always dreaded what I'd find in her rooms or the spare apartments.

When I arrived at Emile's apartment door, I could hear voices on the other side. I knocked and stepped back.

Marc answered, his right hand hidden behind his back. "Sylvia, I wasn't expecting you."

"I come every Tuesday. I don't understand the confusion."

"It's Tuesday?" He threaded ink-stained fingers through his hair. "Right. I've lost track of the time."

Emile came up behind him, smiling. Her hair hung loose around her face. It was messy, and her eyes were red, as if she'd been crying. "Sylvia, our salvation. We wouldn't eat if it weren't for Cécile's German food."

"Marc, would you give us a moment?" I asked.

He hesitated but retreated, and Emile closed the door. I handed her the basket. "I won't take too long. Your sister's driver brought me today."

"It's not the best time to bring the Boche to my home," Emile said. "There's work scattered all over my kitchen table, and there's a family in the apartment next door." She didn't explain who they were, and I didn't ask.

I lowered my voice to a whisper and glanced at her disfigured fingers. "If you think they won't shoot you because you're a woman, don't be fooled. They don't distinguish between male and female disrupters. The authorities deport women like you to the camps daily."

"I cannot sit and do nothing," Emile whispered. "You know how passionate we are about this."

"We've had a great success. I caution you to be careful. Oberst Schmidt is having you watched."

"Let them follow me. I refuse to cower. We must force change and win this war."

I gripped her damaged hand in my gloved fingers. "You'll change nothing if the police or Germans arrest you."

She snatched her hand back. "I can hold my head high, Sylvia."

"So can your sister. So can I."

She glanced at the basket. "Is there anything special for me?"

"Not today."

"Then keep it. Today I have no appetite for Nazi food."

"Give it to the family in the other apartment. They must be hungry."

My comment silenced her retort, and she took the basket. "Marc's sources are pressing for more bombing locations."

"As soon as Cécile has information, I'll tell you." Outside, the heavy thump of footsteps reverberated on the stairs. "The captain is coming."

"Let him in. Marc will take care of him, and no one will find the body. We've done this many times before."

Heat rushed through my face as I struggled with frustration. If they killed the captain, he would be reported missing, and the Germans would initiate a search. How many French people would they kill as they went from apartment to apartment?

"Go on," Emile coaxed. "Call to him."

I shoved the basket in her arms, hurried out the door, and found the captain halfway up the stairs. I paused and drew in a breath, knowing he would notice my mood shift. Finding a slight smile, I descended toward him.

"Everything all right?"

"A quick visit. Emile has bread to bake."

He blocked my path on the stairs. "You look upset."

A faltering smile tugged at the edges of my lips. "No, I'm fine."

He didn't move. "I know your moods, Sylvia Rousseau. You're not as guarded with me. Is Emile in trouble?"

The heat in my face rose, and my skin burned. The captain was inches from me. If I allowed him to continue up the stairs, Emile would be ready for him.

"No," I whispered. "It's nothing like that."

"Then what is it?"

I leaned forward and pressed my lips to his mouth. He tasted of tobacco, surprise, and desire. His hand came to my waist. I drew back, knowing a kiss witnessed by others would seal my fate as a traitor. "I was thinking about you."

"Were you?" The hand remained on my waist.

Cécile had insisted that men, all men, could be distracted. She could make men melt where they stood with a look. But I wasn't a movie screen seductress.

The captain pulled back and descended the stairs before waiting for me at the bottom. My hand firmly on the railing, I climbed down the remaining risers. We crossed the sidewalk. He opened the car door, watching closely as I settled into the front passenger seat. He hesitated, his arm resting on the open door as he displayed his large frame. It was a silly moment of male posturing.

My cheeks burned with fresh heat, but this time, it wasn't fear or fury but a surprising jolt of sexual desire. I'd had a lover when I first arrived in Paris, but he'd always rushed the sex. I suspected the captain was a patient man, and he would take his time in bed.

"Ah, those red cheeks." He winked. "I'll never forget that look."

CHAPTER TWENTY-SIX
RUBY

Sunday, July 6, 2025
7:00 a.m.

I woke to the sound of a door opening and then the smell of coffee. When I rolled on my side, I glanced at the pillow beside me and at the imprint of Jeff's head. Jeff. So much for boundaries and keeping my distance. Last night had been great, but it would make the ending all that more difficult. And if life had taught me anything, endings were inevitable.

Sitting up, I found a smile as Jeff wrestled a coffee cup holder with three large cups and a bag from the Union Street Bakery.

"Three cups?" I asked.

His thick hair was finger-combed back now, but I'd fisted it in my hands last night as I'd come. Twice. "You could always drink more coffee than most humans."

The strap of my silk cami fell off my shoulder, exposing a little side boob and my PICC line scar. "Guilty."

"A sugar and two creams, unless that's changed."

"That thankfully has not."

He sat on the edge of the bed and handed me a cup. A slight smile tipped his lips as he raised his cup to his mouth.

"Feeling pretty proud of yourself, aren't you?" I teased.

He grinned. "I like to think I have a few moves."

"You do indeed." I took a long sip of coffee, wishing he weren't such a great guy.

He opened the bakery bag and peered inside. "A couple of cookies, bagels, and cinnamon buns."

"You're trying to make me fat."

"You have a few pounds to gain back."

He was right. When I was sick, I'd lost thirty pounds, and as of this week, I'd gained twenty pounds back. "You keep feeding me, and I'll have the last ten back in no time flat."

"That's the plan." He kissed me gently on the lips.

"I hate to break up this party, but I have an appointment with Madame Bernard today. She's told me she has letters for me."

"Letters?"

"She didn't say from whom, but she sounded anxious to share them."

"She's embraced this project, hasn't she?"

The coffee cup warmed my fingers. "Sharing her mother's story with me has been like opening Pandora's box. She expected a quick peek, but now all the unsaid memories are flying out."

"She has no one left to discuss her mother and the past with. You've been a gift for her."

"She's been a gift to me. Last year, I felt alone in my life-and-death struggle, but Sylvia's diary entries have shown me many have suffered far worse than me."

His brow knotted. "I'm sorry you felt alone."

I took his hand in mine. "It's no one's fault. Survival, the will to live, is a solitary sport."

"What time does she want to see you?"

"Noon."

He raised his brows. "Four hours. It only takes you three hours to get dressed?"

I smiled. "Give or take."

"That leaves a little extra time."

My skin warmed as he rubbed his thumb against my palm. "Aren't you tired?"

"No. You?"

I'd have to end this with Jeff. It wasn't fair to saddle him with a life of uncertainty. "Not exactly."

He waggled his brows. "Oh, really?"

I leaned forward and kissed him, tasting cinnamon and sugar. "I can get dressed in two hours."

He took my coffee cup and set it beside his on the end table. "I thrive on deadlines."

※

When I arrived at Madame Bernard's town house, the clock in a nearby church rattled off the first of its twelve chimes. I knocked. I ran my fingers down pearl buttons skimming the length of a green dress with butterfly sleeves, a fitted bodice, and a skirt that brushed below my knees. Beige espadrille wedge shoes, gold hoop earrings, and a straw purse finished the look.

Madame answered the door seconds after I knocked, as if she'd been waiting. "Bonjour," she said, kissing each of my cheeks.

"Bonjour. How are you doing?"

"Very well." She regarded me closely. "And I would say you're doing very well. There's color in your cheeks. The fireworks over the Potomac keep you up?"

"A friend met me for dinner. He's quite charming."

"I would say he's more than charming." She waved me inside.

I chuckled. "It was a lovely evening."

"I miss being young and enjoying evenings like that." As she closed the door, her gaze grew wistful. "My mother was always careful about who I dated. I didn't experience real romance until I could study in London."

"How did your mother feel about you traveling to England?"

"She wasn't happy, but my father talked her into letting me go. I didn't understand, but now I see that her worries were justified. When I went abroad during college, she warned me not to cross the English Channel to France."

"But . . ."

She led me down the center hallway toward a large kitchen. Our prior meetings had been in the house's formal parlor, but now she'd invited me into the kitchen, the space reserved for family and close friends.

Madame set out a plate of small sandwiches, soup, and a pitcher of iced tea. "I thought if I was going to drag you here during the lunch hour, I should at least feed you. You and your friend didn't have an early lunch, right?"

I set my purse on a tall chair. "Just time for coffee."

"Good for you."

We sat at the table and talked as she served me two small sandwiches with the crusts cut off. "My mother said sandwiches were so American. But I've always loved them."

"They look amazing." I poured iced tea for us both, opened a white cloth napkin, and spread it over my lap. "You didn't have to go to all this trouble."

"It's no trouble. It's refreshing to have someone to cook for. Cooking for one is never quite as satisfying."

I dipped a spoon into the soup. Leek and onion. "So delicious."

"My mother wasn't much of a cook. She could do anything with a needle and thread, but cooking wasn't her gift. But she loved food. We often went out to eat, and she would put a lot of thought into the restaurant, their specialties, and even what day they had their fish delivered."

"In her diary, she speaks often about hunger, the food lines, and the women desperate to feed their children."

"The war didn't leave any ordinary Parisienne unmarked. The women were alone. Their husbands, fathers, and brothers were either at war, dead, or in a labor camp."

"Sylvia had been alone for some time when the war started."

Madame's expression softened with sadness. "She remained alone because of her Jewish heritage, and the German army that she knew was marching toward France. Anyone who might have loved her would have been at risk if her heritage was revealed."

"Most in 1930s Paris believed the destruction in the east would never reach them."

"It's difficult to accept that the world is turning against you."

How long had I ignored my growing fatigue, headaches, and muscle pain before I was forced to see a doctor? "Did your mother ever talk about her father?"

"She reminisced about the days when she was very young, but she never discussed the war times or her heritage."

I hesitated before I broached my next question. "Your mother was attracted to a German soldier."

"Ah, Hauptmann Otto Wolfgang. A complicated man."

"How so?"

"Paris was a dream for him. He was a simple man handed a platter of the ultimate pleasures."

"He didn't know Sylvia's family history?"

"My mother could hide her identity because of her fair complexion and her perfect French. Few asked many questions about her past, and when they did, she said she was from Alsace. An easy lie in those days. Everyone in Alsace had a slight accent, and most could speak German."

"I'd love to ask what happened between Sylvia and Otto."

She dipped her spoon in her soup. "Again, the story must unfold."

"Will your mother reveal what happened to Cécile?"

"You shall see."

We ate our lunches, shifting our conversation to polite topics. We shared our favorite haunts in Paris and our longing to return to the city.

"When will you return?" she asked.

"I will one day, but for now, I must stay close to home."

"Because of your illness?"

"I used to be so brave, but cancer reminded me I'm very human. I have a big checkup in a few weeks. After that, I might be able to release the breath I've been holding for the last three years."

"I have decided to return to Provence," she said. "I'd come to believe I was too old, but going through all the papers and clothes has rekindled a desire I thought long dead."

"When will you leave?"

"October. It's my favorite time of year. I have rented a house near Avignon and plan to stay for a month. I don't want to rush this trip and must savor it all."

"Will you go to Paris?"

"I think not. Paris was an ending for my mother. Avignon was a beginning for her."

"She lived in Avignon?" This information was my first clue to her future, which I'd become very invested in.

"You'll see."

I couldn't help but laugh. "You're quite the tease, madame."

She looked very pleased with herself. I suspected she'd longed to tell this story for some time and wouldn't rush the ending. "Glad to see I haven't lost my touch."

Madame took one bite of the sandwich. Our conversation shifted to fashion and movies, and when we finished, I cleared the plates as she set coffee on the table. While she arranged cookies on a plate, I poured the coffee.

When she retook her seat, she set a stack of letters on the table. "These are letters between Cécile and her prewar Avignon lover. The first letter is from him, but she only saved one of his. The rest are hers, written to him."

"She never mailed the letters."

"When Germany divided France, it became tough to exchange letters over the line of demarcation, which divided France in two. The censors read everything. But she must have needed to put her thoughts onto the page."

The collection must have contained twenty letters, held together by a fading purple ribbon. The faint scent of lavender rose from the yellowing, brittle pages.

"All these memories are very precious to me," madame said softly. "I thought I would never share them with anyone other than my daughter. But she's passed, and then you arrived. A miracle, I think. It's time to turn over the memories so people don't forget women like my mother and Cécile. They risked their lives to resist the Germans."

"I'm sure there are very private moments in these letters."

"There's no more reason to keep them secret any longer," she said. "And sharing them will remind the world that there are those who rose above the masses and did great things without anyone noticing."

"I'm honored."

Her left shoulder lifted in a slight shrug. "It's time."

CHAPTER TWENTY-SEVEN
SYLVIA

Tuesday, March 24, 1942
11:00 a.m.

As the captain drove me to the boulangerie, he chatted about our upcoming dinner tonight and his selected restaurant. I wasn't familiar with the establishment, but he assured me I'd be pleased. Dinner between a man and a woman shouldn't change anything. It was a meal. But I was crossing another invisible line and turning back later might not be possible.

Alone, I climbed the stairs, wondering if the family in the extra apartment was still there. Once, I'd heard children giggling, but now the room was dark and silent.

After knocking on Emile's door, I stepped back, the basket held close to my body. To my surprise, Emile opened it right away. Most days she took her time, as if she was busy hiding Marc or whatever it was she was working on.

Today, dark circles ringed under her eyes, her hair was disheveled, and her face was pale.

Sitting at the small table in her flat were two of the three boys I'd seen out front playing with the ball. The oldest, who was absent, had kicked the ball into the captain's leg. Each of the smaller boys was now nibbling on crackers.

When Emile saw the basket of food, her gaze brightened. "Is there anything special inside?"

"Not today. Perhaps next time."

"Where is the captain?"

"Waiting for me in his car outside."

Emile glanced over her shoulder to the boys. "The children would appreciate whatever you have."

"Of course."

The threadbare carpet dulled my heel strikes as I crossed to the children. "I hear there might be someone looking for a bit of cheese and sausage."

Both boys looked up, nodding. I took two dishes from Emile's cabinet and made a plate for each child. I set them in front of both, and they stared at the food as if they weren't sure if it was real.

"Go on, enjoy it," I said.

The boys each took a large slice of cheese and slipped it into their pockets and then began to eat.

"Where is your cousin?" I asked.

"He's working today," the oldest said.

"Where does he work?" I asked.

"At Les Halles," the younger boy said.

Many young children found small jobs to make a few coins that now bought so little, but, like Rupert, work often put them in the path of Germans. "Take food for your cousin. He'll need more than two slices of cheese."

"Thank you," the boys said, their mouths already full.

I crossed to Emile. "Where is the mother?"

"Waiting at the market, hoping to spend her ration stamps. She left early to beat the lines."

"And the cousin is working at the market?"

"He delivers messages."

"For the Resistance?" I whispered. "The Germans will shoot a child as easily as an adult."

"He is smart and quick. He knows all the shortcuts and places to hide." Emile folded her arms over her chest. "Something is brewing in the city. The SS are making more arrests, and I fear there'll be more."

She didn't mention the target of these roundups. But I knew most were Jews. "I feel the tension in the air."

"What about you?" Emile said. "Aren't you worried?"

Suspicions about my heritage lingered behind her words. "Always, but I'm used to it."

"Are you ever leaving Paris?"

"I'll stay as long as I can."

The door opened, and the boys' mother appeared. She looked shocked and then scared, as if my presence was a threat. She'd no doubt seen the captain's car parked out front. Only when she saw the boys eating did her eyes soften. "Bonjour."

"I had extra food," I said. One thing to ask Emile about the cousin's Resistance work, but another to discuss it with a stranger. Spies were hidden all over Paris. "I hope you don't mind. I'm Sylvia."

"Pleasure." She wisely didn't offer her name as she set down a small parcel on the table. "The clerk at the market would only let me buy a little cheese. There was more stock, but she wouldn't sell it to me. They save the best for themselves."

Emile's face bore no resentment. "The women working the market counters are as poor as the rest of us, but they delight in telling others what they can or cannot have. It's a small slice of power, but they guard it with care."

The occupation had brought out the best and worst in us. "I can't stay long. I have plans for this evening."

My plans. I had a dinner date with Hauptmann Wolfgang, and I couldn't bring myself to tell Emile or the Frenchwoman. My association with my German driver afforded me small privileges that had made my life easier. I wasn't so different from counter ladies guarding their own small luxuries.

※

I'd delayed having dinner with the captain for weeks, and now here I stood dressed in a smart navy blue suit, polished heels, my mother's pearls, white gloves, and a small hat. I should have escaped this path, but I couldn't find a way clear.

I stepped outside and found Hauptmann Wolfgang standing by his Mercedes. He was dressed in a dark suit, white shirt, and a silver tie. His shoes were polished, and a handkerchief peeked out from his breast pocket. He wasn't a classically handsome man, but when he looked at me with appreciation, I'd be lying if I said I wasn't flattered.

The captain handed me a small lavender bouquet. "You look lovely."

I accepted the flowers. Raising them to my nose, I inhaled their delicate scent. "Thank you."

He opened the car door, and I slid inside. When he angled behind the wheel, he sat tall as he put the car in gear and pulled into traffic. "The café I selected is not the Ritz, humbler, but the food is perfection."

"Sounds wonderful. I've been to the Ritz and find it overrated."

A slight nod acknowledged a shared kinship. "Exactly."

We drove through the near-empty streets. Neither of us spoke, and I think he was as nervous as me. We arrived at the café, and he parked on a side street. He met me at the passenger side and opened the door. I rose, and he offered me his arm as we walked inside. The perfect gentleman.

Inside the café, the maître d' greeted us. He was a rawboned man in his sixties with black hair streaked with gray. If he was casting judgment on me, he gave no sign of it as he escorted us to a back table.

The waiter explained what the chef had prepared tonight as he filled our water glasses. The captain looked at me, but I demurred to him, suggesting he make the choices. He made our selections, and soon we were sipping wine.

"When I first arrived in Paris, the pace of the waitstaff frustrated me," the captain said. "So slow. For years in Germany, we had terrible food shortages. Whenever I had the opportunity to eat, I was always too rushed and anxious to enjoy the process. In this last year, I've learned to slow down."

And everyone else in Paris struggled not to rush when they ate what little they had. "It's indeed special."

I savored the wine and, like my Cécile, asked enough questions to keep him talking. I'd watched her do this so many times with Monsieur Archambeau. Her questions always had a way of steering the conversation and tugging him out of a sullen mood.

The meal began with an aperitif; then we progressed to soup, fish, main course, and salad. By the time the cheese arrived, despite my best efforts to eat small portions, my stomach was ready to burst. The captain, however, had cleaned his plate at each course, and when the cheese arrived, I sat back with my wine, watching him consume each morsel. He did the same with a chocolate crepe.

As we lingered over coffee, I asked him about the places he still wanted to visit. He listed several countries and confessed he was hungry for more adventure.

When he tried to coax me into conversation, I described the plot of *Secrets in the Shadows* and the excitement over its production. I talked about making Cécile's costumes; however, I didn't mention that I often sneaked out and visited Rupert's contacts in the black market in search of fabrics.

Once our meal was complete, he escorted me to his car. We drove, not back to Cécile's apartment but to another, unfamiliar building.

"This is where I stay," he said.

I understood the implication immediately. He'd been patient with me over the last few months. My toes touched another more dangerous line.

"You don't have to come up," he said.

The wine had softened the sharp edges of my nerves. "I want to."

Later I would look back on this night with some shame. That night I'd told myself I was sleeping with him in the hope that he'd be distracted from Emile and her activities. But the truth was I missed a man's touch. I was tired of being alone.

His rooms were large and overlooked the Seine. Stars winked in a clear sky as a full moon dripped light on the river.

I didn't want to think about who'd once lived here and enjoyed this view or who was hungry when my belly was full. He offered me a drink, which I accepted. His eyes darkened with desire. He set my drink aside and pulled me into his arms.

His touch was gentle but full of authority and purpose, two elements missing from my life. I wish I could say that sex was him was unpleasant, but that would have been a lie. I enjoyed his touch, his scent, and the brief moments of feeling connected.

As we both lay naked in his bed, he suckled my breasts as his fingers teased my wet folds open. When he pushed inside me, he moved with a force that was thrilling. In those moments, there was nothing but the feeling of us, and I welcomed it.

How could I open myself to a man who, if he learned my truth, could turn me in to the Gestapo? I had no doubt that the captain would be as loyal to his country as I was to my adopted land. We were each in this fight to the death, yet my mind and body separated as I gripped his shoulders, arched toward him, and climaxed.

Later I dozed, and when I woke, he asked me to stay the night, but I refused. Cécile typically arrived home by 2:00 a.m., and it was always better if I was available to help her undress.

"I'll be busy for a few days," he said as he drove me back to the apartment. "Oberst Schmidt has many important meetings, and he requires a driver."

"Then you must be available to assist him."

"I would rather be with you."

As Cécile did so many times with the men circling around her, I dropped my gaze. "Coquettish" was what Monsieur Archambeau called Cécile. "If you have free time, then send word to me. Perhaps we can steal some time."

He leaned toward me and kissed my lips. "I will."

The captain didn't call me for five days. When he did, there was no time for dinner. No time for talk or a drink. I met him at his apartment, and this time, his hands were on me as we passed a large dining table. He paused, kissed me, and then bent me forward until my cheek pressed against the polished mahogany. Rough, impatient hands raised my skirt and pulled down my silk panties over my very precious stockings.

"I've been craving this for days," he said.

He drove into me with a force, startling a cry from me. He hesitated, reaching his hand around and placing it against tender swollen tissue. He began to rub. I moaned. He drove harder. When he finished, I could hear the quickness of his breath.

I stood, pulled a handkerchief from my pocket, and dabbed away his semen. I hadn't thought about the consequences of our actions the first time, but now I wondered if I'd end up like the women with bellies swollen with German babies.

He adjusted his pants, his cheeks full of color. "I'll see you again soon."

I straightened my skirt, surprised by my primitive reaction to him. Shame warred with satiation. "Where are you and Oberst Schmidt going this week?"

"Brittany," he said.

"So far away." The west coast of France had been closed to the French since the Germans arrived.

"It's where the U-boats are docked."

I moistened my lips and kissed him gently. "What is a U-boat?"

He rested his hands on my hips. "An underwater vessel. Very efficient at sinking ships. The Americans are sending cargo vessels full of supplies to England, and they must be stopped."

His manner was candid. Perhaps later he'd look back and wonder why he'd been so open with me. Perhaps he sought a human connection. Or perhaps he was baiting a trap with information hard for a spy to resist. "It isn't dangerous, is it?"

"No." He smiled as if my worry pleased him. "You've never used my given name."

I had not. Thinking of him as "the captain" created distance for me. "I haven't?"

"Say my name," he insisted.

Another line crossed. "Otto."

"Thank you, Sylvia."

CHAPTER TWENTY-EIGHT
RUBY

Sunday, July 6, 2025
8:00 p.m.

I sat in the middle of my bed and laid out the letters Cécile had written to a man named Daniel but never mailed. I'd spent the last few days getting to know Sylvia, and though she was helping me see Cécile more in a better light, the actress still felt distant. She was a summation of others' opinions.

Letters home were often filtered, but because she'd known she couldn't post these, she'd been somewhat candid. There were twenty-one letters in total. Only one was from Daniel to Cécile, while the remaining twenty were written by Cécile and signed with a *D*. Dominique.

October 15, 1939

Dominique,
It's good to hear you and Emile are settled in Paris. The old women of the village still grumble about

your decision to leave and most likely will for the next decade, but I suspect they all long to have you back because you were such a rich source for gossip on market day. The local men insist that your move north won't last. They say southern men are far more robust than the city males. As you may have guessed, the world outside Avignon has not changed.

The olive harvest is complete, and the pressing begins tomorrow. It's been a good year and I hope to see a hefty profit. It might be the last one for a while. Perhaps you'll see the olives from my farm in one of your Paris markets.

The harvest and pressing was difficult without the extra workers. Many of the young men have enlisted in the Army and marched off in their new uniforms, ready to defend France against Germany. I confess that I tried to enlist, but the local officer told me I wasn't fit to serve. The French seem to prefer soldiers with two working legs. So now my duties are on the farm during the harvest and in the port of Marseilles the rest of the year. Unsettling to be at war again. I thought after the last great one we were finished with the killing.

Know that you are missed and if your films are shown in Avignon or Marseille, I'll be the first in line to buy a ticket. If you should ever decide to abandon Paris and return home, I will be waiting.

Yours truly,
Daniel

Daniel's handwriting was bold and crisp, the letter's folded creases sharp. A man of precision. Practical. Accepting the blows life had dealt him.

If Daniel had served in World War I, he would have been in his late thirties at the time of this writing. Though he sounded solid and sure, to a young woman like Cécile yearning for an exciting life in Paris, accepting the role of a farmer's wife could have felt like a trap.

Dominique had made a bold choice to leave a secure life in the late 1930s. Few women would have dared. In those days, those who stepped outside their traditional roles weren't welcomed back to their old provincial communities.

I folded up Daniel's letter and tucked it back in the envelope. The first letter from Dominique to Daniel in this stack was dated September 1940. I could only assume any letters she'd written before had been posted.

By the fall of 1940, Germany would have entered France and taken over Paris, and the country was then split between the northern occupied and southern free zones. Dominique might not have feared remaining in Paris, but she was smart enough to respect the dangers around her.

September 15, 1940

Dearest Daniel,
I've missed your letters. I've missed seeing you. I would love to show you Paris. It's still a city of wonders, and I feel as if I've barely tasted its beauty. It's quite empty now. Everyone has fled the Germans, but I gave up so much to be here, I refused to leave. Emile is in love, and she will not leave for her lover's sake.

My first two movies were quite popular, and I've now been signed to make another. It should be no surprise to anyone that the Germans now control film production. I have been assured that I'll be cast in a new comedy that begins production next month. The Germans are very fond of me. Many of the officers have asked me to escort them around the city, and I've discovered their company is quite enjoyable. I've seen the Ritz, l'opéra, and the Comédie-Française. As you've always said, I wear luck like a second skin.

Love,

D.

October 15, 1940

Dearest Daniel,

The Germans are polite and careful not to offend. Their uniforms are tailored and their vehicles shine. The soldiers parade every day, their polished boots catching the light. Civilians can't have cameras, but the German soldiers all have one. And like all wide-eyed tourists, they delight in taking pictures.

Make no mistake, the barbarians have entered the city. They remind us often that they are the victors. Their arrogance has grown tiresome. Some French now go out of their way to confound and confuse the soldiers.

The Parisians who fled the city in June are beginning to return. Many confess that life on the road turned out to be harder than they'd imagined. And with the coasts and borders closed, there is nowhere to go.

I have hired a new costumer, who is a friend of Emile's. This woman can make magic happen with a needle and thread. She is quiet, misses little, and hasn't been associated with a whiff of gossip. Her French is perfect, but she's not French. Most don't detect the slight accent, but I've developed an ear for these things. I think Eastern Europe. Pity her family if they are in Warsaw.

Emile remains at the boulangerie, refusing my offers of a job on the next film. She despises the Germans and is often sneaking away to secret meetings. She never tells me where she's gone. Once we shared everything, but the war has started to divide us.

In my heart, I believe we both want the same thing. The Dupont sisters love France. There is a reason I'm in Paris now. I feel my excellent memory and gift for languages is divinely inspired, and I can't ignore my God-given talents.

The next film is a silly comedy, but I'll have better roles soon. You know I get what I want.

Your love always,
D.

Given what Sylvia had said in her diary, Cécile calculated her smiles, her gestures, and her kisses. As early as 1940, she'd already decided to work against the Germans.

The more I learned about Cécile, the more I realized she was a clever and calculating woman. Anyone who thought she was a silly blond was a fool.

CHAPTER TWENTY-NINE
SYLVIA

Monday, July 6, 1942
11:00 a.m.

The filming of *Secrets in the Shadows* was within days of wrapping. Cécile and her costar, Louis Lambert, had brought a rich intensity to each scene. And everyone was surprised.

Most believed Cécile had not earned this role. She was not a trained actress. She'd never studied the craft. And many industry insiders declared it was her bedroom skills that had won her the part. If she cared about the gossips, she didn't show it. Once she'd joked, "I've heard the same *Secrets in the Shadows* since I was thirteen."

Critics also had concerns about Louis, the dashing star of a dozen comedies. He was the exact opposite of the hard-drinking Guy LeRoy, and most believed he couldn't become Guy. But when the director shouted "Action!" Louis's easy smiles vanished, and he became Guy. And as soon as the director yelled "*Coupez!*" Louis's grin reappeared.

The two were committed to these roles, and they rehearsed often. Cécile knew her lines and those of everyone else in the film, but she kept practicing. And each time they recited their lines, the words sounded more natural. They shared a desperation. Cécile craved critical acclaim and the Germans' goodwill, but I couldn't think of what drove Louis.

Oberst Schmidt was back in Paris, and Cécile saw him several times a week, but she was on Louis's arm for all the public parties and events. Monsieur Archambeau believed the buzz of their "affair" would help the movie. Oberst Schmidt didn't appear jealous so far, but I thought that was Cécile's careful management of him. She said he enjoyed talking, especially after sex and a few glasses of wine, even after the March factory bombings. It seemed he did not suspect his lover was a spy.

Though Oberst Schmidt insisted in public that Germany was winning the war, he seemed to have private concerns about the Reich's invasion of Russia and its march toward Stalingrad. It was warm now, but the harsh Russian winters came early and had defeated invading armies before.

Cécile rose and brushed nonexistent wrinkles from her skirt. "You'll have time to deliver Emile's basket tomorrow?"

"Yes. Hauptmann Wolfgang is driving me." He'd insisted when we were alone that I call him Otto, but I'd resisted after the first time. I'd feared I might slip in public. If our relationship became public knowledge, it could create more issues for me. For men of his station, mingling with local women could warrant his transfer to the Eastern Front, a certain death sentence. Oddly, I didn't want to see him hurt. I wasn't sure what that said about me.

"He's very dedicated to you," Cécile said to me.

I looked up at her, rising, the gold locket dangling in the center of my scooped neckline. "He worries that the streets are not safe."

"For you?"

"The Resistance is getting bolder."

She must have suspected that we'd been sleeping together. "Does the captain come upstairs to Emile's?"

"Sometimes, but Emile knows always to expect him. The less I discourage him, the less he seems to suspect."

"Is my sister careful?"

"She's polite to Hauptmann Wolfgang."

"Emile?"

"She can smile like you when she chooses."

A brow arched. "Good. And Marc?"

"Always busy on Tuesdays now. He's either searching for flour, yeast, and salt or baking in his kitchen. I never see him."

"Ah. Marc never imagined a German walking into his building."

A knock on my dressing room door, and a young man announced, "The director needs you on set."

"Thank you, Pierre."

The boy smiled, ducked his head, and vanished. She knew all the names of the people working on the set and always made a point of using them.

I followed Cécile down the hallway toward the set: two cameras, lights, microphones dangling from booms, and cables snaking over the concrete floors. All the chaos fed into a down-on-his-luck private detective's office.

Cécile searched the set, hands on her hips. "I need to find Louis. The last time we ran through lines, he struggled to remember them. He was distracted, and my patience ran thin. I was rude, and he stalked off. Now I need to make amends. We have a love scene next, and I don't need him in a foul mood."

"I would guess his dressing room."

"Ah, he's always worried about his costume. I'll find him," she said. "You come along. I'd like you to spread a few rumors that you caught us kissing."

We moved toward Louis's dressing room, at the end of the hallway. It was twice the size of Cécile's, and when she'd complained, Monsieur Archambeau had reminded her that Louis, being the male lead, must have top billing and the best dressing room. Usually she would have argued, but she wanted this role so much that she didn't complain.

Louis Lambert appeared in block letters on the actor's dressing room door, and Cécile knocked. When he didn't answer, she huffed her impatience and opened the door.

"He's either sulking or screwing a young starlet," she said.

Louis was discreet when sleeping with young women, so no one questioned his actions.

"If I find him with a woman, I'll share it. His prowess will enhance his reputation as a great lover, and the world will see me as the jealous mistress. For the press, we will become the embattled Françoise and Guy."

The door opened to an empty room, and I heard a man grunting from the bedroom. Smiling, Cécile moved toward the door and flung it open with a dramatic flair the gossips would love.

Louis sat in a chair, his pants puddled by his ankles, his muscular legs spread wide. His eyes were closed, and his face contorted with that sweet agony before release. But there wasn't a young woman on her knees fondling him, but a young man.

Immediately, I closed the door behind me, and Louis's eyes popped open. Ecstasy shifted to panic. He pushed the man's face away from his genitals and reached for his linen trousers.

Louis turned away from us as he zipped his pants and hooked his belt. His dressed companion wiped his hand over his mouth as he looked away.

Louis shoved long fingers through his thick dark hair. "I didn't hear you."

"No, I can see that," Cécile said.

The young man, Lucas, had been hired a few weeks earlier as Louis's assistant. He had a wiry frame, golden-blond hair, and an aquiline nose the Germans so admired.

"This is not what it seems," Louis said.

"It's exactly what it seems," Cécile said. "Where is the discretion, Louis? You know the Gestapo visit our set often now."

Louis's hands were outstretched, fumbling for an imaginary lifeline. "It wasn't planned."

Cécile's brow arched. "I can see that as well." We all understood that if the Germans discovered his predilection, they would send him to a concentration camp. If he wasn't executed when he arrived, they'd ensure he'd suffer.

"Please," Lucas said.

Cécile didn't spare him a glance as she snapped her fingers in his direction. "You'll be silent."

"Yes, ma'am."

Cécile walked up to Louis and fixed his twisted belt buckle. "I couldn't care less who you share your free time with, but I must insist that you be extremely careful. This movie is very important to me, and it should be to you as well."

"It is," he said. "I don't know what came over me. It's never happened before."

"I saw a man enjoying a familiar pleasure," Cécile said.

"I was in shock," his voice rasped.

She walked to his dressing table, reached for a silver case, and removed a cigarette. With a matching lighter, she lit the tip. She pulled in several deep breaths and allowed the smoke to curl serpentlike into the air. "This is how we're going to handle this."

Louis's shoulders slumped a fraction. "What do you want?"

"Sylvia will not say a word."

"You trust her?" Louis demanded.

"I do." She pointed her cigarette toward him. "You're going to fire Lucas. Keep him locked in a country house and do not see him until after the movie is finished. But none of this," she said, waving her fingers between the two of them, "while we're shooting this film."

"How can you judge me? You're fucking that German," Louis said.

"I don't judge you, my dear. Your passions drive you, and you enjoy them. I use sex for gain. And my dalliance with the German might cost me later, but for now it helps us all." She drew in another lungful of smoke, holding it for a fraction of a second before releasing it. "You and I are going to kiss and touch every chance we get in public. No more speculation as to whether we are lovers. My building's concierge will see you sneaking in and out of my apartment. She's a horrible gossip, but that'll work to our advantage."

"Is this necessary?" Louis demanded. "If no one talks—"

"It's necessary." She moved toward him. "I have no interest in you sexually, Louis, but I do care about our film. And so do you. You want fame, like me."

Lucas began to speak, but Louis held up his hand, silencing him. "Continue."

"As I said, we'll be seen at more parties at the Ritz and the private clubs. Everyone will believe we cannot keep our hands off each other. I've seen your acting. You should be able to do this."

"What about your German colonel?" Disdain rumbled under his words.

"Worry about us making this movie and turning it into a hit. I'll take care of him."

Louis stared at her a long moment and then said, "Lucas, you need to leave now. It's a matter of minutes before someone comes looking for us both."

Once Lucas had left us alone, Cécile unbuttoned her blouse until the V widened and exposed her lace-trimmed breasts. "Louis, mess up your hair a little."

"We need to be on set," he protested.

Impatient, she crossed to him and ran red-manicured fingers through his thick hair that moved like silk. She drew a strand down over his forehead. "Such a beautiful man." She kissed him on the cheek, making sure her red lipstick smeared his tanned skin. "Our 'love affair' is the best move for us."

A muscle pulsed in his jaw. "I agree."

"And Lucas will keep his mouth shut?"

"I'll take care of him."

"Make him understand that his silence is key to staying alive."

"He knows this."

She folded her arms over her chest. "Locked doors. They'll save your life."

"I know. I wasn't thinking."

She patted his chest. "I've always kept tight control of my passions. I use them to my advantage. You do the same."

"I'm not so disciplined."

"But you will be until this movie is a great hit, no?"

"I will."

I wondered if Louis was capable of caution. An unlocked door wasn't only sloppy; it tempted destruction. Some people who were weighted down by secrets justified their gambles. *My righteousness will protect me. I deserve pleasure. Loneliness hurts.* But no matter the reason, once discovered, there was always a price to pay.

Like Louis, I hid my true self from the world. I'd become a devout Catholic, taking weekly communion and wearing a locket that displayed the cross, a Star of David hidden underneath. I hadn't sewn a gold star on my jacket or followed the new laws for the Jews. I had told no one my true story, and yet I now risked it all by taking a German lover. What price would my hubris cost me?

Footsteps sounded outside the door. As Cécile smudged the lipstick on his cheek with her thumb, I rushed toward the door and opened it to find Louis's makeup artist. Laurette was in her fifties and had worked in movies even before there was sound. She regarded my shocked expression and then looked past me to Cécile and Louis. A movie set was a very small town, and gossip traveled fast.

"They were rehearsing," I said.

"Of course. I understand," Laurette said.

Cécile faced Laurette, making a show of buttoning her blouse. I glanced at Cécile as if I was a tad embarrassed while she sauntered out of the room. I followed her.

Cécile entered her dressing room, and I closed the door.

"By the end of the day, the set will buzz with rumors of your affair with Louis."

"It won't take that long."

I helped Cécile dress in a dark, sleek dress that hugged her curves. I pinned a black pillbox hat on her head and fanned the netting over her face. She slipped on black shoes, and I arranged a fox stole on her shoulders. When Cécile stepped on set fifteen minutes later, she was pulled together as if nothing had happened.

Two Gestapo officers stood on the sidelines watching, saying little. They knew their black uniforms, knee-high polished boots, and hats evoked fear. No one dared ask why they were here or what they wanted.

Drawing in a slow breath, I was more than ready to hear the actors run lines and mark stage positions on the set. I wanted to work and focus on this small world the set designers had created.

When Louis appeared on set again, he was dressed like Guy, and there were no traces of lipstick on his face nor signs of the man who'd stared at Cécile with desperation in his gaze.

Today, in this moment, we were doing our best to hide what we didn't want the world to see.

In this scene, Françoise needed to convince the cool, distant Guy that she was innocent. But Françoise wanted to break through Guy's facade so she could manipulate him.

Like Cécile herself, Françoise used her sexuality to get what she wanted. Neither woman pretended to be innocent, because each knew men like Schmidt, Monsieur Archambeau, and Guy craved a wicked escape.

The director told everyone to be quiet on the set, and after a moment, the silence was complete.

"Action!" the director shouted.

Cécile pressed her fingertips to Louis's chest, and as Françoise she said in a husky voice, "Your heart is beating so fast."

Guy's face was unreadable. "It's not."

Françoise edged closer and then brushed her lips against his, testing. "My heart is ready to burst from my chest."

"You're afraid," he challenged.

Dropping her gaze, she pressed her cheek against his. "I've been afraid all my life until this moment. With you there is no fear."

He cupped her face, tipping it up. He stared at her a long moment, his doubt and hesitation reflected in his eyes. Under Guy's cynicism was loneliness, and he was on the verge of showing Françoise his true self. His fingers gripped her arms, and anger joined with frustration.

Guy sought his own version of a dangerous release in a forbidden love that could be his undoing. He was no different from Louis or me.

As if giving in, Guy kissed Françoise hard on the lips. She wrapped her arms around him and pressed her body against him. The sexual chemistry was palpable, and there wasn't a sound on the set.

When Monsieur Archambeau yelled "Cut!" he looked very pleased with himself. "Excellent job! You two are magic on the screen."

Slowly, they released each other. Neither seemed ready to drop the facade of their character or face the real-world dangers waiting for us all.

It was after nine in the evening when Cécile left the set seconds after Monsieur Archambeau had wrapped production for the day. In her changing room, I helped her out of her dress, and as I hung it up, she poured champagne into a tall flute. She drained it and then refilled it.

"I thought today went very well," she said.

"The Gestapo are watching you."

She took another gulp of champagne. Her cheeks flushed in an uncharacteristic blush. "They're always watching, aren't they? It's a given. We must keep our masks in place."

Discussing the dangers around us didn't do either of us any good. "What will you wear tonight?"

Cécile glanced into the full-length mirror. She ran manicured fingers through her blond hair. "I don't recognize myself sometimes. I've transformed into a stranger. No hints of Dominique exist anymore. And I fear she's gone for good."

"Hiding. Not gone."

She caught my gaze in the mirror. "Do you miss the past?"

"Every day."

"What was that version of you like?"

My chest squeezed with memories of my lost life. "Happy. Optimistic. Naive."

"Dominique was always restless, and so fearful she'd miss out on life. She was always searching for adventure."

"She's found it."

A bitter smile tipped her lips. "But at what cost?"

I understood the cost of choices. "We might not ever know."

Her gaze dropped as she released a sigh. "I think I'll wear something dark and seductive. Schmidt will be at the Ritz tonight."

"Will Louis be at the party?"

"Yes. We'll make a show of it and appear to leave. I'll meet the colonel in his room."

"Tomorrow is Tuesday. I'll be paying a call to your sister."

"I might not be home tonight, but I'll return by noon."

I dropped my voice to a whisper. "Does the colonel suspect you?"

"No."

"But the Gestapo," I hissed.

"They are everywhere. No need to worry." She seemed to swallow her worries with another gulp of champagne.

I didn't know if she was being honest or if she was acting. If today had taught me anything, it was that she was very skilled at her craft.

I suggested a long silk black dress with a back neckline that dipped to her waist. It was one of the costumes Françoise wore in *Secrets in the Shadows*. It was as close to undressed as a woman could be in public.

"Good choice," she said. "I'll have to be very persuasive with the colonel tonight as the rumors about Louis and me swirl."

Back at her apartment, I pressed the dress while Cécile bathed and applied fresh makeup. When she joined me, she was wearing her silk undergarments and stockings held up by garters. The dress slid over her body and hugged her like a second skin. I wrapped the diamonds Oberst Schmidt had given her around her neck and covered her shoulders with a fur stole.

Hauptmann Wolfgang's glistening black Mercedes pulled up in front of the building, and Louis stepped out and strode through the main doors. Seconds later, there was a knock.

Odd that the captain, and not Louis's driver, was transporting them tonight. I wondered if Oberst Schmidt was behind the order.

I opened the door and found Louis standing with his feet braced. He was wearing black slacks, a white dinner jacket, and polished shoes. Diamond cuff links winked from his wrists. His confidence projected a magnetism that would catch any woman's attention. His gaze met mine, and no hints of recognition flickered. "I'm here for Cécile."

"Of course." I went into the bedroom and paused as if I were announcing him, and Cécile smiled and followed me to the living room.

When Cécile emerged, Louis's eyes shone with appreciation. If Oberst Schmidt hadn't heard the rumors about them, he wouldn't be able to ignore them after tonight.

"You look like a scandal," Louis said.

"That was the idea. Champagne?"

"No, not yet."

"We're going to be on magazine covers next month. We should toast our new notoriety. This will be good for both of us."

A muscle pulsed in his jaw. "Lucas has been let go."

"Good."

"He didn't take it well."

"Will he be a problem?"

"No. He has no desire to rot in a camp."

"Nor do I. If this deception is discovered, you and I will both risk arrest."

"You'll be set free."

"I don't count on that."

I understood her worry. An arrest for a small thing could lead to an interrogation that would reveal the bigger deception.

"We should be on our way," he said. "Wouldn't want your concierge questioning what I'm doing here."

"We couldn't have that."

He pressed his hand to her bare back and guided her out of the apartment. From the window, I saw them walk toward the car. Louis opened the door for her, and as she lowered herself onto the leather seat, her white fur slipped off her shoulder, exposing skin. Lights flashed, popped. A group of reporters stood on the corner. She looked over her shoulder and smiled. She hesitated so the photographers could snap more pictures, and then she vanished into the car.

The captain closed the door and glanced up toward the apartment window. He moved to the driver's side door. My cheeks flushed from the heat of the fire I now danced so close to.

Later, the papers printed several images of Cécile dancing with Louis at the Ritz. According to the reporters, a string quartet played Strauss as uniformed Germans and their dates ringed the ballroom. Nazi flags dangled from the balcony as a crystal chandelier winked with a hundred small lights.

After Cécile departed, I set about picking up and folding her clothes and putting away jewels she'd chosen not to wear. I'd just finished putting away discarded high heels when the phone rang. The maid had again been given the night off, so I answered it.

"Hello?"

"Sylvia?" Marc's voice sounded sharp with panic.

"Yes. What's wrong?"

"Can you come to the boulangerie? It's urgent."

My mind raced with possibilities. I didn't dare ask, knowing the telephone operators listened in on calls. Had Emile been detained again? Was there a new Polish family who couldn't speak French? Had there been another bombing? Marc's emphasis on the word "urgent" told me I had to hurry. I still had two hours until curfew, which would give me time to reach the boulangerie. How I would return here in time, I didn't know. "I'll come immediately."

CHAPTER THIRTY
RUBY

Monday, July 7, 2025
8:00 a.m.

"I have a surprise for you." Jeff's voice echoed through the phone.

I sat in the center of my hotel bed, and Cécile's letters surrounded me. As glad as I was to hear Jeff's voice, I was annoyed by the interruption. "And what is that?"

"I traced the official travel papers of one Dominique Dupont. Want to know what I found?"

I shoved my glasses back on my head. "Shut up! You didn't find her."

"I did." He sounded very pleased with himself.

"Are you going to tell me?" I coaxed. He enjoyed the drama of a big reveal, and as much as that drove me crazy, I was going to give him this one.

"Want to know how I found her?" A chair squeaked in the background, and I imagined him leaning forward toward his massive computer screens.

I didn't. I wanted the punch line. "Yes, tell me every single detail."

He chuckled. "Am I driving you crazy?"

"I'm going to reach through the phone . . ."

"Okay, okay," he said, laughing. "I won't bore you with the technical details of computer programming."

I reached for the cup of coffee I'd made in the room and discovered it was cold. "Bless you."

"Long story short, I wrote a program to search for travel data from the French ports between 1941 and 1944. The Germans were excellent recordkeepers, and much of the old documents now have been digitized."

"And?"

"Escaping France at this time was difficult. The Germans had locked down the Atlantic and southern coasts because they were considered German military assets. Some people skied or hiked into Switzerland, and some walked south over the Pyrenees Mountains into Spain."

"But likely no written record of that, correct?"

"Very clever."

"Does that leave the port of Marseille?" I asked.

"Bingo."

"The port was controlled by the Germans in 1942."

"As with all things, there were always exceptions. If someone had connections at the docks, there were ways to smuggle any goods or person in or out of the country. And Daniel worked at the port," he added.

"Exactly," I said.

"Any traveler was required to report to the local Nazi office in the port city and present a passport and exit visa."

"Said visa might have been possible for a well-known actress," I said.

"Yes," he replied. "And that's what happened. On July eighth, 1942, port officials approved Dominique Dupont's exit visa from Marseille. And on the same day, she boarded the *Sea Angel* and set sail for Portugal."

"Portugal."

"The port of Porto. From there, she vanished."

"How? Why?" I asked.

"I suspect she swapped her identity papers for a new set. I would bet she was carrying extra papers."

"Emile's lover was a forger."

"That would fit."

"So, she disappeared?" I asked.

"We know she escaped France alive in July 1942. And Porto was a good place to vanish from."

"What about Emile?"

"No records of her leaving France. The records of the 1942 Paris police have also been digitized but can't be accessed online. I've requested the report. It'll be a couple of weeks."

"I know Marc lived until 1969," I said.

"As a forger, he could slip into the shadows and stay ahead of the police."

"Sylvia hasn't mentioned in her diary that the police raided the boulangerie. I've reached the passage when she mentions Marc suggesting there's an emergency. Something happened, but I don't know what yet."

"I'll also check the records for the Ravensbrück camp for Emile Dupont. Records for the camps were spottier. Many were destroyed as the Allies closed in on Germany."

The idea of Emile's life ending in a dark cell, in tortured pain, was heartbreaking.

As if sensing my mood shift, he said, "Emile was living with a forger. Marc could have created exit visas for her as well. She was familiar with the southern routes out of Paris. Maybe she trekked over the mountains into Spain."

"I don't think she left Paris willingly. She wouldn't turn her back on her cause."

"When her sister left, maybe she decided to leave as well."

"Maybe. What about Sylvia Rousseau? Her daughter said she arrived in the port of New York in June 1944."

"I'll have a look into US immigration records."

"You're amazing."

"How amazing?"

I smiled. "Very."

The keyboard keys clicked. "Are you in Alexandria much longer?"

"I'm headed home tomorrow. Time to pull all the pieces of this article together and tell Cécile's and Sylvia's stories."

"Want to have dinner?"

It would be dinner, and then it would be sex in my hotel room, which would be awesome. And then we'd create more emotional ties, and then we'd try to pretend that my health was perfect.

"I hear the gears turning."

"I'd love to have dinner and whatever comes next."

"But."

"No buts." Sylvia and Cécile had faced death like me. They'd lived their lives to the fullest for as long as they could. And there was no reason why I couldn't do the same. "See you at six?"

"It's a date."

I changed and hurried to Madame Bernard's house. After I knocked, the steady clip of footsteps echoed in the hall. It wasn't polite to come unannounced, but I needed to talk to her about what Jeff had told me.

"Ruby?" She made no effort to hide her surprise. "How nice."

"I'm sorry I didn't call ahead, but I had to tell you about something I discovered."

She motioned me inside. I followed her to the kitchen, and she began making coffee.

"You don't have to make coffee," I said. "I don't want to be any trouble."

"Nonsense. We'll sit at the table and sip our coffee like civilized women, and then I'll hear your revelation."

Something in her tone made me think she hadn't told me everything. I moved to the back windows, which overlooked a long, thin backyard encased in an old brick wall. There were dozens of varieties of flowers, all well watered and pruned. A wrought iron table with two chairs sat atop a stone patio. A mossy angel figurine in the garden looked as if it was centuries old.

Madame set the coffee carafe and cups on the table, along with sugar and cream. "Sit."

I sat at the table, doing my best not to rush, and allowed her to pour my coffee. I filled my cup with plenty of cream and sugar.

She took a careful sip and set her cup down in the saucer. "What is your great revelation?"

"My friend Jeff discovered that Dominique Dupont boarded a ship in Marseille during the summer of 1942. Cécile escaped France."

Madame didn't look surprised by my revelation. "Keep reading."

"Are you saying she didn't escape France?" I asked.

"Keep reading." Again, she sipped.

"Did your mother tell you about Cécile's fate?"

She brushed away my worry with a flick of her fingers. "No. My mother hid her past for her entire life. She wanted me to know the truth. Otherwise, she'd have destroyed the diaries and letters. But she couldn't tell me herself for reasons I don't understand."

"The early forties in Paris were a difficult time."

"Have you finished Sylvia's diary?"

"Almost."

"When you reach the end, you'll understand how complicated life can be."

"You knew about Dominique's departure from Marseille."

She circled a manicured finger on the marble countertop. "Yes. But it's more than you realize."

"Tell me."

She traced the rim of her cup. "You must hear it from Sylvia. I could never do those days justice."

"I know what Cécile did for Louis. She covered for him. A Google search told me he lived until 1980."

"It was one of the small brave moments that no one will ever know about."

"She did it for her career. To hide her spying."

Madame's shoulder lifted and then dropped. "Maybe. But turning Louis in would have deflected attention away from herself. She would have gained favor with his arrest."

The unanswered questions nudged me, demanding to be satisfied. "Can you at least tell me where Dominique Dupont is now?"

"You must read."

CHAPTER THIRTY-ONE
SYLVIA

Monday, July 6, 1942
10:00 p.m.

When I arrived at the boulangerie, it was dark. I climbed the stairs to Emile's apartment and found Marc standing in the dark by her window, peering through the curtains, holding a cigarette that was little more than ash.

"Were you followed?" he asked as he stubbed out his cigarette on a small saucer.

"No. I was careful." I'd taken several back alleys and avoided all the German and French patrols.

"No German driver escorting you?"

"No. Why did you call?" I asked.

Shadows bathed Marc's face. "We received word that the police are going to be conducting roundups of Jews in the next week. We don't know when, but it will happen."

"There have been roundups before."

"Not like this one," he said. "This one will be massive. Emile and I were in the neighborhood knocking on doors, trying to warn the families we know." He clicked on a small lamp. "No one was listening to us."

"Why did you call Cécile's phone?"

"When the police arrived, Emile and I were separated. I made it back here. She hasn't returned. I went out looking, and an old woman told me several police officers tossed Emile into a car."

"When did this happen?"

"Ten hours ago. I have contacts in the police department who aren't offended by a bribe. They told me the police were instructed to take Emile to 11 Rue des Saussaies, the Gestapo headquarters. If they haven't started questioning her by now, they soon will. If she breaks, the police will come for Cécile and you." Marc lit a fresh cigarette.

"And you'll be arrested."

"I know how to vanish." Lamplight sharpened the angles on his face.

"Emile is tough." I hoped saying the words out loud would add weight.

"You and I both know the Gestapo can break anyone." He looked out the window. "The irony is that no one was listening to our warning. No one."

I'd wanted to believe the worst couldn't happen even as my father had escorted me to the train station in Warsaw seven years ago. He'd seen it coming, and I hadn't believed him.

"We must both leave this building now. It'll be overrun with officers soon."

"I'll talk to Cécile. She has contacts."

"Tell her about her sister and caution her that saving Emile will be difficult." Marc drew in a slow, steady breath. "It's time for you to leave France. They'll find out the truth about you sooner or later."

I reached for the door handle, knowing the sooner I found Cécile, the better.

"There are others I can bribe," he said. "I'll try to find out more."

"Leave any information in the compartment under the carpet."

Outside, I hurried down the side steps. On the street, shouts and a gunshot cut through the darkness. Across the street, I saw a policeman standing at the corner. I hurried down the sidewalk as footsteps echoed closer. Walking faster, I wondered if my luck had run out. I'd always believed I would be fine if I was careful. But I'd begun to take more risks with Cécile, Emile, and the captain.

I hastened down the stairs of the Bastille Métro stop, bought a ticket, and ran toward what was likely the last train of the night. When I spotted a collection of German soldiers boarding the train, I hurried past the car and up the stairs opposite. Ducking my head, I moved swiftly. I was grateful I knew the city's shadows and shortcuts so well.

When I arrived at Cécile's apartment building, it was after eleven. Hauptmann Wolfgang's car was parked across the street, but his head was slumped back. He was sleeping.

I angled through the front door, but as I moved toward the central staircase, the building's concierge opened her first-floor apartment door.

Though Cécile used the old woman's penchant for gossip to her advantage, I wasn't sure she wouldn't turn into a police informant.

"Mademoiselle Rousseau."

"Madame Balzac."

The concierge was a slender woman with thin, graying hair and long bony fingers. Weariness lingered in the curve of her stooped shoulders. "What are you doing out so late?" she asked.

I turned and descended the two stairs toward her. I stood at least three inches above her. "I lost track of the time."

"You broke the curfew."

The old woman glared at me with narrowed eyes. She'd lived in this building for decades and had known the family who'd lived in our apartment. I'd always assumed she saw Cécile and me as interlopers.

"It was a mistake. I was working late," I said.

"Cécile returned an hour ago."

"I know," I lied. "I used the extra time to scout fabric sources."

She glanced at my empty hands. "After curfew."

"I'd been told a shopkeeper had a rich yellow silk that would be perfect for a costume I'm making. But he'd swapped it for cheap cotton. It was a waste of time."

Madame Balzac pursed her lips. "I know liars. And you're a bad one."

To disagree would have underscored her suspicions. "You're right. I wasn't working. I saw my lover. He didn't want me to leave."

"The German driver? The one always parked out front?"

"He's not the only one I see," I lied.

The old woman's scowl deepened. "Be careful, girl. You and the actress are playing with the devil. The Boche will turn on you both. They're all hungry tigers circling and ready to eat every one of us alive."

Lifting my gaze, I was surprised to see concern etched around her eyes. "Yes, ma'am."

"Get up to your room and be more careful next time."

"Yes, of course."

I ran up the stairs and was breathless when I reached Cécile's apartment door. When I entered, I closed and locked the door, allowing myself to release a breath I'd held for hours.

Cécile emerged from her bedroom, tightening the folds of a silk robe. "Where have you been?"

"With Marc. The French police arrested Emile. Marc and Emile were warning families about a pending roundup when the police arrived. They were separated, and the police took her."

Cécile drew a slow, steady breath as she removed an envelope from her robe pocket. "I'll return to her apartment and put this in her hiding place. Then I'll go to Henri."

"You're expected on set this morning, and Hauptmann Wolfgang is parked out front. He's sleeping for now, and I snuck past him when I approached the building. Madame Balzac is awake and watching. I'll deliver the letter. I'll wake up the captain and have him drive me to Emile's."

She considered my offer and then handed me the letter. "That's valuable information. Much is about the U-boats."

"What do we do about Emile? Are you going to see the colonel?"

"No, the colonel is finished with me."

"Why?"

"He's jealous of Louis. I couldn't calm him." She seemed more irritated than hurt as she moved past me toward a table sporting my delivery basket. "There are extra francs in the basket if Marc needs to pay more bribes. Stuff the letter in the bread as we always do."

"You'll go to the studio?"

"It's the last day of shooting, and Henri will be waiting. Henri has contacts in the city police and with the Germans. He'll help me. He owes me a great deal. He'll call in favors and save my sister."

"I should be at the studio to help you with your costumes."

"Today is the seduction scene. I won't be wearing much." She studied her manicured fingers. "When I first arrived in Paris, a nude scene would have shocked me. Now, it seems trivial."

"But if I alter my routine . . ."

"Then you do. Charlotte manages Louis's costumes, and she can help me. Louis never argues when I ask for a favor like that. Your delivery is more important."

"Once I've dropped off the basket, I'll come to the studio. It's more important that nothing appears amiss. And perhaps Marc knows more now."

She considered my statement but didn't look encouraged. "Perhaps."

"Do you think Oberst Schmidt or Monsieur Archambeau suspects anything?"

"I've been cautious. But who can say? Emile's arrest might not be linked to my letters, but I don't trust coincidence."

When I rushed outside, the captain was waiting, leaning against his gleaming car, staring at the building. Faint moonlight glistened on the car's shiny exterior. He walked toward me, his footsteps steady and sure. "Where are you going?"

"To deliver Emile's basket."

He leaned closer. "It's very late."

"I must be on set by nine. It's the last day of shooting."

His gaze lingered on me. "I'll drive you."

"Thank you."

He opened the door for me, and I slid into the front seat. He closed the door with a hard thud and moved around the car. He sat behind the wheel and started the engine.

The weight of the basket felt heavy on my lap as the captain drove through the quiet streets. There was a sullenness about him that was troubling.

"You're worried," I said. "What's the matter?"

"I'm concerned about you," he said.

"Me? Why?"

Gravel popped under the tires as the vehicle moved through the dark streets. "You're in trouble."

I struggled to keep the tension from my face. I pushed aside thoughts of Emile's arrest and the hidden compartment under the threadbare carpet. "What do you mean?"

"You must know the police questioned Emile last year. The marks on her hands. Did you see them?"

"She told me it was an accident," I lied.

Shadows smoked the edges of his clenched jaw. "The police did it to her as a warning."

It wasn't challenging to feign shock or fear. "Why would the police arrest Emile?"

"She has ties to the Resistance."

"Those meetings? She told me she stopped," I lied.

He didn't look convinced. "She didn't. She was arrested in the Marais last night."

"Why?"

"She's trying to warn families of a coming roundup. She's interfering with Reich policy."

"Roundup of families? Why?" I wanted to hear him say what the Germans planned.

He countered with his own question. "Why were you sneaking into Cécile's building?"

I said nothing.

"I saw you." He gripped the wheel tighter as he drove through the darkened and narrowing streets. He wove past the Marais's ancient stone buildings. "You were at Emile's." When I didn't answer, he said, "I turned a blind eye to Emile. But she's pressed too hard."

"She's done nothing wrong."

As he parked in front of Emile's building, he glanced ahead, staring down the street toward a group of three women who were breaking curfew. One glanced up and saw him, and the women dispersed.

The captain kept his gaze trained ahead as a muscle in his jaw pulsed. "Stay off the streets as much as possible for the next few weeks. There are going to be arrests. Be very careful."

I dug my thumb into the basket's brittle wicker.

The captain placed his hand over mine, startling my gaze up to his. "I care about you, Sylvia. I don't want to see you dragged into anything that causes you trouble."

"I sew. I visit Emile. I sleep with you. That's my life." I touched his arm, wondering if he was being truthful.

His frown deepened as he dropped his gaze to my hand.

I added, "It's been too long since we've had time together. Let me deliver this basket, and we can take care of that. I have several hours before I need to be on set."

He studied my face.

As I ran my hand over his thigh, his body tensed. I could sense his desire for me clouding his mind and blurring his growing suspicions. But he could regain his clarity very soon. "I'll be right back."

"I'll come with you."

"I won't be gone more than five minutes. Stay with the car." I opened the door and hurried up the side staircase. When I knocked on Emile's door, there was no answer. The other two apartments were quiet and dark. I twisted Emile's doorknob and pushed open the door.

Silent shadows bathed the small space. The only sign that Marc had been here was the lingering scent of cigarette smoke. A disturbing hush wrapped the room, and when I flipped on a light switch, I realized the apartment had been ransacked. All the drawers had been emptied out on the floor, feathers lay near ripped pillows, and the bedding had been dumped into a heap next to pieces of a clay urn.

Who had been here? Had Emile already been broken and confessed?

My heels clicked across the parquet floor as I checked the closet. Emile's few meager outfits had been shredded and tossed on the floor. Two well-worn shoes lay on their sides.

The captain's warning rattled in my head.

I crossed to the round rug and, with trembling fingers, pulled up the carpet and opened the small hiding hole. Waiting for me in the hiding space were several sets of identity papers and a note from Marc. It read: *Run!*

With a shaking hand, I dug Cécile's letter out of the bread and placed it in the compartment. I shoved the new identity papers in an inside jacket pocket. Beyond the front door, heavy footsteps echoed on the stairs. I covered up the compartment and smoothed out the rug. As I set the basket on the table, the door opened.

The captain stood on the threshold. I was gone only a few minutes, and yet he was checking on me. Was he hoping to save me or catch me? His gaze surveyed the destruction, and he didn't appear surprised.

"She's not here," I said. "Something terrible has happened."

"Leave the basket. If Emile returns, she'll know you were here. Don't leave a note. If this was the work of the SS, they'll question everyone who knows her."

I left the basket on the table, and as I walked, a tremor ran through my body. I had no one to rely on in this moment other than this German.

On Tuesdays, I dressed for him, choosing the colors and fitted bodices that caught his interest. Today, I'd had no time to prepare for him, and I felt shabby.

He watched me as I passed by. He closed the door with a hard click.

"I'm terrified," I said.

"I'll ask around. I might be able to find out where the police took Emile."

I took his hand. Powerful fingers gripped mine.

"Thank you," I said.

I wanted to run back to Cécile and tell her what I'd seen in Emile's apartment, but to do so would have alerted the captain even more. I needed to remain calm.

He released my hand as we approached the bottom of the stairs. Without a word, he escorted me outside and to the car. The perfect gentleman, he opened the door and waited until I was seated.

He said nothing as he drove through the Marais to the brothel where my refugees had hidden. Fear ripened by years of deception swelled in my chest.

The captain revealed none of his thoughts. He shut off the car engine. "There will be fewer prying eyes here," he said.

"Why here?" How many times had I passed the lobby's shabby red wallpaper and climbed to the third floor with frightened families in tow?

"You do not like it? I thought you were familiar with this area."

Was this a test? Or was he showing me my worth to him? "It's an unorthodox choice."

The captain walked with me into the building. The woman at the front desk, who'd seen me many times, was accustomed to discretion and didn't say a word or give a hint she recognized me. I looked to my right into the familiar gilded mirror in the green parlor. I didn't recognize this version of me. The girl from Poland was gone. She'd been erased by a thousand choices that had created the woman staring back. A woman who now belonged in this brothel.

The captain requested a room, gave the woman a generous sum of francs, and was given a door key.

We climbed the center staircase to the second floor, and he unlocked room 22. The place smelled of desperation and sadness.

It wasn't until our door was closed and locked that the captain reached for me and pulled me roughly toward him. All traces of the gentleman vanished. In his place stood a man starving for something I doubted even he could name.

I didn't flip on the lights. I didn't want to see the shabby carpet or the stained bedspread.

An undercurrent, intimate and foul, surged through the narrow space between us. And then he grabbed me, hiked up my skirt, and pushed down my silk panties. The sudden force ripped fabric and the last of my dignity.

Before I could catch my breath, he pushed me onto the bed. He fumbled with his pants and braced a hand by my head. He used the other to shove inside me with a despair I'd never felt. Desire flowered out of my shame. And it grew with each of his thrusts.

I knew the end was here for us. And he seemed to sense it. What did he know? Was he turning me in to the police after we left the brothel? His anger, fear, and frustration became mine as my desire peaked.

After we both had finished, he dropped his head into the crook of my neck. His panting, ragged breath was as labored as mine. Our sex was not love but a fulfillment of a primitive need.

He raised his head and reached for the charm around my neck. Rough fingers ran over the cross and then against the star on the underside.

I froze, unable to breathe, teetering on a tightrope.

He released the charm. He rolled off me onto his back and lay beside me. He stared at the water-stained ceiling. "You should have left the city two years ago."

"I couldn't," I said.

"Then go now," he said. "I might not be in Paris much longer. My superiors have ordered me to the Eastern Front."

"Where?"

"Poland and then to Russia."

Poland. The Germans had decimated my home country. I lay beside him. Our shoulders pressed against each other, and I drew comfort from the simple touch. "Why are you being transferred to Russia?"

"Germany will move on the city of Stalingrad soon." The lines furrowed his brow. His dread had the consistency of futility.

Cécile had said a few German officers had privately expressed their concerns about the Russian invasion. They whispered that hubris would devour the Reich.

I knew what it was like to see your country fall. But I had no pity for the Germans. Nothing would have given me greater pleasure than to witness Germany's ruin.

"When will you leave?" I asked.

"Next week."

Perhaps in a different world we could have cared for each other. Perhaps we'd have met on the German–Polish border. He'd have wooed me in a proper courtship with poppies. Our families would have witnessed our vows.

But in this world, I'd given his secrets to the Allies. And he could turn me over to the police.

CHAPTER THIRTY-TWO
SYLVIA

Tuesday, July 7, 1942
11:00 a.m.

The captain drove me back to the studio. For the first time, he took no detours. There was no easy chatter about his love of Paris. Silence hummed around us.

Out of the car, I'd taken two steps when his car engine roared. I watched as he drove away without a glance back.

I hurried through the movie studio's main gate and stopped to show my papers to the guard. Then I made my way through the maze of offices to Cécile's dressing room. Her discarded clothes littered the floor, but there was no sign of her.

When I approached the main studio, Cécile stood in the center of the set, now surrounded by several Nazi officers. She wore a slim-fitting black silk robe that skimmed all her curves. I'd had to refit the robe three times because she'd lost so much weight.

Dressed like a siren, she'd also adopted Françoise's vulnerable air. Cécile had always excelled in the lost-orphan roles. At this point in the movie, the audiences assumed that Françoise was innocent. She was the waif in need of rescue.

Cécile moved toward several Nazi officers, smiling as if they were old friends. Black uniforms, glistening knee-high boots, and calm expressions churned fear in the crew, all looking uncomfortable.

We all knew someone like Emile who had been charged with resistance and taken to the old jails commandeered by the Germans. The facilities' reputations were now rife with tales of torture and horrific conditions.

But none of that seemed to concern Cécile now.

She appeared at ease with these men as she wished them well and moved to her mark on set. The officers chuckled to each other. It was clear they were charmed by her.

Louis stood off to the side, the well-worn script gripped in his hand. His gaze was downcast as if learning the words on the page was the most pressing problem in his life.

Cécile made a show of picking up her script and reading through several pages. Lately, she'd misremembered a few lines that she could have recited backward.

Footsteps sounded on my left, and I felt a gaze heavy with interest land on me. Its source was the tallest Gestapo officer. His blond hair was neat and short, and his angled cheekbones had a cruel elegance that any camera would love.

"Good morning," the officer said in perfect French.

"Good morning. Can I help you?"

Sharp hawk eyes locked on me. "No, I came to observe the filming. I'm a fan of Cécile's."

I couldn't picture him in a darkened theater watching a romantic comedy. "I'm glad you could join us. We should begin soon. Can I introduce you to anyone on set?"

"That would be nice, thank you."

"And your name, sir?" I asked.

"Hauptmann Rudolph Hertz," he said.

"Pleasure," I said, extending my hand to him.

He gripped my fingers, tightening to the point of discomfort. "No, it's my pleasure."

I beckoned Louis over with a flick of red-manicured fingers. A muscle pulsed in his jaw before he grinned and moved toward us.

"Monsieur Lambert, I would like you to meet Hauptmann Hertz. He's a fan of our work."

Louis clasped his hand. "It's a pleasure, sir."

"Can you tell me about this movie?" Hauptmann Hertz asked.

"The movie features a down-on-his luck detective and the rich woman in jeopardy who hires him." Louis angled his head toward Cécile. "As you can see, our heroine is quite the seductress."

"A wonderful woman," the captain said. "I suspect your detective has no chance against her."

Louis chuckled. "I have no defense against her."

I smiled, ducking my head as if the suggestion was embarrassing.

"She represents degeneracy, something all good men must combat," the captain said. "And the detective personifies old-world authority. She'll be his ruin if not controlled."

The undertones coiled around me, tightening with unspoken threats.

"That's very true," Louis said.

"Does she win?" the captain asked.

"I don't want to spoil it for you," Lambert said with a smile.

"It's a classic story of Adam and Eve," the captain said.

"You're a biblical scholar, Hauptmann Hertz?" I asked.

"I enjoy reading the Bible whenever I can."

"Ah, then I'm sure the actors will welcome your opinion after they've filmed this scene."

"And what's this scene?" the captain asked.

"Seduction." Louis's innuendo was intended for another man. "It's the last one we'll shoot."

"Well then," the captain said. "I'll let you begin."

"Thank you," I said.

As Louis walked away, I didn't dare glance at the captain. No one believed that Hauptmann Hertz was a fan of the Bible or Cécile. The Gestapo was here for other reasons.

Monsieur Archambeau gave Cécile and Louis basic directions. But neither seemed to pay close attention. Both were lost in their thoughts and fears. The director stepped behind the camera and yelled, "*Silence, moteur, action!*"

Cécile abandoned the last of her persona and became Françoise. As she moved closer to Guy, she let her robe slip from her shoulders. Beneath the robe, she wore only a gauze sheath that left nothing to the imagination. Most women couldn't expose themselves like this, but she didn't seem to give it any notice. I knew from the script that the camera would catch enough glimpses of her naked body to tease the audience.

"I didn't kill him," Françoise said. "I loved my husband."

Guy took her arm in hand, squeezing harder than ever. "You're a liar."

Françoise tried to twist free of his grasp. But she was trapped. When she realized this, she edged closer and slid out of the sheath. Her bare breasts brushed Guy's chest. A muscle in Guy's jaw tightened. He knew Françoise was manipulating him. And yet he couldn't pull away.

Françoise bit her bottom lip, allowed tears to well in her eyes, and gripped his shirt. Guy's hands came to her waist. The set was chilly, hardening her nipples. In the final film, audiences would only catch glimpses of her nudity. But on the set, there was no hiding.

Paris was Françoise. The Germans were Guy. The invading soldiers had been seduced by Paris's restaurants, hotels, art, and brothels. Now, the Germans and Guy realized their siren was more dangerous than they'd ever imagined. The only way to win was through the destruction of the temptress.

Françoise pressed her lips to Guy's. If she didn't win him over, she would be lost. In an unscripted moment, Guy cupped her face in his large hands and pulled her lips away from his. He glared into her blue eyes. His expression mirrored desire and resentment.

When Guy kissed Françoise, his touch was hard and bruising. He pushed her against the wall and trapped her hands over her head, kissing her neck and breasts.

The moment reminded me of the one I'd shared with Hauptmann Wolfgang hours earlier. My heart thundered in my chest as tension rippled through my body. When I looked up, I noticed Hauptmann Wolfgang for the first time. He had returned to the studio and was staring at me. Shame reddened my cheeks as desire twisted around hate.

The set went silent. Françoise and Guy's hopelessness and futility echoed in all our lives.

And then a gunshot broke the silence.

I cringed.

Françoise stared into Guy's eyes as tears slid down her cheek. She gripped his shirt. He kissed her on the forehead. And then, she began to slide to the floor, revealing the small revolver in his hand. Guy dropped to his knees and scooped up his dead lover in his arms and kissed her.

When Monsieur Archambeau shouted "*Coupez!*" Lambert didn't break the kiss. The two actors remained locked together.

Monsieur Archambeau yelled "*Coupez!*" again, and finally, the spell broke.

The crew would reset the cameras up at different angles and the actors would reshoot the scene, but I wondered how they'd re-create that intensity.

I carried Cécile's robe to her, covered her near-naked body, and helped her stand.

Hands clapped as Cécile righted her shoulders.

Louis ran his fingers through his dark hair and offered a sly smile. He shrugged, suggesting *Boys will be boys*. The men, even the Gestapo captain, smiled with appreciation.

As I followed Cécile to her dressing rooms, Monsieur Archambeau barked orders at the crew. Cécile closed her eyes as I cleaned her smeared lipstick from around her mouth. "What news do you have of Emile?"

"Someone searched her apartment, and there's no sign of Marc. But he left us identity papers and a note instructing us to run."

CHAPTER THIRTY-THREE
RUBY

Monday, July 7, 2025
5:00 p.m.

I spent the afternoon reading Sylvia's journal, then rereading how she'd compared her seduction of her captain to the scene between Françoise and Guy. Shame and desire went hand in hand with her after she'd found satisfaction in the arms of her enemy.

There was another complication I'd never considered until this moment. Sylvia had worried about an unwanted pregnancy. Could Madame Bernard have been the product of this affair?

When my phone alarm went off, I realized it was time to dress and meet Jeff for dinner. I didn't want to leave this room or Sylvia's Paris, but after months in hospital isolation, I'd learned the value of fresh air and people.

I changed into a navy blue sheath dress, my favorite trio of gold necklaces, and hoop earrings. My makeup was minimal, but I painted on bright-red lipstick and spritzed on some Miss Dior perfume.

When I saw Jeff, he was dressed in another neat, clean outfit that looked amazing but went against his type. I wondered if his toes felt cramped in the polished loafers.

I kissed him, holding him close. "You look amazing."

"Thank you." He straightened the small cross nestled in the hollow of my neck.

"You don't always have to dress up for me. Don't feel you need to be someone else to make me happy."

He waggled his eyebrows. "Missing the Star Wars T-shirt?"

I chuckled. "No. But I know you love those shirts. And I don't want you to feel like you can't be you."

"Very deep. Where's this coming from?"

I shuddered a sigh. "Sylvia donned a mask to survive. The pretense kept her alive, but it also cost her. No one can live a lifetime with that kind of weight."

"I don't consider closed-toe shoes a heavy lift, Ruby." Despite the quip, his tone was severe before a small smile flickered. "But if I ever feel the urge to dress like a college geek, I will."

"Promise?"

"I do." His head cocked. "Will you wear a Star Wars T-shirt if I bought you one?"

Smiling, I tamped down a shudder. "The idea goes against everything in me, but for you, I would."

He chuckled. "I have a vintage one that dates to the midseventies—never been worn. Princess Leia. A pop of pink in the center."

"You had me at 'vintage.'"

"On our way to dinner, then?"

It was all so easy between us. There seemed no reason why we couldn't build a great relationship. Sylvia had risked discovery and death so many times. She might have escaped France carrying a German officer's baby. With all that Sylvia had managed, I could enjoy what I had with Jeff now. "I want to be fair to you."

"How are you not being fair?"

Maybe I assumed too much, but I needed to say the words out loud. "I could get sick again, Jeff. I'm in remission now, but Jason was given the all clear, and look at him now. He's dying. Be careful how much you like me."

He looked at me and sighed. "Too late. I already like you too much. I have since that first day you came one winter break in college."

My heart scraped with fears that always lingered close. "I can't give you the kind of life you want."

He looked curious. "What do I want, Ruby?"

"Children. I've seen the way you were with the kids at the hospital. You're great with children. You've said you wanted children."

He laid his hands on my shoulders. "I have all I want right here."

That was so easy to say. Scott had been so clear that he'd stand by me no matter what. Looking back, I could see he was telling the truth, but he didn't understand what committing to me meant.

"I can smell the circuits catching fire in your brain," he said.

A frown furrowed my brow.

He looked annoyed. "I'm not Scott."

"I know."

He regarded me. "You aren't convinced."

"I want to be. But I don't want you making promises that can be impossible to keep."

"I'll have to show you for as long as it takes."

Tears welled in my eyes. Jeff meant what he said. He did. But this disease could eat away the strongest bonds in my life. I kissed him.

He cupped my face. "I'm not going anywhere, Ruby."

I wish I could have believed that.

CHAPTER THIRTY-FOUR
SYLVIA

Tuesday, July 7, 1942
7:00 p.m.

Hauptmann Wolfgang parked by Cécile's apartment. Cécile left the car immediately and hurried into the building. I lingered.

The light from the dashboard sharpened the lines on the captain's stern face. "I'll make inquiries about Emile."

"Thank you."

"Do not hold out hope." His voice was low and firm.

His hand rested on the seat. I leaned forward and laid mine over his. Usually, I didn't dare a kiss with so many prying eyes. But I sensed this was our end. I pressed my lips to his. He kissed me back. A hot breeze gusted sharp through his open window and brushed my cheeks.

"Take care," he said.

"You as well."

The taste of him lingered on my lips as I opened the door. When I closed it behind me, I didn't look back, but as I rushed toward the building's entrance, I felt his gaze on me. The captain would be good to his word. He would ask about Emile. But if Emile was in prison, she was likely being tortured, and every second mattered. No one knew how strong they were until they were tested.

I found Cécile sitting at her makeup table, applying red lipstick. As soon as I entered the room, she glanced up at me.

"The captain's going to ask about Emile," I said.

A skeptical brow rose. "He won't turn on you?"

I thought about our violent lovemaking. His thrusts had channeled as much desperation as his last gentle kiss. "I don't think so, but it's a risk."

"The Gestapo lingered on the set long after you left," Cécile said.

"They must know about Emile."

"How could they not? I think the captain was playing a game with me." She stood, stripped off her silk robe, and removed a simple dress from her closet. "I never found Henri alone on the set. I think he was avoiding me. I must see him now and ask him to help with Emile."

"I thought he planned to leave town after the film wrapped?" I knew he kept a home in the country near Bordeaux and escaped Paris whenever he could.

"He hates to travel at night. I might still be able to catch him. He has friends in the police department."

"I'll go with you. But you must not wear that."

She glanced at the black dress made of a delicate fabric. "This is my simplest outfit."

"Let me give you something of mine. We need to blend in. And my jackets are all fitted with pockets. Take money, jewels, anything you might need. Assume we aren't returning."

"It can't be that dire," she said.

"We must assume it is." I moved into my room and collected a brown suit. She took it and inspected the pockets in the lining.

"I've heard nothing of the roundups yet. Perhaps it was just rumor."

"The Germans will strike. It's just a matter of time," I said.

Cécile left with her suit to change. I found my diary and tucked it into an inside jacket pocket. The weight of the last seven years felt heavy. I stuffed a roll of francs in another pocket and a knife in a small one on the right.

Minutes later, Cécile had changed into the simple suit I'd made years ago. Neatly tailored, the suit had a humble cut and fabric and echoed what most struggling women in Paris wore now. She ran her hand over the fabric, shaking her head.

"Not silk, but it functions well," I said.

"I pass no judgment. Nothing changes. And then in a blink the world transforms into something I don't recognize." Cécile entered the living room, her hands brimming with money and jewels. Letters were tucked under her arm. She handed me several diamond bracelets and more francs. "Take these. In case we get separated."

"I can't even calculate the value."

She pushed letters into an interior pocket. "Bribes are not cheap."

As we descended the building's main stairs, Madame Balzac opened her apartment door and regarded us. Our humble appearance must have raised questions. But instead of chiding us, she said, "Use the back door."

The older woman hurried down the dimly lit center hallway. She fumbled with her ancient ring of keys and then opened the back door. On the other side was a dark alley that smelled of trash.

Silent, we set off toward Monsieur Archambeau's apartment. It was two hours before the curfew, so we had some time.

It took an hour of walking to reach the director's town house in the fifteenth arrondissement.

Cécile glanced up at the grand old building, studying it closely. She and Monsieur Archambeau had known each other for four years and had been lovers for three. "This is the home where he lives with his wife and children. I've never been here before."

I rang the bell. We waited as footsteps clicked in the hallway. The door opened to a young serving girl in a black uniform trimmed with a white collar. When she met Cécile's gaze, her eyes sparked with recognition.

"Mademoiselle Cécile? This visit is unexpected."

Cécile pushed past the girl. "Where is he?"

"He's not here."

"He wouldn't have left yet. He doesn't travel after dinner." She marched toward the dining room, the maid on her heels.

"Mademoiselle," the maid rushed to say. "You can't be here. The police were here. They are looking for you."

"Then we'll be quick."

Cécile opened the pocket doors. Henri's first reaction was shock at the unexpected intrusion. Then annoyance tightened the lines of his face.

"We need to talk," Cécile said.

He grunted as he dropped his knife and fork on the china plate piled with roast beef and potatoes. Red wine filled a crystal glass.

"This isn't appropriate," he said. "This house is where I live with my wife and children. It's sacred. Even you cannot have everything you want."

As if he hadn't spoken, she said, "Emile is missing."

Monsieur Archambeau glanced toward me and then back at Cécile. "She's not missing. She's being questioned."

She moved toward him. Her fists were clenched. "And you didn't tell me?"

"You knew this day was coming. She's been pressing the police and Gestapo for a long time. You can't save her. If she's smart, she'll cooperate, and the questioning won't be too extreme." He sipped his wine. "The police won't have patience with her this time."

Cécile grabbed his arm. "You must make phone calls, ask for favors, and save her. I'll do whatever you want."

He jerked free of her grasp and stood. "What was she doing this time?"

"She was in the Marais, talking to families."

"Talking. To Jews? Warning them."

"It doesn't matter."

I closed the dining room door behind me as Monsieur Archambeau walked toward a sideboard. I had no idea if the maid was listening in the hallway, or if she'd call the police. I prayed she'd go upstairs and ignore us.

Monsieur Archambeau scoffed. "That section of town has been targeted."

"I don't know about that."

"But I'd wager Emile did."

"I would tell you if I knew, but I don't." Cécile channeled Françoise's desperate tone as a tear slid down her cheeks. "I still love you. I'll always love you."

Monsieur Archambeau leaned closer and touched her face. "I almost believe you, Cécile."

"Henri, it's true. We have meant so much to each other."

"You could have gone far. You really are a talented actress."

"Find my sister, and I'll send her away. She won't be a bother to you ever again."

"Your sister has never liked me. I tolerated her for you, but now she's not worth the trouble. The Germans have lost all patience with anyone who interferes with their plans. She chose the wrong side."

Fists clenched at her sides. "She's my sister! I cannot abandon her."

His eyes glistened with dark glee. "Did you know the Gestapo have been watching you? I was barely able to buy enough time so I could finish this film. Now the movie is finished, I don't need you."

"What does that mean? I'm the one that made you. I'm very popular with the audience and our benefactors."

Monsieur Archambeau reached for a crystal decanter beside two gold statuettes of Louis XIV, the glorious Sun King of France who'd died over two hundred years ago. He poured two glasses of sherry and handed one to Cécile. "What do you think the police will learn from Emile when they question her?"

"She knows nothing," Cécile insisted. "She's involved in nothing."

"Does she know about the March bombings of the Renault factory?"

Cécile never hesitated. "What are you talking about? She was shocked by the explosions like the rest of us."

Monsieur Archambeau's eyes narrowed. "You have a very, very good memory, and I'd wager that whatever you heard at a party or in bed with Schmidt imprinted on your brain. Did you pass on secrets to her via your dressmaker?" He looked toward me. "Hauptmann Wolfgang told me she makes deliveries to Emile every Tuesday."

I shouldn't have been surprised that the captain had been spying on me. My seduction powers were amateurish, but that didn't change the fact I'd been using him.

Cécile showed no signs of shock or worry. "Sylvia takes my sister food and a bit of money. And of course, I had my driver take her. The streets are not safe."

"The driver your dressmaker is sleeping with?"

I'd told no one about our affair because I'd been as afraid of retaliation as I was ashamed of my sexual satisfaction. He'd enjoyed me in his bed, but he appeared to have had no misgivings about who knew about us.

Cécile rested her hands on her hips and managed to look offended. "You're sleeping with me and at least three other women. If sex is a sin, then you will join me in hell." She smiled. "Unless you have a bias against German lovers?"

Tension tightened his haughty expression before it vanished. "Many said you'd be the ruin of me."

The mirror behind Monsieur Archambeau caught her bitter smile. "We both will suffer the wrath of God."

"Maybe." He downed the amber liquid.

She chuckled, the sound bitter and broken. "We'll make a fine couple in hell, no?"

An unpleasant smile twisted his lips. "There was a time when I was fond of you. And you've made me a great deal of money. So, I'll do you this favor and give you a warning. The Gestapo will be arresting you. They are likely at your apartment now. Your dressmaker will also be detained."

"Why her?"

"The high command suspects that you, your dressmaker, and your sister passed on secrets to the Allies. You three are quite the resisters."

Had the captain known my arrest was imminent when he'd taken me to the brothel early this morning or kissed me in the car hours ago?

"You're wrong about us," Cécile said. "We did nothing to help the Allies."

"You, my dear, must convince the interrogators, not me." He sighed. "Because you meant something to me once, I'll give you this chance. Run while you can. You have just hours. And then you and Mademoiselle Rousseau will vanish into the hole where Emile has fallen."

Cécile stilled for a moment, took a sip from her glass, and set it next to one of the gilded Louis XIV statuettes. She reached for it and swung.

"What're you—?" Monsieur Archambeau said.

Monsieur Archambeau's question halted midsentence as the statuette struck him hard on the side of the head. He staggered back a step and then dropped to his knees before falling face first onto the floor. Blood from his head oozed on the white marble.

I rushed toward Cécile, took the statuette from her, and replaced it on the sideboard. Grabbing her shoulders, I forced her to look at me. Later, I would deal with the shock of this, but for now, there was no time. "We must go. They'll kill us if we don't run."

She stared at the blood seeping toward her shoe. "Where is my sister?"

I clutched her cold hands in mine. "There will be no saving Emile if we don't go now."

Cécile looked at me, her gaze vacant. For the first time since we'd met, she looked lost.

CHAPTER THIRTY-FIVE
RUBY

Tuesday, July 8, 2025
Noon

The drive back to Norfolk was exhausting. Traffic on I-95 jammed up north of Fredericksburg, and by the time I neared Norfolk, I was stopped again by Hampton Roads Bridge–Tunnel traffic. I could barely carry my suitcase up the stairs when I reached my apartment. After dropping my bag and laptop bag by the front door, I crossed my small living room to the bathroom. I stripped and turned on the hot shower. My head pounded, and I felt like I'd caught a bug in Alexandria.

I had more pages of Sylvia's diary to read but couldn't focus right now. I plunged under the water and let the heat massage my face. I'm not sure how long I stood there, but when I turned off the tap, I had enough energy to dry off, climb into bed, and text Eric and Jeff: **Home again.**

When I woke, dawn was breaking. I'd slept for sixteen hours. My head still pounded, and my mouth felt dry. As I sat up, I swung my legs over the side of the bed. Had I just overdone it the last few days?

I'd been more active than I'd been since I'd gone into remission. Maybe I was tired.

How many excuses had I made when I first got sick in Paris? Too much wine? Too many tours? The shift in weather? I'd found endless excuses until Scott insisted that I see my doctor. If not for Scott, I'm not sure when I would have asked for help.

I drew in a breath and ran my hand over my spiky hair, sticking up like a bristle brush. I rose and glanced in the gilded mirror resting against the bedroom wall. The woman staring back at me had jagged hair, pale skin, and fading mascara ringing under her eyes. Normally, I would have laughed, but now a rising sense of panic silenced all traces of humor.

With effort, I swung my legs over the side of the bed and returned to the shower. I dampened my hair and rinsed my face this time.

I found sweats and a T-shirt in a bottom drawer, and it took most of my energy to get dressed. I sat on the couch and immediately dozed.

When my phone rang, it took me a second to figure out where the ringing was coming from. Once I found my phone under a pillow, I realized I'd missed a call from Jeff. I'd been napping for two hours.

I stared at the display. Jeff deserved a healthy partner. No matter what he said, he didn't understand what he could be facing if we stayed together. I called my brother.

"Hey," he said. "I heard from Jeff that DC was a lot of fun."

I rolled my head from side to side. "It was."

"What's wrong?"

"I'm not feeling great," I said. I ran through all the reasons, but then I quickly added that it could have been nothing.

"Call your doctor. I'll pick you up in fifteen minutes. He's going to see you this morning."

Hearing the concern in my brother's voice magnified the small doubts I'd been pushing aside. I wanted to believe I'd been overreacting, but his concern suggested I wasn't. "You're a bigger worrier than me."

"Guilty as charged. But I'm still taking you to the doctor."

"I probably overdid it." If I stayed positive, the world would be okay, right?

"Probably. I'll be there in fifteen minutes."

"Don't tell Mom and Dad."

"Not yet. First, the doctor."

It took effort to comb my hair, get my purse, and slip on flip-flops. Eric was pulling up when I stepped out onto the sidewalk in front of my apartment building.

I crossed to the passenger-side door, opened it, and dropped into the seat. I pulled on my seat belt but didn't have the energy to hook it. Eric took it from me and clicked it into place.

"How long have you been feeling like this?" He pulled into traffic.

"I was pretty beat yesterday, but whatever this is didn't hit me until I got home." City blocks passed as he angled toward the Beltway. "You haven't told Mom and Dad, have you?"

"No. Have you told Jeff?" When I didn't answer, he added, "I talked to him yesterday. He's fallen head over heels, Ruby."

"I warned him I'm a hard case," I said. "You need to tell him I'm too big a risk."

"He's been in love with you since your senior year of high school. He won't listen. All he sees is white picket fences and rainbows when he's around you."

"I know. And you'll help me convince Jeff I'm not the horse to bet on."

"I'm not going to do that," Eric said. "You deserve to be happy, Ruby."

"But it's not fair to Jeff."

"It's not fair to you either. Jeff is a grown man. He can make up his mind."

I'd have argued if I felt up to it. Instead, I tipped back against the headrest and let the sun warm my face. When we pulled into the parking lot of the Norfolk hospital twenty minutes later, it felt as if I'd barely closed my eyes. Eric parked the car and came around to my side. With care, he walked me toward my doctor's office. We entered the waiting room and sat down. Five minutes later, the nurse called my name.

"Ruby." Nurse Becca glanced at my chart. "What're you doing back here?"

"I'm feeling kind of rough," I said.

Becca regarded me a beat and then opened the door to an exam room. She quizzed me on my symptoms, and I gave her a recap as Eric listened, his frown growing. "Well, Dr. Mitchell will be right in to see you. Slip on a gown and sit on the table."

"I know the drill."

"I know you do," Becca said.

She closed the door, and Eric turned his back as I wrangled out of my clothes and into the gown. When I'd first gotten sick, I only wanted my mother to help me undress. But somewhere, as I was passing through Cancerland, I'd lost my modesty. So, if I required help from Eric or my dad, I took it.

The paper gown crinkled as I settled on the table. "There's nothing like a backless paper frock to make a girl feel helpless."

"I should text Jeff," Eric said.

"There's nothing to tell him yet," I said.

"That's not the point, Ruby. He'd like to be here."

"He has a big meeting this morning. Let's see what the doctor says first, and then I'll call him with facts, no worries."

"Okay. But not a second later."

The door opened to Dr. Mitchell, a man I'd grown to know very well. He was in his late fifties and had salt-and-pepper hair. I'd learned along the way that he was married with three grown children, and he loved to cycle.

"Hey, stranger," he said. "What're you doing back here?"

"Hopefully, I'm overreacting." I recited my symptoms.

"You could have done too much. We talked about you making more time in your days for rest."

"I know. And I have. Until last week."

"To be on the safe side, I'm going to run a few tests this morning."

There was no need to ask how long the tests would require. If lucky, I'd lose a day, maybe two. "Eric, you don't have to stick around. This crisis is not my first rodeo."

"No, I'm staying."

"Don't," I said. "I have my phone and plenty of notes to read over from my interviews. I'll be sitting around."

"Eric, you're welcome to stay, but we'll take good care of her," Dr. Mitchell said.

I knew this was a crazy time with him at work. "Leave," I ordered. "I can't focus on these tests if you're hovering in a corner."

"I'd be working too," he said.

"Leave. Your office is less than a mile away. If I need you, I'll call." I smiled, trying to look bright, but I suspected I looked a little crazed.

He drew in a slow breath. "I'll be back. Dr. Mitchell, when you finish your exam, call me. She isn't to leave alone."

Dr. Mitchell nodded. "Understood."

When Eric left, my smile vanished. "Dr. Mitchell, this sucks."

"I know, Ruby. We'll go as easy on you as we can."

I glanced at my naked arm and the green-blue lines of veins still marred by faint scars from IVs past. "Tell me I picked up a flu bug."

He laid his hand on my shoulder. "Tests first. Then we talk."

He left, and Becca returned. I lay back and she placed a ball in my hand. I squeezed.

"I'll be right back with vials," Becca said.

"Thanks." Classical music played over invisible speakers.

My phone rang, and I half expected to see Eric's number. But it was Robert calling. I sat up, ignoring the dull ache in my head. "Robert."

"Ruby, I'm sorry to bother you, but I have news."

"You aren't bothering me." My voice sounded soft and small.

"Jason passed away an hour ago. He wanted me to call you."

Tears welled in my eyes. I closed them, hoping in vain to keep them from spilling. "I knew he was so much sicker, but I had no idea he would go this fast."

"He didn't want you to know."

"I'm so sorry, Robert."

"I'm glad you had a chance to see him. Your visit made him smile, something he hasn't done in a long time." I'd been on the receiving end of so many kind words and well wishes. All were spoken with good intentions. None had inspired me. I wanted to say something that would let Robert know I understood his pain. But all the words rambling in my head sounded meaningless.

"Remember when Jason and I re-created the final scene of *Secrets in the Shadows*? He was Guy, and I was Françoise?" We'd performed for the ward. I'd worn a red hat with netting on my bald head, and he'd worn a fedora.

Robert chuckled. "I've seen the videos. You both pulled it off until the kiss."

"We couldn't stop laughing."

"Jason and I have played that tape a dozen times. It'll always be one of my fondest memories of him."

"Me too." I drew in a breath. "Text me the funeral information."

"I will."

"I love you both."

"Back at you."

When I hung up, Becca arrived with her needles. "You okay?"

"Jason passed."

Her expression tightened. "I'm sorry."

"Me too."

Becca was one of the best nurses I'd worked with. She was a goddess when it came to blood draws. That had never meant much to me until I became a human pincushion. I'd developed a knack for spotting the techs and nurses who knew their way around a needle.

After Becca drew my blood, she promised to return soon. Our next stop would be an MRI.

I could have predicted the testing lineup, which always followed a similar pattern. After three hours, I was back in this room, glancing at the clock. It had been several hours since Eric had left.

The last few days had given me a taste of living life again, and I found this current limbo irritating. I didn't want to be here. I didn't want to deal with this again. Once was enough in a lifetime.

But as Jason had once said, bad luck didn't come in threes. It came as often as it damn well wanted to. When the door opened, I expected to see Eric with a milkshake, my favorite after-treatment treat.

Instead, Jeff entered the room, looking harried and worried. He wore the Star Trek T-shirt he'd bought at Comic-Con about fifteen years ago, faded jeans, and flip-flops. This was the Jeff I knew and loved.

I sat straighter, aware I wasn't wearing makeup and that my hair was now half-flattened and half-spiked. "Hey."

He crossed the room and kissed me. "What's the deal? Did you start the party without me?"

"Eric called you."

"A few hours ago. I was on I-64 and stuck in traffic or would have been here sooner."

Worry etched lines on his smooth face. "I told Eric not to call until the test results were back. This is a party no one wants to attend." Having him here eased my anxiety and made me feel less alone and scared.

"I'd be mad if he hadn't called." Jeff looked exasperated. "I told you I was in it for the duration."

I clasped his hand in mine. "Jeff, I love you for caring, but places like this will be a part of my life forever. That's why I'm going to find you someone else."

Before he could answer, Dr. Mitchell entered the room, my file in hand.

CHAPTER THIRTY-SIX
SYLVIA

Tuesday, July 7, 1942
11:00 p.m.

I closed the door to Monsieur Archambeau's dining room, searching for the maid. She was nowhere to be seen, so Cécile and I left.

Everything looked different now as Cécile and I hurried into the night. The shadows were deeper, the sounds of footsteps sharper, and the air thicker with humidity.

It was tempting to return to Cécile's apartment and pack a travel case. But we could never return to the apartment. If the police were ready to arrest us, they'd be watching the apartment. I'd helped people hide all over the city but couldn't think of a place for us to go. It was one thing to conceal a faceless immigrant, another to hide a movie star. Many people would be willing to turn us in to win the favor of the Germans.

"We need to become simple Parisiennes struggling to navigate an occupied city," I said. "It's too late for the Métro."

"When is curfew?"

She'd never had to worry about it. "We are almost out past it." Even if the Métro lines had been running, the cars would be crowded, and someone would notice Cécile.

Cécile locked arms with me. "If I'm recognized, I want you to run. You have a better chance of escape alone."

"We're stronger together." My thoughts skipped to methods of travel. "Marc keeps two bicycles locked in the kitchen. We can ride the bikes out of the city to a train station south of Paris."

"Returning to the boulangerie is a risk."

"It's more dangerous if we stay on the streets."

We avoided the Métro and walked toward the Seine and moved east until we crossed at the Pont de Sully to the Right Bank. From there, we walked north down shadowed side streets in the direction of the boulangerie, in the Marais.

Several times, we heard men talking, and Cécile tensed as if tempted to run, but I cautioned her to remain steady and stick to the shadows. Quick actions, I warned, were more likely to catch attention.

"At this time of night, French police and German soldiers patrol often," I said. "If they stop us, keep your gaze down and hand them your papers."

"My identification papers will betray me."

I unzipped a small pocket and removed a set of papers. "Use these."

She looked at the documents with her image. "How?"

"Marc is clever and one of the best forgers. He knew this moment might come."

"I should have been nicer to him."

"He's taken many risks for people in need."

"He's also made a great deal of money creating forgeries."

Ahead, I saw three German soldiers standing on the corner. As I did with the refugees, I willed myself to relax. "Being seen on the street this late is noticed. We could either receive a reprimand or be arrested. It depends on the whims of the man stopping us."

Cécile squared her shoulders. "I'm clever with men."

"Not too clever. We don't want you recognized." As we approached the Rue Michel-Ange, the German soldiers approached us, each sporting a long rifle.

Cécile offered the soldiers an innocent, even lost smile. She was the Adèle from her last romantic comedy. "Good evening."

"You are out past curfew," one soldier said.

Cécile offered a meek smile. "We're lost."

"How can you be lost?" the soldier asked.

She giggled as she reached into her purse for her papers. The documents slipped from her fingers and fluttered to the ground. As she knelt to pick them up, she arched her back, driving her breasts upward. "I don't know. I get confused. Are we on the Rue du Temple?"

The man watched her brush a curl from her forehead and then glanced again at the worn pages. "Mademoiselle Dupont?"

She smiled. "Yes."

"And who is this with you?"

I stepped forward with my documents. The soldier took them from me, but I didn't hold his interest like Cécile had.

"It isn't safe for you to be out," he warned.

Cécile edged closer to him. "Forgive us. We should be only blocks from my mother's apartment."

"There's been Resistance activity on the streets," he said.

Cécile looked distressed. "We noticed a collection of men near the river under the Pont de Sully."

"What were they doing?" he demanded.

"They were standing around," I said. "Each had suitcases."

The soldier's expression grew grave. "Get going now."

"Thank you," Cécile said. "You're very generous."

As we hurried south toward the river, the wails of a woman echoed. She was pleading, calling for help. Her cries tunneled down a side alley before they ended in silence. Air charged with an edginess pressed against my chest. So far, no new extensive roundups had taken place. It was impossible to know when or if they'd happen.

We moved fast. Neither of us asked how we'd get into the boulangerie or what we'd do if there were no bikes. We tucked our heads and kept walking.

When we rounded the corner onto the Rue du Temple, the boulangerie came into view. The building was dark and quiet. My heart rattled, and Cécile's face was flushed and sweaty as we moved closer to the front display window. A **Closed** sign hung from the door.

Before the Germans invaded, I was here often in the evenings collecting identity papers. I'd knock four times on the alley door. Marc would appear, clothes dusted with flour and fingers stained with ink.

Over the years, I grew bolder, visiting the boulangerie in the middle of the day. Before the Germans, the streets were filled with people moving through their lives. The Marais had been vibrant and full of life. Now it was silent and sullen.

As we slid down the alley that smelled of garbage and urine, a trash can crashed over, and a cat screeched. We both flinched and froze. Neither of us dared to inhale until it had grown quiet again.

We continued down the alley to an iron gate, which I pushed open. The boulangerie's alley door was wide enough for delivery carts, at least when the flour mills still had grain to grind.

I knocked four times. No one responded. I grasped the door handle, pushed it down, and discovered it was locked.

Cécile stepped back, rested her hands on her hips, and stared at the building. "I don't remember this place being so dismal," she said more to herself. "When Emile and I arrived in Paris, I was so excited to be here. The Marais and the boulangerie were our new home and the first step to putting us on a new path."

"It hasn't changed much over the years."

"You're right. It's me that's changed."

I searched the alley, spotted a square carved stone, and lifted it. The door lock was old, and I guessed I had two or three strikes to break it before someone would call out from one of the windows or summon the police.

From the main street, I heard the deep rumble of men speaking German. The scent of cigarette smoke drifted down the alley. Cécile moved to stand in front of me as if she could block their view. I gripped the rock and listened, hoping the sound of their voices would fade. One soldier paused to light a cigarette, and the smoke snaked down the alley toward us.

Finally, the soldiers moved along, leaving us alone in the dark silence. I drew in a breath. Traveling by bicycle at night was a risk, but staying here was far more dangerous. We'd have to find a darkened alley nearby and hide until the curfew lifted in the morning.

I struck the lock hard, the impact radiating through my clenched fingers. Hesitating, we both listened for a nosy neighbor or a passing soldier. No one appeared and the silence held.

"Again," Cécile whispered.

I hit the lock with greater force, and this time, the handle gave way and dropped, swinging back and forth as if dangling from a hangman's noose. I pushed on the door, and it opened.

"No locks or chains on the inside?" Cécile said.

"He's always cautious when he's here." Boulangeries were becoming targets for hungry thieves willing to eat flour scraps off the floor.

I didn't dare switch on a light, but it was impossible to get my bearings in the darkness. I tripped over a wooden bowl on the floor, and as I moved deeper into the kitchen, I realized it had been ransacked.

"They searched the boulangerie too," I said. I thought about Marc's small printing presses and inks hidden in the secret little room. Had the police confiscated them? Had Marc escaped, or was he in prison?

Cécile stared into the shadows, and as her eyes, like mine, adjusted to the diminished light, we saw every bowl, spoon, plate, and knife littering the floor.

"I wonder if they returned to Emile's apartment?" Cécile asked. "What if they found her hiding spot?"

"It's too late to worry about that," I said. "We are going to be arrested in the morning. Why they torture us doesn't matter."

Broken pottery crunched under Cécile's feet as she walked through the debris. "Dead is dead."

"Do you see the bikes?" I looked back and saw the spokes of a wheel hidden under an overturned table. "Help me right this table."

We each grabbed an end and, with some effort, lifted the old wooden workbench. Under it were the two bikes. I righted the first and realized only a few spokes were broken. It was rideable. The second had a bent wheel, which would slow the tire rotation, but it would work.

"We must leave now," I said.

She took the first bike, and we wheeled it out the back door. As I took my first steps, a car's headlights shone down the alley, blinding me. The few vehicles on the streets now belonged only to the police and Germans.

The alley deadened into a brick wall, so running wasn't an option. And no matter how fast we pedaled, outrunning a bullet was impossible.

"Keep calm," I whispered.

I pushed my bike toward the car. When the driver's side door opened, I recognized the captain's stern face. He had driven me here countless times. And it was natural for him to look for me here. Word of Monsieur Archambeau's death must have reached the Germans.

"Hauptmann Wolfgang," I said.

The shadows sharpened the angles on his face. "They're looking for you both."

"I know."

He looked past me to Cécile. Seeing her so plainly dressed appeared to take him by surprise. "Leave the bikes."

"We need to get out of the city," I said.

"You won't make it far with those. All the roads leading out of Paris are blocked."

Cécile moved forward and stood shoulder to shoulder with me. "We can try."

The muscles in his jaw pulsed. "Get in. Now."

The car blocked the entrance to the alley, trapping us. The captain and I had shared tender and explosive moments in bed. But I couldn't say what he thought about me now.

"Where are you taking us?" I asked.

"Do you not trust me?" he challenged.

"I don't know who to trust anymore," I said.

"I'll drive you both out of the city. Orléans, I think. There you can catch a train."

I moved close to him, but he grew rigid as I approached. He'd said his commander had ordered him to the Eastern Front. Was he willing to turn us in to the authorities to earn himself a reprieve from the battleground? Either way, we had no choice but to get into the car.

"Do you have travel passes?" he asked.

"Yes," I said.

"With your name?"

"Different names."

The captain frowned as he opened the back door. We slid into the car. There were no handles on the inside of each door. They could only be opened from the outside.

The captain said nothing as he backed the car out of the alley and pulled onto the street. As we moved toward the city's southern outskirts, we approached a roadblock.

He glanced in the rearview mirror. "Have your papers ready," he said. "With luck, they won't recognize Cécile."

When he slowed, he rolled down his window and showed one of the soldiers his identification. He spoke quickly and calmly, and when the man looked in the back seat, Hauptmann Wolfgang joked that he was taking us to a party in a villa outside of town.

The soldier knocked on Cécile's window, and she rolled it down as she dipped her head and dug worn papers from her purse. Everyone in France knew Cécile, but darkness, combined with her new name and plain clothes, made her invisible at first glance. He glanced at the documents, looked at our faces, and then handed them back.

The two joked about the captain's ability to satisfy two Frenchwomen. He grinned, promising he was up for the challenge. "Would you be willing to share?" one of the men asked.

"On the return trip," the captain said. "I won't be long."

All the men laughed and then waved us onward. The soldiers on duty were young and naive, and if we'd crossed more experienced Gestapo, we wouldn't have been so lucky.

We traveled in silence for the next hour until the captain broke it with "The Gestapo have issued arrest warrants for you both. I only know because they questioned me."

"Did they mention Emile?" Cécile asked.

"She's been taken to Fresnes Prison. The Gestapo is interrogating her."

Cécile's expression was stoic, and I couldn't name her mood. But I sensed violence and vengeful thoughts crowding out fear.

"They've had her at least twenty-four hours," Cécile said. "Is there someone we could bribe to get her out?"

"No one would risk a bribe now," he said. "They have no reason to kill Emile right now. They're very good at keeping people alive when necessary. If she survives questioning, she'll be transported to Ravensbrück."

We'd all heard about Ravensbrück, a camp located north of Berlin that housed female political prisoners. Emile wasn't Jewish, so she would not be executed on sight. If she survived interrogation, the camp would offer starvation, beatings, and backbreaking work. Most who were transported there died.

"What can I do for her?" Cécile said.

"Nothing," the captain said.

"Do you have any contacts in the camp?" Cécile asked.

"No," he said. "I find that kind of work distasteful."

Cécile sat back and gave no sign of upset as he angled the car around the curve in the road. "The police are corrupt. It's a matter of finding one willing to take a payoff."

"And if you contact the wrong man, you'll be in prison by sunrise." He was so practical. "Emile pushed too hard. And you shattered any chance of getting her out when you killed the director."

Neither of us denied the statement.

"Are there going to be roundups?" I asked.

"Yes," he said. "In a matter of days, weeks at most."

"The Jews," I asked.

"Yes."

The captain said nothing as we continued to drive. When we arrived in Orléans, it was well past 2:00 a.m. He parked in front of the train station. It was quiet. The curfew had chased everyone into hiding. At 5:00 a.m., it would fill with passengers.

"You have money for tickets?" he asked.

"We do," I said.

He opened the back door on Cécile's side and let her out. "Go on then, get out. Find a place to hide." He watched as I slid toward him and rose out of the car.

He blocked my exit. His gloved fingers captured the locket. He turned it over, exposing the star. He wasn't surprised. "The first time you dozed in my arms, I turned the charm over because I wanted to know more about you."

He'd known this for months but had never exposed me. "Why didn't you tell me?"

His hands slid to my waist. "Get out of France. You're not safe here anymore."

His gentle touch belied the tension straining his features. I leaned forward, resting my forehead against his chest. "Thank you."

I broke contact and hurried toward Cécile. Neither of us looked back as we rushed toward the shadows.

CHAPTER THIRTY-SEVEN
SYLVIA

Wednesday, July 8, 1942
5:00 a.m.

We stood at the closed ticket office for two hours before it opened. Being exposed was risky, but we were confident the ticket demand would soon outstrip what was available. If anyone was heeding warnings of a roundup, they'd be trying to flee.

German soldiers were patrolling the platforms, but they stifled yawns and moved slowly at this early hour. I wasn't fooled. As sluggish as they might appear, they could spring into action.

By the time the ticket master opened his window, several people had lined up behind us. Cécile was the first of us to push her identification papers toward the clerk. He glanced at the name, seeming to scrutinize it more than he would the others, and then studied her face. She arched a questioning brow as he stared. Finally, he sold her a ticket, and she stepped aside, not bothering a glance in my direction.

I slipped my new identity papers through the slot. Though they looked worn and had all the right stamps, using new papers always came with a risk. The clerk took more time with me, flipping back and forth between the pages, inspecting stamps and seals.

When I purchased my identity in 1938 and became Sylvia Rousseau, I paid Marc his premium price, knowing a simple mistake could cost me my life. Afterward, I'd returned to my flat, set a fire in my small cast-iron stove, and burned all traces of the young, proud Polish girl who'd left her past and father behind forever. To have kept those papers was too great a risk. Keeping the locket marked with the Star of David had also been foolish, and my nostalgia could have cost me my life.

"Lili Allard," the clerk asked. "Where are you from?"

I'd read the papers while we were waiting for daylight and had memorized all the details. "Alsace."

"Why are you traveling south?"

"To visit a fabric supplier," I said. "I'm a seamstress."

"Do you have special permission?"

I handed him a generic travel permit issued by Henri Archambeau. It allowed me to move about the cities and regions when securing fabrics for movie set costumes. Like Cécile, I tried to look annoyed and somewhat offended. The clerk turned from the window and disappeared into a back room. My stomach tightened, but I resisted the urge to shift or fidget. The world around me shrank to this narrow space my body occupied.

When the ticket clerk returned, he handed back my permits and identification without a word. He asked my destination, and I announced "Marseille" as I tucked my credentials into my purse. Once I had the price, I paid him.

Gripping the ticket in my gloved hand, I walked through the train station toward my track. Cécile and I waited for the train for the next hour. We pretended not to know each other as the platform started to fill. When the crowds grew thick, I moved toward the edge of the platform. Even a ticket didn't guarantee a spot when the train was overcrowded.

Finally, the old train engine chugged into the station, black smoke belching from its stack. When it stopped, I stepped through the open doors and found a seat in the back by a window. Seconds later, Cécile sat beside me. Across from us was a young couple with their sleeping infant outfitted in pink cotton and wrapped in a blanket. The man and woman were nicely dressed and looked like they could have come from Paris.

There'd been a time in Poland when I would've wished them a good morning. But since arriving in Paris, I did what I did best. I remained invisible. The goal was to reach Marseille.

More German guards walked along the platform. They stopped random people and demanded identification. I was unsure if they were looking for us or intimidating travelers just because they could. Several guards boarded the train and walked down the aisles. They said nothing but held their machine guns close to their chests.

The mother across from me dropped her gaze to the baby, who slept soundly. She fussed with the infant's crocheted pink jumper and cap as if its position were far more critical than the presence of the guards. The soldier paused by our seats and looked at us.

Of the four of us, Cécile was the only one to look up and offered a demure, standard "orphaned character" smile. It was timid but sultry, and men loved it. The guard nodded toward her as he passed.

After the soldiers had departed the train and the doors closed, I allowed the breath trapped in my chest to release. The woman across from me seemed to relax, too, whereas the man who traveled with her remained stiff and sullen.

More black smoke belched from the engine's stack, the wheels scraped against the tracks, and the train rolled down the rails. We made our way out of Orléans and across the Loire River.

The steady rocking of the train was relaxing and seductive, and soon, I was lulled into sleep. I'd been on the run and hiding for over seven years, and the adrenaline that had fueled me for so long wanted to wane. How long could I keep running and hiding? I couldn't afford to lower my guard now but keeping my eyes open was too tricky.

As my eyes closed, the woman sitting across from me jostled me awake. I blinked away fatigue and sat up, glancing out the window. We were approaching a train station, but I'd lost any frame of reference and didn't know where we were.

Cécile's eyes were closed, her gloved fingers knit over her flat belly. I sensed she wasn't asleep but was paying close attention. The man who'd been across from us was gone.

The woman settled her gaze on mine with an uneasy intensity. "Pardon," she said.

"Yes?"

"Could you hold the baby for a moment? I need to visit the toilet by the platform."

"I've never held a baby."

"She's an easy child. Very sweet." The woman's voice carried hints of desperation.

Before I could offer another excuse, she was laying the child in my arms. "She's been fed and has a clean diaper."

The baby nestled in my arms. "What's her name?"

"Michele." The woman rose and smoothed her skirt flat. She left behind the baby's bag and her suitcase, squaring her shoulders. She never once looked back as she exited the train along with other departing passengers.

Cécile opened her eyes. We both stared out the window toward the platform, where German soldiers had gathered. The woman walked past them, but they demanded she return and show them her papers. She opened her purse, pretending to search. The train engines hissed, a sign we were leaving. The woman didn't appear rushed as she continued to dig in her bag. The train whistle blew.

"What's she doing?" Cécile asked.

The woman's hand emerged from the purse, holding her papers for the guard. His frown deepened, and he summoned more guards. Her expression tight with panic, the woman took a step back and reached again in her purse. This time, she held a revolver and, without hesitating, fired at the guards. Her shots caught one soldier in the shoulder but missed the other one. The crowds scattered. Women screamed. The woman turned and ran down the platform, racing through the parting crowds.

The engine hissed and the wheels ground forward as the train pulled out of the station. Unmindful, the woman evaded a man's grasp as a soldier aimed his handgun at her. He fired once. The bullet struck her in the back, dropping her to her knees at the train station entrance.

The gunfire triggered more screams and chaos as the train picked up speed. The man who'd been sitting with the baby's mother appeared, cuffed and surrounded by guards.

I held the baby tighter, my body stunned into silence. Neither of us spoke for several minutes as we sat still, waiting for the train to stop and the guards to board again. A woman sitting to our left stared at the child and then me. She'd seen the exchange.

"She knew," I said.

"'Knew'?"

"When the guards first came on the train, she wouldn't look at them," I whispered. "She knew they were looking for her and the man."

"That's why she left the baby behind."

The war had forced so many terrible decisions like this. "What a choice."

"There is an orphanage in Marseille," Cécile said. "We can deliver the child to them."

I glanced at the baby's small pink face, reached for her bag, and searched. There were diapers and bottles ready to be filled, but nothing that identified the woman or the child.

"If the child had papers, her mother had them."

"She appears very young, a few weeks old. The mother might not have secured papers yet."

"The man traveling with them. Is he the father?"

"The Germans have him now. But he seemed to give the woman and child no notice."

Cécile sighed. "Daniel will help us find the orphanage."

"What does he know about orphanages?" I asked.

"Daniel is well connected."

"Can you trust him?"

"He would die for me. He and I were lovers once. He wanted to marry me." Cécile stared at the passing landscape.

"How do you know he's still alive?"

"I can hope," she said.

"And he won't be angry with you?" Negotiating with ex-lovers could be treacherous. I thought about the captain. He'd been duty bound to call the authorities, but he had helped us instead.

She raised her chin a fraction. "Daniel will not be angry."

Neither of us spoke as the train rumbled on. The baby woke as we pulled into the Marseille train station. I had no idea how to care for a child, but when we departed the train, Cécile strode toward a small area where several local women had gathered. She spoke to them briefly and then vanished for twenty minutes. I jostled the child, shifting her in my arms as we struggled to find a comfortable arrangement. As the minutes passed, I began to worry about Cécile. How long before the Germans arrested her?

When Cécile returned, she had several diapers and fresh milk. "Cartier would be appalled at what his gems are selling for these days."

She took the fussing baby from me and moved us to a bench under a shaded tree. She changed the infant with unexpected ease as she explained how to fasten the pins.

"You're full of surprises," I said.

"When I was thirteen, I worked as a helpmate to a woman in town with five children. I didn't enjoy the experience, but the work and a few stolen kisses with the father earned me some of the money that got me to Paris. One does what one must."

She filled the bottle and, after securing the top, nudged the nipple into the baby's mouth.

The baby fussed louder even as she rocked her from side to side. "I think she prefers you."

"How could she?"

Cécile settled the child in my arms. She placed the bottle in my hand and guided it toward her mouth. Without hesitation, the baby suckled. "People trust you. There's something about you."

My eyes locked on the child as she suckled.

"Keep the end tipped up so she doesn't get too much air in her stomach. That will make her cranky."

The baby drank greedily.

Cécile stretched out her legs and tipped her face toward the warming sun. "I've forgotten how clear the air is here. Already, I feel cleaner."

Under this beautiful sky, I couldn't picture the woman who wore silks, furs, and diamonds dancing with German officers.

Her gaze roamed the station and the mountains beyond. "When I was sixteen, I couldn't wait to leave and do something real with my life."

"You did. You owned Paris."

She sank into a silence and then said, "And then I lost it all, including my sister."

"Will they look for you here?"

"I don't know. I've never discussed my life in the south with anyone other than Monsieur Archambeau. He erased my humble past as he built me up as a movie star."

"You're safe for now."

Cécile's brow furrowed. We both knew that very few people could withstand intense German questioning. "I won't be at peace until I find Emile."

"She could already be dead."

Her face hardened. "The Germans won't be in a rush to kill her. They want to squeeze her dry. But my sister is stronger and more stubborn than me."

"She'll be transported to Germany if she's still alive."

"I'll find her."

The baby made a soft mewing sound as she suckled. The child appeared willful, and her cheeks were smooth and rosy. "Why was the mother running from the guards?"

Cécile reached for the diaper bag. With no one watching us now, she had more time to search. She removed spare cloths and a blanket. As she ran her hands along the bottom of the bag, she tugged at the lining until it separated. Inside was a petite pocket. She removed a black-and-white picture of the woman, pregnant, standing by the man who'd been on the train. On the back were the names Ruth and Antoine.

I looked at the picture and saw the Soviet flag behind the couple. "She was a communist. She had to be Resistance."

Cécile regarded the image and then tucked the picture back in its hiding place. "Take care no one sees this. We must get the child to the orphanage."

I'd lost my mother, but I'd had her for fifteen years. My father had sent away his only child to save me. I knew they'd loved me. I knew they'd sacrificed for me. This child would never know what her parents had done for her.

Cécile opened her purse and held out her identity papers. "We need to swap. Your papers are excellent forgeries, but they almost didn't stand up to the scrutiny of a local train clerk."

"I cannot take your papers."

"If you take them and leave the country, the world will soon believe that Dominique Dupont has left France. Perhaps they'll stop searching for me then."

"What will you do?"

"I'll become Marc's Adèle," she said. "And you'll become Dominique. With Daniel's help, you'll leave France, and I'll return to Paris and find Emile."

"You can't go back to Paris."

"I'll change my hair and demeanor. Becoming someone else is what I do best. And thanks to your jacket, I have enough money tucked in my pockets to buy my way into any prison."

The baby continued to nurse, and when she finished, Cécile showed me how to lay the child over my shoulder and pat her until she burped.

"We'll buy one more milk to get you to the orphanage."

"Will they protect her?" I asked.

"It's not an ideal life, but she won't starve."

The chaos would swallow this child up. What kind of life would that be for her? "I'll take her with me. Perhaps another orphanage in a different country."

"They are all much the same." Cécile regarded me. "And the journey will be much harder with a child."

"I know."

"Do you?"

"Does anyone know what's waiting for us?"

She sighed as if there was no need to argue. "On board the ship, you must rely on canned milk."

"And if there is none?"

"Daniel will help you figure it out."

I had no idea how to escape this country, let alone care for a child, but that's what I had to do.

A train whistle blew in the distance. "Let's get that milk and get you to the port. The baby might be of help. If the police are looking for us, they're searching for two women traveling together and not a single woman with an infant. The Germans seem to enjoy babies, and she's charming. Use that to your advantage."

"And you just walk away alone?"

"I won't be alone for long. I'll find Emile."

As we stood, she brushed the leaves from my skirt. "You have been a true friend, Sylvia."

"Zofia." I hadn't spoken my real name in so long, and it sounded awkward, as if it no longer fit me.

"What a lovely name. And now you're Dominique." She smiled as she smoothed her hand over the baby's head. She reached into her pocket and removed a packet of letters. "I wrote these to Daniel but never mailed them. Show them to him. He'll believe your story. He will also know I thought about him often."

I took the letters. Wrapped in a purple bow, they smelled of lavender. "Thank you."

"We won't hug or make a fuss. That might draw attention. The port is only a few blocks from here. Walk toward the water. Daniel works for the North Star shipping line, if he's still alive. He'll find you passage. Leave this country behind."

"I'll never forget you."

CHAPTER THIRTY-EIGHT
RUBY

Wednesday, July 9, 2025
2:00 p.m.

When the door opened to Dr. Mitchell, all thoughts fell out of my head. Jeff set down his phone, and I sat a little straighter. Jeff stood, extended his hand to the doctor, and introduced himself. I assured the doctor he could discuss my medical records with him. I had no idea what was about to land in my lap, but Jeff needed a strong taste of what life with me would be like.

"The MRI and bloodwork are negative, Ruby," Dr. Mitchell said.

I'd braced for disaster, and when it didn't hit, I still couldn't relax. "Are you sure?"

"No cancer has returned. I'd still like to see you back in three months so we can retest, but as of today, you are in the clear."

His assurances didn't quiet my worries. "Why do I feel so awful?" I asked.

"You have been busier than usual?" he asked.

I glanced at Jeff. He shrugged as if he wasn't going to narc on my adventures in Alexandria. "I've been working on an article. Burning the midnight oil."

"It's a great article," Jeff said.

"You've been going nonstop for how many days?" Dr. Mitchell asked.

"At least a week," I said.

"Dehydrated, rich foods, no yoga, not enough sleep?"

"That sounds about right," I said.

The doctor smiled. "That can make anyone sick. I'm glad you're living your life, Ruby. It's good to see. But like I told you before you left the hospital last year, less is more. You can do a lot but can't do it all at once."

Relief rushed over me with a ferocity I'd never felt. Tears burned in my throat. "Got it. Won't happen again."

"If it does," Dr. Mitchell said, "it's not the end of the world."

"Sure felt like it this morning," I said.

Jeff took my hand. "I'll take some of the blame for the extra nights out."

"I'm glad she wasn't overdoing it alone," the doctor joked. "But slow and steady is better if you're with her."

"Understood," Jeff said.

The doctor chuckled. "Ruby, get dressed. I'll see you in three months."

"Perfect. Thank you."

When the door closed behind him, tears trailed down my cheeks. I swiped them away and found a crooked smile. "Sorry for the false alarm."

"Next time, call me first," Jeff said. "I don't want you doing this alone. Eric is great, but if you and I are going to have a real thing, we need to share the good and the bad."

"Jeff. This visit today was tame compared to what it has been. And I could very well end up here again. Better we stick to the plan and let me find you the next Mrs. Jeff."

"I don't want another Mrs. Jeff. I like the one sitting right here."

Tears welled in my eyes. "Jason died this morning."

He drew in a deep breath. "I know you hate hearing 'sorry,' but I'm sorry. I know Jason was a good friend."

"It would break my heart if I got sick again and all the drama drove you away."

"Robert was at Jason's side, wasn't he?"

"Yes."

"I'm a Robert, not a Scott. I'm in it for good."

I took his face in mine and kissed him on the lips. "I'm not being fair, but I love you so much."

He stilled. "Love as in love or LOVE?"

"LOVE," I said.

He kissed me back. "When did you fall for me?"

I swiped away a tear. "When you hired the marching band to play outside my hospital room."

He grinned. "That was a good move, wasn't it?"

"You were the talk of the ward for weeks."

"Go big or go home." He pulled me into a hug. "We're going to be fine. You need to stop worrying."

A nurse came into the room and unhooked my IV, and I slid out of the bed. Jeff handed me my clothes. For a moment, I hesitated to strip in front of him and then laughed at my modesty. I dropped the gown and dressed in my sweats and T-shirt. A glance in the mirror was enough to make me grimace.

"I wish I'd picked something cuter."

"Given the circumstances, give yourself a break."

I shrugged. "Cécile did escape Paris in Sylvia's old clothes."

"See. Even Cécile didn't dress up. Time and a place, Ruby. Balance."

"We need to tell Eric," I said.

"He's already texted me eight times. I've responded to all, and he's been updated."

"Good. I need to remind my brother not to tell Mom and Dad."

"That cat might be out of the bag."

The nurse arrived with a wheelchair and forms for me to sign. Once the hospital had discharged me, the nurse wheeled me out toward the elevator, where Jeff took over. He took me to the lobby, and then we headed out to the circular parking area.

"They aren't flying home, are they?"

"No, but it would be good to call them."

"I'll do that now."

"I'll get the car."

Mom answered on the first ring, and I spent five minutes assuring her I was okay and that I wouldn't overdo it again. She asked how Jeff was doing, and I wondered aloud if this family had any secrets. There were none, she said. After several "I love yous," the call ended as Jeff pulled up.

I rose out of the wheelchair and settled into the front seat. As Jeff pulled away, I asked, "Did you find out what happened to Louis?"

He chuckled. "So much for taking it easy."

"I'm just talking here. Nothing fancy."

"He had an unpublished memoir auctioned about a decade ago."

"How did you find that?"

"A friend of a friend. I've only had a chance to skim it, but he's very open about his life and choices. He ended up moving to the South of France, where he obtained work as a hotel manager in Nice. He died in a car accident in 1980. His memoir mentions an actress who saved him during the occupation."

"Does he name Cécile?"

"No, but in 1980, the world might not have been ready for that news. The war was still an open wound for many."

"Did he say what happened to her?" I asked.

"He suggests the actress retired to a quiet life in southern France. She could have returned to the farm near Avignon."

"It would have been a natural place to vanish."

As far as the world knew, Cécile had collaborated with the Germans and lived better than most during the occupation. No one knew that she'd passed German military secrets on to the Allies.

Cécile had noted to Sylvia that her decisions in Paris, no matter how noble, would have had repercussions from those who didn't understand her entire story. "I hope home was as welcoming as she hoped."

CHAPTER THIRTY-NINE
SYLVIA

Marseille, France
Wednesday, July 8, 1942

In the end, Monsieur Archambeau's death and an abandoned baby saved me.

Finding the port of Marseille proved more complicated. When I took a wrong turn, I stopped to speak to a shopkeeper. He scowled when he looked me over. Even in old clothes, I didn't look like a local and presented as a Parisienne. I'd spent so many years hiding in Paris that discarding the old persona wasn't as easy as I'd thought.

Seeing the baby cradled in my arms softened the older man's expression. Even after he'd given me directions to the port, I couldn't visualize the way. Frustrated, he walked me several blocks and told me to continue west along the Rue Saint-Pierre. When the road ended, I would smell the Mediterranean Sea and hear the gulls squawk.

It was past three in the afternoon, but the day's heat lingered. When the baby noticed the heat and began to cry, I found a small side street and stripped off her sweater, which I tucked in her bag. I took one of her blankets, ripped it, and tied the ends together, creating a sling. She fit nicely inside and seemed grateful for the change. I removed my hat and tied a scarf around my head.

I walked along the crowded streets past police and German soldiers. Marseille was a city of immigrants, and I looked like a thousand other mothers looking for food or work.

When I reached the end of the road, the old farmer had been correct. The air turned briny, and I saw the blue waters in the distance.

We arrived at the port ten minutes later. Entering the port was another matter, however. I walked up to the dockmaster's place by the main gate. I told the man, with as much arrogance as Cécile would have mustered, that I was Dominique Dupont and wanted to speak to Daniel LeClaire.

The little man behind the gate told me to wait, and I found a shaded spot under an awning. I waited at least an hour, and in that time I discovered that when I sat, the child cried, but when I stood, she fell back to sleep.

A tall, thin man limped toward me. He wore dark pants, a white shirt rolled past his elbows, and scuffed shoes. His face was expectant, but when he saw me, that hope vanished.

"You aren't Dominique," he said. "Is this a trick?" He braced as if ready for trouble.

I adjusted the baby's pouch. "I'm Sylvia Rousseau," I said. "I was Dominique's dressmaker in Paris."

The man didn't look convinced. And I didn't blame him. The Germans were clever. And as far as I knew, he could have been a spy sent to trap Cécile and me. "She hired me in 1940. I was a friend of Emile's."

"Her cousin?"

He was testing me. "Sister."

His reserve didn't soften. "Where is Emile?"

"She was arrested in Paris on Monday. She was trying to warn families of a coming roundup."

"I've heard of no major roundups in Paris."

I could have explained that Hauptmann Wolfgang also knew of the roundups. But my association with the captain would not help my cause. "She believed they were coming soon."

Frustration etched his face. If he'd known Emile, he'd also understand her desire to fight. "And Dominique?"

I'd never met Daniel and didn't know this man. "We parted ways. She's returning to find her sister."

He drew in a breath and stared out over the bustling port. "Whose child is this?"

"I don't know. The mother abandoned her on our train. The Germans killed her." Remembering the letters, I fished them out of my pocket. "Dominique said to give you these."

He accepted the packet and studied the handwriting. A deep sigh filled his chest. Slowly, he exhaled and handed the letters back to me. He beckoned me through the gates and along the water until we reached a salt-weathered building. Inside, he took me to a small office filled with piles of papers, schedules, and sea logs.

Cécile had trusted Daniel, but it had been four years since they'd seen each other. The world had changed so much, and priorities shifted. "She said you could help us get passage out of the country."

A slight shrug lifted his shoulder. "Why should I do a favor for a woman who abandoned me years ago?"

"She said you had great honor. She still loves you. Read the letters. She said that they show she thought about you often." The baby shifted in my arms and mewed.

His frown deepened. "What are you going to do with the child?"

"Keep her."

"There is an orphanage in the city."

"No."

A brow arched, and he leaned closer and inspected the child. "She's barely weeks old."

"Yes." I eyed him, suddenly unsure.

"I don't know if I can help you."

Cécile had been so sure of her Daniel. Now his hesitation stirred a fresh set of worries for me. He'd been limping, suggesting he'd lost a leg, but that wasn't solid proof. "How do I know you're *her* Daniel?"

He raised his left pant and revealed the wooden leg and the letters *DD* carved into the prosthetic. "Why are you using her papers?"

"Hers have a better chance of getting me onto an outbound ship."

Amusement danced in his eyes. "She thinks me a miracle worker. She believes I can get anyone out of Marseille so easily. If either of you hasn't noticed, the Germans control it."

"Cécile said you could get passage. She said you are very clever."

"Cécile? The famous actress? Not Dominique?"

"They're the same. You know this," I said. "You were lovers. You know she left Marseille for Paris in 1938."

He appeared impressed by the bit of information but said, "The Germans would know that. They could have stolen the letters from her."

"She's filming *Secrets in the Shadows*. It's a crime drama. Filming ended days ago."

"That's common knowledge in Paris."

"She has a mole at the base of her spine. I don't know what else to tell you."

"Why do you want to leave France?"

"It grows more dangerous by the day."

He expelled a breath. "There's a freighter leaving tonight. It's bound for Portugal. From there you can book passage to England. We must hurry if you're going to make it."

"I have no papers for the child."

"I'll ask the captain to certify she was born on board. He owes me many favors."

"Just like that?"

"Ah, that's the power that Dominique has over men."

CHAPTER FORTY
RUBY

Saturday, July 19, 2025
11:00 a.m.

Jeff and I were in my apartment living room. I sat on my couch. The keys of my laptop clicked. Jeff was beside me, his feet propped up on my coffee table as he worked on his laptop.

My article for Cécile had taken over a week of solid writing, but I was pleased with the final product, save for the ending, which wasn't an ending. I knew she hadn't traveled out of Marseille in July 1942. It had been Sylvia Rousseau, a.k.a. Zofia, born in Poland, daughter of a Jewish tailor and a French seamstress, who'd fled Poland in 1935 and spent her time in Paris delivering false identity papers to refugees and later Jews. She left carrying a baby thrust into her arms by a mother who knew the Germans were closing in on her.

What Sylvia's journal didn't reveal was Emile's and Cécile's fates. Jeff was the one who'd found Emile. He'd dug deep into digital archives and discovered that Emile had been transported to Ravensbrück in July 1942. She'd perished in the prison camp six months later.

Cécile, née Dominique, had vanished from a Marseille train station in July 1942, and there was never another record for her. She and Sylvia didn't see each other again. I wondered when Cécile discovered that her sister had been transported, where she'd gone, or what she'd done. She'd been stripped of her influence, cut off from contacts, and on the run from the police. Where did a woman like that go?

"I think I found her," Jeff said.

"Who?"

"Cécile."

"No way!" I kissed him on the lips.

"You said Daniel's family came from a farming community near Avignon."

"The LeClaire family grew olives."

He shifted closer to me, turning his screen in my direction. Displayed was the website of an olive oil farm. It had existed for 150 years and still grew and pressed olives. It also now catered to tourists who wanted to tour its facilities, buy olive oils from its shop, and eat lunch in its small café.

The farm's website featured an image of stone pillars with flowering purple jacaranda trees dripping over a graveled driveway leading into a courtyard. In the center was a stucco building with a clay roof and two sizable hunter green garage doors. The backdrop was a vivid blue sky. Off to the right was a small picnic area with red tables, white chairs, and an arched pergola with a roof made of woven branches.

"It's beautiful."

"It is. But that's not the main event."

He clicked through the website until he found a section dedicated to the farm's history. There was a black-and-white photo showing ten members of the LeClaire family. In the center was an older couple who appeared to be in their early seventies. Surrounding them were several children who shared the same dark hair and wide grins. On the right was a couple in their forties.

Jeff pointed to the couple on the right. He zoomed in to the woman's face. She had salt-and-pepper hair twisted into a bun, and she wore a neat dress that fit her slim frame. She grinned, but her head was turned down as if she didn't want the photographer to catch her entire face.

"Cécile?" I asked.

"Looks like her, doesn't it?"

I gently punched his arm. "You found Cécile?"

"If it's not her, it's a close relative."

I leaned toward the computer screen. "Dominique went home."

The caption below read *The LeClaire family*. But there was no mention of the individual names. "No names!"

"Unless you know where to dig."

I hugged my arm around him. "Do tell."

"In the center are the grandparents. To the left is a brother and his wife. The children are theirs. And to the right is the older brother, Daniel, and his wife, Dominique."

"Dominique." Relief rushed over me. "She did make it home."

"She did."

"How did no one know about what happened in Paris?"

"The war was heating up, the roundups began, and the detectives working Monsieur Archambeau's case were looking for a glamorous actress, not a farmer's wife."

The longer I stared, the more I saw traces of Cécile. Though gray streaked her dark hair, there was no missing the high cheekbones and cutting eyes.

"Dominique and Daniel were married in 1945," Jeff said. "They never had children. He died in 1980, and she died in 2012."

"Sylvia never returned to Europe," I said. "And I doubt Dominique left France again."

"They crossed paths at a critical time, and neither wished to return to that period."

"Yes."

"And the baby?" Jeff asked.

"Michele. Sylvia's daughter. Madame Bernard. I was supposed to speak with her again before I left Alexandria, but I felt so bad. I need to see her again."

"Do you think she wants the world to know this?"

"I'll call her, but I think she's ready to tell her mother's story."

"How did Sylvia meet her husband?"

"Sylvia found work as a seamstress in the city of Norfolk, in southeast England. She met an American pilot, and the two married in 1944."

"And he adopted the child?"

"I assume so. Madame said they were the most loving parents."

Jeff rose and crossed to his backpack, which he carried to the sofa. "I don't know how to do this sort of thing. I should have hired a consultant."

I laughed. "What are you talking about?"

He fished out a small black box. Slowly, he opened it. In the center was a solitary diamond. "Marry me."

I stared at the diamond's angled edges, which caught the morning light. It was the most beautiful ring. "I can't."

"Why not?"

"You know why."

"You just learned the fate of two women who took incredible chances in the face of terrible danger. Sylvia accepted an infant from a stranger and escaped Marseille and made it to England, and then the United States. The odds don't get much worse than that." He plucked the ring from the box and took my hand in his. I watched as he slid the ring on my finger. "It'll work with any outfit."

Tears welled in my eyes. "That's not playing fair."

He chuckled. "All's fair."

I drew in a breath. "For the record, I want to say yes."

"Then say it. We'll get married and honeymoon in Provence. We can visit the LeClaires' olive farm."

I kissed him on the lips. "You're sure?"

He traced my cheek with his finger. "Very."

I didn't want him to be sorry. I didn't want him to feel saddled with me. But I loved him. And if illness had taught me anything, it was to grab every moment when it presented itself. "Yes."

CHAPTER FORTY-ONE
DOMINIQUE

Avignon, France
Tuesday, October 2, 1945

The roundups in Paris began July 16, 1942. The police arrested thirteen thousand Jewish men, women, and children and packed them into the sports arena, the Vélodrome d'Hiver. After grueling days and weeks in hot, unsanitary conditions, they were transported to concentration camps and executed.

I thought about my Emile, trying to warn people. She'd given her life in vain for people who couldn't or didn't heed her warnings.

I'd sold all the gems I'd stowed in Sylvia's jacket pockets and used the money to bribe officials. After months of questions and searching, I'd learned in the fall of 1942 that my sister had been transported to the Ravensbrück concentration camp.

I never knew what the police had done to her in the local prison, but after the Germans left Paris in 1944, I returned to the city and tracked down the few survivors from Ravensbrück. I'd learned that Emile had been broken and battered but defiant when she'd arrived in the camp. Soon after, she contracted typhus, and she died six months later.

When the Allies entered Provence through Marseille in August of 1944, I decided to go home. The Germans were either dead, captured, or returned to Germany.

I'd arrived at the LeClaire family farm on foot, not expecting to see Daniel. I'd planned to rest for several days and head to Marseilles, but I found him standing at the front gate as if he'd known I was coming.

He had left the port of Marseille and returned to his family farm when the Allies landed. I wasn't sure how he'd take me, but he wrapped his arms around me and held me tight. I cried, never more grateful to be there.

Daniel told me about a woman and her baby he'd smuggled onto a freighter bound for Portugal. I knew he'd help Sylvia escape France. If only I'd been able to save Emile.

Daniel and I became lovers again, and unlike the first time we'd been together, I was content in his arms. We married one month after my return.

The departure of the Boche had unleashed the anger simmering among the French. France no longer had the occupiers to hate, so the fury turned inward.

Angry citizens hunted collaborators, and soon, there were executions and the public degradation of women who'd worked with the Germans. Images of the actresses Arletty and Cécile became the faces of Frenchwomen who'd betrayed their kind to the Nazis. Arletty was publicly humiliated and sent to prison. But Cécile had vanished.

In the last few weeks, that hatred had ignited again in Provence, and I'd heard stories of Frenchmen attacking women who'd slept with Germans. Last week, an angry mob stripped a woman to her undergarments and shaved her head.

Though I'd done my best to shed Cécile's skin and lose myself in the role of the farmer's wife, rumors stirred every few weeks that the famous actress was alive and well, living in disguise.

Daniel encouraged me to stay away from town, but after months of hiding, I became restless. Would I ever not want more?

So today, I rode my bicycle into town. It was a stunning, beautiful day, with vivid blue skies and warm, dry air. The olive harvest had been pressed and bottled, and many in the valley were optimistic that next year would be so much better. These were some of the sweetest days in Provence.

And now the cold, hard knife blade pressed against my skin. "I know you all," I said. "You know me. I'm Dominique LeClaire."

"We know you," Charles said. "We know what you did in Paris."

"You have no idea what you are talking about," I shouted.

Reasoning with drunks was always a gambler's game.

Harsh lines now angled around Charles's mouth and across his forehead. He twisted my hair in his fist as he pulled at the roots. He sneered as he raised a knife to my face. "Those Boche made my life hell. And you spread your legs for them and lived like a queen."

"Let go of me, Charles. The war is over. We should not be fighting each other."

"Easy for you to say." He pulled my hair so hard that strands pulled free from my scalp. I refused to cry out. And when I met his gaze, I spit on him.

Charles slapped me so hard across the face I dropped to the floor. He was on top of me seconds later, pinning my arms flat with his knees as he grabbed my hair and sliced off a chunk with the sharp blade. A blood fever took control of him as he held up the locks of hair like a prized hunting trophy. I kicked my feet, trying to wrestle free as other men grabbed my bare ankles and pinned me to the floor. The men cheered.

The knife scraped my scalp, and warm blood oozed through my remaining hair. I'd survived Paris, the Germans, and the police, and now I would die at the hands of my neighbors.

A shotgun blasted into the room. The sound was so loud in the small space that it echoed in my ears. The knife eased away from my scalp as Charles whirled around.

I couldn't see past him. But I sensed the shift in mood from the men as reason tamed some of their uncontrolled anger.

"Get off of her." Daniel's voice rang with a rage I'd never heard.

When none of the men moved, Daniel stuck the barrel of his shotgun to the first man's head. The man raised his hands and left the cottage. The gun trained on another intruder, and as each man left, he moved closer to Charles and me.

"We've all suffered, Charles," he said. "I know you lost brothers and a son. I'll give you this one mistake if you leave now and never touch my wife again. If you do not listen to me now, I'll splatter your brains right here."

Charles's breathing slowed as his grip on my remaining hair eased. He raised the hand with the knife, and Daniel took it. "You know what she is," he said.

"She is my wife. Get out."

With Charles's weight lifted, I drew in a deep breath and sat up. I tried to shield my hair and face from him. I'd done what I'd done over the years. Perhaps my choices were questionable, but I'd never felt shame. Now, in front of my husband, I was humiliated.

After Charles left, Daniel closed the door and locked it. As he came toward me, I rose on shaky feet and turned away from him. When I'd returned home, we'd found a way to pretend that the last few years had never happened. Now, there was no denying it. I didn't want to see the disappointment on his face.

He placed his hands on my shoulders. "Look at me."

Tears welled in my eyes and then spilled down my cheeks. "I can't. There are too many sins."

He turned me to face him, and I began to weep when I saw the compassion in his gaze. I hadn't cried even when I'd learned Emile's fate, but now all the wounds opened wide, pouring out sorrow.

Daniel held me close, enclosing me in an embrace that smelled of olives and sunshine. "There's nothing to forgive. Now is all that matters." He ran his hand over my chopped hair, which, until moments ago, had been thick and lush. "It'll grow back. We'll grow together, and life will go on."

I met his gaze. "People will always whisper about me. Always."

He wiped a tear away. "Thankfully, my hearing was never excellent."

"It can't be that simple."

He kissed me on the lips. "It can."

CHAPTER FORTY-TWO
JEFF

Alexandria, Virginia
Monday, June 6, 2033

I had become adept at braiding hair. My daughter Sylvia was now five, and her long, thick blond hair needed to be tackled daily, or it would become a tangled mess. She had Ruby's brown eyes and sense of style. But she wasn't petite like her mother. She was already in the ninety-ninth percentile for her age group and was projected to be five foot eleven inches, maybe even six feet.

Ruby and I had been married a year when we decided to hire a surrogate. Scott sued Ruby, but my attorneys then tied him up in numerous legal and very expensive knots. I was told his new wife refused to finance the suit any longer, and he was forced to drop it. My team threatened to sue him for my legal expenses unless he signed a document declaring he would never sue again. He'd signed.

The doctors had implanted several embryos. They'd fertilized all her eggs with my sperm, and for added insurance the medical team had also used one of the embryos she'd made with Scott. It didn't take a geneticist to see who had the winning ticket. But Sylvia had been my child from the moment she'd come squealing into the world. Genetics would never change that. And whenever I looked at my daughter, I only saw traces of Ruby.

Two months after Sylvia was born, Ruby's cancer returned. She'd fought hard to beat the disease the first time, and they were hopeful she'd win it again. But the journey back to health was rocky and rugged. It was a grueling five months as I watched my wife grow weak and sick from the chemo.

"Daddy, there's a bump in my braid."

I looked in the mirror and searched for the ridge. My daughter liked her hair perfect, just like Ruby.

I unknotted the braid and brushed out the locks until they were as smooth as corn silk. I pressed my hand on her crown, concentrating on lining up the tresses in a soft, even sheet. I glanced in the mirror. "Okay?"

"Braid carefully, Daddy."

"Roger that." I divided the mane into three neat rows and wound them together. In my mind, the braid was perfect. I fastened the ends with a twist. "I should work in a hair salon."

Sylvia giggled. "No, Daddy."

I admired the blended hair. "It's a perfect braid."

She inspected the wrapped band at the bottom. "It's okay."

"Okay" meant "perfect" in my world, and I'd won. "Ready to go to the park?"

She glanced in the mirror and studied her blue dress, trimmed with small yellow flowers at the waist. "Should I change?"

I chuckled, shaking my head. "You're your mother's child, Sylvia."

When the hotel room door opened, I glanced over my shoulder to see my wife. She wore a sleek black pencil skirt, gray silk blouse, and tall chunky heels. Diamond stud earrings winked. Thick black hair skimmed her shoulders.

"Mommy!" Sylvia ran toward her mother.

Ruby knelt and hugged her daughter close. "I've missed you."

I didn't point out that it had been less than an hour since they'd been together. "Daddy tried to do my braids, but he didn't get it right."

She skimmed her fingers over her daughter's hair. "They look pretty perfect to me."

"Maybe," Sylvia conceded.

I crossed to Ruby, and as she rose, I kissed her on the lips. "How was the funeral reception?"

"Very elegant. Very French. Friends packed the church's reception hall. Madame Bernard was buried next to her husband, daughter, and mother."

Ruby had stayed in contact with Madame Bernard over the years, and as my business expanded, we bought a condo in Old Town Alexandria. Whenever we were in Alexandria, Ruby and Madame Bernard had coffee at least three times a week. They'd collaborated on a book about Sylvia and Cécile, but madame had died before they'd completed it.

Ruby had been cancer-free for four years, and we never talked about illness again. We'd agreed to focus on our daughter, and now.

"We're going to the park," Sylvia said.

"Let me change, and I'll join you," Ruby said.

Sylvia arched a brow. "Don't take forever. You always take forever when you're picking out clothes."

Ruby chuckled and gently pinched her daughter's cheek. "Look who's talking."

From the moment I'd met Ruby, I'd known she was the one. And, as I often told my business partners, my first impression was always accurate.

"I'll be quick," Ruby said. "I don't want to miss a moment of this beautiful day."

CHAPTER FORTY-THREE
SYLVIA

Last entry
Friday, August 10, 1945

The baby and I arrived in England in June of 1943, after wintering in Portugal. Finding piecework in Portugal was easy, and I made enough to keep us fed and housed. I'd sold a diamond bracelet in the spring and secured passage for us to England. The crossing was harrowing, with the captain and crew keeping a sharp eye out for U-boats, which often weren't detectable until the torpedo was fired.

I'd thought when we docked in Yarmouth that we'd be safe and that we'd left the war behind. But the city had then been devastated by bombs. We continued on foot until a truck stopped and allowed us to sit in the bed. He took us as far as the town of Diss, which I'd heard was near an air base.

In Diss, I rented us a small room in a house owned by a war widow. Her name was Kathleen, and she had a one-year-old boy. She needed money from a boarder, but I think she also took pity on me. She assumed I was a widow like her. I didn't tell her otherwise because a husband lost to the battlefield softened many hearts. From Susan I learned that the

Americans would hire me for piecework. With Susan watching Michele, I set out for the base. It took me several hours to reach the airfield.

When I arrived at Thorpe Abbotts air base, it wasn't much to look at. The soldier on guard duty didn't care about my offer of work and, given my accented English, assumed I was a spy. When I realized I would have no luck that day, I was turning to leave when a jeep stopped at the gate. The driver, an American, judging by his uniform, asked me to state my business. I explained myself and my situation as a war widow. He wrote down my name and address.

Two days later, Lieutenant Ross Talbot pulled up in front of Susan's cottage. It was a lovely day, and I was watching Susan's young son and my daughter while I weeded her garden. Lieutenant Talbot asked if I could mend several of his shirts. The man had such a beautiful smile, and there was a brightness in his gaze that I liked very much.

He didn't return for another week. There'd been work delays, he'd said. I'd seen the bombers flying over the village and knew he had been on one of those planes. I gave him his mended, cleaned, and pressed shirts. I offered him tea, and we sat in the garden with the children for an hour.

His visits became as regular as they could be, and in August, he asked me to marry him, cautioning that the war was far from over for him. I could easily become a widow again. Despite the risks, it was very easy to accept his offer. We married two days later.

I decided not to tell him about Paris or how Michele had come to me. Some secrets were buried so deep there was no resurrecting them.

But at night, I often thought about the past. I remembered the captain who'd saved my life twice. I remembered the young couple who had loved their Michele so much that they'd been willing to die for her. I remembered the actress who'd vanished into the crowds in Marseille. I always felt sorry I didn't have the courage to tell their stories beyond the pages of my journal.

My redemption would have to rest in a sacred vow to dedicate myself to Ross and Michele. And after I closed this book today, I would never speak of the past again.

ABOUT THE AUTHOR

Photo © 2017 Studio FBJ

A southerner by birth, Mary Ellen Taylor has a love for her home state of Virginia that is evident in her contemporary women's fiction. When she's not writing, she spends time baking, hiking, and cycling.